LINDA

NEW YORK TIMES BESTSELLING AUTHOR

BRODAY

> "LINDA BRODAY'S HEROES
> STEP RIGHT OUT OF HER BOOKS
> AND INTO YOUR HEART."
> —JODI THOMAS,
> *New York Times* bestselling author

Texas Redemption

THEY SWORE THEY WEREN'T THE MARRYING TYPE.
PREPARE TO MEET...

THE BACHELORS OF BATTLE CREEK

When Delta Dandridge shows
up claiming to be Cooper's
mail-order bride, he scrambles
to set her straight...and send
her packing before she worms
her way into his wounded heart.

On the run from outlaws,
widow Callie Quinn takes
shelter in the arms of a man who
swore never to love—confirmed
bachelor Rand Sinclair.

Brett Liberty has always lived
straddling two worlds: white
and Iroquois. He'd never ask
anyone to share his fate, but
when he crosses paths with
troubled beauty Rayna, he
struggles to remember why he's
better off alone.

ISBN-13: 978-1-4926-46440

50799

EAN

Praise for *Redemption*

"Broday understands the West and its lure. Without stinting on the gritty reality of a rough Texas life, she brings strong characters and deep emotion into a very realistic Western romance that hits no bum notes."

—*RT Book Reviews*, 4 stars

"Not only does Ms. Broday deliver a well-written story, but she'll keep you on the edge of your seat in this passion-laced tale that will have you alternately laughing, crying, and sharing in the joys and sorrows of real people seeking redemption."

—*Historical Romance Writers*

"Linda Broday is a wonderfully talented author who has a knack for bringing the West to life."

—*Roundtable Reviews*

Praise for *Texas Mail Order Bride*

"Linda Broday's books always take me back to a West that feels true. Her love stories run deep with emotion. A delightful read."

—Jodi Thomas, *New York Times* bestselling author of *Promise Me Texas*

"Broday introduces readers to three memorable heroes, a small town, and one feisty Southern beauty. She spices up the sweet and gritty tale with plenty of adventure, meddlesome townsfolk, and some ruthless villains."

—*RT Book Reviews*

"[A] great story about growth, pride, love, and care... All the ingredients for a fine new series."

—*Fresh Fiction*

"Readers will enjoy the witty banter, the colorful descriptions, the mystery of the villain's identity, and, most of all, the obstinate hero and heroine... Broday will appeal to fans of such authors as Georgina Gentry, Leigh Greenwood, and Jodi Thomas."

—*Booklist*

Praise for *Twice a Texas Bride*

"Broday crafts a richly atmospheric Western complete with the grittiness of the frontier as well as the tenderness of blossoming love... With a touching and gentle, yet rugged and real story, Broday captures the West—and readers' hearts."

—*RT Book Reviews*, 4 Stars

"A well-written, evenly paced, feel-good yarn with all the requisite ingredients... Linda Broday is spot-on with her setting, story lines, and superbly drawn characters. *Twice a Texas Bride* is pure enjoyment."

—*Fresh Fiction*

"Tension, treasure, treachery, terror, tenderness, and trust or the lack thereof make *Twice a Texas Bride* a captivating story... Love, on so many levels, makes the story shine."

—*Long and Short Reviews*

"[A] spellbinding romance that will win your heart."
—*Addicted to Romance*

Praise for *Forever His Texas Bride*

"Broday's Westerns always captivate with realistic settings, rugged cowboys, and feisty heroines. Broday ends her Bachelors of Battle Creek trilogy with a bone-chilling thrill. Two lonely hearts come together against vigilantes determined to destroy all they hold dear."
—*RT Book Reviews*, 4 Stars

"The Bachelors of Battle Creek is a shining example of the talent of one of the best historical Western authors."
—*Fresh Fiction*

Texas
Redemption

LINDA
BRODAY

sourcebooks
casablanca

Published by Sourcebooks Casablanca, an imprint of Sourcebooks,
Inc.
P.O. Box 4410, Naperville, Illinois 60567-4410
(630) 961-3900
Fax: (630) 961-2168
www.sourcebooks.com

Originally published as *Redemption* in 2005 in the United States of
America by Leisure Books, an imprint of Dorchester Publishing.

Printed and bound in Canada.
MBP 10 9 8 7 6 5 4 3 2 1

To Mom, who instilled the love of reading
and taught me to dream big. I miss you.

"When we cannot find contentment in ourselves,
it is useless to seek it elsewhere."
—François de La Rochefoucauld
(1613–1680)

One

East Texas, 1869

WHEN A MAN LOSES HIS SOUL, HE HAS LITTLE CHOICE except to try to find it again. Unless he wants to stay lost. An old Chinese proverb claims the journey of a thousand miles begins with the first step. Lord knows he'd found plenty of reasons of one kind or another to avoid taking that first one.

Brodie straightened in the saddle at the edge of town. He squinted into the noonday sun and let his gaze drift to the wooden sign declaring the name as Redemption, then to the row of establishments lining the main street.

White egrets flew overhead. In the distance, giant cypress stood in silence. Spanish moss draping them gave added ghostly tears. They cried in silent harmony—an army of unheard voices in the face of more death and destruction than he dared number.

He'd come home.

They say to become whole, a person must return to the beginning, to the place where his soul was born.

Redemption?

A one in a million chance of that.

He sighed. He'd had worse odds, he reckoned. A click of his tongue moved the big Appaloosa forward.

The town had doubled in his absence. That meant a lot of new folks. Old acquaintances likely wouldn't recognize him anyway. Eight years had a way of changing a man. War could do things to make him unrecognizable...even to himself. The musket ball, compliments of a Yankee soldier, had only shredded his leg. Other scars lay hidden, never to see the light of day.

Those he'd nurture until his dying breath.

The aroma of fresh-baked bread drifted past his nose, assuring the moment of leaving this vale of tears had yet to arrive. Mingling smells of home cooking originated from an untidy little restaurant that, according to best recollection, hadn't stood there years ago. Rumbles in his belly reminded him it hadn't gotten anything in a while.

Besides, he needed to plan what to say before he visited the house on State Street...if such words existed. In response to an unspoken command, Smokey turned and stopped at the hitching post in front of Ollie's Café.

A quick glance through the window revealed wall-to-wall patrons. The steamer tied at the pier probably accounted for a good many, he reckoned. He didn't miss the cluster of men in front of the barbershop who openly stared.

Brodie climbed from the horse and looped the reins over the wooden rail. He'd come to expect rude welcomes.

Maybe it was the devil's scorn that shadowed him or the deadly hiss of rattles from his hat that created such aversion. Or perhaps they spied the apparition that insisted on sharing his saddle—the kind that belonged in graveyards and tombs.

Still, unwanted attention roused pinpricks. He adjusted the thin rawhide strip around his thigh that secured the holster and let his palm rest for a second on the polished walnut grip of his Army-issue Navy Colt.

The gawkers gasped when he nodded toward them, but they didn't turn politely away. They never did.

He held the door for the couple who came out, stepped inside, and removed his Stetson that had seen better days. A quick glance located the table the man and woman had probably vacated.

It hugged a wall in the far corner, perfect for needs requiring an unhindered view of the premises—where a man could blend in easily. This suited both counts. His movements were unhurried as he swept the room for trouble. He breathed a sight easier when he slid into the seat and dropped the hat at his elbow.

A woman well past the mourning of her youth jostled him as she cleared away dirty dishes left by the previous occupants. "What'll you have, mister?"

Before he could reply, a man yelled from the far side, "Hey, Ollie, where's my lunch? Did you hafta go butcher it first?"

"Son of a bluejacket. It'll be ready when it's ready and not a goldarn minute before." The rough talk put a grown boy to shame. Judging by unfazed customers, they'd likely gotten an earful on any given weekday.

"Can I count on that anytime soon?" the man persisted.

"If'n you don't like it, go home and cook your own."

She was a most peculiar female, both in name and appearance. She'd evidently made someone mad as hell when they took a hatchet to the faded russet hair. What remained stood in short uneven porky-spines all over her head. The good Lord must've squeezed in her nose and mouth at the last minute or she'd have wound up nothing but large eyes. Smoke curled from the corncob pipe clamped between her teeth. Except for the smoking apparatus, she could've passed for an organ grinder's monkey he'd seen in San Francisco.

Short wiry females had a way of making him tread extra lightly. He'd rather tangle with a hardened mountain man.

The skinny termagant never spared him a glance. Her gaze flitted over the crowd the whole time she worked as though expecting them to toss coins her way and wanted to make sure she didn't miss one if they should.

Yep, just like that trained monkey.

"Well, mister, I don't have all day."

He assumed she spoke to him, although he based that merely on the lower volume with which she spoke, nothing more. Her arms full of dishes, she turned toward the back.

"I'll have a steak. Biggest you've got." Brodie didn't know if she heard him. She didn't acknowledge the fact.

The monkey impersonator faded into the dark interior. He contemplated leaving…until a younger woman strolled from the kitchen.

Sweet Jesus. Of all the luck.

Her image haunted his dreams much too frequently for forgetting. He'd lost count of the nights when memories jerked him from a sound sleep. And days when familiar yearning pulled deep in his gut, leaving a chest full of misery and bleary eyes.

From across the crowded café the violet-eyed beauty still made him pray for impossible things, promising each desire could come true despite the meager coins in his pocket.

Strange how she wound up here in Texas. He'd never thought to see her again after leaving St. Louis.

She blew away a strand of fallen hair, struggling under the load of plates piled with food. She concentrated on her footing and aimed for the complaining patron's table. With their griping satisfied, she went back for more. She carried armload after another without noticing him. He doubted she'd recognize him anyway after so long.

The years had treated her kindly. She'd changed in small ways—all of them favorable. A mature woman with rounded curves stood in place of the slender young girl he'd known.

His throat clogged when she came close enough to touch.

Tiny lines hugged the lush mouth that once invited, daring him to resist. A block of stone might've. But he bore no kinship with rock. In him she found a randy soldier who liked to taste.

Ahh, those kisses. More an angel's than flesh and blood.

Brodie would stake good money she could make him believe he held the key to her heart even now.

He wouldn't make that mistake twice. Still…

A crooked smile formed when he considered his good fortune.

⁕

Laurel sent the clock a silent cussing. She swore it hadn't moved in the last hour. Her feet and back paid no heed that impatient customers waited for their lunch.

She lifted a plate containing a large cut of beef and strode for the dining room of Ollie's Café ever mindful of her purpose. Marriage to Murphy Yates offered answers to her dream.

The devil take anyone who stood in the way. She clenched her jaw. She'd worked too hard.

Miles of ground lay between Missouri and Texas. Trouble wouldn't find this town at the swamp's edge.

"Let the last day of your past be the first day of your future." Olivia, or Ollie as she preferred, had given the first of much advice the night she sprang Laurel from that hellhole.

The dear woman had seen something worth saving. The chance to make a new life would come just once. Laurel gripped the plate tighter. She meant to grab hold and ride until someone pulled her, kicking and screaming, from the saddle.

A dull ache between her shoulder blades reminded her what she stood to lose. She weaved between the tables, sidestepping sweaty cowboys and their heavy boots.

She'd do whatever necessary to keep her secret buried.

In the midst of noon madness, someone grabbed her arm, sending the plate crashing to the floor. "Spit and thunder. Now look what you've done."

"Don't worry none about that, sweet thing."

A man pulled her onto his buckskin lap. She found herself staring into the cold disdain of young Jeb Prater.

"What do you think you're doing? Let me go." Dear God, she'd thought to rid herself of bold hands and heavy breathing. Pounding in her head reminded her of things she tried to blot out.

"When I get good an' ready." Jeb squeezed her waist. Lust glittered in his stare.

"I think you're ready now, boy." The dark warning tore through the room like scattershot, instantly muting clanking forks, conversation, and noisy chewing.

Laurel struggled to see the owner of the steely voice.

"What's *good* for you is letting her go," the stranger spoke again, a threat in his low drawl making the goose-flesh rise on her arm. She strained for a better view.

The shadowed corner beyond reach of lamplight hid his face. But not the long, lean legs propped out before him. The way he lounged so easily in the chair stirred the embers in her mind of someone she'd known long ago. Like this one, his quiet bearing had carried much weight.

Jeb shot to his feet, upending her. His mouth flew open, then snapped shut in disbelief. Laurel scrambled to safer territory, clutching the back of a spindly chair.

"You're not from these parts so I reckon you don't rightly know who you're dealin' with, stranger."

"I recognize a mealy-mouthed swamp rat when I see one." The man straightened, lifting his black felt hat from the table. The deadly hiss of snake rattles filled the silence. Slowly, he angled it on his head. "I've crossed paths with far too many."

Only one man wore a hat banded with snakeskin from which diamondback rattlers dangled off the back. He leaned forward into the lamp's glow. Someone stole all the air.

Shenandoah.

Laurel's gaze traveled to the tall loner's features. Her dry mouth fought for moisture. Creases beneath his high cheekbones had deepened into valleys, underscoring the grim set of his mouth. And the dark hair sported a few streaks of gray at the temples.

She sidled toward the obscurity of a group who had jumped to their feet. Trouble had a way of making folks edgy. Some already headed for the door, their stomachs forgotten.

"I give you three seconds to apologize for that name-calling." The young bully shifted, a bit of the swagger fading.

"And I'll give you two to scrape that steak off the floor." Shenandoah rose lazily. "I believe it's mine, and I haven't eaten in two days."

"What'll you do if'n I don't?"

"Choice is yours." The icy glare never faltered. "The easy way or the hard. Make it light on yourself, boy."

The Colt weighting Shenandoah's hip apparently gave Jeb plenty of concern. He flung an angry scowl about the room. If hoping for support, none came. Color drained from his face when he slapped holster leather and found empty air, realizing Ollie had confiscated his revolver at the door. Laurel wouldn't sympathize. Jeb had dealt out plenty of misery.

"What's all the goldarned commotion?" Ollie propelled her petite frame between the towering men.

Shenandoah continued to hold Jeb in his stare. "This boy owes me a steak. Mine's on the floor. We're settling up."

Ollie lobbed a questioning glance her way. Laurel cringed but answered, "Jeb made me drop the plate."

The wiry woman swung back, directing a pointed stare to Shenandoah's hand resting on the butt of his Colt. "Shootin' irons ain't allowed in here. No exceptions. Didn't you see the sign that said to leave 'em on the counter?"

"I saw it."

Though he spoke to Ollie, his granite gaze never wavered from Jeb. Laurel knew if the overgrown boy twitched he'd shake hands with St. Peter.

"Means what it says. That's my rule." Wiggling the pipe between her teeth, Ollie stood on tiptoe to get a better look. Furious puffing sent plumes of smoke toward the ceiling. "Don't I know you, mister?"

"Might."

"Ever been to Missouri?"

"Among a few hundred other places."

"I never forget a face." Ollie rubbed her chin. "Might you be the fellow they call Shenandoah?"

"Depends on who's asking."

Laurel's stomach churned. When she could take a breath, she wondered how Ollie knew him since Shenandoah left years before the woman arrived at Taft's establishment.

Ollie swung back to Jeb. "You chuckle-headed shavetail. You don't have the sense God gave a pissant. Here's a man you don't wanna mess with. You're mighty lucky he hasn't already filled you so full of holes your own mama would mistake you for a flour sifter."

Jeb bristled. "Gimme my forty-four an' we'll see who's able to see daylight through."

The pipe flew from her mouth. Ollie slapped Jeb's arm. If she thought to jar his feeble brain, she needn't have bothered.

"Pick up the man's lunch."

"I won't. He called me a mealy-mouthed swamp rat."

"I'd call that awfully kind. Now pick it up, I said." Few would've ordered such. The brash woman didn't frighten easily.

Red-faced, Jeb plucked the meat from shards of earthenware. He juggled the hot steak as though auditioning for a traveling circus act before shoving it at the newcomer. "Here."

Tense quiet stretched. Shenandoah didn't move. A tic in his jaw spoke of supreme effort to curb his anger.

Finally, Ollie snatched the slab of beef. "Never mind. You're buying him another. Laurel girl, go throw one on."

A growl rumbled in Shenandoah's throat. "We're not finished. He owes the lady an apology."

"Boy, whatever you done, better own up to it before it gets you killed. And next time you come in here, bring some manners, dadgum it. Else you're not welcome."

While the majority of folk kowtowed to the young bully, Olivia Applejack b'Dam didn't let her short stature or the fact of her gender tie her tongue in knots. Over the months, Laurel had witnessed that courage many times. Most learned too late the folly of going toe to toe with Ollie. Still, one day her friend's ornery nature could earn her a one-way ticket to the other side.

Jeb turned beet-red. Shenandoah had dethroned him in front of fidgeting patrons he'd lorded over. The protective confines of the kitchen would take scant seconds to reach.

If not? Laurel could despair of saving her new life.

Good fortune and hope deserted. In the space of a heartbeat, Shenandoah wrenched Jeb's arm behind his back. "Where I come from a man don't treat a lady like some common saloon girl. Show respect or I'll break it in half."

Unease pricked worse than a stiff horsehair petticoat. Reference to a lady of ill repute might've been pure chance had it come from another.

A diner named Mabel averted her gaze. No one ever said how the woman made a living. Her manner and eyes full of shame gave her away. Those things Laurel recognized.

Beads of sweat dotted Jeb's forehead. "Didn't mean no harm, Laurel."

"Miss Laurel. Call her miss."

"M-m-miss Laurel." Jeb's face twisted into an ugly caricature.

Shenandoah dipped into Jeb's pocket. "For my steak."

Prater stumbled for the door, forgetting his confiscated revolver. Shenandoah straightened his leather vest.

Laurel whirled from the searching gaze that had the ability to heat each cold corner inside. But she couldn't outrun the pursuing hiss of snake rattles.

"Show's over. Go back to eatin'," Ollie shouted.

Memories of the pungent stench of sulfuric bath water drenched the taste of her spit. Others equally as tormenting rose.

How long before she could sleep without fear?

And how much time to erase the hurt of betrayal? She pushed through the door. Sagging, she buried her face in her hands.

What rotten luck. She'd thought nothing would find her in this town tucked quietly on the banks of Big Cypress Bayou.

Ollie breezed in minutes later. "Someone die, girl?"

"Shenandoah… I know him."

"Every man, woman, and child west of Kentucky's heard of the legendary rebel spy."

"I enjoyed his company toward war's end." A brittle laugh broke free. "I learned the value of his word to return. He'll destroy everything."

"Maybe he didn't recognize you."

"And maybe I've grown horns from the top of my head."

"You worry too much. He's simply passing through."

"And if not?" Her bones didn't lie. She couldn't stop the tremor in her heart much less the quake in her voice.

Ollie patted her shoulder. "If he thinks to hurt my little girl, he'll have to step over my dead body first."

"That's cheery." Despite the image of Olivia lying cold and still, the loyalty touched a deep chord in Laurel.

"Relax. Got you this far, haven't I?"

Tightness squeezed. The irascible lady had delivered

her from wretched hands when no other dared. Laurel could never repay that.

Laurel kissed the weathered cheek. "You truly have."

"Now quit your brow-wrinkling and cook that steak. Hunger makes a man meaner than a lop-eared polecat. I'll serve the rest of those whey bellies."

Laurel eyed stacks of dirty plates lining the sideboard and ladled simmering soup into a bowl. "Most left. Take this to old Jonas and we can get Shenandoah out of here quicker."

"Ring the bell when that cow quits mooing and I'll fetch it."

A fine mist covered her eyes. The meat on the grate covering the hot coals could've been a fence post for all she could tell. An unbreakable bond existed. Risking your life for someone tended to do that. Not that Ollie spoke of it. Laurel respected that, same as the gut feeling that Ollie ran from something, too.

With no destination in mind, the wind carried them to Texas. Murky swamps and marshes had righted an upside-down world.

Redemption was a place of being. What lurked in the bayou's water lilies and deep shadows had reborn her spirit. Majestic cypress knew her here and sympathized with the raw break she'd gotten. They forgave her sins.

She could become a whole person. Peace lay within grasp.

Damn Shenandoah. Damn him for appearing from the blue and scaring her witless.

Two

MYSTERY SURROUNDED THE FUNDS OLLIE HAD USED TO buy the café and small living quarters overhead. Seemed strange for a parlor house cook to fork over such a sum. Still, that was neither here nor there. Laurel respected another's affairs. Besides, a desperate lady shouldn't look a gift horse in the mouth.

Everyone had secrets…some more than most.

She flipped the meat and stirred the hot coals.

Hungry flames licked the raw edges of the steak, consuming, scorching. The hiss and spit of juices dripping onto the fire mimicked her heart's loud protest.

A proper marriage to Murphy Yates could disappear into the thin air of a desert mirage. Instinct urged her to flee somewhere, anywhere safe from the familiar gray-eyed rebel.

Yet such a place didn't exist, not even in her dreams.

Through a haze she watched until an evenly dark color signaled the meat's doneness. She pulled it onto a plate and shook the cowbell.

The door swiveled on the hinges almost immediately.

From the corner of her eye, she watched Ollie plummet. The pipe flew from the woman's mouth, skidding across the floor. Laurel rushed to her side.

"What's wrong?"

Frightened eyes in the chalky face stared up. Ollie clutched her chest, gasping for air.

"Oh Lord. What can I do?"

Laurel stretched her on the floor then wet a cloth. Loosening the top of the threadbare bodice, she placed it on the clammy brow.

If only the town had a doctor instead of a dentist. Jake Whitaker would have no inkling how to treat anything more than the usual chigger bites and earaches.

A lifetime passed before the pain eased. At last Ollie managed to speak. "Didn't mean to let you see this, girl."

"I'm going to get help. Even Jake—"

"Might as well dig a grave and throw me in."

At least the suggestion put a bit of color back in the wan cheeks. "He's better than nothing. At least give him—"

"Hmph! Reckon you don't recollect how that quack gave me pyrexia poisoning when he pulled my tooth."

Darn the ornery woman. Ollie suffered a grievous problem and it was no time to split hairs. Besides, she couldn't prove Jake made her puke up her toenails and put her abed with a fever. But the stubborn set of her lips left no room for mind-changing.

"We're closing the café. I'm taking you to Jefferson." Laurel wouldn't let Ollie die and leave her all alone again. "I've heard they have fine doctors. The *Lizzy Belle* will come through tomorrow morning. We'll be on that steamship or else."

With considerable effort, Ollie sat up. "I dadgum

sure am *not* going. A pure waste of time an' good money. Ain't nothing wrong with me. Besides, if I'm gonna die, I don't want the good Lord to find me with those carpetbagging leeches and riffraff."

"I beg to differ about the time and money part."

"Just my old ticker wearing out, something to look forward to when you get up in years," Ollie wheezed. "Nothing to fret about. Help me up so's I can get to business. Be a good girl and hand me my pipe if you can see where the goldarned thing went."

"You're going upstairs and I won't hear a word about it."

Pain distorting Ollie's face matched the dull ache in her heart. Laurel lifted the frail form into a chair.

"Cain't abide a girl more contrary than me. Don't let Shenandoah get a good look, you hear? Give him his meal, then skedaddle back here." Ollie stopped for a breath.

Thankfully, it left a small crack to get a word in. "Yes, General Applejack b'Dam. I'll handle things."

Perhaps the root of their worry had left.

After Laurel located the errant pipe, she peeked through a crack in the door. Most of the patrons had vacated, leaving coins behind for their meal.

Yet there sat Shenandoah pretty as you please, with his back against the wall, Colt within easy reach. If trouble called, it'd not take him unawares. A glimpse of his hat again brought chills up her spine and a shiver through her bones.

He'd developed into a calloused, toughened hired gun. And she'd become a lot wiser. The question remained how wise.

Nothing short of divine intervention would help in surviving this meeting. And Laurel had learned at fifteen that miracles didn't happen for someone in her shoes.

Whispering a desperate plea, she slid her arm under Ollie's shoulder and helped her stand.

No, the good Lord reserved such things for the good and pure of this earth. That pretty much eliminated her.

Occupied with propelling Ollie up the narrow stairs, Laurel's heel caught on an uneven plank when she stepped onto the landing. Her shoulder jolted into the wall, causing her tongue to scrape the small chip in her front tooth. Anger of that long ago night flashed as she slammed open Ollie's bedroom door. The crack of it bouncing off the wall recalled the noise of her head hitting the floor. She clenched her fists.

Miracles? She'd gotten only one—getting away from Taft alive. And at the moment she questioned the blessing in that.

A few minutes later, with Ollie tucked in bed, she braced for the chore at hand. Down in the kitchen she lifted the plate and took a deep breath.

One small hope stood between her and salvation.

Perhaps Shenandoah truly hadn't recognized her. She'd worn her hair loose and flowing in those days, not pulled back in a severe knot on the back of her neck as she did now. She straightened her shoulders and strode into the dining room.

Walk briskly. Feel nothing.

Shenandoah's intense gaze burned, luring her concentration from the brisk, firm walk she'd planned. The faint smell of leather, bay rum, and cheroots jogged her memories.

Nights when her world seemed less hopeless.

Nights when she first dared thoughts of a new life.

Nights of passion.

Her steps lagged.

The crooked half smile disturbed her far more than the shock of hair that dangled rakishly across his forehead. Rivulets of sweat trickled down her back. That devilish grin touched a longing deep in the locked chamber of her heart where she could lie to herself and pretend she was worth saving.

Laurel willed herself forward, a desperate prayer sticking in her throat. She plunked the meal onto the table and turned on her heel.

Not quick enough.

He captured her hand.

"Much obliged. Sit with me a spell, Lil."

Cold fingers of doom clawed their way inside, wrapping around what remained of her soul.

Lavender Lil. No one had called her that since…

She gave the other two patrons a skittish glance. Their forks never slowed from plate to mouth, indicating they'd not heard.

"Sorry, cowboy." She meant to add the layer of flint. The bitterness surprised her though. "You've got the wrong person."

Shenandoah pulled her into the chair beside him. Not a forceful tug, but one that offered no escape. The gentle touch spoke of remembrance and insatiable desire.

A crack in the floor came under her intense scrutiny.

How could so much dirt get into such tiny places? It would take a good scrubbing to get it clean.

"Nice try. I'd recognize that silky black hair and those violet eyes in the midst of a horde of saints at a church social, the last place I'd expect to find you... even if I wore a blindfold."

His husky drawl lodged somewhere in the vicinity of her fickle heart. *Dear God, for another lifetime, another chance.*

"You're mistaken."

"And certainly if you spoke." He brushed aside her denial. "I've never heard another with your throaty voice."

She swallowed the lump. "My name is Laurel James."

Release of his hold gave false hope, for he merely changed locations. She flinched when he cupped her jaw. Damning the touch that bound without rope or chains, she had no choice but follow where he led. His rebel gaze reflected the futility of her lies. Her stomach twisted into a knot.

"Surprised to find you here. A bit far from St. Louis, aren't you, darlin'?"

"Please...don't—"

A loud yell from outside interrupted her desperate plea.

"Hey, you in there! I'm calling you out."

Jeb Prater. Shenandoah shifted in his seat. A glimmer of disquiet crossed his features before it vanished, replaced by the cold, hard mask of a seasoned warrior.

"Face me now, meddler. I double-dog dare you. I'm gonna show a yellow-bellied, chicken-livered maggot we don't cotton to your kind here."

Shenandoah sighed and gave the succulent meat on the plate a longing glance before reaching for his hat. The rattles shook, filling the silent room with foreboding as he settled it on his head. Prater was the worst kind of fool, Laurel decided. *And I'm the second, without a doubt.*

"Keep this warm." He towered above her when he rose to full height. "You and me have unfinished business."

The soft trousers clung to lean thighs. His long stride and easy calm spoke of a man who had no need to prove anything to anyone. He knew who he was and didn't give a tinker's damn about the rest. Laurel drank in the sight.

Of all the ones they'd forced her to entertain, he was the only one who gave of himself. He fit into a special class. She thought his caring genuine. In the long nights and wee hours of the mornings she fantasized he'd come for her. What a foolish notion.

He never had.

Until today.

When she least needed rescuing.

Blue blazes. His appearance destroyed the belief he'd died a hero on some battlefield, a preference to the bald truth.

Still, despite fear he'd ruin her new life, she couldn't help wishing for something that could never be. Crazy but true.

Though she abhorred the practice of gun play, she pressed her nose to the café window. Suppose Jeb got lucky. Suppose Shenandoah's pistol misfired. Suppose the man she hadn't been able to forget found his place in the hereafter before her eyes. Her stomach landed in the middle of her throat.

A piece of lead would keep her secret intact. Her heart hammered. A weakness swept over her for allowing thoughts that aroused more panic than did his sudden arrival.

"You don't have to do this." Shenandoah's voice carried through the thick glass. "No way to settle a score."

The familiar hand hovered over the polished grip of the revolver. Solid and firm, he projected confidence in abilities that could prove most dangerous to a body's health.

"Scared, mister? Afraid now that I've strapped on a six-shooter?"

"It'd take more than a snot-nosed kid. Don't do anything stupid. Back away and we'll both win. You draw that iron and one of us will lose. Care to gamble it might be you, boy?"

He presented a powerful argument. For a moment, Jeb wavered, appearing to listen. Shenandoah must've shared her thoughts for he turned slightly toward the café. The small motion set the rattles hissing in the quiet street.

"Watch out!" Laurel clutched her apron into a wad. She was afraid to look but found it impossible to turn away.

Before Jeb's pistol cleared his holster, Shenandoah pulled and fired in a fluid movement. A thick puff of gray smoke enveloped the figure from her past. Prater lay moaning in the dirt, gripping his bloodstained leg, and cursing the men who came to carry him into the saloon. The scene sickened.

War had ended and men continued to fight. They'd never learn that violence only dug more graves.

Sudden nausea had her running toward the back before she lost the contents of her stomach.

Gulps of air and a glass of water helped. Ten minutes later, she eyed the mess left by the dinner crowd, mindful of the ticking clock. Only a few hours before suppertime. Besides, Jeb had asked for what he got. And avoiding Shenandoah seemed more prudent than before. Ollie would spout she couldn't lollygag around. Speaking of which, she needed to check on her.

Heavy-hearted, she climbed the stairs.

"What was all that ballyhooin' down there?" Ollie asked before she barely crossed the threshold to the room.

"Stupidity." Laurel straightened the frayed patchwork quilt. "Jeb discovered his mistake in drawing down on Shenandoah. Probably walk with a permanent limp from now on."

"A man goes spewing his mouth, he's liable to get it filled with something besides a chicken leg. Reckon he found lead a bit harder to swallow." Ollie cackled, puffing on the pipe. "Jeb never cast a shadow across anyone of this caliber."

Laurel veered away from that subject. "How do you feel?"

"Fit as a four-legged mule." She threw her legs over the side of the bed, dodging Laurel's attempt to feel her forehead. "Don't need any mothering neither. Save it for your younguns."

"Don't have any." Nor did the prospect seem likely. Laurel lowered herself onto a chair beside the bed.

"Won't get any either, less'n you learn to stifle that god-awful sassy tongue."

"No use trying to change my ways now."

"What happened to Shenandoah?"

"Eating, I suppose. Jeb interrupted his meal again."

"Fool boy. Just ain't right in the head." Ollie stared into her face. "Well?"

She knew what Ollie asked, but recognized what more worry would add to a bad heart. "Well, what?"

"Did he remember you, that's what."

No use trying to plead ignorance with the crusty dear. "He called me Lavender Lil. Spoke about unfinished business."

"Son of a bluejacket."

"I tried to deny it, but he wouldn't listen. I don't know how to fix this mess." Her nerves were tightly stretched bowstrings. Each breath rasped over them in a quivering rush.

"Appeal to his better side. Did you ask for his silence?"

"Jeb stole that chance." Even had she found the words, she couldn't have gotten them out.

Smoke curled about Ollie's head. "Gotta find out his plans. Don't reckon he gave any hint of how long he's staying?"

"Not hardly."

"What's holding you back, girl? Get busy."

Hotness scorched the back of her throat. It had taken too much strength, time, and planning. She wouldn't let one steely-eyed drifter snatch it away. If he thought her a daylily, she'd make him change that opinion quick. In twenty-one years she'd already lived several hundred. A person couldn't go through what she had without acquiring survival skills.

"I'm waiting for you to not die on me. Luckily, I see far too much mule blood in you to let that happen.

Much as I loathe the thought, I intend to satisfy your curiosity and mine."

"I'm coming." Ollie's boots struck the floor.

"It's my past I have to face." Laurel stared horrified as the woman danced a jig around her and wondered if Ollie's brain had sprung a leak. "What in heaven's name are you doing?"

"Proving I'm not ready for the undertaker yet."

Ollie wobbled when she stopped. Quick reflexes kept her from falling. Laurel held tight, glancing about for a piece of strong rope. She spied none, not even a speck of yarn. "I do this alone. By myself. That doesn't include you."

"Well, of all the ungrateful nerve," Ollie sniffed. "It's not as if I wouldn't let you do all the talking."

"Only a case of lockjaw would save that from happening, I'm afraid. I'm ordering you back to bed. Don't make me lock you in."

"You're mighty bossy, you know that?"

"I had a good teacher." Laurel hugged the dear lady.

"I'll be more than happy to wring that fellow's neck."

What a picture: Ollie squared off on tiptoes in front of Shenandoah, her bandy legs stretched, hands struggling to reach his throat. Yeah, the man had real trouble on his hands.

Laurel kissed her thin, hollow cheek. "I love you. Don't know what I'd do if I lost you."

"Quit your dadblasted worrying. I ain't some favorite shoe that's likely to fall out the back of a wagon first time it hits a rock."

Foot apparel and people didn't bear much similarity, but both could fall from a wagon, and Ollie had run smack into a boulder once that day already. Laurel counted her blessings on the way downstairs. Minutes later, she cautiously pushed open the door to the dining room. Thank heavens. The steak and the man had both disappeared, only a shiny silver dollar left behind.

This time the money paid for an honest living, not services of another nature. At least until they ran her out of town.

She dropped the coin into the pocket of her yellow dress and smoothed the white apron over it. Her clothing ranged in many shades…except one. She'd rot in hell before she wore purple again. That hell she'd not revisit again.

Shenandoah could already have spread his venom. Her quiet, respectable life might crash around her any minute.

Her stomach felt as if she had eaten a belly full of lead instead of the town bully doing it for her.

The bell tied to the door tinkled merrily. Laurel whirled.

⚬⚬

From the shadows, Shenandoah's mouth set in a firm line as he watched his beautiful Lil drop the silver dollar he'd left into her pocket.

His chest hurt from trying to fill his lungs with air.

She'd tried to deny their acquaintance. She'd not shown a flicker of happiness to see him. Nothing to indicate she remembered the feel of his arms, the taste of his kisses. A corpse would've welcomed him with more warmth and feeling.

He'd thought he meant more than simply a body who shared her bed. She'd become someone he never would've imagined.

The pain spread out in a searing arc.

What Lil and he once had should've been enough to at least warrant a "Hello, how are you?"

The rudeness rankled. Back then she'd have rekindled the fire right there in front of God and everybody. Unless…

Sweet Georgia clay.

Maybe she'd married and left her heart in someone else's keeping. That would explain her attitude.

Quick, jabbing pain almost doubled him, as if someone put both fists into his gut.

He didn't know if he could stomach her on another man's arm. The special tenderness he cherished inside no marriage vow to another would sever.

He had half a mind to march in there and demand answers. She owed him that much. He tossed aside the matchstick dangling from the side of his mouth and straightened. Before he could translate the thought to action, a figure strolled past.

His mouth went dry as the man pushed inside the café. The passing of eight long years didn't dull recognition.

Shenandoah untied Smokey. "Might as well get you bedded down, boy. No use waiting around for hell to freeze over."

One last backward glance assured him the moisture on his face wasn't from melted ice. It was way too warm and he'd run out of wishes.

Three

LAUREL PIVOTED, EXPECTING TO ENCOUNTER ROGUISH disdain. Relief bathed her to find Murphy Yates instead.

"Is that any way to greet your betrothed? You'd have thought you'd seen a ghost." Long strides covered the short space. He pulled her into his arms.

Little did he know how accurately he described what the afternoon breeze had spirited down the main street of town. She shuddered to think how quickly this man of the finest cloth would put her from his life at the mere hint of scandal.

She forced cheery lightness. "Nothing more than a devil in disguise. That's certainly not you. I'm frazzled, that's all. Dueling in the streets tends to do that. Did you see or hear the shooting?"

"Bank business kept me busy inside, but Sheriff Tucker gave me the gist of it. I'm surprised someone hasn't taken the wind from Prater's sails before this. I always suspected his bluster would get him in deep water sooner or later."

A gentle touch on her back strayed lower to pat her behind.

"My goodness, Murphy." Laurel stepped back.

A pair of rebel gray eyes could easily set disaster in motion. She wouldn't give Shenandoah any more provocation than existed.

"I don't care who sees. We'd have tied the knot days ago if I had my way."

She juggled dirty dishes and tried to ignore the grumbles. Bothersome thoughts plagued her as she hurried toward the steaming washtub. Wedding Murphy would bring everything she coveted.

Why then did she drag her feet, pushing the date further away?

The question barely formed before guilt rose. The gentle man had waited his whole life for the right woman to come along. He deserved the best. Lord knows she wasn't even in the running for that distinction. She owed him more than the high road to hell she would saddle him with.

Sure, he'd probably try to whitewash over her past at first, being the true gentleman he was, but regret would show with each new day.

Murphy tagged behind with a load of plates. "Let's go to Jefferson right now. Within two hours you can be my wife."

How tempting to muzzle each rational thought and just accept. Perhaps through enough trying and hard work he'd never realize he'd gotten a jaded lady instead of the noble wife he sought.

Respect and caring came near enough to love. Didn't it?

Close perusal revealed nothing displeasing. Never mind that everything was worn a bit too perfectly and to crisp precision. Murphy's nicely trimmed hair brushed his collar in rich, sandy waves, each strand neatly in place. The bow tie and starched white shirt added a distinguished air. A gleam came from below.

Her reflection glimmered in the high gloss of his shoes. …the face she couldn't bear to see in the mirror.

Laurel jerked away, setting the dishes in the washtub. "We've discussed this. We can't rush—"

His mouth smothered her objections. The earnest kiss caused no disruption in her heart's steady rhythm. She wiggled away, trying not to notice hurt in his soulful gaze. Plain ordinary wouldn't satisfy her and to be fair, it wouldn't him either.

"I hope that settles any questions you have regarding my true feelings. You're the lady that I'm going to build my future with."

"I believe you care for me. That's not at issue."

"Goes a hell of a lot deeper than that."

For now. Rueful whispers would dodge her attempts to bottle them.

"What's wrong with wanting everything fitting and proper?"

"Enough fuss and bother. Seems an odd reason for concern."

Before a reply came to mind, Ollie ambled in from the alleyway door, blocking a furry blob with a quick foot. "Durn cats. They break their fool necks to get inside. At least something likes the taste of your cooking, Laurel girl."

The woman slapped her sides, enjoying the joke. Except for a slight pallor that remained, a body would have mistaken her for the picture of health.

Murphy covered his awkward position. "Afternoon, Ollie."

"You're just the one to put the bloom back in our girl's cheeks. Reckon you heard about the ruckus?"

"Yeah, didn't get the particulars though."

"Started right here over a man's lunch. Laurel got caught smack dab in the middle of the whole shootin' match."

"Sheriff mentioned the stranger stood up for her."

"Dadgum truth of it. And he did a fine job."

"Horsefeathers." Laurel had to damper the steam before the train jumped the track. "You both know by now I'm fully capable of taking care of myself. Misplaced heroics caused two grown men to put pride over common horse sense."

Ollie turned a deaf ear and squinted at Murphy. "Do you know that fellow, Shenandoah?"

"Might say so. Puzzles me why he's come though."

Laurel choked and collapsed into a chair.

"You do? Who... How?" Ollie's words echoed her own.

Murphy pulled out a pocket watch and flipped the lid. The gold chain's jiggling motion matched her thoughts. "Certain matters demand my attention at the moment, I'm afraid. Our discussion isn't over. I'll be back soon so be thinking about what I said."

Shock of his admission had scattered her thoughts. She'd taken all the jolts she could stand. "But what about—?"

"Later, Miss Curiosity." Murphy tweaked her nose.

"Men! How infuriating to leave me in suspense."

"Ain't no changing 'em. That's God's own truth," Ollie grumbled.

An hour later Murphy returned wearing a happy glow. "If you won't marry me today, will you accept a supper invitation?"

"I truly don't see how it's possible, Murphy."

"I have a surprise for you, my love." His eyes twinkled.

He'd snagged her interest. Besides, she needed to get some answers. "In that case, I can't very well refuse, now can I?"

"How's six thirty, after you serve the crowd?"

It wouldn't leave time to clean up the mess until after she returned. It would mean a late night. "Six thirty it is."

He cast Ollie a cautious glance before giving Laurel a quick peck on the cheek.

When the tinkling bell announced his exit, Laurel exploded. "That low-down, four-flushing, two-bit gunfighter!"

"Simmer down. Murphy wouldn't give you a supper invite if he'd gotten a hint of your dealings with Shenandoah."

"He might if he were baiting a trap."

Ollie lit the pipe before she argued. "Oh, stop. If either believes for one measly second I'll stand by while he destroys you, he's got another think coming. Hell and be damned, I'll fight Satan himself…with his own pitchfork."

❧

A handful of regulars wandered in that Tuesday evening, along with a dozen passengers from a steamer bound for Shreveport. Laurel's shoulders ached by six o'clock. Only after she made sure Ollie could take care of a few stragglers did she dash upstairs to freshen.

"I can beg off or make a tardy appearance," she'd offered.

"Go get gussied up now." The woman had swatted, shoving her toward the overhead quarters. "I ain't gonna keel over."

That particular worry moved in bag and baggage, the uninvited guest accompanying Laurel to her room. Being alone again haunted every waking minute. Her tongue scraped the reminder of what she'd escaped. She shuddered.

Cold bumps on her flesh rose when she stripped off the yellow dress. St. Louis and death bore the same name. She clenched her fists. They'd best come armed and expecting a fight.

She stood gasping until the ticking clock finally penetrated the terror. Better hurry or Murphy would wonder what happened. Her gaze strayed to the wardrobe. She opened the doors, fingering the green calico print. Too plain. The pale blue with a row of lace around the high collar? Too girlish.

Her most prized—a rose-colored silk Ollie bought to celebrate her freedom—settled it.

The fabric rustled when she smoothed down the skirt. Giving her hair a quick brush, she pulled back the sides and secured them with shell combs. The rest rippled down in a mass of loose curls. She gathered her shawl, not once glancing toward the mirror hidden behind a drape of heavy black cloth.

Out in the street, light fog rolled in from the bayou, like quiet tears of a lost soul that yearned for things it couldn't have.

She picked up her steps and lifted the heavy brass

knocker a few minutes later. Deep in the house, the grandfather clock boomed the half hour. Murphy opened the wide portal.

"Sweetheart." He pecked her cheek and led her inside. "I see you've worn my favorite. What a happy occasion."

A tall man stood with his back to them, gazing into the courtyard in which Murphy took pride and joy. Had the fog not muted the colors, bright flowers would've splashed warmth into the room. She wondered who the guest was and why Murphy's secrecy.

"I've waited a long time for this homecoming." Murphy beamed and tugged her forward. "Laurel, meet my prodigal brother."

The stranger turned, the soft hiss of rattles disturbing the tranquil mood.

"You!" The word spewed from Laurel's mouth before she could stop it.

Brother? Blood pounded in her temples.

Murphy's gaze swung from one to the other while Shenandoah glared.

"You're going to leg shackle yourself to her?"

The barb pierced the small bubble of hope for sealed lips.

Suspicion etched Murphy's face. "You act as though you've met somewhere before."

"No... I mean, yes... I mean..." She rushed to recover. "I've never laid eyes on your brother before."

Fingers crossed behind her back should bring forgiveness for the lie. She'd admit nothing.

"Don't look at me." Shenandoah's dark glower promised no help. He'd given her enough rope to hang. The rat.

"Well, of course I met him a few hours ago, although I didn't know who he was. The shock of coming face-to-face with the object of the day's turn of events took me aback. I never expected to find such a man here. Then to discover he's your kin... Ollie called him Shenandoah."

"It seemed prudent to take that name during the war," the familiar voice answered for Murphy. "To protect us both."

"Yep, he's my brother, Brodie Yates." Pride lay in the tone. An affectionate grip rested on his brother's shoulder.

Of a heartening nature—Brodie hadn't known of betrothal plans. That translated to mean he hadn't yet spread news of her tarnished reputation. Before the evening expired she'd finagle a private word with Mr. Insolent. She'd protect her secret if she had to beg, cajole, or strike a deal with Lucifer to do it.

Laurel forced a smile and stuck out her hand. "A pleasure to make your acquaintance. Murphy speaks highly of you."

More fibs added to the list. A magic lamp granted three wishes. What did three lies get you other than a splitting headache? She rubbed a throbbing temple with shaky fingertips.

Although Murphy did mention his brother once in passing, he hadn't provided a name. And she could classify seeing her old love again as pleasurable. At least the bumping of her heart against her ribs indicated proof of it.

The man who aroused excitement and irritation, both at the same time, hesitated for the barest of seconds. Her hand got lost in his large palm. Unexpected warmth sent delicious shivers up her arm to that darn fickle heart of hers. Thank goodness he couldn't see the mess left in its wake.

"Which name do you prefer, Mr....?" Good heavens, was that squeaky voice hers?

"Brodie will do while I'm here."

"How long might that be?" She wished her words didn't burst in breathless rushes. "If you're at liberty to say."

The happiness of several lives depended on a clear head. She tugged her hand free of his hold, relieved when he didn't press the issue. She backed away.

"Until I wear out my welcome, I suppose." He smiled.

He'd worn that thin at the outset, so he might as well move along. She rubbed dampness from her skin. Her annoyed gaze tangled with his. The sudden quirk of a brow relayed satisfaction in knowing the mayhem his touch had left. The room grew overheated.

You're going to leg shackle yourself to her?

Recollection of his curt disdain aroused bristles anew. He was the pot calling the kettle black.

Murphy interrupted her thoughts. "Dearest, I know you'll come to love my brother once you get to know him. He's not always a prickly-tongued cactus. You'll soon think of him as family."

Laurel certainly doubted that. Family man numbered at the bottom in the ways she remembered.

"All horns and rattles, am I, little brother?"

"Only on occasion." Murphy wrapped an arm around her waist, drawing her against him. "This lady's the best thing that's happened to me. I'm forsaking bachelorhood for her."

Again an elevated eyebrow and quiet reply. "Indeed."

The one word said enough. She prayed he'd not add more.

Murphy didn't give him a chance. "About time I tied the knot. You, too, Brodie. When are you going to settle down?"

"I've yet to meet the woman I wish to lend my name to." A dangerous glint sparkled in his eyes. "Laurel? Is that what you prefer? Or is there another?"

Her ire grew faster than the water hyacinths that strangled the life from Big Cypress Bayou. He toyed with her. Loss of control would simply egg him on more. She breathed deep, swallowing the biting remark on the tip of her tongue.

"Laurel's the name I was born with." His cold stare raised her temperature another ten notches. "I have no other."

"If you insist, *Miss Laurel James*. Tell me…is it true you're partial to lavender?"

Blood drained, leaving limp remains of long-dead memories.

A feeble reply finally crept past the double-cross. "I can't imagine who would've spread such a preposterous tale."

"What brought this on?" Murphy blustered. "Makes no difference to you or anyone else what color my Laurel wears. If you have a burr under your saddle, just speak your piece."

Tucked within Murphy's arm, tension suspended her heartbeat, freezing the moment in blocks of ice. Sure as the moon rose in the sky Brodie intended to blurt everything. She flinched, awaiting the doom.

"Thought she resembled someone I once knew." He removed his Stetson. The lethal rattles commenced their clatter, sending a war party of chills through her. He laid it on a polished mahogany credenza. "Now that I've taken a second look, I can see I'm mistaken. That woman wasn't the marrying kind."

Her knees nearly buckled. With the night just beginning, she'd put nothing past this murdering desperado. More than likely, he wished her to sweat plenty before the ugly moment of truth.

Murphy apparently bought the half-truth. "That's better. Annie's outdone herself for this special night of thanks. You're home, and beautiful Laurel is about to become my wife."

"When's the happy occasion, Murph?"

"Four weeks—unless my powers of persuasion kick in." Murphy's warm squeeze released crashing waves of guilt.

Laurel almost favored ending this charade now rather than go on pretending. Murphy would thank his lucky stars she refused to rush to the altar. The town would soon forget his disgrace. Memories fade. Sometimes. Well, nearly always.

"We didn't want to do anything rash. After all, we have the rest of our lives to spend together," she hurried to add.

The pressure at her waist brought mist to her eyes. No man more noble walked Redemption's streets. The landslide election confirmed popular sentiment. Besides mayor, Murphy served as the town's only banker. He enjoyed a stellar reputation as a fair-minded businessman. More than one farmer would've lost his land in foreclosure if not for genuine caring. She sensed unique compassion the first moment they met.

Were her needs greater to justify bringing him down? Naked truth plunged like a dagger. She hadn't willingly chosen to become what she had. It wasn't Murphy's but her debt to pay.

William Taft alone bore responsibility and she hoped he roasted in a fiery pit for it.

"Shall we?"

Murphy escorted her into the dining room. Showing manners and good breeding, he pulled out her chair. His scoundrel brother seated himself across the table without waiting. Even while she reduced Brodie to beneath the rank of barbarian, the noontime incident had sprung from the blue. He'd forced Jeb's apology for rudeness and made him call her miss. A strange code he'd adopted.

Her mind wandered back. Shenandoah once wouldn't have thought it so tragic to tie her name to his.

She glanced up to find him staring as if he read her thoughts and dared her to deny them. Her mouth went dry. The tilted grin on his lips seemed more suited for foxes in hen houses than a civil dining room.

"Some yams, my sweet?" Murphy passed a dish.

Thankful Murphy had broken the spell, she scooped a small portion onto her plate.

"I must say. This is something." Brodie steepled his fingers over full, sensual lips.

She didn't care to explore the hidden meaning. The statement boded ill. She aimed for another path. "I get the impression you've not visited in a while. Have you been away on…business?"

"At least the kind that keeps a Johnny Reb spy two steps ahead of a Union rope."

A hated spy. Yet, he'd risked death to return. Why now? What made the gamble so important? Hearing firsthand what she'd dismissed as disgruntled Southerners sent a jolt of surprise.

"I assumed those who hunted Confederate soldiers long after the war's end bore more fiction than truth."

"Andrew Johnson's pardons were the fictitious part. I have stories to curl your hair. I assure you they are not mere babblings by toothless old men."

She crumpled the napkin in her lap. "Why did you take up arms in such a horrible war you had no hope of winning?"

"Anyone ever warn you of what happens to little girls who ask too many questions?"

"But now you've come back, knowing full well the thick army presence." Her tongue stumbled over the words.

"I did for a fact."

A wry smile formed. She fought the urge to rush from the table when he tilted forward. The younger Yates brother, having turned his attention to the meal, seemed unbothered by a charge in the air.

"Brodie joined up with the South when the smoke cleared after the first Battle of Bull Run. Nothing I said kept him from leaving." Murphy gestured with his fork. "He sent several letters letting me know he'd escaped Yankee bullets and prison camps, but only one since Lee's surrender."

"It seemed better that way," Brodie said.

"That was four years ago," Murphy reminded him.

"Give or take a few lifetimes." Brodie's mood darkened.

The answer spoke of deep remorse, like hers, that ate from the inside until it destroyed everything, leaving only an empty shell. Regardless the uproar his arrival brought, she sympathized with the man who'd evidently lost his way.

Laurel swallowed hard. Going home appeared next to impossible. For them both.

Four

THE CORK FROM THE WINE BOTTLE EXPLODED INTO THE chandelier, setting the sparkling crystal prisms atwitter. Brodie filled the goblets while considering the value of a piece of blue belly hot metal. He preferred a quick end to this torment that whipped his insides into a frothy mess. Murphy's endearments, the tender touches, knowing Laurel would never be his Lil spiraled him into a dark pit. Of all times to listen to the cry of his soul.

He should've stayed gone.

"I believe if a man drinks wine, he should offer a toast," he said.

"That's a fine notion." Murphy rose. "A salute."

A frown marred Laurel's beauty. Brodie had given her every right to mistrust him. Tilting her stubborn chin, she extended her glass, meeting his antagonism.

Only a demented man would recall silky curves rippling beneath a light caress…and her unbridled response.

Brodie disappeared down a forbidding slough,

haunted by faces of the lost and damned. A mental shake returned him to the present. His glass clinked against theirs.

"May the South rise again. And to beautiful ladies who made the fight worthwhile."

"Long live the South."

Their subdued rejoinder paled beside his boisterous one.

"I've heard a louder show of patriotism from dying Rebs."

Murphy flushed. "What damn good did that war do except leave a bunch of families with holes in them? Children will grow up without fathers. Wives have no husbands. Is that victory? Hate between North and South runs deeper than before. That's why we have to watch what we say and how loud we speak. Federal troops will lock you up for looking cross-eyed."

"I saw the heavy military occupation in Jefferson. Carpetbaggers, scalawags, and Union Army overrun the place." Brodie tossed the contents of the glass down his throat. "Hell and damnation!"

"They're trying to redeem us poor Southerners and save us from ruin," Murphy said sourly.

"The situation should improve with the upcoming election," Laurel put in quietly.

"Readmitting Texas to the Union won't fix the sort of ills plaguing us." Murphy set down the wine and resumed his seat.

"But if we have a real governor, the military will pull out. We can make our own laws again. Isn't that the best thing for us and the state?"

Laurel always had a knack for getting to the bottom line.

He remembered wetness spilling down her cheeks. *I need you. We need each other because apart we're nothing but an unfinished painting, bodies without heads. Promise you'll return for me.*

That night was the last time he'd been a complete person. Yeah, she had expertise in pointing out the obvious.

"Edmund Davis will hardly bring us back to the land of milk and honey." Brodie let out a snort. "He's nothing but a Union puppet, and a bastard to boot."

"A free election would be a start," she argued. "Anything beats military appointees. Maybe A. J. Hamilton will beat him."

"Hamilton doesn't stand a prayer. Davis will get in if President Grant has to stuff the polls to do it." Murphy took a piece of bread and buttered it. "Politics gives me indigestion. Forget those fools and focus on this happy reunion."

Laurel quibbled over the happy occasion part. "It's evident no amount of discussion amid china and cut crystal will change what's happened."

Or was about to.

The wayward brother tossed down the contents of another glass. Sheltered by lowered eyes, she saw him refill it.

For a man who claimed a few hours ago to have gone without food for two days, he ignored the succulent roast hen, creamed peas, and yams. What had happened to the steak—the one that almost caused a man's death? Had he eaten it or fed it to the strays?

A raised gaze floundered in the brooding stare across from her. A strange light turned the gray soot of his eyes into sinful black.

Dangerous and defiant, the rogue lounged easily as if waiting in a parlor house for his favorite lady, intent on taking pleasure for the night.

She sucked air into her lungs, blocking hysteria. "This feast puts the café's to shame. Better try it."

"Later. The steak I had earlier filled the hollow spot." He leaned forward, propping his elbows on either side of the imported porcelain. "Don't sell yourself short. You're a mighty fine cook, Lil… Miss James."

Simple slip of the tongue, or did he persist in some game? She feared what might emerge each time he opened his mouth.

"Nothing special. Just plain cooking."

"Skill in the kitchen first attracted me to her," Murphy said. "But then, how could I overlook an angel when I saw one?"

"Indeed." Swirling red liquid in Brodie's goblet held her captive. Only when it sloshed out did he release her stare. "She certainly appears the innocent."

"Pure as the driven snow. My Laurel's worth more than all the gold in California."

"Do tell."

Ice filled her veins. Brodie's quirked eyebrows said he had nothing to lose. What gall to sit in judgment. He hadn't wanted her. And unless things took a drastic turn, neither would the youngest Yates brother once he discovered who she was.

"Spit and thunder. Stop talking about me as though I'm invisible." Her fork clattered against the plate when she dropped it. "And get one thing straight, Murphy Yates. Don't put me on a pedestal. I'm no saint. Don't try to make me into one. I've committed my share of mistakes and I'll make plenty more before they put me in the ground."

"I'd listen to her, Murph." Glints sparkled in the dark scowl. "The lady knows what she's talking about."

Heaven help the scoundrel. He'd need it if she could put to work the murderous plans spinning in her head.

"I believe I smell pie." She tried to steer the conversation from the storm-tossed waters of her character.

"Your favorite. Pecan praline." Murphy's warm smile elicited undying gratitude. He rang the brass bell beside him, signaling Etta. "I do know the way to your heart, my love."

"Sweet Betsy. Had I only known, it might've made a difference in my marital status. Pecan praline pie. Smooth, sugary sweet, and ahh, so desirable." Brodie stretched, raking back the errant lock. The strand stayed put for an entire half second before it sprang back in a disrespectable salute. The soft drawl didn't hide belief he held a royal flush and he'd suffer no guilt when he plunked it down for all to see.

Laurel's stomach plunged.

Etta took Laurel's plate and slid the first slice of pie before her. The cook and housekeeper waited expectantly for her reaction. "It's delicious. I have no secrets around you and Murphy."

Of all things to have said. She needed a good kicking to Main Street and back. Brodie grabbed the opening.

"Speaking of secrets and sugary sweet things... I remember a certain young lady in St. Louis. At the

Black Garter, to be exact. Ever been to St. Louis, Miss James?"

Her heart froze and she choked on the flaky morsel. She downed a full glass of water before dislodging the bite.

"You all right, sweetheart?" Murphy pressed her hand.

"I'm such a ninny. I apologize for causing concern."

Murphy lit into him. "What a dumb fool question to ask. I doubt Laurel's been out of Texas, and I damn sure know she wouldn't go anywhere near a place called the Black Garter."

"Hold your horses, Murph. Can't fault a man for reminiscing. I met a woman there I could've shared more than a few nights with had Lady Luck smiled my way." The molten stare said Brodie remembered every detail of their encounter.

And God forbid, so did she. With indelible clarity. But he hadn't cared enough to find his way back.

How proper to adorn his hat with snake rattles. The man had two deadly skills—his pistol and his tongue.

She wondered how a girl went about trapping a cagey diamondback. And more important, how could she escape its kiss of death in the attempt?

One thing she knew: it never paid to let a scoundrel know he'd drawn blood, something she'd learned about survival.

She flashed her best smile and drawled sweetly, "I do declare, if I don't detect the makings of a pitiful tale. You'll never know whether it was a twist of fate or misfortune of your own choosing. Do you ever wonder what happened to the lady after you moved on?"

"Quite often."

"For the record, I believe she landed on her feet."

Brodie's flash of surprise turned into a half smile. "Touché."

Murphy glowered. "Are you right sure you've never met?"

Laurel doubled efforts to keep things far removed from the state of Missouri and a certain gaming house. She gave Murphy her full attention. "Etta outdid herself tonight. Perhaps I could wheedle the recipe for the roasted hen. And the pie surely topped the meal. Ollie would dearly love a piece."

"Shoot, take the whole pie, sweetheart." He lifted the back of her hand to his lips. "Your every wish is my command."

Her throat tightened. Devotion wrapped the declaration and tied it with a bow.

"Speaking of Ollie, I noticed she looked a bit puny today." Murphy smoothed the inside of her palm, but didn't release it.

"She had a spell with her heart after the run-in with Jeb." Laurel shot Brodie a withering glare, for the dear lady wouldn't have suffered it had he chosen another town to disgrace with his presence. Her voice broke. "I force myself not to think about losing her one day. She's like a mother to me."

"We had one of those. Didn't we, Murph?"

Brodie's bitter remark puzzled Laurel.

Her betrothed explained, "Our mother died when we were youngsters. Without a father, that made us orphans. Aunt Lucy saw fit to step into those shoes." Sadness seeped between Murphy's words like the cold wind of a blue norther. "She took us under her wing. In fact, we were all the family each other had."

Brodie suddenly straightened. "A true genteel lady if I ever saw one. I assume she's away right now?"

"Died last winter. Pleurisy and pneumonia."

"You should've—"

"Found you? I tried. Knew you'd want to know." Murphy's hand shook in an effort to keep control. "That's what happens when you stay gone for a coon's age."

"Double damn."

Torment deepened the crevices in Brodie's face. Laurel turned away, unable to bear the pain that ripped open his soul. Her reflection stared back from the crater. Losing family left a wound that never healed. She knew about that.

Replenishing his empty goblet, the man who lived by the quickness of his hand raised it high. "I salute you, Aunt Lucy, the finest woman God ever created. Rest in peace."

"Amen," Murphy added softly.

"Brother, you have anything stronger? This stuff makes lousy tonsil varnish. Not fit to drown a man's sorrows."

Putting sympathy for the motherless brothers aside, that's not all Laurel wished Brodie would drown.

"I've a bottle of sipping whiskey in my study." Murphy flashed her a wry smile. "Purely for medicinal purposes."

"That'll do." Brodie pulled himself from the chair.

Laurel eyed his easy stride. Long and lean, he moved as a man with a purpose but all the time in the world to get there.

A heavy sigh left her lips. His exit meant prolonging the inevitable. Until she knew his intentions, distasteful and ugly though they might be, time would stand still.

"Forgive my brother. He's not the same man who left."

She found it difficult to focus on anything beyond getting out of there. She slid from the chair. "It's getting late. I must go."

"Please, a brief moment in the garden then I'll see you home. While Etta gets that pie for Ollie?" Murphy cajoled.

"I suppose it won't hurt." Laurel accepted his elbow.

The night air whispered of coming trouble when they stepped into the lush paradise. Late-blooming chrysanthemums, asters, and brown-eyed Susans intoxicated her with their fragrance.

Murphy pulled her against him. "The moonlight must be jealous of your beauty. I want you so badly."

Her thoughts scattered like naughty children. His breath ruffled the hair at her temples, adding to her guilt. Anyone with a shred of decency would tell him the truth.

He ran his fingers through her curls, tilting her head. His kiss sent pleasing warmth coursing through her.

Not earth-shattering.

Or passionate.

Just…pleasant.

A man's lips should make the woman he marries hot and sultry as an August night. They should take the breath right out of her body and make her wonder if she truly needed air to begin with. His mouth should elicit a tremble, like the powerful grip of an alligator's jaws, knowing they could crush or set her free.

Laurel had that once. A long time ago.

Soft clapping jarred the stillness. They jerked apart as two lovers caught red-handed.

"Nice, little brother. Thought I might have to come out and give you some advice in the ways of women."

She whirled. A cigar's red glow outlined the shadowy form. Brodie stepped toward them. A whiskey bottle dangled from his fingers. How long had he watched? No doubt he'd witnessed their embrace. She squirmed at that thought.

Murphy huffed. "Brodie, can't you see we're in the middle of…"

"Business? Yep, that's what it appears."

"Then you must know it doesn't require a third party."

Murphy's sharp tone took her aback. He'd revealed a side she'd not seen. A cool wind rustled the foliage. She shivered.

"Cold, my love?"

"I left my shawl inside. I'll get it."

"Let me. I'll only be gone a second."

He vanished into the house. No article of clothing could give her the warmth she sought.

Without question, nothing other than the interloper's backside riding out of Redemption would put her world to rights. He unnerved her more than anything had since becoming free. The future, the lives of several people lay within his power. Still, she'd not tuck tail and run as he'd done.

A slim-to-none chance was all she had. It'd have to do.

Her tongue found the edge of the sharp tooth. She moistened her dry lips and stuck out her jaw. "What low-down, spiteful game do you play?"

The shadows darkened the day's beard growth. The devil-take-you saunter brought him within touching distance. He knew full well what he did to her. He tucked a curl behind her ear.

"Protecting my brother is all."

"From me?"

"Far-fetched, I know. I'm only looking out for him. Murphy's the only salvageable part of Samuel and Elizabeth Yates."

"Don't you think I know that?"

"What assurance does anyone have you'll not move on to another once you tire of the thrill of conquest?"

"Your worry isn't for Murphy, it's about yourself. You don't want me, yet you'll stop anyone else from having me."

"Have you told him about your chosen profession? Does he know your penchant for good cigars and billiards?" Brodie took a long swig from the bottle and wiped his mouth with the back of his hand. "Does he know you've probably had more men in your bed than he or I both can count?"

The verbal blow sent her reeling. Pride kept her from crumpling to the ground. She'd die rather than let him see.

"So this is about revenge." She tried another tack. "If you truly care as you claim, you'll stop before it destroys the very thing you wish to save. Whether you believe it or not, I've changed."

"From what? Way I see it, you're still trying to lure

men into your bed. The method is the only difference I can tell. The institution of marriage may not be sacred to you—"

"You of all people dare to speak of sacred oaths and decency. At least I've not killed anyone."

Laurel strained to hear his soft reply.

"Maybe not with a six gun, darlin'. Your weapons are far more devious and devastating. You're not content unless you steal a man's soul."

A gush of breath left a painful throb in her chest.

"Once you were warm and oh so willing, Lil."

He fingered wayward strands of hair that spilled over her shoulder. She winced at the touch that burned through clothing to the skin beneath. Damn him. Damn them both.

"I believe you stated earlier, that was two lifetimes ago."

"More or less. I reckon the faces blended together until they all looked the same. I understand that. Yep, mighty easy for someone who had eyes focused solely on the color of their money."

He grabbed her wrist before she got it raised. The depth of anger had taken her by storm. She'd not meant to lift her hand, only wipe the knowing smile. One minute he despised her and the next tried to rehash old memories.

"How dare you!"

His hard, glistening eyes challenged her. Laurel finally lowered her stare, unable to compete with the man who could look another in the eye and send him to his death.

"Dare?" Brodie let her arm drop. He tapped ashes from

the cigar and stuck it in the corner of his mouth. His calm tone deceived. "I'll allow no one to trample Murph's tender feelings. Mark my words, I won't sit idly by."

Hostility thickened the damp air until it clung to her skin. The things he must have endured during the years to be so embittered. But it didn't give him cause to attack her.

There was no excuse.

Before tears could gather, she stiffened her backbone. He'd not humiliate her, or revel in her shame. Not now, not ever.

"Telling him will do irrefutable harm. He'll hate you, not me. I can't think you'd risk that."

A frown crossed Brodie's face. "That's why I held back when the opportunity arose."

"You're wasting thinly veiled threats. I'm trying to start fresh, build a new life. Half a chance is all I ask."

Smoke swirled about her head, tickling her nose. Of the hardest cravings to stifle, cigars stood at the top. Proper ladies didn't indulge in that vice. Achieving that goal ranked highest on her list of priorities.

"I'll see your bet and raise it. One week to break off the engagement. Speak the truth or tell a lie. Doesn't matter, as long as you walk out of Murphy's life."

Thoughts of sinful cravings fled. "One week?"

"That's the deal." He widened the gap between them when footsteps sounded on the stone path.

"Ahh, the two of you are getting acquainted." Murphy draped the shawl across Laurel's shoulders, then put an arm around both her and Brodie and pulled them close. "My two favorite people. How lucky can a man get?"

Five

BRODIE REMAINED ON THE STONE GARDEN BENCH LONG after his brother walked Laurel home. Distant fog horns emerged from the thick soup, along with chattering river otters and mockingbird chirps. Deep croaks of a frog clan sang bass in the chorus.

Why did he have to run into her here of all places?

Despite what time did to thicken a person's memory, he'd recognized Lil right off. Those eyes, that voice, could do unforgettable things to a man. When he'd spied her in the café, he'd gotten the same tight squiggle in his chest. It'd taken several seconds for his lungs to remind him they had emptied.

Great Johnny Reb. He'd wanted to kill that fool boy for pawing her that way. No one treated his lady with disrespect.

Except you, a little voice whispered.

He wished he had some excuse for his crass behavior. Every wrong word had left his mouth, creating a disastrous evening.

Over the years he'd imagined crossing paths again

with the beauty who'd stolen a piece of his heart—the tender things he'd say, the taste of her lips.

He'd done none of those, despite an urge so powerful it gnawed at him still.

The shock of finding her engaged to his brother of all people had plunged a dull blade into his heart.

Brodie sucked in a ragged breath that hurt all the way down to his toes. Present state of mind aside, he found peace here among the trimmed hedges and bordered flower beds.

Neatness and order. A far cry from the bloody killing fields that haunted his dreams.

Some called him a high plains drifter, among other less polite names. He'd given up on finding a place in which a man could hide, in hundreds of towns that all came to look alike.

His damnable reputation.

He'd tried to avoid the fight with Prater that could've ended in his worst fear: that someday, luck would run out. When that time came, he wished to be able to feel it, to know he had more than the cold stone heart of a warrior.

From inside his shirt, he withdrew a soft deerskin pouch, sliding his thumb across the supple texture warmed by his skin.

A handmade memory bag that protected items near and dear.

With care, he removed a scrap of lavender lace.

Thoughts whirled inside his head, a roulette wheel of sorts that stopped on the color black. St. Louis, the Black Garter, and a raven-haired beauty. He'd never met anyone, before or since, equal to Lil.

Had she missed the torn piece from one of her ruffles? Brodie raised the sacred reminder to his nose, imagining it still bore her scent and nights of wild passion. With her he'd escaped the horrors of a war that raged with no end in sight.

Lil made him forget a lot of things when her body curled next to his. And spoiled all other women for him.

For a price.

Everything came with an almighty price.

Shrouded by darkness, he remembered things he shouldn't. Then paradise became pure hell, hurtling him headlong into its pit. That blasted war had ruined all hope. Under General Price's orders, his regiment had marched from St. Louis, and at Pilot Knob he ran smack into a piece of shattering hot lead.

He'd always wondered what happened to her. Meant to find out one day…

After he got the hole in his heart mended first.

Well, now he'd found her. Funny, he still had that hole, and a body with no head.

Why did she have to belong to Murphy?

Truth to tell, her soft curves bewitched even now.

Damn. She'd never believe the pricks he'd uttered had sprung out of deep pain, not from passing judgment. No one would ever nominate him for sainthood. Not with his record.

Albeit chipped and cracked around the edges, Lil was china nonetheless, while the blood of too many men stained his name. Many only boys, their faces etched into his rotten soul, who had become as much a part of him as breathing. Even if he dared confess that the thought of her with another man made him crazy, that he'd give anything to spend the rest of his life wrapped in her arms, what right did he have?

Men in his line of work couldn't entertain ideas of love, a home, and children.

He'd not ask Lil or any other to share the danger riding in his saddle.

The accusation about not wanting her hit a sore spot. It was safe to say he desired her in every way imaginable.

Nope, Brodie regretted a lot of things, but meeting her skipped the long list of remorse.

Hell and be damned if he'd let her marry his brother.

"One week, Miss James." He folded the fragile lavender lace back inside the deerskin.

The memory bag held other treasures. Cold metal of his mother's simple gold ring brushed his fingers. A lock of Murphy's hair spoke of a brotherly bond. Aunt Lucy's faded note right after he'd joined up completed the accounting.

A creak of the garden gate announced Murphy's return. Brodie secured the bag in its secret place. Wouldn't do to let baby brother find him pining over a scrap of lavender.

"Nice night." Murphy settled beside him.

"Sight better than most I've spent. You get Miss James tucked in all nice and cozy?"

"I don't recognize the person you've become. Makes me wonder if I ever knew you at all."

Brodie held the cigar, watching the red glow. "War does things to a man's mind, changes priorities—rearranges his life. I apologize for tonight. Didn't mean to be a jackass."

"I suppose. Don't do it again, and I mean it. Keep disrespecting her and you'll force me to turn you out."

All I'm asking is a chance. Her plea brought unease.

"That's clear enough. I was sitting here thinking about leopards and their spots. Do you think he—or she—can change, Murph?"

"Anything acquired at birth, they're probably stuck with. Like you and me."

"I'm relieved you think we're stuck with each other."

"But if the spots are painted on, I'd say they could. Where are you going with this anyway?"

"No place, little brother. No place at all."

The shake of Murphy's head suggested Brodie suffered from weakness north of his ears. Hell, he'd lost any sense he had a long time ago…to a silken-haired seductress.

"I've missed you. Never got accustomed to being alone. When we were boys, I tagged not more than three steps from your shadow. I'd wake up shaking with fear that you'd die on some battlefield and I'd never know."

"Scared me, too, being by myself. For a while I walked around thinking a mule had stomped on me and left me for crow bait." Brodie tilted the bottle and found a measure of comfort in the trail of fire it left to his belly. "Believe it or not, I still do."

Matter of fact, even more since arriving in Redemption.

"I own there's good reason to build a wall around you. Men who stare death in the face and have seen enough spilled blood to float a steamer would." Murphy shifted. "You can tear it down though. Unlike that leopard, your spots can come off. It's never too late."

He found his brother's advice an ill-fit. Murphy

should save it for one more worthy of change. "I'm tired of running, trying to do no more than survive. You know how many times I've cheated the undertaker by being a split second faster?"

"You're safe for a while. Rest while you can."

How could he when she waited beneath his closed eyes? His thoughts, his blood, his very soul echoed her name. Brodie fought the recollection of Laurel's exquisite features bathed in pale moonlight. Moisture left his mouth.

"Do you truly love her, Murph?"

"More than I ever thought possible."

An ache in Brodie's chest robbed him of air. How could he in good conscience steal their happiness? Dearly as he wished, he suspected Lil's past had become as finely ingrained as his own sorry one. And maybe she truly did return Murphy's affection.

"Guess you do at that."

"I still gather you don't approve. Care to say why?"

"It's my job to make sure you don't get your heart broke."

"Quit upsetting her. You were way out of line tonight with that hogwash about St. Louis."

"Would another apology fix things?"

"Just watch it. I protect what's mine, even from you."

Brodie gave a low whistle. "So I see. You've grown up."

"About time you noticed." Murphy leaned forward, resting his arms on his legs. "I want to warn you about another matter. Despite enjoying your company, it's dangerous for you here."

"I know." The measured words came low.

"I don't think you appreciate fully the hotbed we're

in. Soldiers itch to capture the infamous Confederate, Shenandoah. But frankly, I'm concerned about other areas as well."

"I'm tired of the chase. I'll end my days here."

"White citizens have formed pockets of resistance, groups called—"

"Knights of the Rising Sun, Cullen Baker's Knights of the White Camelia, or any number of similar organizations?"

"You've heard. Any plans on joining them?"

"Nope. Have they converted you, Murph?"

"I'm not their kind. I respect all people no matter the color of their skin."

"I figured that, since you have Etta and her boy here."

"You and I never cottoned to slavery. She earns triple what anyone else would pay. She's part of this family."

"She should've gone north to safer climes after the war's end. The Freedmen's Bureau gives precious little protection. Countless men and women wind up dead each day."

"Etta has nowhere else to go. I look out for them." Murphy stood and stretched. "Remember what I said. Be careful and watch your back. You coming to bed?"

"Believe I'll sit a bit longer."

The prospect of lying in bed across the hall from the room in which Murphy and Laurel would soon make love held the appeal of eating a fistful of juicy grub worms.

Brodie stopped his sibling. Thickness rose, making his voice hoarse. "I'm sorry I left you, Murph."

The kitchen sparkled by the time Laurel wearily climbed the stairs. No sign of Ollie, which answered a prayer. The catastrophe might go down better with bitter brew come morn.

She took off her shoes and padded silently down the hall. But outside her door, guilt set in. The dear woman could be lying in the agonizing throes of another spell. Pausing to carefully listen, the racket brought a wry smile. The snoring recital from beyond stifled any worry.

Inside her room, she became all thumbs as she undressed and pulled on her nightgown. Shaking hands betrayed the turmoil.

Shenandoah...Brodie Yates seemed hell-bent on yanking away everything, and she hadn't the power to prevent it.

A mental list of options ran through her head.

To call his bluff, if indeed it be that, held unknown risk. Pushing him could lead to a dire, quick end.

No greater satisfaction came to mind than to beat Brodie at his own game. It would destroy him though. She couldn't do that to the gentle man.

The gamble could cause them both public disgrace.

Maybe she should quietly break off the engagement as Brodie advised. While that wouldn't spare Murphy hurt, it might be the best hand to play.

A third solution chilled her bones...leaving Redemption in the dead of night, never to return.

And that meant giving up what she'd gained in a final, everlasting way.

In addition, Brodie would win a decisive victory.

Locked in the desperate tug-of-war, Laurel reached

for a small music box. Through pleading, bargaining, and tears, she'd managed to hold on to the gift from her mother long ago. The feather mattress sank with her weight. She cradled the treasure. Fighting back a crush of images, she wound it.

Strains of the old childhood favorite fed a starved soul.

She imagined Mama's soothing touch and murmuring, "It'll be all right, my sweet darling. Everything will be right as rain."

Ollie knew of Mary and Ben James. Laurel had talked for hours about them and the piece of land between Marshall and Jefferson—the same farm from which Taft and his cohorts abducted her. Strange how Ollie sensed her desire to be near her family again, as if somehow their spirit would lend healing and strength. That is if they still lived there.

She hadn't gotten up enough nerve or spent enough time forgetting to find out.

Six years away from those she loved. An eternity.

They'd had seven hungry mouths to feed when she left, quite possibly more now. And suppose her father had perished in the war?

Her family presumed her dead and she'd leave it at that. Far too much pain and a mountain of shame to regain what Will Taft stole. Besides, he'd first look for her there when he came.

No, it was better this way.

A soft rap made her jump. Never one to stand on ceremony, Ollie barged in.

"Dadburn it. Knew the minute I heard the tinkle of your music box trouble's come a callin'."

Laurel brushed tiredness from her eyes. The

comical woman's nightcap drooped over one ear, half on and half off, giving the fading reddish tangle a life of its own.

"Sorry I woke you, although it seemed unlikely judging from the snores raising the roof."

"Trying to get smart with me, aren't you? What's wrong?"

"Nothing. Merely getting that homesick feeling again. You know."

"Yep. But this lump in my chest says it's a bit more than that." Ollie plopped down and forced Laurel to meet her gaze. "My grandpappy, bless his poor soul, always warned, 'Girl, lying will only git you to hell on a fast horse. If you don't have good reason, it pays to speak the truth.'"

Did it count that Ollie suffered from a bad heart and required peace and quiet to live out her days? Or that their hard work had come to naught? Laurel bit a trembling lip.

"Go ahead, spit it out. I ain't leaving until you do."

"It'll keep. Go back to bed."

"Yours is sturdy enough. Reckon it'll hold the both of us." Ollie patted the covers. "Appears comfortable, too."

"Pity's sake. Remember you insisted, so if you keel over, don't blame me." Laurel took a deep breath. "Shenandoah is Murphy's brother."

There, she'd said it. And hearing it from her lips brought more misery than when it sat quietly in her head.

"He's *what*?"

"Murphy's brother. His true name is Brodie Yates. Shenandoah is an alias he took up."

"Well, I'll be a suck-egg mule."

"Brodie gave me a week to break off the engagement."

"Or what?"

"He'll tell everyone and run me out of town."

"The dirty, low-down rascal. One week, huh?"

"That's the threat, and no doubt he'll do it."

"That's right charitable of him," Ollie remarked dryly. "Any stipulations on how you go about it?"

"He left that up to me." She fidgeted with the soft cotton threads. "I suppose I could claim second thoughts."

"Wouldn't work. Men pester the living daylights out of you unless you kick 'em right in the seat of their pants."

"That's awfully shabby treatment."

"No other way. Want your own heart, your dreams, dragged through the mud?"

"They already have been. I thought this time I might succeed in trying to break free."

"Stop with that. Never thought I'd see the day you'd give up without a fight." Ollie squeezed her shoulders. "A body can have anything they desire as long as they have fire in their belly."

A sob lodged in Laurel's chest. She clenched a fist. "I want to outwit Brodie so bad I can taste it."

"From my dealings with men, actually quite a few, what sends them packing faster than anything is to let it slip you're sweet on someone else. They normally don't stick around long once another has stolen your affections. Hard on their pride."

"And who can I pretend to love?"

Anyone except a rebel-eyed gunslinger with a searing touch. She couldn't pit brother against brother. The war had done that.

"Just tell Murphy you was set to marry years ago

and your beau joined up to fight. You got word they buried him on the battlefield, but recently learned of the mistake."

Lord knew how close Ollie came to the truth.

"I suppose it might work. I'm no good at fibbing though. He'll see through me like daylight through a windowpane."

"All's you gotta do is dirty up the window a little."

"Easy for you to say."

"Never underestimate the value of tears and lacy handkerchiefs. Worked for me. We'll buy one of them fancy hats with dark net that hides your eyes. He'll never suspect."

A flicker of hope rose. The plan might save them.

Suddenly, diamondback rattles and the two-legged snake who wore them flashed across her mind. How long would he keep silent?

"I just had an awful thought. Brodie might demand something else after we go through with this charade. Or he could have a slip of the tongue. The right word in the ear of a busybody like Florence Kempshaw, and everyone in fourteen counties will have the news."

The petite woman whistled through her teeth. "I see what you mean. Some gents take pure delight in watching you squirm. Cain't trust Yates far as we can spit."

Once, in a dark room that reeked of filth and broken spirits, she'd thought she'd found a true man of honor. Maybe somewhere deep inside him, that man still existed. She'd like to think so.

"He taunted me throughout the entire evening. This is a game to him. Each moment the words threatened to spill, he'd pull back. Despite everything and no matter how much she rebelled against it, she was still in love with the man she'd known only as Shenandoah."

Memories in the midnight hours were still steeped in passion and lustful cravings she couldn't deny. When she'd seen him standing there with Murphy, it had been all she could do not to run her hand along his stubbled jaw.

God help her.

"In my world, that means he intends to make your life worth nothing more than one of them goldarned Confederate notes."

Ever been to St. Louis, Miss James?

"You hit the nail on the head, Ollie."

Ollie shot her a sharp glance. "You think it's high time to whistle up the dogs and douse the fire?"

Six

"LEAVE? GIVE UP?" LAUREL COULDN'T BELIEVE HER ears. The Ollie she knew would find the idea preposterous. "You made it clear from the start you had no sympathy for quitters."

"Those strong words don't apply here." Ollie pulled the blasted pipe from within the folds of her nightgown. "Son of a bluejacket. Left my tobacco and matches across the hall. Don't suppose you'd be a good girl and traipse over there?"

"Smoking is bad for your health. Besides, it's late."

"If I wanted a sermon, I'd go to church." Ollie stuck the cold pipe between her teeth. "I ain't calling it quittin', mind you—merely moving on. A world of difference between the two."

"You're splitting hairs. It's the coward's way out no matter how you cut it."

"Back in my dabbling days with betting and men who did, I learned a true gambler knows when to ride out a bluff and when to toss in the whole damn bunch of cards. This may be the time for foldin' and laying 'em down. I won't fault you for it."

"I can't expect to run from trouble all my life. Once a body starts, they have to keep on until there's no place left."

For her, Redemption represented the end of running.

"Girl, I've known you the better part of a year and you have no shortage of courage. One day you'll stand your ground and dare the world to knock you cross-eyed. No harm in waiting until you get more wind in your sails. Until a big gust comes along, there's merit in getting while the getting's good."

Laurel rested wearily on Ollie's shoulder. A loving pat on her cheek chased the chill. Damn the runty skinflint for sneaking under the barricades when she wasn't looking.

"My heart says stay—my head urges run and hide."

"You're the closest thing to a daughter I'll have. We're sailing this ship together. If you want to plant your feet here, I'll fight alongside and dare anyone to come get us."

A curtain of tears blocked her vision. "You're quite lovable…for a crusty old coot."

"Now, don't get all-fired mushy on me. I love you, too, but I don't need to go around saying it." Ollie snatched off the nightcap that drooped onto one ear before it finished its slide. "I don't know why I wear this fool thing. No need for a rash decision. Sleep on it. Like my grandpappy always said, 'Never jump off a cliff less'n someone pushes you. A feller could find himself eyeball-deep in dirt.'"

❧

By daylight the next morning, Laurel's churning stomach matched the deep whirlpools on Big Cypress

Bayou. A sleepless night had brought more questions than answers. Six days left.

Ollie was sipping a cup of black dredge when she went down. The woman's idea of a drinkable pot of coffee resembled thick river bottom. Although Laurel tried her best, Ollie wasn't prone to taking instruction. At least not with any degree of patience.

Avoiding questions in the eyes staring over the chipped cup, Laurel lifted her apron from the nail and tied it around her waist before she marched to the dwindling brine barrel.

Meat supplies had gotten awfully low. The promised shipment should've arrived by now. Odd that it hadn't. She fished out a piece of tender beef, wishing it was the scoundrel's head she plopped into a large pot.

Spit and thunder, he could ruin a day.

A week.

...A life.

The squeaky pump handle broke the silence as Ollie drew a pitcher of water and handed it to her. "Morning, girl."

"At least you didn't add 'good' to it." Laurel emptied the pitcher into the pot, splashing water onto the stove's cast iron plate.

"That can wait a minute. Have a cup of my coffee. I brewed it exactly the way I like it."

Contention dripped from the statement. Ollie delighted in jabbing her with a sharp stick merely to test her mettle. She raised her head from the vegetable bin only after filling the draped apron with onions, carrots, and potatoes.

"That stuff you drink might plug the hole in a dyke, but it won't stop lunch from coming."

"Nothing sinful in asking for a measly bit of conversation."

Vegetables spilled onto the table. The smile gracing Ollie's face when she complied told who had won that round.

"We're family, and most of the ones I've known parlay over breakfast." Ollie shuffled to the stove to pour Laurel a cup. "Worriment won't go away simply by pretending it ain't there."

She pushed aside the thick liquid. "If we must talk, I'll have hot tea, thank you."

"Well, forevermore. You never let on you had something against my concoction. It'll learn you to stick your tongue to the roof of your mouth."

The laugh dispelled the gloom, at least temporarily.

But by noon Laurel's nerves had knotted into one huge ball.

"You're jumpier than a horse thief in a noose," Ollie remarked. "Think I can't see how you watch the door?"

"Brodie will likely make an appearance if for nothing more than to keep me off balance. He favors that tactic."

"This old gal might have a few tricks of her own to teach that gun-totin' blackmailer."

A record number of customers kept her hopping. When she watched the last of them depart without Brodie Yates darkening the café, Laurel drew a sigh of relief.

Busy clearing away the remains of chaos, she barely

heard the late arrival. The sound drawing her attention came no louder than the whimper of a mouse caught in a trap.

She whirled, her heart sinking.

The deep husky tone enveloped her in a heavy embrace. "Too late for a man to get a bite to eat?"

Laurel tried to turn away from the smoky warmth, but found her focus riveted to the shadowed square jaw and damnable crooked smile that made her remember all that she'd lost.

"Never too late...for feeding a rumbling belly." Ollie had wandered in from the back. "What'll be your poison?"

"Another beefsteak, if you will, Miss James."

The petite war wagon swelled in height over the dismissal. Laurel tried to speak, but instead floundered in his stare.

Once more Ollie interjected, "Leave that hogleg of yours on the counter and we might consider it. Don't allow shootin' irons in here. I done told you that."

The knot in Laurel's stomach grew. She held her breath, unable to wrench herself from the bold scrutiny. The familiar hiss followed each twitch as he pulled out a chair and sat down.

Ollie crossed her arms. "Go fetch the sheriff, girl."

Long seconds ticked by before Brodie finally unwound his tall frame from the seat. His hand slid to the muscular thigh. The thin leather strap keeping the holster secure on his leg fell away with a gentle tug. Inching back to his waist, he unbuckled the wide belt with one hand. Only after he handed it to Ollie did Laurel dare move...or swallow.

"That suit you?"

"See? It's painless," Ollie said. "Now, we'll rustle up some grub."

Laurel strode for the kitchen.

"Do you want to get yourself killed?" She pulled Ollie behind the door. "You succeeded in antagonizing him further. He came to start a fire and you provided the match."

"Men like Shenandoah don't need reasons. They wake up with 'em every morning. Don't worry. I got him under control."

It sure looked like it. A gnat meeting Goliath.

"You have got to quit thinking yourself bigger…" Laurel's sentence trailed, cut short by a vanishing swish through the door.

Ollie stood on the other side, full of purpose and righteous vigor. She squared her shoulders and marched straight for the threat who'd propped his legs on a chair in front of him. The gun-toter's carefree pose didn't fool an old war horse like her.

"We need to come to an understandin'."

Brodie removed his feet and pushed the chair. "Whatever you have on your mind might best be said sitting, ma'am."

"Olivia. Olivia Applejack b'Dam." She perched on the edge. No need to get comfortable. This wouldn't take long. "My friends call me Ollie, only you don't qualify for that."

"Something eating you, Olivia Applejack b'Dam?"

Ollie narrowed her gaze. "Take that silly grin and those nice manners back where you came from, mister. I'll thank you to leave Laurel alone."

"Lil, you mean?"

"I didn't stutter. Name's Laurel and don't ever forget it." She jabbed the table with a finger.

"No need to get hostile. What did she tell you?"

Heat rose like sweeping fire over dry prairie grass. "Enough to warn you to watch your tongue or someone might happen to put you to bed with a pick and shovel. I'd sure take it as an honor if it were me what did it. When you refer to Laurel, it'd pay to use a big helping of respect."

"Plain language for a short, scrappy pipe-smoker."

"Short or tall, don't need fancy words. My grandpappy, who was a mite taller'n a tadpole, bless his soul, said, 'Say it plain, girl, an' save some air for breathin'.'"

"Awful defensive, aren't you, to not be family?"

"I'm the nearest thing the poor darling's had in a long while. I ain't gonna let you or anyone else sling mud across her good name." She met the scowl without flinching a muscle.

"This is between Laurel and me. It would behoove you to stay out of it."

"You've got a fight if that's what you want, sonny boy."

"Keep her away from my brother, then."

"Give the lady some air. The doing will get done without you hounding her plumb to death."

"No law against protecting my brother. She's hoodwinked him into believing her unsullied. She'll break Murphy's heart."

"Only mistake your brother made is having you as kith and kin. You're not fit to wipe Murphy's boots."

Brodie twitched, arching a brow. Ollie wished

to take back the words. It never boded well to mess with another man's pride or open old wounds. She'd forgotten that in her haste.

Tension hung between them. Though Ollie shook inside, she flexed her hands and readied for a blood-letting.

Laughter caught her off guard. All of a sudden she felt thirsty. Her parched throat welcomed a tall drink. Preferably something stronger than a sarsaparilla.

"Probably right, Olivia b'Dam. Probably right."

Jovial chuckles greeted Laurel when she entered with his meal. What on earth? Peeking through the door at the dogged set to Ollie's chin, she imagined anything but relief.

"Girl, I just remembered I had business to tend to across the way."

Laurel put down the plate, wondering what had thrown Ollie in such a tizzy. The door slammed behind the slight figure. Laurel turned, looking to retreat.

"Sit with me, Lil." The order didn't come with an alternative.

Bittersweet memories rose from their ashes. She'd wished to hear those words about a thousand times. Deep in her heart, an ache throbbed.

"You paid for the steak, not idle conversation." The statement came hard and brittle as she faced him.

Brodie reached into his pocket and flipped a silver dollar onto the table. The heavy coin spun for a second before clinking to rest with the woman's profile staring up.

"I'm paying for the company."

Laurel's lips tightened and her fingernails dug into

the soft flesh of her palms. "Who do you think you are to barge into my life this way?"

"A man no one wants to know. The devil with a six-shooter." His tone held quiet torture. "Someone who's been to heaven and hell and half the stops in between."

Doubting her wisdom, she dropped stiffly into the chair Ollie had vacated, hating the swish as the hem of her skirt floated lazily against his boots. "What does such a man talk about?"

Damn her voice for going soft on her. She blamed the glimmer in his eyes…and the smile that promised sin.

"Pain and regret. Happy times. Four days in St. Louis. Pecan praline pie that I have on good authority is the way to your heart. Should I continue?"

Foreboding swept her down a winding road. To follow would be inviting back the dark, unwelcome nightmares she strived daily to forget. The past lay buried beneath more grief and turmoil than any person should ever have to live with.

Brodie swallowed and laid down his fork when she didn't reply. He leaned forward, his intent clear. Laurel jerked her head aside and drew back. However, such tactics didn't deter a man like him. With a firm grip of her chin, he forced her to meet the hunger in his smoky gaze.

"I recall a hot-blooded woman on a sultry summer night. The wet eagerness between——"

"Please…"

"That's what you said then, too. Begged for more. Pleaded with me to take you with me."

"Lil died. She doesn't exist anymore." A razor-sharp edge flavored the harsh reality. He'd left her in that godforsaken place with never a backward glance.

"You're mistaken. Lil is very much alive." He tapped his leather-vested chest. "She's in here for safekeeping."

With the barest of touches, his fingertips traced the line of her parted mouth, leaving a scorched path. A fine sheen of perspiration pooled in the valley between her breasts.

"Kisses sweet as sun-ripened strawberries. Wonder if you taste the same as I remember."

"Stop." Laurel twisted away and stood. "We can't."

He touched her again, his caress more gentle than dewdrops on an early spring day. She shivered against the contact of his thumb smoothing away perspiration pooling in the hollow of her throat, then across a wildly beating pulse.

"What's a woman like you doing in Redemption? Surely not trying to find salvation."

"Is that so ridiculous a notion?"

Brodie's clear gaze simmered. "Think a leopard can change his spots?"

"I'm not the person you thought. Despite what you choose to believe, I had no control over my situation. I do have that luxury now, however."

"So you say, Lil." Brodie's lazy drawl scraped across raw nerves, silk over sandpaper. "Time does tell all."

Memories tumbled end over end, colliding with temptation that she wasn't positive she had strength to resist.

Her head whirled in tune with a thundering heartbeat as she flew from the dining room into the kitchen. Splashing water from the porcelain bowl beneath the pump, she cooled her heated cheeks.

Please let me come. I promise I won't be any trouble.

Not now, darlin'. Can't, but I'll be back.

He'd heard nothing over the roar of his lust. He'd closed his eyes to her shame. In all fairness, he never knew they'd kept her prisoner. By the time she decided to trust him, he'd waltzed out the door. And left her behind.

The roughness of her tooth scraped her tongue.

Angry rattles coupled with easy footsteps aroused alarm. She pivoted and found herself staring at the man who she wanted more than anything on earth.

He approached with slow, deliberate steps.

"Didn't get my dollar's worth of conversation."

"I didn't ask for or take your money. I owe you nothing." Laurel backed up until her shoulder blades flattened against the wall.

"You saying I can't pay for favors?" He took a step.

"Yes. I told you I'm not the same…" A roar began inside her head. She eyed the approaching storm, knowing it was too late for help.

"You saying you won't give that little moan like you used to if I touch you?" He progressed two steps this time.

She licked her parched lips. Didn't the man understand? Persisting would only awaken sleeping dogs that had no reason to stir from their slumber.

"Do I dare to find out if your lips will remain cold and lifeless?" He inched closer, narrowing the space between them more.

So close. A trickle of sweat slid down her back,

soaking the tight waistband. The fragrance of leather and fresh-cut hay meandered up her nose. God help her. His mouth pressed to hers would rekindle the love she still felt for Brodie Yates. She wasn't made of stone…just flesh and blood and more regrets than she could count.

The lazy half smile indicated enjoyment. He knew his nearness suffocated her thoughts.

He meant to strip every shred of her newfound dignity.

He intended to kiss her.

And perhaps more? She gasped for air but found little.

"Convince me. For old times' sake?" He reached for a dark curl. "Show me I'm no longer in your blood, and I'll leave you alone. I dare you."

A rabbit in a snare had a more reasonable chance. His hand slipped behind her head. Laurel sagged weakly against his chest, tired of fighting forbidden attraction. Beneath her ear, his heart raced, perhaps chased by memories on a fast horse.

"I've dreamed of this for so long." His breath stirred the hair against her throbbing temple. "I've relived every detail of those nights in my mind. The faint scent of rose water behind your ears, the tiny pulse in the hollow of your throat. I remember every whispered endearment."

"Please…stop. I don't—"

His mouth smothered the plea. Her body betrayed her, responding to desire born from hopeless fear long ago.

Laurel welcomed the thrusting tongue, and when her breasts ached for his caress, he covered them with his palms, rolling the nipples to hard peaks. Delicious, shameful thrills played tag up her spine.

Soft mewling escaped from somewhere deep inside, a place where lies could not hide. A place she'd never thought to revisit in this century.

The arousal bulging from his trousers into her soft belly spoke of equal need. Passion became a raging inferno that threatened to scorch everything in its path…including her lofty goals of good intentions.

Low moans rumbled in his throat when she wound her fingers in the thickness of his hair.

What she wouldn't give to pretend he meant nothing. Simply a man she used to know. Or maybe just some nameless wanderer who'd ridden into town looking to put food in his belly.

Truth and lies, pleasure and pain. Seemed she couldn't have one without plenty of the opposite. She'd pay any price if he'd up and disappear from her life one more time.

But wasn't the greater sin in denying that he made her feel alive again?

Abruptly, he pushed away. "Got my answer. The fire still burns hotter than ever. Cloak yourself in self-righteous claims that mean nothing. You still care for me. Admit it."

Laurel recoiled, wishing him into the nearest grave.

"You low-down double-crosser. I didn't throw myself into your arms. You came to me. You took what belongs to your brother."

The imprint of his touch lingered on her skin like a hot brand.

He barked a laugh. "I didn't notice any resistance."

Seven

LAUREL STEELED HERSELF AGAINST THE HURT AND knowing Brodie was right about loving him. Still, she itched to wipe that grin off his face.

"It's in your blood, darlin'. I've no doubt should I want you in my bed, you'd come willingly...for a price."

"My, you flatter yourself, Yates," she said wryly. "Given a choice of jumping into a pool of quicksand or crawling up beside you on dry land, I'd choose the quicksand and meet my fate. Your bed? Not for any price."

The lie left a foul taste in her mouth. Admitting his kiss, his touch, ignited embers of a long-cold fire courted disaster. She couldn't say what she wished, even though it meant denying her heart.

"Stay away from Murphy."

Warmth where he'd pressed against her belly still burned.

"And you?" The whisper gorged the space between them.

"I'm immune to your tricks, Lil." Brodie flashed a crooked smile. "But should you find yourself sinking in that quicksand, my door is always open."

The brimstone glare she shot should've blistered the tall broad figure that left the same way he came.

Laurel collapsed into the nearest chair, emotionally drained. She wouldn't have known Ollie bustled in were it not for scurrying movement too loud for mice.

"I hope you enjoyed your little refreshment."

"Reckon you got a right to spit nails for me deserting you."

Remorse nicked her anger. Ollie needn't bear the brunt. Laurel had unfettered the bridled desire to be kissed and caressed the way a woman yearns.

The fault lay with no one but her.

In all fairness, Brodie would've backed away had she positively insisted. She knew that.

He'd never exhibited cunning or evil.

But devilish, maddening, and charming?

Always.

Honest truth never hurt a body. She hadn't wanted to deny the pleasure that enveloped each tiny, sensuous nerve ending and made them throb with life after a long sleep.

"I'm not mad at you." Laurel marched to the brine barrel and reached in.

"You're ready to throttle someone. Only one other name comes to mind. Better tell me what that rascal did. I'll badger you until you do." Smoke billowed from the overworked pipe. "Is he the one making you cry?"

A sweep of her sleeve brushed away tell-tale signs. "This darn brine makes my eyes water. To which rascal do you refer?"

"Shenandoah or Yates, whichever name he's using today."

A band of soothsayers had to sit on a branch of Ollie's family tree. The way the woman braced a hand on her hip made Laurel suddenly curious. The pose appeared natural for someone comfortable with strapping on a pistol. How odd to consider it.

"What makes you think he did anything?"

"I can see it on your face. Then there's the tears."

Laurel sighed, dropping the meat she'd plucked from the barrel onto the counter. "I give up. After you left, he waylaid me."

"The sneakin' skunk. Yates didn't pay no more mind to my warning than to a flea. What else?"

"Nothing."

She dare not speak of warm breath that nuzzled the corners of her mouth and weakened her knees.

"Spit it out," Ollie demanded.

"He talked about leopards and spots. He said I'd never wash mine off." That was close enough.

"Did you haul off and wallop him?"

Hiding her face, she lifted a long knife and set to work slicing the slab of pork. "It wouldn't have done a lick of good."

"Thought I taught you to have some gumption, girl."

"I'm facing facts. Despite how hard I try, I may not save the woman William Taft turned me into after all."

Ollie closed her right eye and squinted with the left. "Unless you fight, you ain't fit for toad spit."

"Years of struggle don't buy back a stolen life."

Or keep crumbling dreams from falling about her feet.

"Like grandpappy said, 'There's a lot more to buildin' a fire than pickin' up a couple of sticks.'"

The knife slipped. "Darn it, you're distracting me."

"Then put it down for a minute. Changing things means you gotta do more than just say it. A good fire takes finding the right kind of wood. Then you gotta get some leaves and such to stuff underneath it to catch the flame. But picking the right spot is most important of all. Cain't—"

"Spit and thunder. I don't need fire-building lessons."

From Ollie's openmouthed stare you'd have thought Laurel had sprouted horns.

"I ain't no big bag of wind." She took Laurel's hand, stroking the back. "Pick the place you want the change to begin. Start with the little things to get your flame to catch, then add big logs gradual-like. Gotta warn you, though, let that fire get outta control and it'll burn you alive."

Considering the inferno inside, it already had.

"Are you finished? I have work to do."

"One thing you gotta do before anything else and that's change the opinion of yourself." She released Laurel's hand and jabbed a finger into her chest. "Inside here."

"I'm making headway." Whenever she didn't feel like a cross between someone's dirty laundry and a shrinking bar of soap.

Ollie took her face in her hands. "Girl, I wish to high heaven I could turn back time to the day Will Taft took you. I'd do it in a heartbeat."

"That's why I love you despite how difficult you make it."

Had she only stayed with her brothers and not wandered off to pick blackberries alone. How quickly life can change.

Ollie sniffed at the backhanded sentiment. "You're a fine woman, Laurel girl. Sometimes I think it'd be a sight easier for you living with a broken neck. All I'm saying is you gotta make do with what'cha got. And one other thing…a feller would have to be blind as a bat not to see you have rare beauty both inside and out."

Suddenly she wasn't that scared little kid clutching a stranger's coattails anymore. She stuck out her jaw. "I've made my decision, Ollie."

"How soon you want me to saddle the horses?"

"No one's going to threaten me into leaving. I'm about to prove to the world, including Brodie Yates, who Laurel Lillian James is and what stern material she's made of."

❧

Murphy strolled into the café that evening. Laurel turned a deaf ear to Florence Kempshaw's grumbles and met his wide grin. She dodged his reach, tucking her hands into the apron.

"What a pleasant surprise. Did Etta forget to cook?"

"I prefer yours, particularly when I might steal a kiss." Eager light flashed. "Etta can't do that for me."

Florence lifted her fork, cocking an ear toward the table Murphy took. Each nasty rumor in town originated from her.

"Shh." Laurel nodded toward the old spinster.

"Sweetheart, we don't have to hide. I'm going to marry you. Tonight if I could." His hand joined hers inside the apron pocket. The glint in his eyes said he wanted her more than ever.

Guilt settled faster than layers of silt in Big Cypress Bayou. How could she tell him? And yet the words wouldn't come.

Cluttering Murphy's life with someone like her would not repay the debt she owed him. But neither would she let his flinty-eyed brother dictate to her. She had rights.

"Murphy, I have to speak to you after everyone leaves."

"Sounds serious, my love."

Before she could go further, Florence began furiously waving her arms in the direction of the window where two young boys flattened their noses against the pane. The silly woman resembled General Lee ordering a dozen regiments into battle.

"Shoo. Get away, you little heathens." Florence turned. "I wish to finish my grits and fatback in peace, Miss James."

"I'll see what I can do. Most likely they're hungry."

Laurel expected them to scatter when they heard the knob rattle. Instead, two sets of sad, brown eyes stared up. The oldest child couldn't have seen his eighth birthday.

"Anything I can help you boys with?"

The spokesman wiped his nose on the sleeve of a torn, dirty shirt that hung from his thin bones. "We ain't hurting no one."

"I'm sure you wouldn't harm a soul. You look a little lost though. Want to come inside?" She smiled warmly.

A sob broke the quiet, earning the smaller one a

punch to the arm. The forlorn, wan eyes gave her heart a jolt.

"Where's your mother?" she asked gently.

Again the same boy replied. "Back at the wagon. Maw'd skin us for sure if she knew we was here."

"You must have an awfully good reason to disobey."

"We's hungry. Thought you might give us some scraps if you had a mind to feed the cats in the alley."

Her stomach lurched. She caressed the tops of the tow heads. "I just happen to have some stew that someone must eat tonight or it'll spoil. Think you might help me out?"

The light in exchanged glances flared in communication of a silent language. The boy spoke, "If'n it's no bother, ma'am."

Laurel's chest swelled at the way their small palms fit naturally in hers. They pressed against her skirts when they neared Florence's table.

"Don't know what this world's coming to," Florence said an octave shy of a foghorn. "Can't eat without sniveling brats."

"I certainly believe feeding starved children will help make this a better place, Mrs. Kempshaw." She led her charges and marched past with her head high. "Murphy, we have guests."

"I see." He caught on instantly and pulled out chairs. "Will you gentlemen honor me with your company?"

"You mean us? No one ever said that to us before."

"They are now." Murphy smiled brightly.

The smallest brother bit his lip to stop the tremble. Florence huffed loudly. The spinster had evidently developed a nosebleed, judging from how high her nose stuck in the air. Bumping her shins on a table leg, she hobbled from the café.

Smothering a laugh, Laurel smoothed the apron to keep her hand from wandering to places that would worsen the ache.

"I'm Miss Laurel. Do you have names?"

"Edgar Lee Cole," the more talkative one said, "and he's Andy."

"Glad to meet you, Andy and Edgar Lee Cole." Murphy extended a hand.

Swiping his hand on a pant leg, Edgar Lee accepted it. Andy mimicked his brother before sliding his palm forward.

"I'll get that stew we talked about. Don't go anywhere." Laurel flew to the kitchen and hurried back with steaming bowls and a loaf of bread. It must've appeared to them like manna from heaven. Andy rewarded her with the barest hint of a grin.

"Thank you, ma'am." Edgar Lee punched his brother, who shoveled a bite into his mouth. "What'dya say?"

The small forehead wrinkled. Andy stared as though fearing she'd snatch the food from his mouth. "S-s-sorry. T-t-thanks, l-lady," he stuttered.

Edgar dipped his spoon into the stew. "We ain't got no money, but Maw says we're rich if we mind our manners."

Sudden mist clouded Laurel's vision. A loving mother had taught these children important things—lessons that would remain for a lifetime despite meager subsistence.

"My goodness, I completely forgot your milk. And, Murphy, you haven't ordered."

Brodie rested against a hitching post in front of Jake's barber shop. The vantage point provided a clear view. What he saw through the café window softened his war-toughened hide.

Two hungry, ragged boys.

The warm kindness of a special woman.

And a man who'd give most anything for a wife and children of his own.

Forty lashes with a bullwhip would've stung far less than did the memories. He blinked hard and finally lit the cheroot he'd toyed with for the last ten minutes.

The group inside could almost pose as a family of sorts.

He shifted the cheroot to the other side of his mouth.

Only two things wrong with the picture…the man was his brother and the charitable woman was spoken for.

All of a sudden he wanted to get closer, wanted to hear the conversation…

Wanted to be included.

Solitude weighed heavy on a man sometimes. Telling himself for the hundredth time that an outsider could never belong didn't make the stars any brighter or the night less dark.

Brodie had vowed to stay clear of Laurel until the deadline with perfectly honorable intentions. But he just couldn't.

Adjusting the angle of his hat, he sauntered toward the eating establishment. The hiss of rattles seemed in agreement with the decision. Smoke from the cheroot drifted in the breeze. He tossed the remains, grinding it with a worn boot heel.

Honorable intentions be damned.

Making a fool of himself twice in one day had to break a personal record. Still, the small building sorely in need of whitewash drew him.

He opened the door and stepped inside. A quick hush enveloped the room, reminding him his place was with creatures of the night. Not here.

Sudden panic clouded Laurel's glance. He tried to ignore the twinges of guilt, tried to blame the loud clink of his spurs or the ghostly apparition that shadowed him for the tension-charged air.

"Brodie, join us." Murphy scooted an empty chair.

Laurel's gaze labeled him a bastard of the most dastardly sort, evidently assuming he came for no reason except to torment her.

Little did the lady know such affliction belonged solely to him. Some might say he owned prime acreage in the land of torment.

Agony knifed through him with the ease of a well-honed bayonet. A grievous error he'd made today. Strange to have forgotten how one drop of water to a dying man called for more until a thousand drinks couldn't quench the parched tongue.

"I'm not sure there's room. Don't mean to intrude."

"You're not. I insist."

Only a coward would back out now. Besides, he wanted to be there worse than any place else on earth. He dropped into the seat. "Did you pick up a pair of strays?"

Both ragamuffins stopped chewing, a bite freezing midway down the small one's windpipe. Close up he could tell they'd not eaten in a month of Sundays. A striking resemblance to Murphy and him as boys drained his ability to make enough moisture to form spit.

"These are the Cole boys, Edgar Lee and Andy." Murphy's grin spread. "Don't let my grouch of a brother scare you. Brodie is truly harmless."

"You have a brother, too?"

Edgar Lee began the ritual, first brushing away the milk mustache on his sleeve, then wiping a hand on his pants before reaching. Brodie's large grip might easily have crushed the small fingers were it not for the special care he took. An aching hole in his chest made words impossible.

Edgar Lee nudged Andy, silently insisting his brother follow his example. Watching them, the years turned like yellowed, dust-covered pages.

"Where are your folks?" A gruff tone had sneaked into Brodie's voice.

Tears swam in Edgar Lee's brown eyes. "Paw took real bad sick. Maw said the angels came an' flew him to heaven. We buried him under a pine tree. Reckon I'm head o' the family now. Leastways that's what Maw says."

"A bit young to be saddled with that, aren't you, son?"

Edgar Lee pulled up straight, sucking in his breath. "Almost eight. Plenty big to see about things."

"Where's your maw now?" It became imperative that Brodie know.

"We's camped down by the water. Ain't bothering no one."

Silent up to now, Andy found his voice. "W-w-wagon broke."

"Shh. Maw says we gotta be careful. Folks don't wanna hear about our troubles."

"That might apply to some, I suppose, but not us." Laurel's soft reply interrupted Brodie's concentration.

"What happened to your wagon?" Murphy asked.

"Busted wheel. Maw says the Lord'll provide though."

With a little earthly help, Brodie decided.

"Did you come to eat, Mr. Yates?" Laurel's throaty voice broke his train of thought all to hell. And worse, it fanned a tiny sputtering flame…one last flicker he had a devil of a time stomping out.

"I've already partaken, thanks anyway."

Riveting his attention on her middle section seemed safest while he fought the overwhelming desire that left deep ruts all the way down to the holes in his socks.

"I swear, you and Murphy come to a café and don't eat a blessed thing." She threw up her hands. "Think of our reputation."

Murphy looked sheepish. "I'll take some coffee and pie."

"A fine example you set for these children, asking for nothing more substantial than dessert."

"When Ollie spent a good hour this morning raving about your cherry cobbler? It'd make any grown man's mouth water."

His brother's tender gaze didn't escape Brodie. Or the fingers brushing Laurel at the slightest opportunity.

She's just what he needs.

Remembrance of her lips, the pliable curves that perfectly fit, sent crushing pain into his heart.

"I could squeeze in some as well, if you don't mind," he said quietly after the noise in his head dulled.

Quick annoyance didn't surprise him. Brodie

rewarded the flash with a ghost of a smile and a tilt of an eyebrow.

Georgia clay, she was a sight when riled.

Laurel returned with a round of cobbler for them all. He could've imagined the little extra shove she gave his plate, but he didn't believe so. His coffee cup shielded a wayward grin.

She fluttered over the children like a mother hen with baby chicks. She had a certain knack, he had to admit. But before she had children of her own, she'd have to become a wife.

It was his duty to make sure it wasn't to the wrong man.

"Ollie should be here." The brilliant beam caught his breath. "She has a soft spot for ones down on their luck."

"I realized I missed something. Where is the feisty watchdog?" Murphy sipped on the hot liquid. "Generally she hovers over you, growling whenever I come within a mile."

Laurel whispered, "Over at the saloon."

"Never thought she'd wear out her heels on a brass rail."

"Although Ollie imbibes more than she wishes me to know, I'm quite positive her interest runs in a different direction these days."

"You don't say." Murphy's fork paused in mid-air. "Curley Madison, the owner?"

Amethyst eyes twinkled, releasing tiny ripples across his heartstrings. Brodie paid no heed to the conversation. The vibrant beauty absorbed him completely. Although, being near would have to suffice. And unless providence took a sharp right at the next bend in the road, it'd stay that way.

"Curley, that old scamp."

"Don't let her get wind I told you." Lilting humor colored Laurel's admonition.

Brodie thanked the good Lord he'd had sense enough to bust into the party. He soaked up her nearness. Laurel captivated his attention so thoroughly he almost missed Edgar Lee's furtive movement.

The small fingers slid a button through the hole of his shirt to allow the barest of openings before pushing something inside.

Eight

BRODIE GRASPED EDGAR LEE'S WRIST. "NOT TRYING TO steal anything, are you, boy?"

"N-no, sir." The child's Adam's apple bobbed. His big eyes resembled a snagged catfish. "It's only a little bit. Didn't think anyone would miss it."

Edgar Lee drew out his hand. In his clenched fist he held a piece of bread.

"For Maw and Sissie. I'm the man o' the family now. That means I gotta feed 'em. I just gotta, mister."

The plea doused Brodie like a bucket of ice water. He and the boy were kindred spirits, each doing what they must to provide for and protect the ones they loved. Before Aunt Lucy took them in, he'd done whatever it took for his abandoned mother and Murphy. Only it had never been enough. Not ever. His puny efforts hadn't stopped his mother from taking her life, and it darn sure hadn't protected his kid brother when he most needed it.

"You can have all of it you need," Laurel said.

Murphy cleared his throat. "We'll see that your mother and anyone else back at the wagon doesn't starve. That's a fact."

"Maw says we cain't take no charity. Ain't right."
The quivering chin dropped to his chest. Shame over
stealing waged war against necessity. Brodie kicked
himself for even saying anything.

"Call it a gift—an early Christmas present." Laurel
stroked the small proud back. "I'll dish up the rest
of that stew and cobbler to take with you. Also, I've
another loaf of bread that'll mold if someone doesn't
take pity. It sure would do me a favor. I told Ollie this
morning we shouldn't make so many loaves of bread."

Her whispery breath mingled the past and present, blurring the lines between. Everything Brodie
had previously known had changed. This Lil was a
stranger, and the prospect of discovery excited him.
He knew he'd savor every inch of the journey.

Even if it remained limited in duration.

The dress swished around trim ankles. She moved
like a quiet storm. No thunder or lightning, just
efficient steady strength toward completing the task.
He rubbed his jaw. Her quiet calm deceived a man at
first, leading some to take her for some weak, rainwater
woman. Brother, were they ever wrong. The depth of
passion he'd sampled earlier had shaken him in ways he
still tried to sort out. No storm gauge on earth could
measure such wanton abandon or warm generosity.

The small brothers' mouths flew open when she
returned with loaded arms. "For us?" Edgar Lee asked
in amazement.

"I don't see any other little men in here."

"T-t-thanks, lady." Andy ducked his head.

Scooting from the chair, Edgar Lee hugged her
waist. Laurel dabbed at tears trickling down his face.

Brodie was struck to discover a rush of wetness swimming in Laurel's beautiful violet gaze when she looked up. This was genuine caring. A person couldn't fake that. Maybe she had turned over a new leaf.

Except she was determined to marry the wrong man.

After the kiss that seared his brain, he had to prevent a tragic mistake. The lady couldn't possibly love another man. Not when Brodie loved her with every inch of his being.

He halted Murphy, who had pushed back his chair. "I'll take them back to camp. You stay."

"Appreciate it. Seems Laurel and I never get enough time alone. Besides, she has something of importance to discuss."

Laurel flashed Brodie a glittering stare that seemed to promise that tonight she'd do the deed and end the suspense.

And once she did?

A possibility chilled his bones. It occurred to him he could fail to convince her to spend the rest of her days with him.

Lord help him, for he would never get her out of his blood.

Brodie intentionally brushed her in transferring the load, relishing the feel of satiny skin. The contact sent a charged pulse that left a strange heat careening through him.

⚜

Spit and thunder.

Laurel jammed both fists into her apron, surprised they didn't poke out the bottom of the pockets.

The devil take those rebel grays that infuriated, bewildered, and enticed. She'd never been so relieved to see anyone go.

He'd be back though to give her another dose of Brodie charm.

Waves of weakness fluttered. Endurance had limits.

Murphy enfolded her in the circle of his arms. She leaned into him, wishing someone else nibbled along her neck. She wearied of fighting the love she wished to claim.

Your body betrays you. It remembers a lover's touch.

The taunt clanged like a death knell in her head. Although despising herself for owning the truth, she couldn't deny it.

Her fiancé brought pleasant, peaceful moments, whereas Brodie charged each fiber with heightened awareness the instant he entered a room. And while Murphy was a bite of fresh-baked bread, Brodie offered the entire meal—plus dessert thrown in.

Marrying Murphy would be a disservice. Not because she wished to spare him ruin, or out of shame for who she was, but because she must have all or nothing. No half measures.

Not even to satisfy the craving for respect.

Laurel faced her future squarely. "You're going to hate what I have to tell you. I can't—"

Halfway through the chore, the door flew open. "Girl, I brought someone to meet you. Good, I see Murphy's here."

Ollie propelled a large man forward. The light of a woman in love graced her face. Since arriving in Redemption, Laurel never had occasion to cross paths with the owner of the Dry Gulch Saloon until now.

"Don't tell me. Curley Madison?"

A warm blush colored not only the man's face, but painted the bald head as well. He took her hand.

"It's truly a pleasure, Miss Laurel."

"Yep, shore as shootin' is. I told him all about you."

Laurel gulped in sudden panic. "You did?"

"Don't worry, only the good parts," Ollie said. "You already know our fine mayor, who is set to wed Laurel any day now."

The saloon owner grinned. "We've debated the finer points of the subject a time or two."

"Indeed we have, Curley my man." Murphy clapped him on his back.

"Most likely sold you that panther piss he calls beer."

Laurel envied Ollie's twinkling, mischievous eyes.

"Panther piss, huh? Just wait until next time," Curley warned.

The swap of insults with Ollie brought to mind Frenchie Devereaux, cardsharp extraordinaire of the Mississippi. The gambler frequented the Black Garter and became adept at diverting Will Taft's anger. Laurel figured she owed Frenchie her life. More than once the woman's interference had spared her. Curley Madison would do the same for those he doted on.

"Now, sugar, I wasn't aiming to rile you," Ollie wheedled.

"I took it the way you offered—straight up and down the gullet." Curley's smile bypassed his lips to settle in the sparkling gaze. He turned to Laurel. "After finally meeting you, I'm certain I'm in the presence of an angel. Flip that coin over, and my Ollie's more ornery than a buffalo gnat."

The petite woman threw back her head and cackled. "Orneriness is my calling, you big whiskey-pusher. Without some backbone, I'd be dead and buried." A sudden kiss planted on the man's cheek sent a new wave of redness upward.

"Why, darlin', if you don't say the prettiest things. Reminds me of a bald-faced heifer I once had on the farm."

Laurel gave the man whose height must equal the width of his round frame a vote of approval. Whoever named him must've needed spectacles because not one sprig of hair dotted the landscape. A fly would break his neck landing up there. She'd learned not to judge a body by the meat on their bones or the amount of hair they did or didn't possess though. Ollie deserved happiness.

"Goldarned old coot. My grandpappy warned how a body gets plain mean when most of the sand in their hourglass settles to the afternoon side. And by daisy, if he wasn't right."

"Bear that in mind when I turn you six ways to Sunday."

"Now, Curley, no call to get ugly." Ollie patted his arm. "And just think, I was becoming real partial to you."

"If you lovebirds need some privacy, Murphy and I can scoot." Truth of the matter was Laurel welcomed the interruption, although delaying the talk attacked her nerves from every angle.

"We hate to interfere with your courting," Murphy seconded.

"Shoot, boy, just speak up if we're boring you. Thought you might take a gander at someone you'll see a lot of, Laurel girl. Besides, we're gonna help clean up the café."

"We have all night for the pleasurable stuff." Curley began gathering plates off a table. "I know how much elbow grease it takes to run a saloon. This café takes twice that, ma'am."

"Ma'am belongs to a prim schoolmarm. I'm plain Laurel."

"Don't know about you, Curley, but there's nothing plain about Laurel." Murphy draped an arm around her shoulders. "After the last hour I'll never look at her in quite the same way again."

"What's this?" Ollie's ears perked up.

Laurel took the opportunity to slide from Murphy's arm. "Not much, really. Just a couple of starved boys."

While Ollie and Curley cleaned and tidied the café, she told them about Edgar Lee and Andy Cole.

"You would've burst with pride. I glimpsed a side of Laurel I never knew." Wonder lightened Murphy's stare.

"Our girl is quite a lady," Ollie agreed. "But I always saw the compassionate, loving side of her."

"She'll make a wonderful mother for our children."

"All right now, you're doing it again. Quit talking like I'm a million miles away. I didn't do a bit more than any other decent human being would've done," Laurel protested.

Darn Murphy. She couldn't take much more of the adoration and talk of mothering his children.

And damn this attraction for his brother.

Brodie approached the dying campfire with caution. A weary female, probably far younger than her stooped shoulders suggested, stole from around a tilting wagon. She pointed an old musket at him.

"State your business, mister."

"I mean no harm."

The boys slid from Brodie's horse to the ground.

"Maw, wait'll you see what we brung." Edgar Lee's excitement drowned the whispering gentle breeze off the bayou.

Though still leery, she propped the weapon within reach against the shadowy side of a tree.

"Child, I oughta switch you good for running off like that. You too, Andy, for tagging after your brother. Where you been?"

"But Maw…"

Brodie threw his leg over Smokey's back and dismounted. "Sorry, ma'am. I appreciate how they must've worried you, but the boys did what they thought right. Don't punish them for needing to take care of you."

When their mother neared, moonlight etched deep ruts in the hollow cheeks, the sort a man might find in a dry river bed. He'd seen the same hopelessness in countless others who suffered in the war. Long on problems, short on means to solve them.

"I'm beholden for you seeing to 'em. But they know better than to go against me. These two require a tight rein."

"Begging your pardon, ma'am, they also need something to eat." His soft rebuke failed to dent her thick armor. Women sure did mystify him.

He unpacked the fare from his bulging saddlebags. The thin set of her mouth told of a prideful woman who even in desperate times wouldn't accept handouts. He had to convince her. If not for any other reason but the starvelings.

The woman spurned the grub he held out. "You got the boys back safe enough. Now, hop back up on that horse and take your meddling intentions with you, mister."

"Name's Brodie Yates. This isn't much, I assure you. But I'll not ride back with it." He tacked on some force to the statement.

A baby's squalls drew the mother's attention, the noise breaking the standoff. "Edgar Lee, take care of your sister."

The youngster looked from the woman to Brodie, then trudged toward the cries. Andy tripped over a log when he ran to catch up. He sniffled but shed no tears. The ache in Brodie doubled.

"Please, ma'am. Pride doesn't fill hungry bellies."

"Got a watered down cup of coffee. All I can offer."

A glance around the neat camp located a blackened pot beside the fire. It sat alone. Although the family had nothing to spare, Mrs. Cole would take it unkindly if he declined her offer.

"That would be mighty good, ma'am."

The baby's crying ceased abruptly. The little boy who had become a man way before his time continued to spark memories.

Rattles on Brodie's hat accompanied the clink of his spurs. He arranged the crocks and bread on an upended crate and squatted beside glowing embers.

He accepted a battered tin cup. "Much obliged."

"I'm Betsy Cole." With a sigh, she dropped the stiff pretense. "Wheel broke. We're trying to get to my brother's place near Fort Richardson."

"How long since your husband passed?"

Shoulders which bore the weight of the world drooped lower. "A week yesterday. My Daniel had the fever. Me and the boys buried him after we crossed the Red River."

"Please accept my condolences." Brodie sipped on the barely lukewarm brew and fished a small bag of Bull Durham and papers from his pocket. "You mind?"

"Haven't seen a man yet what didn't have the tobacco craving. Reckon I'm used to it."

After he rolled and lit it, he silently blew smoke into the night. Bad luck that had followed the Coles from their former home wrapped him in a cocoon. Or perhaps it was his own luck catching up. Lord knew plenty of that rode his trail.

"Something tells me you fought for the Cause."

From the darkness in his mind, cannons roared. Red flames shot from rifles. Men screamed in agony. He shivered. That special hell remained as vivid as the moment he lived it. Images first born amid the chaos would never fade. Cause? Nothing on earth lent credence to that carnage.

Long minutes passed before he could answer, and when he did his voice cracked. "For a fact, ma'am."

"Daniel, too. A shell of my husband came home. I suppose war does that to a man." She wiped a tear with the hem of her dress. "He was a hero at Chickamauga."

"We buried a bunch of heroes. Not many left

anymore." Brodie tossed the cigarette into the smoldering ashes. It took barely a second to vanish. Just like his life.

"You're a decent man. I reckon you can leave the food."

"A wise choice. You won't be sorry come dawn."

Betsy Cole sniffed. "Don't want some stranger to sit here all night. That's the only reason. A woman likes her privacy."

He rose and dumped black sediment from the bottom of the metal cup before handing it to her.

"I'll be back come daybreak to fix your wheel."

"Reckon you'd be welcome…long as you don't bring a passel of nosy do-gooders."

"You have some special boys. Remember that, Mrs. Cole." His hand brushed the memory bag before he stepped into the stirrup.

❧

"What did you want to tell me, sweetheart? Bet you want to move up the wedding," Murphy teased.

Exactly how did one go about killing a man's future?

The wait, coupled with his tender regard, drove spikes in Laurel's composure.

She took a deep breath and leaped. "I'm not the person you think."

"I know all I need to for now. The rest I'll learn later once we're married. Most married folks don't know everything right off. Shoot, we wouldn't have anything to talk about." He ran a palm up her arm and under her hair to caress her neck.

She gently pushed him away. This was hard enough

without him making it any tougher. "Please, wait until I'm finished."

"My love, whatever it is, I frankly don't care." He nudged her chin upward. She stared miserably into the liquid brown trusting gaze. "You mean more than anything else in this world. Accepting my proposal made me extremely happy. The only thing that can change that is to tell me you don't wish to marry me."

Dry desert sand suddenly caked her mouth. How could she live with the consequences that came with clear obligation?

Laurel licked her dry lips, trying desperately to moisten them. "I have a past, Murphy."

Nine

THERE, SHE'D SAID IT. THE RESULTS SHE'D TACK TO Brodie's hide. Laurel peeked from beneath shadowed lids. Murphy had never mistreated or spoken ill of a living soul. He shouldn't have to bear the price of her dark history.

Murphy's wide-toothed smile didn't make sense.

Anyone in their right mind should be aghast at the bold disclosure. How could he be happy to discover the blight on his almost-wife's character?

"Of course you have a past, sweetheart. Everyone does. None of us got here except through more years than we care to count. That's called living."

Oh Lord, he mistook her words and the delicate situation.

"I'm trying to tell you—"

"You can say nothing that will destroy this love in my heart. Nothing."

Except she'd done damnable things no decent woman would?

Except the truth that she'd never feel clean, no matter how often she bathed?

And except the knowledge his brother heated her blood with a single look and she'd never get him out of her head?

Besides those, nothing stood to break Murphy's heart. She didn't have the courage to poke holes in his bubble. Not tonight.

Perhaps in the light of day…tomorrow perhaps.

"Sweetheart, what dire secret lingers on the tip of your tongue that you can't find words to say?" His chuckle added to her unwillingness to hurt him.

The longer she stood silent, the more guilt burned.

"I…I don't have any parents," she blurted at last. "I just wanted you to know."

"So what? Neither do I. Makes for a smaller wedding."

"And I'm almost certain I snore in my sleep."

Laughter burst from Murphy's throat. "Love, you harbor the most farfetched notions. While we're engaged in soul-baring, I believe you should know that I don't have a nail on my big toe and I'm notorious for cracking my knuckles. In public, no less."

No one could accuse her of not trying. She must carry the burden a day or two longer. Perhaps she'd find the right words when opportunity presented another chance.

After all, she still had five more days.

❧

Laurel and Ollie rose early and stashed staples into the rented buggy. A flick of the reins set the horses in motion. Locating the youngsters' encampment shouldn't pose a problem.

"Giddyup there, you lazy bag of bones." Satisfied, Ollie swiveled on the seat. "Did you remember some hen fruit and salt pork?"

"Of course. I packed the eggs carefully so not one shell would break, and I brought plenty of meat."

"Did you also get the sugar and flour I told you?"

Laurel sighed. General Santa Anna attacking the Alamo would have scribbled a much shorter list than Ollie's. The second Ollie learned about the Coles' plight, she became obsessed. Looking at her now, it appeared the dear woman hadn't caught a wink of sleep.

Neither a salty tongue nor unending questions could hide Ollie's Texas-sized soft spot.

Circles rimming the woman's eyes might hint at lack of sleep upon first glance. Yet, Laurel had reason to know Ollie's weariness was caused by declining health.

Laurel's chest constricted. She couldn't lose the only family she had. Not yet. Fate wouldn't be that cruel.

"You gonna perch there and bore a hole clean through me? If you're itching to say something, speak up, girl." Ollie puffed away on the pipe stuck in the corner of her mouth.

"I'm worried about you. Can't I persuade you to go to Jefferson and let a doc see what's wrong?"

"No sawbones can fix what's ailing me." Ollie covered the back of Laurel's hand. "Don't you lose any sleep over me. I got a whole lot of living yet to do before making the crossing."

Frustrated, Laurel wanted to rattle the stubborn, unreasonable cuss's teeth. But that would merely set her mind in granite, the hardest stone in the state.

Her blood froze.

They carved tombstones from granite.

She banished the thought as quickly as it formed. Someone else might hold more sway over Ollie. Curley Madison?

"I like your man-friend. He obviously cares for you a great deal, although I can't for the life of me see why, what with your rough edges and all."

"That's the living part I just mentioned. That man makes my old bones think they're twenty again. He's taken a notion he can file those crusty patches smooth. Now quit your yappin.' Keep a lookout for those poor little younguns."

The dressing down warned Laurel in no uncertain terms to mind her own business. She buttoned her lip and drank in the beautiful scenery she'd missed for so long.

She'd almost forgotten the mysticism here on the bayou, home to long-legged cranes, loons, and bullfrogs. During summer months, lily pads and purple water hyacinth carpeted the water that gave sustenance to the bearded cypress. The tall trees, stood for decades, silent sentinels against encroachers. Could they sense dishonesty in those who passed by?

"Are you cold, girl?"

"A chill swept over me."

"I told you to bring a shawl, but you scoffed at me."

Tingling premonition crept from the dark shadows of her soul. Building a life on deceit had definite obstacles. A square peg would never fit into a round hole. Not ever.

Heavy thick gloom descended around her. One

little chance didn't seem too large a favor to ask. "The day is warm enough."

"Well, make up your mind." Ollie flicked the reins to urge the horse to a trot.

A clearing upstream produced the camp and broken wagon. A tall figure was hunched over, hammering. He rose when the buggy coasted to a stop. The Navy Colt strapped to his leg caught the sun's rays.

Bare-chested, Brodie Yates gave her a dismissive glance that brushed her face before he resumed his task. A sweep of the site revealed his shirt hanging from the covered wagon's seat.

Her maddening pulse refused to slow in the humid calm.

She adopted nonchalance, finding the buggy's metal step. Who could've predicted her heel would catch when she alighted? A hasty grip of the cracked leather seat prevented sprawling head first. Call her grace and serenity. Heat flooded her cheeks. The oaf probably enjoyed the spectacle. Determined to ignore him, she riveted her attention on the two boys racing to meet them.

"Miss Laurel, Miss Laurel!" Edgar Lee and Andy skidded to a halt, spying Ollie.

Laurel hugged them. "Someone wants to meet you. Ollie's the most special lady this side of heaven."

"You look like a couple of green-broke yearlings to me." Ollie winked and ruffled their hair. "Bet you're worth your salt though."

Each boy scuffed his toe in the dirt and pinkened.

"How about helping unload a few vittles?"

They nodded in unison, turning to the scowling woman who walked up behind. "Can we, Maw?"

The tall thin woman wore disapproval as thick and black as a bucket of hot tar. "We don't need whatever it is you come for."

The cold reception raised prickles on Laurel's neck. "I apologize for intruding. I fed Edgar Lee and Andy last evening. Fine lads they are. You've reason to be mighty proud of them."

"So you're the one responsible." Shards of ice layered her reply.

Laurel didn't take offense. She understood what it was like to have someone run roughshod over her pride. And like it or not that's what they'd done. "I take full blame, ma'am. I'm Laurel James."

"Olivia Applejack b'Dam," Ollie offered stiffly.

"I don't cotton none to charity. We can take care of ourselves." The woman pushed back a strand of hair.

"I agree, ma'am." Ollie nodded. "But ain't no charity, just trading. The boys can wash dishes at the café until you get your wagon fixed. Sounds like good horse swapping to me."

The woman relaxed a bit. "Put that way, I suppose I can make an exception. I'm Betsy Cole. I mind my own business and expect others to do the same."

The blunt statement confirmed what Laurel already suspected. Pride was all that remained for the widow. And Betsy would hog-tie a cougar in order to keep clinging to that.

"We respect your wishes." Laurel spoke loud enough for a certain half-dressed gunslinger's benefit, the gaze she sent flitting his direction.

A babe's lusty cry rent the fragrant breeze.

Mrs. Cole turned. "Guess I'd better go tend to her."

"Awful prideful, ain't she?" Ollie grumbled after the woman left. "I'll get the younguns to unload the buggy. And Yates might need help with that wheel. Come on, boys."

Laurel debated whether to follow Betsy Cole, the troop heading for the horse and buggy, or talk to Brodie who, after the unwelcome stare upon their arrival, now completely ignored her. The need in his kiss that had stamped a permanent imprint on her brain aided greatly in Laurel's decision. Betsy's frigid response seemed far wiser and a thousand times more safe.

"You've raised some wonderful children. I've met few whose manners come close."

"They're a handful at times." Betsy brushed eyes that told of too little sleep, were swollen from crying, or a combination of the two. The woman reached into the wagon, lifting the baby. "Would you hold her while I get dry bundling?"

Edgar Lee's Sissie, she presumed.

Small, tear-filled eyes stared up at her in confusion at the transfer. Alarm plundered Laurel's helpful intentions as well. Wiggling arms and legs hurtled her toward a place she resisted.

The tiny girl twisted and reached for her nose with one hand while the other grabbed a fistful of hair.

Sweet baby's breath dredged up long forgotten portraits, the images chipped from chunks of ice around her heart. Curious, small fingers that clutched everything in sight…a mother's lullabies…the creak of the rocker…the aroma of baking bread that permeated the house and clearing…

Visions of home.

Reminders of family.

Remembering the things she'd lost in the wink of an eye opened wounds the size of Big Cypress Bayou.

"What a waste. Those arms weren't meant for babies, Lil."

The lazy drawl over her shoulder sent memories scurrying to the far corners from whence they'd crept.

Laurel wheeled. The familiar hiss of the snake rattles had failed to warn of Brodie's approach. The black Stetson likely kept his shirt company, she supposed.

Her gaze tripped, falling headlong into a tanned chest. Sparse, damp hairs narrowed into a line that ran down the center of his abdomen and disappeared into the waistband. A bouquet of shaving soap, tobacco, and perspiration aroused more fear than the Colt at his hip.

Blue blazes.

Brodie towered so near that his breath caressed her neck. Corded muscles banding his arms prevented escape, although his presence alone sufficed in holding her captive.

"Don't call me that. It's Miss James to you."

Sissie attempted to stick her fingers into Laurel's mouth, evidently attracted to her teeth. She shifted the babe to one side and shot Brodie a withering glare.

"So you insist." It would be easy to mistake Brodie's lazy reply as friendly and would give anything if a smile accompanied the words. "Your arms were made for other uses. I recall them once holding me close, my face nuzzled to your soft breast."

Her anger flared as she searched for a reply that would put him in his place. She searched for equal weapons and lit upon one.

"Mr. Yates, it would hard press me to remember one face amongst the thousand others. Yours I appear to have far more trouble sorting from the legions of admirers."

His gray eyes darkened. She took great pleasure in the small victory, for admiration peeked beyond the frost.

"Touché. Your sparring skills compare to your talents in bed."

"Insufferable rebel, don't you have someone to shoot?"

Not the most brilliant question considering she stood directly in the line of fire. She sucked in air when he brushed back the errant lock of hair curling onto his forehead.

"Not yet, but the day's young." He fingered the baby's curls. "After seeing you with the children, I almost buy that story about wanting to change. But I can't form the picture of you anywhere except a house of ill repute. That throaty voice of yours, those half-closed eyes that make a man sell his soul for one moment's ride into paradise... It pitches motherhood clean out the window."

Laurel flinched. "I can become anything I must to survive. Anything."

"Even becoming wife to a man you don't love?" The soft drawl flogged her conscience.

"I-I..."

Betsy Cole threw a leg over the back of the wagon. "Sorry it took so long. After Edgar Lee and Andy rise in the mornings, it looks like a hurricane passed through."

"I didn't mind."

The mother relieved Laurel, frowning after Brodie who sauntered back to work. When she spoke all traces of coldness fled. "He's a good man. The war left angry gashes inside men's spirits whether you see 'em or not."

"And every woman, don't forget." Laurel could attest to that.

"True, a person bearing no scars never fought for anything they believe in."

A tender jab without a doubt. Shame branded on her soul would not disappear until she battled hard enough. Even then scars would remain. Those would never fade.

Ollie called, "Hate to break up the tea party, but we need extra hands."

"Mr. Brodie done fixed the wheel," Edgar Lee happily piped up. "We hafta put it back on."

Betsy thrust the infant into Andy's young arms. "Watch your sister."

"Aw, do I hafta?"

Ollie's ashen face and labored breathing caused Laurel concern. Lifting and straining would overtax a sickly heart. "Why don't you hold the baby and let Andy help?" Laurel said to her.

"I'll do no such thing." Ollie jerked the pipe from her mouth. "I'll have you know I'm strong as an ox."

"You're not well."

"Squabbles can wait, ladies. This wheel won't." Brodie's dark scowl ended the argument. He motioned to Laurel and ordered, "Stand beside me. Mrs. Cole, you get on the other side. When we lift, Edgar Lee will take the barrel from under the axle. Ollie, do you think you can set the wheel on?"

"I damn—darn sure can." Ollie amended, flashing the children a guilty grin.

"I don't wanna do a girl's job." Edgar Lee's eyes brimmed with tears. "I'm strong like my paw. See?" He flexed a skinny arm.

Instead of losing patience, Brodie examined the small bulge. "That's quite a muscle there, son. Trade places with your mother. When I give the word, let's all lift."

Against her better judgment, Laurel reluctantly got into position. A finger's breadth separated her from the man who sought to ruin her life. A current leaped across them, sending gooseflesh up her arm. Heaven help her. If she made it through this day, she vowed to limit contact to no less than a country mile. Chewing her lip, she tried to avoid his intense gray scrutiny. She braced her knees for leverage.

"You ready?" His breath teased a strand of hair curling beside her ear. "Everyone lift."

His heady nearness fueled Laurel's need to get it over with. The wood frame cut into her palms, yet it wouldn't yield. Peace would come only by completing the job. Brodie's guttural grunt stole her intentions not to look. When she did, his rebel gaze held her prisoner even as sweat trickled down his face.

The wagon moved, but not high enough.

"I thought you had more in you than that," Brodie challenged, his sinful half smile pulling her.

Laurel's blood became a molten river. An extra surge of power raised it, and the wheel slid onto the greased axle, taking the weight off aching fingers. She relinquished her hold and hurried to escape. Before she realized where she headed, she sank to her ankles in the marshy bayou.

"This is just fine and dandy," she muttered to herself.

The harder she pulled, the more firmly imbedded her feet became in the muck.

"If you weren't too chicken to take my hand, I'd get you out," Brodie drawled from solid ground.

"Go away. My own doing got me in and I'll get myself out."

"There's something between us, Lil. I know it. You know it. You'll come around after you tire of fighting it."

"Get this straight. Were you the last man on the face of the earth, I'd happily die a spinster."

"The hell you say."

Laurel squirmed in the swamp's grip, wishing the man didn't ogle her like some expensive French pastry.

Suddenly she flailed, landing on her behind in the squishy quagmire. His hearty laugh did things to a lady's wounded pride. The miserable glare she shot him failed to squash his mirth.

"My offer stands. All you have to do is take hold." Brodie edged closer and reached.

Resigned, Laurel grasped his palm. The contact sizzled, branding her flesh. A tightened grip and brisk tug did the trick. She flew from the mucky prison into his naked arms.

Thoughts of the indecent kind raced against the beating of her heart. Before she could react, his lips smothered her surprised yelp. Brodie boldly groped her backside, holding her tightly against him. His tongue explored her parted mouth as a strangled moan rose from a powerful need.

Behind lowered lids, Murphy's face floated. She instantly broke away.

"Damn you, Brodie Yates."

Damn them both. Part of her wanted to curl up and stay forever in the circle of his embrace. Painful remembrance had a way of bursting a rosy dream.

He'd left her behind.

Besides that, she was still promised to another.

A quiet sob escaped as she pummeled the tall muscular figure.

His arms trembled but he let her go. Ragged breath ruffled the top of her hair in a faint caress that did little toward helping regain her sanity.

Laurel moved a few feet away and worked to get the roar in her ears down to a low rumble.

"I'm beholden to you." Her stiff murmur competed with a sudden gust of air. She straightened the mud-soaked dress and fastened her gaze on the distant flight of a loon.

"Don't speak of it. Pleasure's all mine." He took several strides and turned. "You once welcomed my attention."

"Well, I grew up and got a whole lot smarter."

And discovered that words of love flowed freely when men had no intention of ever returning. A body learned from dumb mistakes. Or at least they should, she told herself.

A brittle snort conveyed his thoughts. "I assume you shared with Murph your sudden aversion to marriage?"

Fury ricocheted off every good intention known to man.

"Do us both a favor, Brodie Yates. Go ahead and tell him yourself. The sooner the better. I'm fed up with your veiled threats."

Ten

LAUREL'S TAUNT STAYED WITH BRODIE THROUGH THE night and into the next day. The lady changed the rules in the middle of the skirmish.

She didn't fight the least bit fair. What to do now?

He wouldn't reveal her secret, that much he knew. And despite stubborn denial of the attraction, she made him feel more alive than he had in a very long time.

Those lips, the taste of her... Ahh.

Beads of sweat dotted his forehead.

The fact his brother had in all likelihood sampled her sweet delights gnawed at his very fiber.

Brodie contemplated the mess in the walk up the grassy knoll behind Murphy's house to the family plot. A white stone marked Elizabeth Yates' place next to her mother and father.

Heaviness draped his shoulders as he stooped to lay a bouquet of yellow and white blooms. The woman who brought him into the world had asked for pitiful little—a faithful husband and children to love. A lump blocked his windpipe. Pray to God she found peace in death that eluded her in life.

The deerskin bag caught on the leather of his vest. He blinked hard, removing the gold band that once graced her hand.

Memories washed upon the beach of his mind. Elizabeth had gotten a rotten philanderer and a son who'd been better off to have died in the womb. Thickness coated his tongue.

Gossips had plenty of fodder after Samuel Yates abandoned them for another woman, a saloon girl no less. Elizabeth, Murphy, and he bore the brunt of that humiliating nightmare.

Even now Brodie's efforts to turn a blind eye to the pain were futile. No amount of wishing would banish the truth.

The sight on that early September morn remained clear.

A rope rubbing against the edge of the loft permanently creaked in his ears.

His mother's slight form swinging to and fro in the gentle breeze had made him retch, ashamed for not seeing her despair.

Barely ten, he'd learned to be a man. Rope shredded his tender flesh, for after cutting her loose, he lowered her gently to the ground. Then he removed all traces of the suicide so his brother would never know.

"Why did she have to die?" Murphy had asked. "Tell me why."

Brodie had no answers then and none now.

He kicked a clod of turf. They'd thrust a job on him he hadn't wanted. What did a kid know? He needed reassurance and guidance himself... Things parents should provide.

Besides, a body couldn't teach values and self-worth when a mother and father didn't think enough of them to stick around.

Rotten substitute parent Brodie made.

Damn you, Samuel Yates.

Till the day he died, he'd curse the man who passed his bad seed on to him. Surely, sorry blood flowed in his veins.

Every good deed in the world wouldn't atone for that. Fixing the wheel for the Cole family gave him much satisfaction. Still, it changed little when he canceled one right with a wrong by reminding Laurel of things she wished to forget.

But hell and damnation, he hungered for the hot-blooded woman.

Movement below captured his attention. Etta's frantic charge up the incline stood hair at the nape of his neck on end. The ring fell from trembling fingers. He scooped it into the bag and met her halfway.

"Mr. Brodie, come quick. It's your brother!"

❧

Laurel finished serving the last customer and tackled the cleanup. Morning's encounter with Brodie twisted her inside out. The taste of his lips, his searing touch, branded themselves upon her skin.

Odd how fast she'd noted a distinction between Shenandoah and scores of men who'd entered her life back then. The special, inner quiet set him apart. Among a hundred other things, of course.

She plunged elbow-deep into soapy water, surrendering to her wandering mind.

The handsome stranger had given back more than the pleasure which he bought. He led her down a path inside a war-torn soul and the pain there had equaled her own. Her spirits at rock bottom, she despaired of escaping William Taft. Each time she requested help and received the biting end of the lash for her trouble had silenced the asking. She believed she'd die alone far from Texas.

Shenandoah had provided hope of feeling like a woman—a real woman. Someone of worth rather than a commodity.

Nights of sharing precious tidbits of home renewed freedom she could taste. Curled in his arms, strength seeped into her bones. With their bodies entangled in the bedding, she dreamed of pure honeyed passion and everlasting love. Grand ideas of babies and a husband to cherish had taken her on the fanciful journey.

Laurel jerked, returning to the kitchen of Ollie's Café.

"Keep rubbing that plate and there won't be enough left to hold spit." Uncanny the way Ollie read her moods. Laurel tossed her a peeved glance. Lost in reverie, she'd forgotten the dear lady stood waiting with drying towel in hand.

"No law keeping a body from reflecting, is there?"

Warmth in the airless room stuck the clothes to her body, she reasoned. Nothing else accounted for the sheen on her skin.

Besides, recalling certain times in life helped slam doors.

Or open them wider, guilt whispered.

"Never said there was, girl. But your attention's a mite on the scattered side since running into Yates."

Laurel squirmed under the one-eyed squint that pricked. "Lack of dishes wouldn't matter to hungry menfolk. We could serve their food on a piece of tree bark for all they notice."

"What happened at the Coles' campsite?" Ollie asked.

"Nothing, absolutely nothing. You were there."

Silky caresses and kisses wouldn't have an opportunity to occur again. She'd handle Brodie with a firm hand. He couldn't waltz into her life as though he'd never left. She'd show him.

Do us both a favor. Go ahead and tell.

What a dangerous, foolish dare.

"You might oughta consider a few fibbing lessons," Ollie spouted. "I got eyes enough to see."

The porcelain snapped in her hands. Laurel muttered an oath, staring at the jagged cut from which blood pooled. "I can't very well put that man from my mind when you're quite happy to fill in when he's not around."

Ollie huffed, stepping back quicker than if she'd sworn allegiance with the grim reaper and he'd come to escort her to hell.

"No call to get sideways. Grandpappy always said, 'Solving problems is like clearing pasture land. First, pull out the piddly little saplings, the ones that don't make a hill of beans, then set to work on the big ol' stumps. If'n you cain't pull 'em out whole, then chop 'em into small pieces and cart 'em off a chunk at a time.'"

"I'm sick of listening to your dear, departed grandfather. For once speak for yourself, Ollie."

"Quit your bellering. Brodie Yates ain't the logjam blocking your way. I'm saying get rid of the guilt and shame eating you alive." Ollie punched Laurel's chest. "That's the stump you gotta work on. Everything else is pissant little saplings."

Laurel wrapped the cut, muttering beneath her breath. How much patience would it take to wipe away layers of tarnish that had collected on her soul? She sighed. "I'm sorry I took my frustration out on you."

"Denying your feelings can cause nothing but grief and heartache. It's plain you're sweet on the man."

"Horsefeathers. Sweet on a lousy womanizer? He probably tallies the women he's charmed the same way he carves notches in the handle of his Colt for each man he kills." And with as much conscience, she added silently.

She cursed the fact she had only to close her eyes to fetch from hiding every crease, indentation, and pore of his face.

In addition, lest she came close to forgetting those, rippling muscles encased in old leather refreshed her memory.

And the barest of contact melted her firm resolve.

"A body never knows what lies around the next bend until they go down that road. Ain't nothing good comes from denying the truth, Laurel girl."

Commotion beyond the café overshadowed the dire warning. Curiosity took them to the front with aprons flapping. Laurel reached the window shaken by the clamor of hooves filling the street. Gunshots added to the melee.

"Stop them!" a man shouted, running past. Others followed, their boots pounding the wooden sidewalk.

The town's citizens scurried into hiding places. More shots rang out, peppering the glass. Tiny fragments showered them.

"Git down." Ollie shoved her to the floor amid the shards.

"What's happening?" Icy panic raced through her.

"Outlaws would be my guess." Ollie crawled behind the counter where she stashed a revolver in case of an emergency.

"What are you doing?"

"Ain't about to let no sidewinder take what's mine. You wait here and keep your head down."

"But you can't do a blooming thing. Let the men…" Her voice trailed off, for Ollie no longer heard. She'd disappeared, likely charging out the back door, anxious to get into the fray.

A rapid blast of shots, yells, and fleeing horses assaulted her ears. Laurel crouched, waiting for it all to end…or the rest of the world to come crashing down. God only knows what happened to Ollie out in the midst of that chaos. The woman never learned to leave well enough alone. She stood no chance against overwhelming odds, but she'd never listen.

Long minutes passed. When blessed silence came, Laurel almost failed to recognize it. She raised her head.

Ollie burst through the door a second later. "Come quick."

"What's wrong?"

"Murphy's in a bad way. They shot him."

"How? Why?" Trembling legs made her moves unsteady.

"Bank robbers. The Blanchard gang, someone said. Murphy tried to stop 'em. Wounded one before taking a bullet."

Laurel broke into a run. "The sheriff, why didn't he—?"

"Murdering thieves killed Sheriff Tucker." Ollie

panted, trying to keep up. "Snatched little Darcy Hatcher and Willa Carver on the way out of town. Took the girls with 'em."

The news paralyzed Laurel in her tracks. She gagged, tasting the dirty rag her abductors had stuffed into her mouth so many years ago. Sweat and cheap liquor blocked the sun's warmth. A shudder swept her into the swirling, black foreboding of a wild Texas wind. She breathed danger and despair.

"Dear God, no. Someone has to go after them."

"They will. I understand how you feel, but—"

"No one knows unless they've lived the horror."

"Of course, girl. I only meant to point out Murphy needs you at the moment. You gotta be strong for his sake."

A growing crowd jostled them, returning her senses. Laurel and Ollie pushed through to the bank's open door.

Nothing prepared her for the sight. Murphy's pale features contrasted with blood puddling in a circle. Laurel swallowed a sob and knelt, paying no heed that the hem of her dress soaked up the sticky fluid.

"I'm here, Murphy." Shaking, she smoothed back the sandy hair. Eyes closed, he more resembled a corpse. A sudden gasp gave the sole indication of life. "Please don't die."

The pressing sea of faces flushed when she looked up. Each flinched, avoiding eye contact.

All except one. Brodie Yates, who knelt opposite.

"I'll take care of my brother. Nothing short of a miracle can help him." Pain in his eyes did a thorough job of riddling what calm she'd managed.

"A doctor? I assume you sent someone to Jefferson."

"The moment the smoke cleared, for all the good it'll do. By the time one gets here…" The break in his voice said love for Murphy ran deeper than merely shielding him from her.

A man squeezing past intent on leaving the bank caught her attention. "Jake, can't you do something?"

The barber flushed. "Digging a grave comes to mind. Beyond that, nothing much left." He shoved through the gawkers.

"Laurel," Murphy muttered weakly, his eyelids fluttering.

"I'm right here."

"Laurel, I… Don't leave me." His lids drifted shut.

"Don't worry, I'm not going anywhere." She firmly held the limp hand, her glance challenging Brodie to dispute the vow.

The rebel glared, speaking to no one in particular. "Some of you help me carry him home."

Each clearly understood the difference between an order and a request. The teller produced a sturdy board and slid it under Murphy. Half a dozen lifted.

A tortured groan rolled from his colorless lips, ripping open Laurel's heart. The squared set of Brodie's jaw told of a similar effect on him. She ran ahead to make arrangements, praying for a doctor even though Murphy's chances weren't enough to dare mention.

Etta wrung her hands, the whites of her eyes glistening from a mahogany canvas. "Mr. Murphy? Is he passed?"

"He's hurt awful bad. Get water, clean towels, scissors, and…" Her mind whirled, trying to think of what they'd need. "And something to make bandages. A bunch of them."

"My feet's already a-movin'." Etta sped into the house, leaving Laurel holding the door for the men's precious cargo.

"Put him on the sofa in the sitting room." No need to worsen Murphy's suffering by taking him up the stairs.

They gently moved him onto the soft leather.

"Hurry with those towels and water, Etta," Laurel hollered. Time had rendered Murphy's motionless body the color of chalk.

Brodie cut away a shirt no longer crisply white and starched.

"Is he…?"

"Dead? Not yet."

Her tender touch grazed Murphy's forehead. She became queasy when Brodie exposed the wound. A bullet had torn through the right side of the chest wall, from which a trickle of oozing stickiness seeped. Relief swept over her when Etta arrived with a basin of water and a load of towels tucked under her arm. The woman's gasp filled the room.

"Lawsy me. Mr. Murphy's shore in a bad way, ain't he?"

Engrossed in stanching the flow, no one answered.

"I'll fetch them scissors and bandages," Etta said.

Brodie's presence bolstered Laurel to do what she must. "Hold pressure on the wound. Press hard," he ordered.

Without question she followed his instruction, but cringed at the faint pulse of Murphy's heart through the towel. Small signs of life should've brought hope, but didn't. Lack of medical knowledge didn't prevent realizing the obvious.

In tandem they worked, their hands touching frequently in a fight to save the man whose death would bring great loss.

Each fleeting brush prolonged the inevitable. Despite their bumbling efforts, he'd probably not survive. That they simply grasped at air became apparent.

"I...I can't do this. It's no use, I'm afraid."

"Remember your promise to stay with him?" Brodie's bloodstained hands clung to hers. His piercing gaze seemed to recognize the coward in her, but strangely he appeared to sympathize. "We're all he has. Don't buckle on him now."

His intense caring washed over Laurel. Brodie did love his brother, no one could dispute that. His gentle admonition hinted maybe he held a bit of regard for her as well. The brittle edge had vanished, the harsh lines softening around his mouth. She erased the fact that each hope and dream hung in the balance. Everything had changed with the day's events. They no longer played a game. Matching wits had no place here.

Laurel's palm curled inside Brodie's and found new strength. His touch conveyed hope and courage—and home?

"I'm not going anywhere. Long as there's the barest prospect of change, I won't quit," Laurel vowed.

"That's my Lil."

An empty rush of cold air came when he reached for a clean cloth. The broken link left her again bereft and scared.

"Here, take this and give me the soaked one," he said.

The soft squish of the wet cloth landing in her

palm brought chills. She didn't recognize her own red-stained hands.

Quite odd the things to notice at very inappropriate times, like the way blood colored underneath and around, perfectly outlining her fingernails, but leaving the center like unfinished porcelain to paint later.

Perhaps the unblemished portion represented a section of life she'd forgotten to live.

Or maybe it reminded of damaged parts that rejected color?

"Where is that doctor?"

"He'll come. Raise Murphy slightly. Help me get this binding around him."

"This god-awful waiting tries my patience to no end." Thankful for something to do besides reflect on stupid mistakes, she gently tilted Murphy in order to get the binding situated.

Brodie pulled it tight across his brother's chest and went under again. His arm jostled her breast each time, spreading a heat throughout. The innocent, unintentional brushes barricaded the glacial landscape that lurked inside, waiting for the moment to freeze her forever.

Laurel met his blank expression. He pretended well. Yet she knew the carefully orchestrated nimble caresses had affected him. The clumsy tying of the cloth betrayed.

Ollie spoke from the doorway. "Yates, can you spare a minute? Some folks would like a word."

"Not now." He waved her away. "Can't you see I'm busy?"

"Goldarned. It'll only take a minute. Wouldn't ask just to hear myself talking."

"Reckon we're finished for the moment." Brodie sighed and turned to the wash basin. "Make it quick."

Drying his hands, he followed Ollie down the hall.

Bellowing grumbles drifting from the study aroused Laurel's interest. Jake Whitaker and George Adams were hard to miss.

She edged closer.

"We've called a town meeting. The voting was unanimous."

"What the devil are you babbling about?" came Brodie's sharp question.

"We've elected to pin Sheriff Tucker's tin star on you."

"You're not pinning anything on me, you crazy fools."

George became agitated. "Understand something, Yates. There's no one else. It's you or nothing."

"Then I suppose you won't have a lawman."

Brodie's eerie detachment puzzled Laurel. It wasn't some stranger who had leaked red all over the leather sofa. Blood ran thicker than water. Didn't it? It didn't make sense.

But then, not much in this hellish day had.

"Furthermore, you're wasting my time," Brodie snapped.

"That money those thieving varmints took was all these folks had," Ollie spat back. "And there's the matter of those two little girls, don't forget."

"What in Sam Hill are you talking about?"

"The hostages. They took Miz Hatcher's and Miz Carver's daughters with 'em."

"None of us would stand a snowball's chance in hell

of going after them and coming back alive. My God, man." Jake's volume raised a notch. Laurel envisioned his long, twitching mustache. "Bert Blanchard uses men for target practice and laughs about it."

"On top of that, Murphy managed to wound one before they drew a bead on him," came George Adams' nasal twang.

"Gentlemen, I'm sorry. I'd help if I could, but—"

"Son of a bluejacket, Yates!" Ollie exploded. "The savages shot your own brother and left him for dead. An' them poor innocent babes—you want to tell them no one gives a damn? What does it take to thaw the ice around your heart?"

Laurel held her breath. He couldn't turn them down. He represented Darcy and Willa's last hope. His deadly aim and nerves of steel made Brodie more than a match for Bert and his henchmen. He couldn't refuse.

"I'm no lawman, just a two-bit gunslinger."

She peeked through a crack in the door. His wide stance portrayed defiance. Damn his rotten hide.

Brodie continued, "Hell, I've skirted the law most my life, jumping over the line more often than not to suit my fancy."

"Our point exactly. You can get the job done."

"Get it through your thick skulls. No."

Once more he'd betrayed her. Lack of courage or skill didn't hold him back, and he scoffed at fear. His refusal pelted harder than any hailstones she'd seen, making far greater dents.

What halted the air in her lungs didn't come from plunging ice, but bitter truth.

He'd protect his brother from her, but not seek retribution against the men who'd hurled Murphy to death's door and stolen two little darlings.

Living by split second reflexes had changed him into someone she'd sooner not know.

Laurel sagged against the door frame. Slim doubts of the lawless bunch letting the girls live challenged hope they would. Her heart lurched when she touched the broken tooth. Might be a pure blessing should death take them quickly.

"Seems to me it didn't disturb you overmuch when you tried to fit Jeb Prater with a marble hat," Ollie reminded him.

"I answer to no one. This is your town, your money, your problem. Pardon a bit of frankness, but you men need to earn the right to grow hair on your chest."

"It's also your brother who lies still and white." If Jake meant to prick him with the snide comment, he succeeded.

From her listening post, Laurel felt the sting of Brodie's anger. "That's right. And I'm trying to keep him alive. Getting your money back sure won't. Finding a doctor might."

She couldn't put her finger on the cause of Brodie's obstinacy. She'd witnessed his strong, capable hands at work. Mrs. Cole and her children provided ample proof of compassion.

And when she'd found herself mired in the bayou's clutches? Even now she could taste the raw passion of his need.

A cold, heartless man hadn't kissed her.

Eleven

BRODIE'S THOUGHTS STAGGERED TO AREAS TOO agonizing for however brief a sojourn. He rubbed his eyes, but the images stayed, each one splintering off another piece of his soul. His chest ached from a cold that wouldn't leave.

God have mercy.

Wanting to help wasn't the issue. He couldn't.

Not even for Murph. Some things came with a price beyond reach. That knowledge ripped the hole inside even bigger.

"I think I get the gist. You're telling us we might as well toss our hard-earned money to the wind," the barber spat.

Brodie jammed both fists into his pockets to avert disarranging Whitaker's ugly features. "I've had a gut-full of killing."

That they thought him callous and hard rattled the pledge he'd made to himself. Turmoil that had burrowed into his core and taken up squatter's rights had finally begun to ease of late. Making this group understand would use up valuable time.

Besides, they'd mock at a hardened gunfighter's desire to call it quits, to make a stand once and for all here in Redemption, and to find out if his search for a bit of home had not been in vain.

The fight to stay breathing until he found a smidgen of self-respect had taken more perseverance than anyone knew.

"I don't see that ridding the earth of one or two more bad seed should make any difference to your sort." Jake twirled his mustache, shifting from one hip to the other.

"My sort? What the hell's that supposed to mean?"

"You know—someone who kills for the pleasure of it."

Brodie clenched his fists until the bones hurt. He'd never taken a life for sport. Nor would that day ever arrive.

"Find someone else or do it yourself." Let them see how easily they could forget the gurgle of a final breath or the smell of blood after hot lead ripped apart flesh from bone.

"No one says you have to kill 'em, just bring back what they stole," George Adams muttered.

Brodie glared, a derisive snort exploding. "You think to accomplish one without the other? I propose you try it."

Suddenly, a heavyset woman entered the fray. "Mr. Yates, my husband, God rest his soul, gave his life for a cause he believed in. Most of you in this room lost loved ones. I'm tired of losing. How much do we have to sacrifice? My baby is out there with those murderin' robbers. If you have one shred of decency and goodness, I beg of you, please help."

"I respect your grief, Mrs. Hatcher—"

"Mr. Brodie, slavery is all my family has known for generations," a woman of color who he presumed to be Mrs. Carver added softly. "I thought my Willa would finally have a chance to grow up free and enjoy the kinds of things denied black folk. I got nowhere else to turn except you, sir."

"Go tell that to your soldier friends over in Jefferson. They favor darkies. Don't give a damn about any white folk though." Hate spat from George Adams' mouth.

"Yeah, scoot on over there, Miz Carver, and let us take care of our white girls. Anyhow, they probably killed yours right off." A tobacco-chewing, surly man entered the debate.

The mother gasped and tried to muffled her sobs.

Brodie slung the man, pinning him against a wall. Beneath his forearm, the bastard's Adam's apple bobbled in a frantic attempt to stop the brown wad's migration, but the lump edged down the man's gullet anyway.

"What the hell?" Jake's scrawny frame tried to intervene.

Maybe Brodie was hasty in ruling out the "sort" he could be if provoked. He could certainly wring hate from this lickspittle's neck without a bit of remorse.

"Any of you show disrespect of any kind for womenfolk again, I won't stop here." Brodie shoved the man into Jake.

"Hey, you got some nerve threatening Martin and the rest of us," George whined.

"It's fair warning. I don't think you'd care to see what my threats look like." Brodie smoothed his vest and almost smiled at the sudden ashen faces of the self-righteous bunch of bigots. Except for the two mothers and the b'Dam woman. Hell of a name.

"You addlebrained, limp-wristed ignorants. You'd best listen to him." The petite café owner shifted her pipe to the other corner. "And fighting amongst ourselves ain't solving our problem. Remember you asked for his help. Ain't the lot of you with gumption enough to toss a stray cat out the back door."

"But we ain't gonna stand for this," Jake spluttered.

Brodie's train of thought veered south as a slight figure pushed through the small gathering.

Laurel had fire in her eyes and murder in her step as she stalked into the room.

Why did she have to get in the middle of this mess?

"Yates, you're all air and bluff. It's all well and good to overpower a room of slackers." Shocked gasps didn't slow Laurel down. "At one time you might've had reason to call yourself a man. I can't say it holds true now."

"Tell him, girl," Ollie urged.

He caught the finger poking his chest. "Miss James, you're meddling in someone else's bubbling pot."

"Someone has to."

His narrowed gaze should've warned her that she'd overstepped her bounds. Yet, she appeared unfazed by his stony scowl.

"Ollie, pass me your shooting iron."

"You sure of what you're doing, girl?"

"Never more sure. I think this overstuffed goose would fit nicely in a boiling pot once I make a hole to let out a bit of the quackery. Then we're going after those girls."

An icy glare accompanied the bold statement. She couldn't know every slur brought more pain than he could bear.

"And our money, don't forget," George Adams said.

"I could give a rat's hindquarter about that. Frankly, I shame you people for your narrow, selfish minds."

George huffed. "You forget your place, Miss James."

"It must throw you into shock to find a female who won't knuckle under to your stupid rules. Guess I've never been a bootlicker and won't start now. It sickens my gut that green is the only skin color you can see. Except...I wonder how quickly you'd have propped your gluttonous hide into a saddle had they stolen your children. If time permitted, I'd argue the point. Now step out of the way." She pushed past George and lurched for Ollie's pistol.

Brodie's quick reflexes stopped her. She cast a disdainful glance at the grip clamped around her wrist.

"Can't let you do that." He ignored the look that could boil snow off a mountaintop, renewing his hold when she yanked.

"Let me do what? Shoot you or go after those bandits?"

"Take your pick."

Smoke curled about Ollie's head. The porky-spined woman must've tamped the tobacco down good judging from the fog that screened those owl-eyes trying to leap from their sockets. "Looks like you'll have to dicker your way out of this one, Yates. She means business."

"What'll it be?" Laurel's breasts heaved much too near.

He uttered an oath beneath his breath before releasing her. "I'll go. Satisfied? But I absolutely refuse the sheriff job. And, by God, you're not coming with me. Those are my terms."

He brushed her and her victorious attitude aside and stalked back to his brother's side. She hadn't won. No one had.

Truth of it, he could already feel the rip of another piece from his soul. He wouldn't lay odds on those two little girls making their next birthday.

Maybe he wouldn't either.

Nor did Murphy have a fighting chance of seeing sunrise.

A short time later, Brodie sought the serenity of the garden. Air not laden with the stench of blood filled his lungs but it did nothing to help the churning in his belly.

Time appeared to be measured in the ticks of a feeble heartbeat while they waited for a doctor who had yet to show. Helplessness wasn't a role he knew well. Death lurked in the room where the only kin he had left in the world lay and nothing he did could stave off the grim reaper.

Light footsteps on the rock path came from behind. Out of the corner of his eye he caught Laurel's approach.

"I've sent Etta for a healer who lives deep in the swamp off Caddo Lake. Nora Whitebird may be Murphy's last hope." The warmth of her shoulder settled next to his.

"For all the difference anything makes now."

"A horrid thing to say. What happened to your pretty speech about not giving up?"

"I've seen more death in the last five years than you'll see in a whole lifetime. No one can change its course. Same goes for altering the direction of any-one's path once it's set. Wise men call it predestiny."

"Hogwash. Life isn't carved in a piece of stone. If you want something badly enough, you can have it. That's faith."

"Can't buy it at any price." Were that true, he'd gladly pay, even if it cost a king's ransom. Home and family represented impossible dreams he couldn't attain.

"True, a person can't buy their way through trouble. But they can alter destiny with enough blood, sweat, and tears."

"The voice of authority." Sarcasm dripped from his tone.

Why did she have to be so beautiful? And why couldn't he stay away from her? Or she from him? For God's sake, she belonged to Murphy. That throaty voice—the vanilla and spice swirling around his head would drive a sane man crazy. And Lord knows he'd gone there the second he stepped into Ollie's Café.

She studied him for a long minute and shrugged. "Stick to your beliefs, such as they are, and quit belittling mine."

He'd earned a good and proper scolding, but the mildness surprised him after the recent tongue-lashing. Her intense scrutiny made up for it though. He squirmed and tried to look away. A soft touch on his arm sent a sizzle clear to his toenails.

"I appreciate the sacrifice you're making and I thank you for it. Had we anyone else, you'd get your rathers."

"Murphy's the last of the Yates. I want to be here in case he needs me, not off chasing more elusive shadows."

"If fate reversed our roles, I'm not certain I could leave him."

Brodie did a double take. "Still, you made it impossible to say no. You, Lil, no one else."

Laurel hid her violet scrutiny beneath lowered lids. The wrinkle on her forehead deepened from heavy thought. That nice shade of pink flooding her cheeks only made her more desirable.

"There's nothing else you can do for Murphy, except make the Blanchards pay for what they did."

"Peculiar thing about revenge. Once it gets inside, it changes you into an outlander. I wanted to fit someplace, to finally belong. I'm tired of running."

"I'm sorry." She reached for his hand. "That explains why you hesitated. I watched you defend Mrs. Carver. You have a noble heart that will never let you stand by quietly."

Somehow the realization that she regarded him a darn sight better than he deserved increased his longing to hold her close and never let her go.

"That's been my downfall. It baffles me why skin color should lower or raise a person's status. Where do you fit?"

"Alongside you. I'm surprised you had to ask."

"Making sure. You've given me a few starts of late." Especially when she'd arm-wrestled him for the pistol.

"Aren't you wasting precious seconds? The trail only grows colder."

"I'll saddle up come daybreak." He gauged the magnitude of shock by the way her head jerked around.

"You wouldn't drag your heels unless..."

Brodie squirmed under her scrutiny. "I admit I've seen their hideout a time or two."

Laurel gasped. "You knew all along, didn't you? You know the Blanchards."

What he hadn't thought to hear hiding behind the accusation bore a strange resemblance to disappointment. That thorn pricked.

"Sort of."

"Either you do or you don't."

He sighed. "I didn't want to get involved with them unless I had to."

"They shot Murphy!"

"Sweet Jezzie. Folks keep saying that as though it'd slipped my mind, like I was either some senile old man or a simpleton." He kicked a loose pebble into a clipped holly bush. Leaves scattered onto the walk. "You may as well hear this now—me and Luther Blanchard go back a ways. I owe him an almighty debt."

Laurel sucked in her bottom lip. "Whatever it is, your brother and those poor little girls shouldn't have to pay."

Brodie nudged back his Stetson with a forefinger. The rattles added a buffer against the unceasing roar in his head. Without them to ground him, the pain and disillusion riddling every waking moment would hasten his demise. He pulled a cheroot from inside his vest, bit off the end, and lit it before answering.

"Luther saved my life in the Battle of Shiloh. I took a mini-ball in the leg and lay bleeding. A blue belly drew his bayonet, taunting my screams. I clutched the spent rifle to my chest, unable to prevent that soldier from adding me to the list of three thousand other casualties."

Smoke curled up into the breeze, the wisps vanishing.

He wondered at this ebony-haired lady who'd invaded his mind—and his heart. Would she fade into similar nothingness? He'd never spoken of these things to another living soul. The telling didn't come easy.

Strange how tobacco calmed twisted nerves. A filthy addiction. Nonetheless, smoking untangled some of the mess.

"Anyway, I waited, dreading, praying for the moment that would end the nightmare. Luther threw himself over me, taking the brunt of the bayonet. The blow shattered his left leg before he managed to shoot the damned Yank."

"That's how you knew. Bystanders mentioned one of them dragged his left leg." Laurel's whiskey voice became raspy.

"Luther and I recovered in a makeshift Confederate hospital. Had we wound up in Union hands they'd have amputated his leg. It turned out the wound left him a cripple. And me? I'm a—"

"Man with grit and honor," she supplied. "The hellish things you suffered. Yet, you survived. That's what counts."

"Tell that to Luther. He might beg to differ."

"I understand your predicament. Truly I do. But those men rode into this town, kidnapped, stole, and murdered. Don't you care about that? Surely, they deserve what's coming to them."

Not at his expense. Hunger to save the tiny pieces left of his soul beckoned from afar. Killing again would seal his fate.

"Just don't want it to be me who has to mete out the punishment."

But he would...for her. He'd do most anything for Lil.

Even if it damned him for eternity.

Laurel stroked the length of his arm. She paused, her lingering fingertips exerting soft pressure, massaging the hurt.

"You're our last hope. Few stand a ghost of a chance. I still have to ask how you know where they'll hole up." Laden with disappointment, the strangle in her voice unnerved him.

A man couldn't talk about things he knew and still profess ambition to be more than the callous gun-hand she thought him.

A man didn't just blurt out that inside beat the heart of an idealist. The situation made this neither the time nor the place.

Besides, a man could expect complications in explaining exactly what put certain notions beyond reach. The lady had obligations elsewhere and seemed in no mood for what-ifs.

"I stumbled across their hideout once. Luther asked me to join up."

"But you didn't?" He didn't miss the hope in her voice.

"No."

Silence stretched. He focused on the cigar's red glow. To hope for more than belief asked too much. His lungs expanded to accommodate the rush of air. Unfamiliar peace followed the brief glimpse he'd given her into his brand of hell, a place he'd never allowed anyone before.

No matter what he or Laurel had been or done, they were kindred spirits with secrets to hide.

Brodie's bold gaze slid the length of her and drank in the sight of the exceptional woman. Her dark hair pulled back into a severe knot might've brought the word *sedate* to mind had not escaping, wispy tendrils ruined it. They curled about her face with such alluring beauty he had trouble trying to draw air into his lungs. He should've stepped away from the intoxicating fragrance that surrounded her. But he couldn't.

Torturous, insatiable yearning nailed his boots to the spot.

For two cents he'd yank her to him, hold her tightly, and ignore the protest of decency his conscience would cry.

Damn the fool that made a home inside him.

His brother lay dying and all he could think about was the elegant long column of her neck. His gaze dropped to the swell of her breasts, rising and falling rapidly.

Laurel fidgeted, twisting the folds of her skirt. He had experience with those slender hands. They possessed uncanny abilities in caressing away a man's troubles.

Passion wound through his memory like vines encircling the cypress in the bayou, possessing, becoming as one.

Their sultry morning encounter teased. She could rebuke him until she exhausted her vocabulary, but her body couldn't deny this thing between them. He cursed his weakness for her.

"I've a story to tell you," she blurted.

He wrestled his thoughts and his gaze from her lush,

rounded curves. He'd seen many a condemned horse thief with less desperation than he found glistening in Laurel's eyes.

"That is, should you wish to hear it," she hastened to add.

"Seems the day for getting things off our chest. Shoot."

Color drained from her face, leaving it two shades of pale. Maybe he should've left off the joking.

"It happened one day six years, three months, and fourteen days ago."

Brodie had a feeling she knew the exact hour as well. He didn't ask though. Only about something real serious could a person pinpoint the time with such accuracy.

"A young girl picked blackberries along the creek bank. Two brothers went with her, but their favorite fishing hole held more promise than berry picking. They left her all alone." Laurel stopped and moistened her lips.

Ashes fell from his cigar. He paid them no heed.

"A music box her parents had given her for her birthday tinkled merrily at her feet. She could almost smell the pie her mother would bake."

Again she paused, this time to wipe a hand across her eyes as if erasing some horrible scene.

"You don't have to do this, Laurel."

"Three men appeared from nowhere and grabbed her," Laurel continued as if he'd not uttered a peep. "She fought, scratching and kicking as hard as she could. When she tried to scream to alert her brothers, they crammed a dirty cloth into her mouth. These stealers of children took her far away. They gave her a new name, made her do unspeakable things, and kept her under lock and key until they presumed she had no will left for escape."

The rasp dropped to a mere whisper. "I was that girl, barely fifteen."

The cheroot burned his fingers. He tossed it down, grinding it with a heel. Thickness grew in his throat.

Propriety be damned. He pulled her into his arms. She buried her face in his chest.

"I didn't know. I thought—"

"They forced me into what I became." The words tripped over a sob. "I prayed to die."

"I'm sorry, so sorry." He'd been so eager to prove her wrong. The bitter pill that he'd judged, convicted, and sentenced left a bite. He held her, caressing her back.

"I became a cheap piece of merchandise at the Black Garter. Even now I scrub daily, but filth is embedded in my skin."

His gut twisted. He'd helped degrade her. Worse, he'd threatened to tell the entire town and heap further disgrace. "I didn't know."

"They laughed, proud they'd ruined me for any decent man."

"I'll kill every one of the bastards."

She pushed back and leveled an accusing stare. "I kept hoping for a miracle. I thought... I clung to your promise."

Her hands curled into fists. He wished she'd lay into him. A good whaling might take the edge off the disgust and loathing.

"Laurel, I—"

"You made me believe you truly cared."

If she knew of the many nights he'd awakened bathed in a cold sweat. The days she filled his thoughts and gave him reason to keep trying.

"Darlin', I did. I ran into another Yankee bullet on my return. Once I regained my health, I wasn't sure you'd like the man I became, not sure that what happened had merely been a figment of my imagination." He coaxed her against him, resting his chin on the top of her head. "I drifted to California and back, dodging everyone sent to kill the famous Confederate spy."

"That's why Ollie and I settled here. Redemption fit."

Something about the word seemed to offer hope and belief that a man could save himself. It fit snug around him also.

"Ollie helped you escape St. Louis, I take it."

"She worked in the kitchen. We became close and I finally confided in her. She got me out in the wee hours after everyone slept."

"Remind me to thank her. She's a good woman."

"We're family now. We adopted each other."

Laurel's lips enticed. He'd gladly risk life, limb, and certain death to sample them again.

The sun faded below the horizon. Dusk was made for lovers. Her willowy curves snuggled into his arms. She belonged here. He slipped the pins from her hair, breathing into the silk. The moment spoke of everything—and nothing.

Her moist pink lips drew him like a parched man to water. He couldn't resist any longer.

His mouth met hers in a blaze of sinful passion. White dahlias and vanilla, the past and the present, dreams and reality, merged in a single instant.

"You smell of moonmist and gentle rain." He breathed against her ear, reluctant to let her go.

"Moonmist? I'm not certain that's a good thing."

"My lady, a lover's breath beneath the silvery rays creates moonmist. Some claim it carries the aroma of an aroused woman."

"But we're not…and I'm not…" A becoming blush stained her cheeks.

The pulse in the hollow of her throat beat frantically. This among other things he could mention, like the wisps of hair hugging her earlobes, the catch in her whiskey voice, the way she fussed over the Cole boys, made her the only woman he wanted.

"You lie so well."

Laurel's mouth flew open. "I must go."

"Wait."

She dodged the outstretched hand. "This isn't proper."

The lady spoke the truth. He owed his brother a sight more than stolen kisses with his woman. Although nothing that made Brodie feel he'd died and gone to heaven could surely be a sin.

Loving Laurel should never be wrong, he decided.

Ollie chose that moment to open the garden door. "Girl, the healer's come. Thought you'd want to know."

"Thanks, Ollie." She smoothed back her hair, scrambling for pins with which to secure it. She made do with just two.

The crusty woman's disapproving stare kept Brodie from trying to help. He felt as if she'd caught him stealing from the cookie jar. Maybe that's just what he'd done.

"I hope you're right about this Nora woman," he managed.

"One thing's for sure, it won't hurt. We're groping in the dark."

He clutched her hand when she started toward the open door and Ollie. He could've sworn she returned the light squeeze.

"One more thing and I'll let you be." He struggled to keep a betraying tremble from sneaking into his voice. "Since I won't be around the next week or so, will you stay nearby…so Murphy won't be alone when he dies?"

"It goes without saying."

"And one more thing. Should he by some miracle make it, I'll not stand in your way of marrying him. I give you both my blessing."

Twelve

AT DAYBREAK LAUREL STOOD ON THE VERANDA LONG after the gray-eyed rebel disappeared down the road. One last check on Murphy had found him alive, but no sign of improvement. Then, Brodie had silently gathered a few essentials, saddled, and ridden out.

Strangely enough, though she'd prayed for his leaving, she could scarcely breathe from the empty space he left behind.

Through her pounding pulse she heard the rattles dangling from his hat. Those didn't fade despite that he'd passed from view.

Spit and thunder. Didn't Brodie know she'd risk most anything to sleep in his arms again? Surely he felt the earth-shattering desire in her touch. Denying their feelings seemed to have melded the fabric of life that had woven the two of them together into one fate.

Dearly as she hoped Murphy lived, she couldn't marry him. Not now. Not even to obtain status. Not for any reason.

The rumble of thunder interrupted her thoughts. Dark rain clouds that escaped notice in the wrenching agony of Brodie's departure appeared. She hoped his overstuffed saddlebags included an oilskin slicker, although a serious drenching probably mattered least to him. She'd forced him into this dangerous mission. The outcome could end all wrong.

"Please, keep my darling safe," she murmured into the wind. "Let him bring back those girls unharmed... and soon."

Among the lot of Redemption's citizens, only she held insight into the minds of Darcy and Willa. The brand of fear they knew at this very moment blocked her air passage, souring the contents of her stomach. Years had passed since her abduction and yet one incident sent her hurtling back to the moment when the nightmare began.

Hindsight let her see the bad mistake in speaking of it.

For pity's sake, Brodie had already accepted the task when she opened that door.

Clear as day he misunderstood why she had. Giving his blessing to the betrothal confirmed guilt he felt for not saving her. She'd have been far wiser to leave it buried. Bringing those demons into the light of day smashed the odds of reclaiming a lost love into a million pieces.

Damn the familiar chord he struck in baring his own dark corner of his soul.

Only yesterday she'd harbored belief of betrayal, or at the very least that he'd misled her. But their moonlit talk, scented with hibiscus and lavender, vanquished those notions.

Yes, she must've taken leave of her mind.

And for what reason had he shared his secret? Absolution? Acceptance? Or a cry to silence voices from the past? Each pain-filled word had sprung from his gut. The agony that had fractured his deep voice had revealed how deeply rooted in honor those events had grown. The same peace that eluded her eluded him also.

They were truly two of a kind.

The door creaked. Nora Whitebird stood at the white railing running the porch length. "Rain good. Wash away evil."

"I wish it could." She met the ageless woman's piercing gaze. Nora appeared to know things meant for sages. Her smooth, tanned skin gave no hint of age. "How is Murphy?"

"He sleeps. You go. Get rest."

Nora's stare halted on the hem of Laurel's dress where blood had soaked, turning the yellow fabric dull, rusty brown. Laurel realized she wore the same clothes she'd donned yesterday.

"Perhaps I will."

"You do your man no good here."

She felt obliged to correct Nora and explain that she was merely following the promise she made to Murphy, but she didn't.

"I couldn't leave when he could die any second."

Last evening she'd shivered when Nora attached bloodsucking leeches. Though the woman explained their usefulness in keeping the wound clean, Laurel would not soon forget the horrifying sight of the burrowing parasites.

Laurel stopped the sob that tried to rise. "Do you think…?"

"Time tell if he stay or cross river into next life. We wait for Great Spirit."

She touched Nora's arm. "Thank you for coming."

"I am healer. Grandmother passed gift." Nora covered Laurel's hand with her own brown one.

"You must be exhausted after spending most of the night mixing herbs and roots."

"I go long time no sleep."

Large raindrops pelted the ground just then. So much for praying Brodie would stay dry.

Ollie threw open the door. "Come quick, it's Murphy!"

❧

Why did he persist in pushing away the one thing that would fulfill his every longing? He must be daft.

Miles away Brodie uttered a string of curses as big drops fell from the sky. It promised to be a miserable day. He sighed and tugged his hat down low.

"For two cents I'd turn around and go back." He patted the Appaloosa's neck, knowing he wouldn't.

He set his jaw and turned due north toward Stephenson's Ferry on the Sulphur River. He'd follow Trammel's Trace to Pecan Point, then head east to Fulton.

Worsening weather almost had him wishing for one of the yellow slickers most men wore, even though he didn't have much use for them. Bright colors created a wide target for someone like him. Killing Shenandoah would bring instant fame to some unlucky soul with a fast six-shooter. Such name-seekers dogged his shadow, sometimes so close their breath tickled his neck. If they realized sending him to the beyond was tantamount to digging their own grave, they might plot a different course.

But not likely. Most sought glory and fame, thinking it made them more of a man. But all it made them was stupid.

A lot of problems accompanied notoriety, the biggest of which was staying alive.

Brodie had accepted long ago to appreciate every sunrise.

The sudden urge to ride back overcame him again. He'd tempted fate far too often.

He leaned to stroke his horse's neck. "Damn, Smokey. I'll run out of poker chips one day."

Laurel's face swam before him in the cold, gray morn and he remembered why he rode in a soaking rain. He was those little ladies' only hope. And it didn't matter their skin color.

The hate talk of George Adams suggesting he rescue the white one and leave the other made him bristle anew. North or South, black, white, or red, all should learn to coexist. Had those Yanks let him be, he'd have gone back for Lil years ago.

Bigotry, hate, and greed had ruined them all, he figured.

"Georgia clay. We've got our work cut out this time, boy." The horse moved into a canter, perhaps sensing the urgency.

A cent for every mile Smokey had carried his hide would make him wealthy. Two years ago he plunked down twenty-five dollars and knew he'd found a bargain. The Appaloosa had proven the strength of his heart and would again if Brodie only asked.

"Yep, you're a jewel all right."

Smokey snorted and nodded his head as if to say he'd take the compliment and keep 'em coming.

"Don't go getting a swelled head, now. You have plenty of shortcomings to compensate. Maybe I should tell you how often you came to finding yourself saddled by a new owner."

Smokey snorted again.

All of a sudden a slow grin crossed Brodie's face. "I do believe Lil meant to shoot me yesterday evening. She lit into my hide something fierce. Not much left of my hind-end after she got done chewing. Be glad you're a horse."

He didn't recall Lil wearing that fighting streak. Of course, years had a way of dimming a man's memory. But he most certainly remembered she hadn't worn much of anything back then.

Good God a Friday. Such images only worsened his misery.

Not that Lil didn't have good grounds for being mad enough to stomp a wild hog barefoot. She had a whole bunch of 'em.

"I would've broken her out of that place, daring anyone to step in the way...if she'd just confided in me."

Thirty years of road behind him were filled with "if only" excuses. The latest was in a long string of regrets. Ignorance couldn't buy forgiveness. Some things were no use justifying.

Guilt-eaten thoughts turned to her parents and brothers. Despite the passing months, days, and years, they probably still fretted over what had happened to her. He'd make a few inquiries once this distasteful business ended…should he continue to suck air, that is. The Jameses would likely welcome news of their long-lost daughter.

Thunder rumbled, quaking through his bones. Rain peppered his face as he urged Smokey into a gallop.

It was a far piece to Arkansas.

❧

Laurel's heart hammered. Brodie trusted her. He'd never understand if Murphy died alone. She raced past Ollie, almost knocking the woman down. Why hadn't she kept vigil beside the bed instead of thinking of her own wants?

When she reached Murphy's side, his body was shaking violently with chills. Perspiration poured off his forehead, mixing with bloody froth coming from his mouth.

"Dear God."

Nora quickly rolled him on his side to prevent choking. Laurel wet cloths to bathe his face.

Laurel turned to Ollie. "We're going to need more blankets."

Minutes later Ollie returned. "Here you are, girl. There's more if you need 'em."

Between the three of them, they propped Murphy into a half-sitting position and wrapped him snugly.

"Don't you die on me, Murphy Yates. I'm not going to let you get out of marrying me this easy." Her tears blurred the figure until he blended into the patchwork colors of blankets and guilt.

Her arms ached from clutching them so tightly to

her chest. Through the wet haze she saw Nora put her cheek to his mouth.

"Is he…?"

"He have breath."

"Thank God."

"Laurel girl, maybe it's best to let him go. Not much else a soul can do," Ollie said.

"I can't do that." She collapsed against the woman's shoulder. "Not yet. I need to tell him something first."

"Goldarned it. You're a stubborn one," Ollie said, stroking her back. "Some people have got more luck than a cat in a roomful of rockers. Were I of a betting nature, which I'm not, mind you, I'd place my money on Murphy."

Laurel kissed the face that resembled a weathered old boot. Dark circles under Ollie's eyes worried her. "Do me a favor."

"Anything for my girl."

"Get some men to board up the busted window of the café and stick a note on the door. Then, go upstairs and sleep."

"Cain't do that. Good idea about the sign though."

"And the crawling into bed part?" Laurel insisted.

"I'll get all the dadgum rest I need when I'm dead." Ollie shifted the pipe that had long grown cold and gave her a one-eyed squint. "My grandpappy, God rest his soul, was fond of saying that a body born on a Wednesday and lookin' six ways to Sunday is nothing but a no-account."

A wan smile formed. The dear woman would always have the last word. She did, however, hitch up her skirt and make for the door.

Relieved, Laurel stooped to mop blood from the floor.

"I'll do that." Etta took the damp towels from her hand. "You shouldn't worry your pretty head about such. I just took hot biscuits from the oven to go with my Creole omelet and grits. Get along there now and eat."

"I surely applaud Murphy's choice when he hired you." Laurel wished Etta hadn't gone to the trouble though. Now she'd have to force down a bite or two or deal with hurt feelings.

A horse whinny out front set her frazzled nerves on edge. The haste with which Etta hurried to beat the caller to the front door indicated that Laurel wasn't the only one suffering from nerves, including Murphy who moaned. He became calm when Laurel touched his pale face and smoothed back his hair.

Etta returned. "Miss James, you better come."

Dear heavens, what more could happen? Wrestling with dread, she whirled. "What is it now?"

"Out on the front porch... Maybe the doctor."

"What are you waiting for? Show him inside."

Etta wrung her hands. Dismay lined her features. "I cain't. Oh me. Oh my."

Laurel sighed, wondering what demanded her personal attention. She spied trouble immediately from the porch. A man sprawled on the ground beside a horse. Pouring rain had plastered his clothes to his skin. He clutched a familiar black bag in one hand. Besides the satchel, nothing else suggested this must be the physician. Laurel flew down the steps.

"Doctor, did you fall? Are you hurt?"

Snores erupted from his mouth. The stench of

liquor brought instant recognition that an increase in the storm's downpour could not wash away.

A quick gaze located the housekeeper, who remained beneath the sheltering veranda.

"Etta, come help get him inside."

The portly man had to weigh a ton. They tugged and struggled, managing to drag him out of the cloudburst. With not a dry stitch on them, they collapsed on the porch to catch their breath.

"We ain't gonna take him inside, is we?"

"I believe he can recover quite well enough out here." Disgust rippled over Laurel that she couldn't hide. "After the buffoon sufficiently recovers, I'll send him packing. Now be a dear and have Jacob take the horse to the barn. We can't begrudge his poor animal hay and shelter."

"This man cain't do Mr. Murphy any good no how," Etta said.

"Nora has excellent skills and at least she's sober."

Etta bustled off to the stables while Laurel traipsed into the deluge to retrieve the precious medical bag and quiet the animal which became walleyed at a tremendous clap of thunder. The housekeeper's son wasted no time.

"I got him, Miz Laurel." The boy took the reins from her.

She lifted her limp skirts and followed in case Jacob had his hands full with the agitated mare. No telling how long the poor excuse for a doctor had left the mare exposed to the elements. Thank goodness the leather satchel protected its contents. Hopefully, it held something useful.

Inside a dry stall Jacob draped a blanket over the frightened horse and spread fresh hay on the floor.

"There now, isn't that nice and warm," Laurel said softly.

"What happened to the man laid out on the porch?"

"Liquored-up. He'll be fine in a while."

"My mama said she'll knock me in the head and throw me to the gators if she catches me drinking rotgut."

"Your mama's a pretty smart woman."

"I figure long as she don't catch me, I'll be all right." Jacob patted the mare's jaw. "You don't hafta stay out here. Mr. Murphy pays me to handle things. He's a good man. I shore hope he keeps outrunning the angel of death. My mama and me—we got nowhere else to go. Taking care of Mr. Murphy is our life. Wouldn't know how to do anything else, I don't expect."

Laurel pondered the boy's worries on the way to the house. She'd never considered the devastating effects of Murphy's death to people like Etta and her son. The whole town depended on him. It appeared quite a few had a stake in him making it. The lump that lodged in her chest shifted. Her steps quickened.

Hours later, Etta yelled that the doctor was trying to sit up. Laurel took him a cup of coffee, the Ollie-kind that required a fork.

"Mister, drink this, for it's all you'll get here."

Bleary eyes stared up. "Whats'at you say, dearie?"

"I'm not your dearie, you old goat. It'll help ward off the chill to keep you from taking up permanent residence on this veranda. It's coffee, very hot and very stout."

The man shook so badly she helped him get the cup to his lips for a careful sip. He wrinkled his face.

"Ooh, that's awful. Need a little sump'in in it. I gen'rally mix it with spirits."

"You won't get any of that, I'm afraid."

"Got a spoon, then?"

She and the doc shared the same opinion. She hid a smile and helped him down more. "Mind if I ask who you are?"

"If you'll tell me where in hell I'm at. Doc Gates, in case it matters."

"From Jefferson?"

"Gotta gunshot to treat." Unsteady movement sloshed coffee onto his shirt, though it was a pure mystery how the thick stuff managed to escape.

Laurel hastily grabbed the cup when Gates tried to stand. He teetered on the edge of the top step, threatening to topple backward into the mud. She looked for a place to unload the coffee, wishing problems arrived by telegraph where a body could take them in doses they preferred instead of them coming right up to the door and knocking. That way they'd have a right to refuse if they didn't want 'em.

"Whoa there, sawbones." Ollie arrived out of breath from the direction of the café. "Them legs are trying to ride a mighty rough sea. Might oughta sit a spell first."

Gates gave up the folly of balancing and dropped back onto the wooden slabs cut from giant cypress. "I'm sorry, Mildred."

Ollie gave Laurel a bemused glance and circled an ear with her finger to indicate the man had fallen out of his rocker and left it still rocking. "Mildred must be your wife. I'm Olivia Applejack b'Dam."

"Well, I'll be damned, too. You sure favor my Mildred."

"I never found occasion to seek a husband," Ollie sniffed.

"Me neither. It's the wives I can't outrun. Do you know that marriage isn't an occasion but an occupation, and a most hazardous one at that."

Laurel wearily tucked a strand of hair behind her ear. She had a hundred more pressing things to deal with, each one requiring more courage and stamina than she possibly possessed.

"Excuse me. Mister, I leave you in capable hands."

Doc appeared bewildered. "But I have a patient…"

"Not anymore." She made no attempt to hide the anger or brittle tone. "No one here requires your services."

"A banker fellow, something Yates, got hisself shot."

"You're too late. He died."

Thirteen

A FRIEND NAMED HAWKSHAW ONCE ADVISED BRODIE, "When danger comes calling, don't hem haw around. Do what you hafta, boy. A half second often separates driving a hearse from riding in one."

The dead mountain lion at Brodie's feet confirmed that he'd been a watch tick away from having to ride in that hearse Hawkshaw spoke of.

Wafting smoke from the Sharps rifle barrel tinged the scene a familiar shade of lead gray—cannons, Johnny Rebs, storms, and the iron weight of a heart. He shook away fuzzy cobwebs to nudge the lion with a toe.

It seemed irrelevant that Hawkshaw's tutelage pertained to the finer points of killing men instead of animals. But then, making the impossible distinction between those kept Brodie awake many a night. He brushed rain from weary eyes and holstered the Sharps in a leather sling hanging from the saddle. Tendons quivered beneath Smokey's drenched hide.

"Appreciate the warning, boy," he murmured into the horse's neck. "I could've had a lot bigger problem."

Brodie led the Appaloosa toward the thick woodland cover where they'd be out of the rain. Squatting, he rolled up his sleeve where the cat had ripped a jagged gash. He'd bled worse on occasion, he reckoned. The knot in a faded red bandanna took a devil of a time to loosen one-handed. He pressed it tightly to the wound. An experienced eye confirmed darkness would fall quickly.

"We'll pass the night here, Smokey. Good a place as any."

His companion had plenty of horse sense. Soft nickering followed by three nods of his head confirmed that. Smokey earned the name from the white smattering his spotted charcoal flanks, giving his coat a hazy appearance. A trail-rider could ask for no finer piece of horseflesh. Brodie wound the neckerchief tight around his arm, cinching a knot with his teeth and fingers.

At least the rain showed slight promise of letting up. He gathered drier firewood and buried leaves that would catch. With the warmth of a fire going, he addressed a rumbling belly.

"Those steaks Lil cooks would beat coffee and beans all to hell." The horse feasted on a patch of lush rye grass, ignoring his master's chatter. "Appears you've already found your supper."

Cold biscuits Etta had pushed on Brodie and a heated can of beans silenced his growls. He leaned back on the bedroll with a steaming cup of brew. Though September and October days in east Texas heated up, a man had to cozy up to a fire come sundown.

This night's moist air carried an extra chill.

The sting of his arm dredged up thoughts to sort out. The big cat went in the dull gray category—blood, pain, and raw fear. He considered Lady Luck and felt grateful for the sparing.

That road led back to Hawkshaw, who he'd put in the one-of-a-rare-breed department.

Never offering anything more than Hawkshaw, Brodie never knew whether that was his given, surname, actual, or made up name. Not that it mattered a smidgen. The friend took a ride in the hearse shortly after meeting up with the widow, Mrs. Sugarbaker. Brodie sure missed Hawkshaw. Come to think of it, that surely went in the gray section, too.

Brodie next mulled over the Blanchards. The downpour had erased signs, but he knew they came this way and he hated all the reasons for knowing why.

Lust for money numbered among Ike and Bert's worst sins. Even so, Brodie couldn't overlook the debt owed to Luther.

But the other two gang members froze his blood.

Reno Darnell and Nat Jude were natural born killers. Both cut their teeth on Quantrill's terrorizing rampage through Missouri and Kansas years earlier, the experience sharply honing a thrill for torture and murder.

His jaw tightened. They shouldn't have taken those little ladies. And if they hadn't treated them kindly? He jabbed a long twig into the fire and stared into the flame.

One thing for certain, he'd not return empty-handed.

Laurel's revelations had walloped his sense of honor sideways and crooked. She placed a powerful burden on him. In his travels he'd learned of twisted men and their perversions, yet the depth sometimes jarred him. He clenched his jaw.

Gloom threw each scenario into the blackest of corners.

Smokey whinnied softly, the soulful eyes meeting his in the dim light. The animal struck the ground carpeted with pine needles, perhaps conveying similar thoughts, yet Brodie hadn't uttered a word.

"You taking to reading minds now?"

The Appaloosa nodded three times. Brodie set down his cup and rose to stroke Smokey's powerful neck.

"We'll get 'em back. Might strew a few dead carcasses over Arkansas though. Way I see it, they deserve everything coming to them. The weather taking a turn for the better will make it easier."

With a grim stare up into the trees where an owl hooted, he rolled a smoke and lit it. The smoldering tobacco took the edge off most things.

Except his dying brother.

Bleak curiosity wondered if Murphy had made the crossing yet. He'd not seen many survive a hole that large. And yet? After a few minutes, with a final puff, he flicked the short remains into the embers. Dropping to the bedroll, Brodie lay back, forming a pillow with his hands.

Why in the name of Jericho had he told Laurel he'd not stop her from marrying? Maybe he'd gotten hold of some baneberry. Only that tended to kill a man. On second thought—the sharp spasms piercing his heart suggested the possibility.

"You're mine, Laurel James." He muttered it into the breeze, wishing to climb the highest mountain and shout it for all to hear. "Whoever lays claim to you can't change the fact that we have a bond."

Conviction had glistened in Laurel's violet gaze when she'd spoken of changing her life. Though it seemed farfetched, maybe one *could* go from scarlet lady to housewife and mother. That she believed it so sincerely made him believe it, too.

She'd make a fine wife.

Jagged pain enveloped him with that parcel of reality.

Should he return to find Murphy mending, he'd stay not a day longer than necessary. He'd pack up and take himself far from the misery of watching her with someone else—for he'd not go back on his word.

Even if it ripped his heart from its mooring.

But should the pendulum swing the opposite and things didn't turn out with the Blanchards like he planned…

The half-formed thought settled in ice. He refused to dwell on that. While his brother might present the toughest obstacle, it wasn't the sole one standing in the way.

❧

Laurel crimped the edges of the soft dough topping the apple pie. Her mind wandered back to Jefferson's sorry excuse for a doctor. Thank goodness the growing populace had many others from which to choose or they'd get her condolences.

Telling Doc Gates the lie about Murphy yesterday brought no remorse. In her estimation he'd left her no choice. Gates' shaking hands could barely help him climb into the saddle much less aid in the treatment of a critically wounded patient.

She did color a mite at the memory of lifting a few items from his bag. Necessity justified her crime.

The back door opened and Ollie blew in, blustering like a north wind. "I dropped in on Murphy, and Nora says his color's a tad improved today."

"What wonderful news." She slipped the pie into the oven. "I questioned whether we're opening the café prematurely, but we… I need…to get a normal routine going again."

"My grandpappy, God bless him, always said, 'Cowards never start and the weak ones die on the way.'" Ollie took an apron from a nail and slipped it on. "Murphy will be fit in no time. He's got the constitution of a mule. We gotta git on with the business of living."

Bedecked in a frilly apron, the bandy woman appeared more like a hurdy-gurdy dancer. Laurel suppressed a giggle.

"What do you think you're doing?" Laurel asked.

"If it's any of your never-mind, I'm gonna help get ready for the Sunday noon crowd. The *Nancy Belle* will dock in roughly two hours and we'd best have enough for Sherman's army."

"I have a large pot of mulligan stew on, pies baking, and fresh bread cooling. Green beans and potatoes simmering on the back, and I've cut up six chickens for frying." Laurel untied the apron and lifted the frills over Ollie's head. "There is nothing left to do. I want you to rest."

"Goldarned upstart. You must've kissed the Blarney Stone. Since I'm not wanted or appreciated, you'll find me over at the saloon, visiting someone who values my company," she huffed.

"Ha! Wait until Curley knows you better."

The door slammed back, interrupting the exchange. Edgar Lee and Andy Cole ran inside as if a pack of wolves chased them.

"Miss Laurel, guess what? Maw says we git to wash your dishes." The boys hopped around in circles. "Oh boy."

"Whoa." Ollie caught each by an arm. "Were you born in a hurricane?"

"Nope. What's that?"

Mrs. Cole followed, quite breathless, shifting the baby on her hip. "I apologize. They're excited to help in the café."

"No reason in the world for children to be otherwise, Mrs. Cole." Laurel wiped flour off her hands.

"Just call me Betsy, please."

"Agreed. And I'm just plain old Laurel."

"Well, if this don't beat all I'll kiss your foot. Reckon you shore don't need an old woman now," Ollie grumbled.

"Tell Curley I send my regards." Laurel shooed the skinflint toward the sidewalk.

Edgar Lee swiped his face on a sleeve. "Where you going, Miz Ollie?"

The pipe-smoking woman turned three shades of red. Laurel wondered how she'd squirm out of explaining the saloon's star attraction. "Uh, I've got some dadgum business to attend."

"Can we come, too?"

Ollie jerked out the pipe only to stick it back in. For once she was at a loss for words. Laurel suppressed a laugh.

"Edgar Lee, we're here to work, not play," Betsy scolded. "We have a debt to pay off."

Short, bandy legs could move awfully swift when they had a reason to, Laurel discovered. She pulled a chair from the work table and tweaked Sissie's fat cheek. The baby giggled.

"Sit down, Betsy. I'll get the boys started and we'll chat."

"Didn't come to socialize. Where's your broom?" The thin line of Betsy's mouth promised an argument.

Laurel pointed toward the implement in the corner. "This isn't necessary."

"Let me be the judge." She sat Sissie on the floor and handed her a rag doll and string of wooden beads. "I heard about the trouble and Mr. Brodie's brother. It's a pure shame. How's he doing?"

"Murphy is in a bad way."

Bored, Edgar Lee and Andy indulged in playful scuffle.

"Stop it, boys. Remember where you're at." Betsy snatched the broom. "If the young Mr. Yates is anything like his brother, he's some kind of man. And I keep thinking of those poor little girls. Those mothers must be sick to death with worry."

"Mrs. Carver and Mrs. Hatcher do indeed have heartbreak. It'll turn out right as rain in the end, I do believe."

Bitter thoughts turned down a similar path. Laurel's mother would not share such sentiment. Mary James still waited for a whisper of news. There had been no Brodie Yates back then to track Will Taft. Sissie's toothy, silly grin got lost in Laurel's blurred vision.

"If someone took my children, I'd follow them to

kingdom come and make them sorry they ever did," Betsy declared.

The threat didn't seem idle or strange. It came from a woman who'd buried a husband beside a river and had the will to press on by herself. Laurel knew Brodie would catch up with the Blanchards, but what then? The odds were stacked against him. Her hand flew to her mouth. She should've insisted on going along. An extra pistol would help. He needed someone.

Edgar Lee and Andy play-scuffled with each other, but their mother's stern eye quickly brought them in line.

"Mr. Brodie will make them rue the day, never fear," Betsy said, patting Laurel's shoulder. "The man's got plenty of guts."

Manhandling the broom, Betsy stalked into the dining room. Laurel stared, the truth echoing in her mind until it finally stuck.

No one but a fool would accuse Brodie Yates of tucking tail and running or describe his nature as normal. Bold facts spoke of a man special in every way. Grit and determination wouldn't let him quit. The set of his jaw and the steel in his stare made him continue when everyone else gave up. Because he couldn't. Overwhelming numbers meant the job would take a little longer, that's all. Despite great personal risk he'd find a way to win. That's what separated the gray-eyed rebel from the rest.

Edgar Lee tugged on her elbow. "Miss Laurel?"

Impatience lined the boy's face. She put aside her mulling. "Oh yes, the dishes. First, though, I want you to roll up your sleeves."

Andy struggled until she took pity and helped.

Scrawny arms contrasted with tough, stubborn pride to carry his own weight.

Shyness wouldn't let him glance up, although he pressed close to crumple the lace on Laurel's apron. A warm glow that had swept her the night she'd met them again settled inside. She cherished it, despite the reminder of how much Taft had stolen. She had a lot of ground to make up.

"You're a baby, Andy. I can do mine by myself," Edgar Lee crowed.

"N-n-no, I'm not a baby."

"I hate to burst your bubble, Edgar Lee, but you didn't do any better." Laurel wouldn't tolerate unkind talk in her kitchen. "We all do the best we can and don't have to apologize for anything less than what we're capable of. Now, let's hear you apologize."

"I'm sorry, Andy."

"That's more like it."

She adjusted his handiwork and grabbed a block of soap. Hot water from the stove mixed with cold from the pump assured their sensitive skin could tolerate it. Then, she pulled a bench up to the counter for her short helpers. Both wasted no time diving in elbow deep.

Laurel found keeping an eye on Sissie exhausting work. The child not only located every vegetable peel, dirty knot hole, and tiniest insect imaginable, but tasted each treat.

"I think Mr. Brodie must be awful brave." Edgar Lee's startling statement appeared from the blue.

Determined to dislodge a small pebble from Sissie's mouth that Lord only knows how it got into the kitchen, Laurel glanced at the freckled face. Edgar Lee toted far too much concern for a mere lad. She regretted him overhearing her and Betsy's conversation. The little man already took on more than any child should.

Small teeth suddenly clamped onto her finger. She struggled to keep from crying out.

"Mr. Brodie is indeed very courageous, Edgar Lee." Laurel grimaced as she extracted the throbbing digit, leaving the pebble inside. Babies' teeth were razor sharp.

"Those mean ol' bandits might kill him though."

Chills scurried from Laurel's hiding place. "He would never allow that. Let's find something a bit more cheery to discuss."

"M-M-Mr. Brodie'll shoot 'em d-d-dead," Andy stammered, his cheeks turning an angry, ruddy hue. "H-he's f-f-fast."

"When I get big I'm gonna be jus' like Mr. Brodie. I'm gonna own me a shooting iron and get rid of all the bad people." The older brother stuck out a finger covered with soap suds and formed the barrel of a weapon. "Pow, pow, pow."

Betsy stepped through the door. "Stop that this instant, you hear? Your paw gave his life so you kids can grow up in a better world than he did. Over my dead body will I see you turn into a no-account, good for nothing gun hand."

"Sorry, Maw." Edgar Lee ducked his head.

"Heed what I say. I don't want to hear that kind of foolishness." Betsy lifted Sissie from the floor.

To Laurel's utter amazement, Betsy stuck a finger into the child's mouth and plucked out the pebble.

The motion was quick, smooth, and accomplished with no effort. Laurel had so much to learn. She would have little need of the information though. Her kind of life didn't include normal things that some women took for granted.

"You boys get busy with those dishes, and while you're at it, scrub your minds of shootin' and killin' outlaws and such."

"Yes, Maw."

Downcast eyes stifled her spirit. Laurel hated to see children who had no time for playing or believing.

"They meant no harm, Betsy," she murmured low, hoping curious ears couldn't pick it up. "It appears Brodie Yates found a couple of young champions."

"Those two worship the ground that man walks on. I try to explain he's only human." Betsy sighed, pushing back a strand of streaked hair. "But they won't hear it."

"Children need a hero, plain and simple. Adults, too. It's nothing to shame out of them."

"But Mr. Brodie won't fly up to heaven like Paw did, will he?" Edgar Lee's voice held thick tears. "He won't, will he, Miss Laurel?"

She fought back her tears. How could one expert marksman survive the barrage of gunfire of five desperate bushwhackers? "No, sweet boy, of course not. He'll be back with nary a scratch. We must hold that dearly in our hearts."

The murdering Blanchards wouldn't dare snuff out Brodie's life. Besides…Brodie hadn't survived these eight years without learning a trick or two. Hopefully, this bunch should prove no match for him..

The scoundrel who made her pulse pound with excitement was most definitely larger than life.

Even if he didn't want to fight for her.

Even if he gave her up to his brother.

And even if he never again enclosed her in the circle of his arms and whispered fanciful words of moonmist and passion.

A part of him would always and forever remain hers.

Fourteen

"ARE YOU RUNNING SHORT OF STAPLES, BETSY?"
Laurel wiped her hands on the apron and stepped
quickly to the pie safe.

Pausing in the doorway with her brood, Betsy
Cole's stark features stiffened. Her head snapped
around. "We got aplenty."

Betsy's brusque tone stung. And yet Laurel sympathized with the woman's desperation to owe no one
anything.

Tired lines etched fear too deeply imbedded to
disguise. Something put there by hard times, uncertainty, and doubts that one more trial or setback
would do her in. Betsy couldn't see that Laurel shared
the same worries.

Some things a body never admitted to a living soul.

Today, Betsy had scrubbed the entire café from stem
to stern. In addition, she made Edgar Lee and Andy
wash every dish in sight and inspected them afterward.

"Words of gratitude come cheap for the hours of
toil. You must at least accept a custard pie for your
services," Laurel insisted.

The boys' eyes lit up. "Can we, Maw? Please?"

"No, I'm going to make you a nice dessert. We'll return tomorrow to complete our bargain, then me and the children head for Fort Richardson."

Edgar Lee's and Andy's crestfallen glances reflected Laurel's.

The steely-spined woman and her loving children would leave Laurel bereft. They'd distracted her from the rigors of waiting for Murphy to regain consciousness and for Brodie's return.

Each Cole brother hugged her in turn.

"See ya tomorrow. Don't wash any dishes till we get here 'cause that's our job, ain't it, Andy?"

The smaller version nodded. "I-i-it's fun. W-we like it."

"But I 'spect we won't be mad if you wash just a few."

Laurel smiled. Despite pretending to be little men, they couldn't hide the children inside. She shut the door behind them.

"We're gonna miss them younguns." Ollie was seated at the table sharpening kitchen knives on a long razor strop. "Though they can ask more questions than a body has answers for."

"Made you hobble-tongued, did they?" Laurel hung her apron on the nail, thankful lunchtime had come and gone. She dropped into a chair, propping her feet. A record number had passed through the café's doors this day. Their reputation grew by leaps and bounds. Thank heavens Betsy had pitched in.

"I reckon that about says it all right there." Ollie filled the bowl of the pipe, tampered it down, and lit it. "Didn't exactly know how to explain the business a lady has with a gentleman."

"Guess you could've called it monkey business."

Ollie grumbled in her throat. "Making light of an old woman's pleasures, are you?"

A giggle slipped out before Laurel could stop it.

"Does my heart good to hear you laugh, Laurel girl. You faced mighty hard times of late, what with Yates threatening to spill the beans and Murphy getting shot. It's enough to drive you daffy."

"I haven't been altogether truthful about something."

The knife Ollie honed to a sharp edge halted in midair. "Spit it out. Let the hide go with the tallow."

"Remember when you found Brodie and me in Murphy's garden?"

"I wanted to smash his face in for making you cry." Ollie's gaze narrowed. "I also recall how your hair was all undone."

Laurel had wondered when Ollie would mention that. She passed over the mussed hair remark, struggling to keep the trembles inside from spilling into her words.

"Brodie no longer fights Murphy and my wedding plans." Taking deep breaths, she added, "He even gave his blessing."

Ollie resumed the slapping motion of the knife on the strop. "Why the long face then, pray tell?"

Had Laurel not blinked several times, hovering tears would've spilled. "I can't marry Murphy. I don't love him—not proper, the way a wife should a husband."

"I wouldn't have much call to know about them

things, me being a spinster and all, but I reckon tender feelings grow on a body if you give 'em half a chance."

A lump that refused to budge reduced Laurel's declaration to a raspy whisper. "And what if I love someone else?"

"Son of a bluejacket, I figured something like that. You gotta get up mighty early in the morn to fool one of us b'Dams."

"Horsefeathers. You made up that name after a half-deaf Missourian mistook Burrdan as b'Dam."

"Shore, but who's to dispute it ain't real?" Ollie gave her a one-eyed squint. "So does Brodie's change of heart mean he's not reading from the same hymn book you are?"

The harsh reality of offering her to another after kissing her silly opened the gaping wound wider. "Moonmist my eye."

"What in God's name is that crazy babbling about?" Ollie demanded. "And what the devil is moonmist?"

The flowery words meant nothing to the man. They'd only suited Brodie's purpose in getting what he wanted. She'd been foolish enough to think he cared for her.

"Nothing. Getting back to the change of heart. I don't think Brodie knows what he wants. Thank goodness I haven't told him how I feel about him." Laurel crossed her fingers and hoped so, at least. That finely cocked eyebrow of his was something she cared not to witness.

"I swear, everyone'd be better off if I blast that man with my forty-four the minute he steps back into town."

Except her…and the rebel gentleman, of course.

❧

Not one to waste words in idle chatter, Nora's quiet presence comforted. Questions cluttering Laurel's head required concentration. Yet, logic skittered worse than rambunctious children the harder she looked for answers.

This yanking back and forth kept her reeling. She was much too old for such games.

Stellar didn't begin to describe Brodie's record. Lord knows she'd invested a lifetime of emotion since they met. The latest round only heaped fresh pain atop the old. Although to his credit, he had gone after those little girls. No matter what else, she had reason to owe him for that.

When he returned she'd badger him regarding his intentions.

Or none? The possibility left a bitter taste on her tongue.

A stone Nora used to crush dried plants scraped against a hollowed out piece of granite. The woman ground them into fine powder exactly the way her forebears had.

Laurel recognized golden seal, sagebrush, wild ginger, and sassafras leaves. Other roots and bark neatly piled to the side escaped her, yet she knew Nora could tell each and their usage.

Seated beside Murphy's bed, Laurel met the Indian woman's mysterious, dark eyes, wondering what thoughts filled Nora's head. Did the woman share her tepee with a man? Or have babies?

Murphy's hand twitched inside hers. Laurel's returned slight pressure was meant to assure the unconscious man of her presence.

Strange how, now that she knew which path not to take, she had to sit silently and wait for Murphy to wake up. His reaction crossed her mind. For certain he'd be disappointed and perhaps angry. But crushed? Heaven forbid, she prayed not.

"Nora, how long do you think he'll sleep like this?"

"Only the Great One knows. Many moons maybe." Nora shrugged. "I do not guess. Why ask a foolish thing?"

"I have something of great importance to tell Murphy."

Irritation crossed her high cheekbones. "This thing—is it important to the man or you?"

Laurel's face heated. Poor Murphy fought for every breath, yet her need to correct a bad mistake became selfishly paramount. She'd jilt a gentle, kind man to justify ill-fated love for a gray-eyed rebel who seemed more inclined to think her a bothersome fly and would move on when the urge struck.

"It's vital only to me." Shame kept her reply low. "I've deeply wronged Murphy and desire to fix it."

"Then find forgiveness in your heart, not in the eyes of a sick man. It will wait. All things come in time."

Truth of the ages. And even should he regain his senses this second, she'd have to continue with a pretense. No telling when he'd grow strong enough to hear what she must say.

She was stuck in a lie.

❧

Brodie slid from horseback to view a blood-stained boulder where someone had rested. Once bright red, the tacky secretion had begun to brown. With the rain stopping, the horse trail yielded other drops and smudges, none more fresh than this.

Pray to God it hadn't come from one of those girls.

"The bleeding's worsening, Smokey." Whoever it belonged to could die soon, particularly if they'd been gutshot.

The Appaloosa snorted and pawed the ground.

"I swear, if I didn't have so much time and effort invested, I'd turn you out to pasture for being smartassed." He kept his voice low, grabbed the saddle horn and swung up.

"Take that strawberry roan I had. Pearly Gates was one hell of a horse. Unlike you, he knew his place." Smokey bent his neck to shoot a baleful look. "Asked or otherwise, Pearly Gates never voiced an opinion."

That roan did have one fault, Brodie reckoned. He fancied himself a lady-killer. Tried to mount every mare he came near.

The Appaloosa broke into a canter.

"No need to go getting jealous. Pearly Gates met his end when a posse ran us into the Black Hills of Dakota territory."

Brodie draped the reins over an arm while he rolled a smoke. He recalled the day he'd never forget and the horse that had never known his bottom. Pearly Gates thought he could do anything, even jump a canyon to escape blue bellies. They didn't make it. Gravity carried them into a river below. The force broke the animal's legs and he'd had to shoot the roan that'd seen him through the war. The memory sliced through his chest as if it'd happened days ago. How fortunate to own two horses whose hearts were bigger than the great outdoors.

He smoothed Smokey's withers. "I've been mighty blessed and that's a fact. Couldn't ask for more."

Except for Lil's love.

And Murphy had that. She'd never be his.

Brodie wondered if his brother still drew breath. The bond tying them nothing could sever, not even Laurel, not anything. He wouldn't fight his brother. He brought Smokey to a standstill and looked up through the pine trees at a patch of blue sky.

"It's been a long while," he prayed reverently. "And you may have your ears closed to the likes of my kind, but I'm asking a favor. That is, if you've a mind to listen."

He took a deep breath. "I'm willing to strike a bargain. You let my brother live…and I'll forget all about Laurel."

Something rustled the scrub brush. He jerked around, his palm automatically sliding to the revolver.

❦

"Morning, Ollie." Jake finished winding the barber pole in front of the shop. "Care to come sit a spell?"

Ollie skirted mud puddles left by the morning shower and took one of several chairs where she could take in the goings-on. Despite loathing the barber, she took advantage of every opportunity to needle him. It provided untold entertainment.

"Jake, how's the world treatin' you?"

"Cain't complain."

Thumbs stuck inside his galluses, Jake leaned back. From all appearances, his hair, slicked and parted down the middle, might've gotten a dousing in the lard bucket. The mustache hadn't escaped a dipping either. Something had stiffened it into a bow. The twirled-up ends resembled hairy buggy springs. Ollie disguised her laughter behind a cough.

"I've got some tonic sure to cure that," he offered.

"Stuff your remedies into your mustache, you old coot, 'cause I ain't taking none of your god-awful skunk tonic."

"Just being helpful. Why do you insist on smoking that nasty pipe anyway? It's likely what's making you cough."

She puffed away and watched the smoke curl from her mouth. "I could ask why you hafta use lard for pomade, but I reckon you're an expert on those things, you being in the barbering profession and all."

"Do you figure Yates caught up with the Blanchard gang?"

"Can't speculate. But those murdering bushwhackers will wish to God he hadn't when he gets done with 'em." She spied Jeb Prater hobbling from the stage depot on crutches. "Bet Jeb's regretting his smart mouth."

"Wonder if the boy's leaving soon? You know, I still can't figure why Yates gets so riled. Take my friend, Martin. Black is black and white is white. No changing it."

"I ain't gonna waste breath explaining to an ignoramus who's too goldarned stupid. Girls are girls and boys are boys—different but the same. That's all I'm saying on the subject."

Ollie grinned when Florence Kempshaw strolled hell-bent for them. Everyone in town knew the vinegar-tongued busybody had set her cap for Jake, although personally Ollie had no idea what Florence would want with the greasy-haired bag of bones.

"Thank goodness, she left me alone." Jake relaxed his grip on the chair when Florence veered into the office of Thomas Hutson, Attorney at Law. He swatted a fly from his mustache. "Appears the old biddy found someone else to gripe at."

"I swear, you're as charitable as a preacher in a hurdy-gurdy house. If you'd loosen up a mite and sweet-talk her, she might not be plumb soured on life."

"No one has that many words in their vocabulary. Besides, I'd rather spend 'em on you, Ollie b'Dam."

She wished to tell Jake he could kiss her rear end, but only if he washed his face first. Instead she planted a seed to watch what grew. "Reckon you haven't heard. I'm spoken for."

"You don't say. And who would that be?"

"Curley Madison."

"Of the Dry Gulch Saloon?"

She nodded with delight. "The one and only."

"What would a prosperous gent want with an old sourdough biscuit-eater?"

"Why, you!" Ollie kicked the nearest bony shin.

"Ow! I won't be able to stand up now to cut hair."

"I hope you cain't. Teach you to mend your nasty ways."

"Don't know why you get the cream of the crop and I'm left with old biddies."

"I rest my case. With your whiny jabber, you're lucky to attract curdled milk."

Ollie spied Betsy Cole and her towheads heading

up the street. The woman carried the baby on one hip, struggling to keep up with the boys who raced in front.

"Howdy, Miss Ollie," Edgar Lee hollered.

"Morning, boys."

"What's ya doing, Miss Ollie?"

"Mildewing." She cackled when Edgar Lee's hold slipped on the horned toad he held and it leaped onto Jake's lap.

"Good God, what the hell!" The barber jumped to his feet. "Don't you know those things cause warts?"

"N-n-not if you don't kiss 'em," Andy said.

Ollie couldn't resist. "You ain't gonna do that, are you, Jake? Come to think on it, might be more exciting than Florence."

"Are you the town hair-cutter? Why is your hair so wet?" Edgar Lee took a breath and licked his lips.

"Yes, I happen to be the barber, young man. And dentist. Have any teeth that need pulling?"

Edgar Lee and Andy began backing up, their eyes big as dollars.

"Boys, he's harmless. Jake, meet the best question-askingest, ring-tailed tooters in the whole dadgum state."

Betsy arrived, completely winded.

"Mrs. Cole, have a sit-down. You don't look so good."

"No time to waste." Betsy brushed back a lock of hair from her eyes. "We got work to do. Come along, boys."

"Aw Maw, cain't we stay awhile?"

"We didn't come to jaw. We came to work."

Edgar Lee's shoulders hunched with dejection. A twinge of sadness swept Ollie. The tykes hungered for little boy things. They were too young to saddle with such adult burdens.

"You mind your maw and I'll tell you a secret place to catch crawdads."

Their faces lit up before they trudged after their mother.

A dark horse and rider emerged from the woods just then, capturing Ollie's attention. The saunter down the street made her heart shift into a frantic beat.

"Who in thunder do you suppose that is, Jake?"

"Sure hope he's not looking for a shave."

She shuddered as if someone stomped across her grave. Dressed all in black, the stranger sat straight in the saddle. A warning whispered in Ollie's ear too loud to ignore.

Eighteen hands tall if the gelding stood an inch, he high-stepped past lumbering wagons and the bustle of mid-morning business. The shiny coat glistened, matching the funerary black the man wore. They halted across the street. She didn't notice the gray beast, a mix of wolf and dog, until horse and rider came to a standstill. The lean animal bared its fangs at Ollie and Jake, a growl rumbling deep in its throat.

Ollie gripped her hands tightly, giving silent thanks for the Closed sign swinging on the café. Coupled with the boarded window the Blanchard gang shot out, maybe he'd think it vacant. She could hope to God he moved on before he found out different.

The stranger's profile was all she'd seen until then. When he favored her with a frontal stare, Ollie couldn't move past coldness freezing her breath.

A scar, more terrifying than any she'd seen, ran diagonally from his jawline across one eye, vanishing under the brim of his hat. Her mouth went slack. The pipe clattered unheeded onto the sidewalk.

"Dog...stay." The order sprang from a guttural voice.

Though she didn't know him, the stranger brought familiarity of his kind. Frost coated Ollie's breath.

Son of a blue devil.

Whatever name the man bore, it would start with a capital *D* for deadly.

Fifteen

LAUREL PEEKED FROM A CRACK IN THE DOOR FOR A glimpse of the death angel, as Ollie called him, who'd instilled terror. The runty benefactress provided explicit detail of the newcomer who went by the name of Vallens and who now sat in the café dining room with the wolf-dog at his feet.

But she could see nothing except his backside.

"What's ya looking at, Miz Laurel?"

She jumped a foot at Edgar Lee's twang beside her. The door banged into her forehead with its quick release.

"A man—nothing but a man." Thank goodness for roomy pockets to hide her trembling hands.

"Are you skeered of him?"

"For pity's sake, I would hope not." *Liar, liar, pants on fire.* Grim reaper fit the creepy man in dismal trappings even down to the black hat. And according to Ollie, he rode a horse darker than midnight.

"If he hurts you, I'll get Paw's musket and kill him. I'd be real mad if anyone made you dead."

Another David meets Goliath. Laurel's chest tightened. Meager kindness had earned such devotion. Just when speech appeared possible, Andy rushed to throw his arms around her waist. Tears sparkled on the shy brother's cheeks.

"You know what? You're brave little soldiers to take up for me. I think I'd be really angry if someone hurt you, too. But don't worry your heads. That man is harmless. And remember how your maw feels about shooting." She ruffled the towheads, grateful Betsy had found a spot on the upstairs banister to wipe.

Edgar Lee solemnly nodded. "But I'm a man now and men hafta stand up for their fam'ly no matter how skeered they are."

To think of her as kin opened raw sores. She'd not seen her family in ages, nor had much hope of it.

"There's no need to take on so. It'll be right as rain."

Laurel hated the hollow sound in her ears. Ollie had suffered another spell after her encounter with the death angel and had to lie down for a while. It took a lot of persuading to get the woman to take a buggy ride with Curley for a leisurely afternoon. Still, Laurel wished waiting on the stranger befell someone else's lot.

"I'd best go see what he wants, I suppose."

The sturdy, kid leather shoes seemed fashioned of lead as she wound her way toward her unlucky lot. The dog rumbled low, the back of its neck bristling. She drew back in alarm.

"Dog! Quiet or I'll carve out your gullet."

Laurel put the table between her and the beast. The man's glance froze her blood. Ollie hadn't embellished the beggarly appearance or disposition. It took effort to unglue her tongue.

"I'll kindly ask you to leave your animal outside or

vacate the premises," she finally managed, a bit weakly in her opinion.

"He stays." The voice was low and gravelly.

Not a soul to help besides the boys. She stood her ground and met his stare, determined not to shrink into the woodwork.

"I truly can't allow—"

The bell over the door jangled, to her relief. Lars Frederiksen, the burly steamboat captain of the *Mystic Queen*, and four of his crewmen entered the café. Bolstered, she eyed the captain's long Colt Dragoon.

"So be it for now, but I won't have that dog running off business. Furthermore, we uphold a policy of no firearms. I insist you respect the sign to leave it on the front counter."

"Who's going to make ol' Zeke Vallens if he don't? You oughta grow some before you go ordering folks around."

Captain Frederiksen flexed beefy fists and paused before taking a seat. "This gentleman causing trouble, Miss Laurel?"

Vallens glared but handed over the weapon.

"Thank you, Captain, but everything is under control." She placed the Colt in the box up front and returned to the stranger's table.

"Monday's special is pot roast."

"That all you got?" he snarled.

"We also offer mulligan stew and beef steak."

Pray to heaven he didn't want overmuch of any. Their meat stock had dwindled to nothing since the expected shipment was five days late. Perhaps Lars brought it on the *Queen*.

"Two of those steaks, and don't take all day."

"Do you wish those raw or cooked, sir?" Laurel's question seemed legitimate. Nothing this man said or did would surprise her.

Wolf-dog sprang to all fours. Laurel gave a horrified shriek and the riverboat crew jumped to their feet.

"Damn you, I said shut up. You gonna mind me, dog? You can't tear into girlie here before she feeds us. Now lay the hell down." He grabbed a handful of the bristling neck and forced the disagreeable animal to the floor. That it didn't sink powerful jaws around the black-clothed arm surprised Laurel. "Cooked will suit us."

Thankful that the man called Vallens had a bit of control over the animal, she hastened to the others.

"Say the word and me and the boys will roust them out. It would be pure pleasure." Lars flashed daggers at the newcomer.

"I appreciate that." To get sideways with the man would only bring more grief to heap on top of what she already had.

"You change your mind, just nod." Lars winked.

"I hope your cargo contains meat for the café?"

"Nope. Sorry."

Laurel took their request and barely reached the swinging portal to the kitchen when more customers strolled in. Surely Vallens would behave in a packed house.

                          ❧

Smokey's ears perked up at the soft moan. Brodie slowly lifted his hat and hung it on the saddle horn.

It wouldn't do for the noisy rattles to announce him. He slid the forty-four from the holster and eased to the ground.

The moan came from his right. A cautious turn around a stand of cedars gave a glimpse of two men. One lay next to a trickling creek. The other knelt beside him.

"Get your hands up slow and easy." Brodie found instant recognition in the face when the man turned. "What are you doing, Ike?"

"My brother's hurt real bad."

His insides tightened into a hard ball. "Which one?"

"It's Luther." Ike's voice trembled.

Damn his luck.

"Toss your pistol into the creek and don't try anything."

"Ain't got no bullets in it, Shenandoah."

"Throw it in anyway—along with Luther's." The weapons splashed and sank to the bottom. Brodie moved closer.

"He's dying. Some fool man in Redemption gut-shot him."

"That fool was *my* brother."

"If we'd knowed that was your town, we'd never have gone anywhere near it. We respect another man's territory."

"Redemption doesn't belong to me." Except for his name and the clothes on his back, he owned nothing. He hated the brittle, dry feel to his insides. Everything he desired had shriveled. "My brother's dying, too, compliments of your gang. I'd call that brother for brother."

Keeping his six iron on Ike, Brodie knelt by Luther.

Blood soaked the clothing until it bore no sign of the original color.

"Luther, it's me…Shenandoah."

The old friend tried to moisten his dry lips. "Them's angels singing. Sweetest music I ever heard. You hear it?"

Smokey nickering softly was all Brodie could distinguish.

"Ike, get the canteen from my saddlebag." He holstered the Colt and lifted Luther's head. Ike uncorked the tin vessel and passed it. Brodie trickled some onto the man's tongue.

"Paw, is that you?" A thin stream of red oozed from the sides of Luther's mouth. The man's eyes stared unseeing. "Paw, I done some terrible bad things."

Brodie's gut clenched tighter.

"He's out of his head," Ike whispered.

No harm in granting a dying man's wish that he could see. "It's all right, son. You can make amends."

"No time, Paw." Sobs racked the body. "I didn't mean to do 'em, honest. I tried to be good like you and Maw taught me."

The pitiful confession tore a chunk out of Brodie's heart. He took a deep breath. "You did your best and that's what counts. Your maw and me are proud of our boy."

"I didn't let you down? You're not ashamed?"

Tears blurred the familiar face and Brodie struggled to speak. "Close your eyes now and rest. Let the angels carry you home."

Luther's lids drifted peacefully shut. A shudder, a whoosh of air, and the body sagged limp in his arms.

The ache created a hole unlike any Brodie had known since the war. He well imagined the scene repeated when he returned to Redemption.

Damn destiny, damn fate, and damn his sorry timing!

"Reckon I'll carry him on back to Missouri." Ike wiped his nose on a shirt sleeve. "Bury him next to Maw and Paw."

"He'd appreciate that, I reckon."

Together they tied Luther across Ike's horse. Brodie didn't speak until they finished.

"The girls...what happened to those little girls, Ike?"

"Reno and Nat have 'em." The middle Blanchard brother brushed a hand across his eyes. "Bert tried to talk some sense into 'em, but they wouldn't listen. They said they're keeping 'em in case a posse shows up."

Two murdering desperados with nothing to lose. Brodie's jaw clenched. "They'll have hell to pay if they harm them."

Ike jerked back. "You're a man of your word, Shenandoah. Thank God it's them and not me who'll be on the receiving end of your justice."

"Are you saying they've already hurt them?"

"Well, I ain't exactly saying that in particular, but they ain't been none too gentle either. The girls are alive though, or leastways they were when Reno and Nat dumped Luther and rode off." A hard glitter shone in Ike's eyes. "Put a bullet in them for me and my brother, will you?"

Brodie snatched his hat from the horn and jammed it on his head. The rattles' vibration added deadly assurance. Nat and Reno's next stop was the hereafter—and he'd be sure to drag out their departure. First, they'd pay.

"Where are they going?" Hard flint layered the question.

"Arkansas. Said they'd lay low for a while."

Smokey stood motionless while Brodie put a foot in the stirrup and pulled himself up. He spared no parting word or backward glance at the friend he'd owed so much.

◆

Laurel's stomach knotted as she seared the steaks. Dishing up plates of roast and bowls of stew kept her from stealing the nearest horse and running.

Called himself Zeke Vallens, did he?

Keeping busy didn't prevent questions from circling like vultures. Vallens could work for Will Taft. The flesh-den owner probably hired the man to track her and Ollie. If so, he'd come a long way for nothing. Her lips tightened.

"What's wrong, Laurel?" Betsy touched her shoulder.

"I'm fine." *Except for I'm lousy, I've got rotten luck, and I wish Brodie was back.* Never had she imagined the hiss of those rattles would bring comfort instead of dread.

Brodie would protect her if for no other reason than, heaven forbid, to make sure she married his brother.

"Beggin' your pardon, your white face disputes that. Got anything to do with the man in the other room? I almost choked when he gave a plateful of meat to that mean ol' dog."

"I appreciate you taking that to him, Betsy. I

simply have a premonition he's bent on making our lives miserable."

"Ain't asking, mind you, but wondered if you knew him?"

"I can happily state I've never had the misfortune."

"A body would be well off to avoid him." Betsy gazed sadly out the back door where the children waited. "I hate to run off with him sittin' there. Don't see I have much choice in the matter. We roll at dawn. Fort Richardson is a long ways."

Tears lurked behind Laurel's eyelids. "I'll miss you."

"Reckon you've been as good a friend as I've ever had. Time to get on with things." Betsy swung to open the door.

"Will you stop on the way to let me say good-bye?"

Betsy gave her a long stare. "I'd like that."

After she left, Laurel glanced around the spotless kitchen. A lick and a promise was all she'd ever had a second to spare. She glowered at the dining room entrance. "I'd rather rake embers in hell and feed the furnace than face Vallens again."

But she'd delayed it long enough. She just wished the dining room wasn't empty. Vallens sat with both feet propped on a chair as though king of his castle. Wolf-dog warily eyed her but uttered no sound.

"Empty plates generally indicate a good sign," she said, praying he'd not tarry.

"Is that pie I smell?"

"Rhubarb." Her heart sank.

"I'll take some. Got a hankering for something sweet."

Shivers chased up her spine when he eyed her from head to toe. She almost lost her grip on the plates. The statement pertained to more than pie and she'd seen that leer in men's eyes far too often to play innocent. She hurried to do his bidding.

Vallens's gaze followed each twitch, the rise and fall of her steps when she returned. He removed his feet from the chair. The beast bared its teeth.

"Oblige me with your company, girlie."

The sharp order split the air like a thin piece of rawhide. Laurel edged her hand beneath the apron into her pocket to grip the knife she'd hidden. Whether this black-clothed man bore deadly intent or not, she'd protect herself from him. Her clenched jaw and jutting chin should relay that.

"Who do you think you are? You can't come in and treat people as though we're slaves to do your bidding. We have laws here. Change your tune or I'll get the sheriff."

"Be sorta hard, seeing as how he's stiff as a two-by-four and six feet under."

Laurel's heart stopped. The strange man knew too much.

Vallens took a bite and chewed. He waved his fork toward the pie. "You make this?"

She nodded.

"Didn't hear you, girl. Cat got your tongue?"

"I made it." The words came through stiff lips.

"Pretty good if I do say so. You're too pretty to waste your talents on cooking. You appear more suited to parlor houses and such. You got a man?"

Vallens stared through the scarred eye. She'd not run and give him the pleasure. But it took great effort to stand her ground.

"It's none of your affair. I have a kitchen to ready before the supper hour." She pivoted, dismissing him.

The dog uncoiled with killer instinct. His growl and bared teeth terrified her. She stood still as a statue when she wanted only to run.

"Quiet, dog. Lay!" Reluctantly, the animal stretched beside the master's boots. Every muscle tensed beneath its hide. "The lady ain't going nowhere less'n I say," Vallens added softly.

"State what you came for because I have things to do." She eased the knife from her pocket, hiding it beneath the apron.

"All in good time, dearie. Ol' Zeke ain't in any hurry." Vallens finished the last bite. He laid down his fork, wiping his mouth on the back of his hand. "Yep, that's mighty good. What pleasures can a traveler find around these parts?"

Laurel stuck her tongue in her cheek to keep from telling him that the favorite pastime was feeding sinister men like him to the gators. But she doubted even those creatures that ate just about anything would find Vallens a tasty morsel.

"The business of eking out a daily living keeps us far too busy for other forms of entertainment."

"Pray tell, to what business do you refer, girlie?" Vallens's coarse voice sliced into her chest and plucked her heart from its hiding place. He hinted at lurid things.

Ollie's sudden entrance saved a reply. "There you are, Laurel. I see—"

The woman pulled up short, swallowing hard. Clearly, this man scared Ollie more than anyone. When Laurel's gaze drifted from the dear face, she spied a holster slung around the petite hips and the butt of a forty-four. The sight shook her.

"I didn't think to have customers so long past the lunch hour." Ollie's short steps suggested someone who dodged a field littered with dynamite and blasting powder.

"The gentleman is about to leave," Laurel said quietly.

Vallens snarled, "You're interrupting a nice chat, old lady. Not wise for a body to do that. Could prove unhealthy."

"Anything pertaining to Laurel pertains to me as well."

"You're a little on the squatty side to speak so bold."

All four feet nine inches of the woman drew up. "I might be the one to teach an ugly swamp rat some manners." Ollie glared. "Or I might be the man on the moon. And I damn sure might be the one to answer to next time you disrespect my girl."

Vallens returned Ollie's glare. "You her maw?"

"You could goldarned sure say that."

"Then I reckon we got things straight, old woman." Vallens thrust two fingers into a vest pocket. Ollie deftly caught the silver dollar he pitched in mid-air. "For the meal. We'll cross paths again."

Low rumbling came from the dog when his master stood.

Never one to miss out on getting in the last word, Ollie snapped, "You'd best count on it."

Vallens's fleeting grin exposed an evil heart. "For less'n a spit in the eye I'd sic Dog on you. Teach you to leave a man be when he has dealin's with a lady."

Ollie whipped out the revolver, brandishing it. "Get out or I'll see what improvement a bullet between your eyes makes."

Vallens held up both hands. "Just leaving."

"Good choice."

The vermin paused to throw Laurel a cracked stare. "A pleasure, ma'am. Let me know when you get tired of wearing your fingers to the bone here. There's easier ways...but then, I suspicion you already know that."

Sixteen

"I oughta pepper that smug rear end for such a remark," Ollie hollered.

Despite the sort of dark gloom that had visited frequently back in St. Louis, Laurel couldn't help notice how Ollie waited until Vallens collected his pistol and left before voicing the latest threat. Although she did more than plenty to his face.

"Taft sent him. Otherwise, why say what he did?"

The gleam in Vallens's eye left no room for coincidence.

"Aw, the walleyed polecat was just trying to rattle you. Honey, he'd have snatched you in a second and been halfway back to Missouri if Will Taft employed the likes of him."

"The man may work for the highest bidder, then, and wants to see if we'll up the ante."

"Don't go borrowing trouble. Girl, let's go see Murphy before the supper hour. Nora might appreciate company."

Afternoon sun filtered through the mossy cypress, creating lacy shadows that swayed this way and that. Welcome warmth dispelled chills that the disfigured visitor left. The stroll to the trim clapboard house at the end of State Street provided for a bit of teasing.

"Perchance could I blame Curley for your rosy glow? You came back bursting with happiness until Vallens ruined it." Laurel threaded her arm through Ollie's.

"Don't have any idea what you're gabbing about."

"Stop playing coy." Laurel gave her dear friend a sideways glance. "Finding the man of your dreams is worth howling at the moon about."

Except if the lady was bound to the man's brother. Guilt twisted Laurel's stomach. Sometimes the things one most wished to fade only tended to grow more vivid the harder a body tried to forget.

That low, lazy drawl.

The unpretentious scuffle of his boots on the floor.

The hiss of snake rattles on a well-worn Stetson.

Most of all, though, she remembered the storm of flutters he unleashed…the barest touch of his breath mingling with hers and the quirk of his mouth in a crooked smile.

"Ain't ashamed of a blooming thing. I just ain't one to kiss and tell."

Things of passion made the sun's rays extra warm.

"Ollie, how long do you suppose before Brodie returns?"

The petite woman came to a standstill and squinted at Laurel. "You're pining for him, ain't you?"

Laurel developed a sudden fixation on the condition of her broken nails. "No crime in wondering."

Another sidelong glance said she didn't fool Ollie, who divined each thought that popped into her head before she even had them.

They climbed the steps and crossed the veranda.

"I reckon Yates should be back in four, maybe five days with luck," Ollie said.

A lifetime when the death angel had taken up squatter's rights in the hotel. Laurel quaked, lifting the brass knocker.

"My land, don't stand there like common folk. Come on in," Etta greeted them, taking Laurel's shawl. "How's Murphy today?"

"Doin' right smart. That Nora's of a mind he'll come around soon. Ain't that something?"

"I'll be my mama's stepchild," Ollie proclaimed. "See? I told you, girl."

"It's a miracle," Laurel said, kissing Etta's cheek.

"Mr. Brodie's gonna be tickled to death when he gets back, all right." Etta beamed. "That's a fact, sure, 'nuff."

A much lighter step carried Laurel to the bedside. Though Murphy lay unmoving, a more natural color had replaced his skin's ghastly pallor.

Nora met her questioning gaze. "It is good."

"I'm here, Murphy. Do you hear me?" She squeezed his hand gently. "I'm waiting for you. I've much to say."

Amazement almost knocked her over when he moved his fingers. "Did you see that?"

"He come from the land of sleep. Talk to him. Your voice help guide him through the fog."

"We've been so worried. You have no idea how sick you've been. Brodie went after the gang who shot you." Laurel touched the angled jaw that sported beard growth.

Murphy's eyes fluttered, struggling as if weighted down. Seconds stretched. Her breath held suspended. Finally they lifted and he stared into her face. The wan smile was beautiful to behold. She leaned to press her lips to a cool forehead.

"I knew you could do it," she whispered. "You've come back to us. You're going to make it. Thank God."

The effort became tiresome. After a brief instance, he drifted back to dreamland from whence he came. He'd passed through the shadow of death and returned.

With luck, Brodie may not have burying to cope with.

...Unless the black-clothed stranger and his wolf went to work.

❧

Weary clear to his soul, Brodie reined Smokey to a halt. They'd ridden straight through except for brief moments. Ike's description of Darcy and Willa's harsh treatment didn't allow for dawdling. Rosy dawn broke overhead when he slid the Winchester from its sling and dropped to the ground. Inching through a tangle of wood fern, Virginia creeper, and red foliage of yaupon, he pushed aside thick clumps of switch cane. A shanty stood in a clearing amidst the Arkansas woods.

Memory hadn't failed. He'd come to the right place.

A crow's shrill caws broke the early morning slumber. A wisp of thin smoke from a flue on the roof gave sole indication anyone occupied the shack. A child's muffled sobs reached his ears and closed a fist around his heart.

He studied the layout carefully as the door opened. Bert Blanchard emerged with a bucket.

The man's grumbles carried in the stillness. "Don't know why I hafta draw the water. Hell, I gotta do everything, even to leaving poor Luther behind."

Brodie didn't hesitate. He crept behind and, before the robber-turned-kidnapper got wind, cracked the thick skull with the butt of his Colt. Bert slumped to the ground in a heap. Emptying the man's holster of its hardware, he tossed it down the well. When Bert came to, he'd not pose a threat. Brodie reached for the man's arms to drag him from view.

"Don't take all day with that water," Nat called. "We need coffee. You know how quarrelsome Reno gets without it."

Bert would have to lie in the open. Brodie raced for cover, beating Nat Jude who came to investigate. The speed with which the man reached inside for a rifle said he spied the body beside the well. Quickly, Brodie squeezed off a shot, slid another cartridge in, and sent it behind the first. Both caught the ruthless child-stealer and murderer in the shoulder.

Nat fell back inside, slamming the bolt on the door. *Christ a Friday.* He'd just put the odds in their favor.

"Who's out yonder?" Nat called.

"Shenandoah."

"Hell, you should've said something," Reno broke in. "We took you for a lawman. Why'd you hafta go and shoot Nat for?"

"This is no social call. I came for the children you took."

"You been smoking dandelion weeds? Ain't no little girls in here."

Nat added, "That's right. It's just me and Reno."

"You'll go to hell for lying." And for lots more…

"Reckon I've been thinking we might already be edging on down there," Reno spoke again. "You bring a posse?"

"Naw, I figure I can handle you boys by myself."

"We're not going peaceful-like," Nat snarled.

"I didn't expect it, you sorry piece of manure," he muttered into the wind. A faint shape crossed the dingy, broken window. They were trying to rig up a plan, in addition to drawing a bead on his position. Brodie shifted further into the undergrowth.

"Who sent you, Shenandoah?"

Tall, dry grass swayed around the shack. Laurel's gaze, awash with unshed tears, flashed from between each dead clump. Impassioned pleas of a pretty lady sent him, nothing more. Failing to find the abductees dumped along the trail, he now shared Laurel's fear. Those girls might end up ruined for life.

Damn, he should've torn himself away sooner.

Jude and Darnell had no idea of the justice he'd inflict. Brodie tightened his grip on the Winchester. They'd earned a free trip to Glory Land this fine September morn.

"It purely seems to me you should worry about why, instead of the who part. Get the wax out of your ears and the lead out of your britches. Send the captives out and we'll call this a day free of bloodletting."

"Don't know why you're raising all this fuss over a darkie and her carpet-bagging playmate." Hate spat from Nat Jude.

Anger ricocheted but Brodie didn't rise to the bait. A rifle poked through the window. Three flashes burst from the barrel. He leaned back. No use burning powder until he had a target. Reno, the hothead, would be his guess.

"We ain't giving back the money. You can forget that."

A high-pitched scream of a youngster suddenly pricked the morning chill. Gooseflesh rose on the back of his neck. His hardened stare never left the tumbledown hideout.

"Boys, you better hope a panther made that cry. Otherwise, you'll be real sorry."

"We ain't scared of you," Nat Jude answered. "Men say you're not so fearsome anymore. You're getting old. Do what you gotta do or shut the hell up and leave us be. I don't think you've got guts to take what you want."

Slight adjustment of the accurate weapon and a keen sense of where Jude stood would deliver the answer. Brodie aimed just a hair or two right of the window. An orange ball, a puff of smoke sent the bullet on a mission. The wood splintered when it hit. Groans and cussing punctured the tranquil Arkansas hills.

He figured Nat's opinion of age and guts might differ now.

"Damn you, Shenandoah. Now you've gone and made us mad." For the first time, Reno's bravado cracked. "Hold onto your rattlers. We're coming out."

Precious minutes came and went with no movement. Brodie dare not sit idle while they did God knows what. Reno and Nat could simply wait him out or hope he made a mistake.

But his birth certificate made no mention of patience.

And he didn't make too many mistakes.

Except where Laurel was concerned.

The dry grass danced. One spark would create an inferno. A family of squirrels cavorted along the limbs of a mighty oak towering above the hideout. They scampered down an overhang and dropped easily to the flat tin roof, giving him a better notion.

Dense foliage concealed Brodie's wide circle. Blocked from the window's limited view, he reached the structure's rear.

Rough tree bark scraped his palms. Crawling out on a limb, he swung silently to the roof. The stained bandana stuffed into the flue wouldn't take long for the ol' smoke-'em-out strategy.

And he was right. He'd barely shimmied down and positioned the shack firmly in the middle of his sights in time to see a figure run from the shack.

A child strained against the man's grip as he dragged her along by an arm.

Brodie aimed for the bulky upper body and made his peace. Then, he introduced Reno Darnell to a chunk of hot Winchester lead. The girl screamed while her captor sprawled face down.

Inside the cabin, the other child coughed and sobbed but no one poked out their head.

That could mean only one thing…

◈

Five o'clock sneaked silently into Laurel's bedroom the following morning. She squinted at the unwelcome thief, her thoughts on Murphy's miraculous awakening. Though it brought happiness, she couldn't risk saying what she needed to tell him for days or perhaps weeks.

And the matter of Vallens entered into the equation. The man might steal the luxury of waiting.

Fear shook the length of her. She jerked the bed sheet over her head and burrowed deeper.

The death angel had not sought their town for his health. A specific goal lurked inside that black heart. Something frightening, something deadly known only to her sixth sense.

Lord help if they didn't get rid of him soon.

Hinges on the door squeaked.

"Why in tarnation are you lazing around in bed at this hour?" Ollie shook her. "And what are you doing under there?"

Laurel lifted her head, glaring through a curtain of hair. "For your information I'm hiding."

"It ain't working too well."

"Everyone doesn't have your sharp wit, General b'Dam."

"Maybe you should stick with cooking and such. You have more skill at that." Ollie peeled back the sheet. "Remember the Cole family? They'll be here shortly."

She groaned. "I completely forgot."

Another reason for the ache sitting on her chest. She would dearly love to pile in and go with them. Escape Vallens and that evil dog of his.

But then…it might be worth hanging around to give Brodie an earful that she'd not be doled out to anyone.

She alone would decide who to marry. And love.

Although the rebel hadn't appeared to give that much thought.

"Ollie, why does fate always have to switch things back and forth and upside down the moment you get comfortable?"

"Girl, don't do a damn bit of good to rant and rave and blame fate. Change is a fact of life. Without a shake-up occasionally, things'd get about as dull as a bunch of widow women knitting long johns."

"Fine thing for you to say. I prefer boring."

"Better accept what is, dearie, and go on. Asking all these goldarned questions won't bring any peace that I know of."

"Do you know how long it's been since I had reason to be carefree? I miss that and lots more."

Ollie patted Laurel's cheek. "Happiness is nothing but a state of mind. Joy comes from tiny details, not how perfect life is. Girl, you gotta keep your eyes peeled or it'll slide on past you." She swatted her leg. "Get dressed, lazy bones. I'll make some of my special coffee. It's purely a waste of energy fuming and fussing over stuff you got no control over."

"Don't make that horrible brew of yours on my account," Laurel yelled at the closing door.

The stench of that vile coffee swam up her nose halfway down the stairs. She knew Ollie would have a cup waiting and persist in feigned innocence.

"About time. Thought you'd sleep the whole day."

Laurel spied a steaming cup at her usual place. She slid into the seat, wrinkling her nose at the dark contents.

"An extra ten minutes doesn't quite equal twelve hours."

"Might as well." The corncob pipe between Ollie's lips jiggled up and down with the statement. "Drink up, girl. It'll pop those eyelids open good and proper."

That wasn't all it'd pop.

"You know I can't stomach it."

"How do you know if you don't try?" Daring sparkled in Ollie's round eyes.

"You're not about to shush until I do." Laurel glared, lifting the cup. Funny, it didn't smell all that bad. And this liquid actually moved. A cautious sip slid onto her taste buds. "This is tea. You should be ashamed."

"Well, I ain't. Now, about that hiding nonsense… I reckon the death angel put your head under the bedcovers."

"He makes my flesh crawl. I can't help it."

"I'd lie if I said he didn't make me shake in my boots. We can't let him know it though. Think what he'd do to cowards."

"I realized that while I dressed. I'm not admitting he came to take me back or anything, but he'd better know right now I'm not a little girl anymore. I can fight a whole lot harder this time."

She kept a knife under her pillow and one in her pocket.

"That's the spirit." Ollie cocked her head, listening. "Unless I miss my guess, that's Mrs. Cole and those younguns."

Laurel grabbed the basket of food she'd packed last evening, trying to quiet the uproar inside that railed against the lousy ungraciousness of life, love, and losing.

Ollie beat her to the door. The woman would deny

how attached she'd grown to the pitiful family, only Laurel saw it.

"Morning, Miss Laurel and Miz Ollie." Edgar Lee hopped down, almost upending Ollie who wasn't much taller.

"Well, I'll be slickered, if it ain't the two tadpoles." Betsy climbed from the high seat and reached inside the wagon for the baby. "Kept my word like I promised."

"W-w-we wanna stay here." Andy fought back tears.

"But we cain't." Edgar Lee kicked a clump of dirt. "Maw says we gotta live with Uncle John."

"U-U-Uncle J-John has a r-r-r-ranch."

Laurel put her arm around the small shoulders. "That'll be exciting. You'll have great adventures and learn how to brand cattle and rope."

"I reckon," Edgar Lee grudgingly admitted. "Only I bet we don't have more than we got here."

She offered Betsy the basket of goodies. "Ollie and I packed a few things to help get you there."

"You have no call to think I changed my mind about accepting handouts and such."

"It won't do a dam…darn bit of good to refuse. I'm sticking it in when you roll outta here," Ollie blustered.

Laurel jolted when Andy threw his small arms around her waist.

"I-I-I love you."

Laurel kissed the top of his head, wiping tears that trickled down Andy's cheeks. A big lump choked her.

"I love you and Edgar Lee, too. I'm already missing you."

"Shore shooting right. Don't rightly know who's

gonna wash them dishes now." The blustering voice
cracked. Ollie turned to address Edgar Lee. "Boy,
you're might near a grown man. Watch after your
maw and brother and Sissie, you hear?"

"I will," the little man sniffled.

Laurel breathed a sigh of relief when Betsy took the
basket. It would be downright shameful for Ollie to
engage in fisticuffs with the woman.

"I don't know what I'd have done without your help
and your kindness," Betsy admitted. "It truly saved us."

How strange to hear something other than the
hard flint in Betsy's tone. Seems their acquaintance
benefited everyone.

Ollie rested a hand on Betsy's shoulder. "If we
managed to ease the weight of your burden a mite,
then we done what we should've."

Baby Sissie reached for Laurel, cooing happily
when she took her. The child snuggled against her
breast. Laurel blinked hard and buried her face in the
soft curls.

"I'll never forget you." Betsy collected the minia-
ture copy of herself. "Back in the wagon, boys."

"You're always welcome should you ever need a
place." Laurel's arms and heart felt so empty.

"I appreciate that." Betsy handed up the baby to
Edgar Lee. Before she climbed to the seat, she hugged
Laurel tight. "You're real lucky to find a man like Mr.
Brodie. He loves you, you know. Be patient. War's a
terrible affliction."

Tears blurred the last glimpse of the family. Though
Ollie shuffled back inside, Laurel waved until the
loblolly pines and river birch swallowed them up.

The demonic laughter of loons from the bayou mocked her loneliness. Hundreds of long-tailed grackle settled in treetops, adding lusty calls.

She didn't hear the footsteps until they crunched directly behind. She dabbed her eyes before turning.

"Never took you for a sappy, weak-willy sister." Zeke Vallens, with a matchstick propped in the corner of his mouth, gave her a start. His wild animal was at his side.

"What I am is of no consequence to you."

"Been checking around. Asked some questions. Folks say you're about to marry the town mayor. That is, if the poor devil lives. That true?" The man's gaze absorbed the sunlight, yet gave back none of the warmth.

"You're the one with the information. Now, excuse me please. I won't feed your curiosity."

"Cain't imagine you wasting all that softness on one man. Nope, just can't figure it." Vallens shifted the matchstick to the other side of his mouth.

Laurel clenched her fists. The smirk on the feared face angered and terrified her at the same time. Wolf-dog's sharp eyes glittered, his long tongue hanging out one side, exposing razor teeth.

Dear God, Ollie should've let her hide under the sheet!

"Good day, Mr. Vallens." She turned carefully, slowly, measuring how many strides it would take to reach safety.

"It's my duty to remind you of your place, little missy. You don't belong in a two-bit town feeding hungry bellies. Bet you don't make enough to buy a dead man's supper. Ain't that right? Just saying there's easier ways."

Seventeen

LAUREL WHIRLED ON HER HEELS, FORGETTING THE folly of sudden moves. The animal lunged for her. Had Vallens not snatched a handful of gray neck the wolf would've torn her to shreds. Her pounding heart told her how close the beast had come.

Sometimes being that frightened helped unleash old-fashioned fury. If a fight he wanted, then one he'd get.

"What do you want? How much will it take for you to leave and forget you ever stumbled upon this town?"

"Ain't your money I'm wanting, little missy. Got more than enough from selling wanted men's sorry hides."

"You're a bounty hunter?"

"By trade. I'm not above dabbling in other persuasions should the job require."

Blood drained, leaving her stone cold and faint. "In case you think that pertains to anyone here, there's not a soul who'd pay one shiny copper for Ollie or me."

But what about Brodie? The army would pay dearly for him.

The thought slid down sideways. Prayers doubled for Vallens to ride on before Brodie returned.

Wolf-dog's powerful body strained against Vallens's grip. "I wouldn't be too sure, girlie. You might fetch a handsome price."

The pitiful attempt to approach him with logic withered. "Over my dead body, that's the only way."

"That's purely a shame you feel that way. A crying shame."

Laurel's stand took every ounce of strength. She flew inside the café, slammed and locked the door behind her. Only then did she sink to the floor, shaking.

Ollie glanced up from peeling onions. She threw down the knife and knelt beside her. "Who's chasing you?"

"That...that horrible man." She let Ollie help her to a chair.

"Who? The alley was deserted when I came inside."

"Your grim reaper."

The woman's lips narrowed into a thin line. She whipped the pistol from the table, then fumbled with the door latch. When it finally opened, sheer force sent it thundering against the wall. Ollie glanced up and down.

"Dadburn it. The devil's gone." She shut the door.

"Thank God." Badgering Vallens would cause more danger and possibly trigger events no one wished.

"What did he say?"

"He's a bounty hunter. Leastwise that's his claim."

"Any idea who in hell he's sniffing after?"

"Maybe me." Or Ollie. Or Brodie. Or all three. Who knew? Taft taught her well to distrust the obvious. The walls seemed to close in when Laurel repeated the conversation.

"Son of a bluejacket. He'd better not try it or he'll find himself on the hurting end of this six iron, trying to plug a few leaks. I ain't about to let him get you."

"You'll do your level best." The assurance didn't comfort.

"I need to come clean about something, girl."

The solemn statement brought ghostly silence inside like when a person had to own up to a secret even though they hated to but couldn't see a way to dodge it. Laurel knew it would bring change that would serve no practical purpose.

"Please, we should get lunch cooking."

Ollie continued, unfazed. "That night we snuck out of the Black Garter…I struck Will Taft, rendering him almost dead. Then I stole the money he was counting."

"You didn't." Laurel covered her mouth.

"I ain't sorry. He deserved it for his devil ways. That's what brought us to Texas and how we purchased this café. Vallens is here because of me."

"It could be any number of reasons."

"Stop humoring a sick, old woman. You know I'm right."

The revelation made sense. Despite agreeing, she wouldn't admit that Ollie had unwittingly put them both at great risk. By finding one, Taft would find the other.

"We'll think of something."

"I'll go to Vallens and fix it. Don't worry about them taking you again. I'll protect you."

The heart and will of a crusty lady didn't equal out the difference. Only one man had the ability to boot

Vallens out of their lives and heaven only knew where he rode this day.

&

"Help! Help me!"

Brodie pried Darcy's arms from his neck and gripped the Colt. "Wait here. I'll be back."

Shielding his mouth with a shirt sleeve, he ran into the billowing, gray plumes.

Suffocating haze robbed his sight. Panic rose. A man could get turned around real fast when blinded. For a second he gave thanks he didn't set the grass afire. Smoke filled his lungs, but at least he didn't have a blaze to fight.

He nearly tripped on a form on the floor. Kneeling, he saw Nat Jude. Dead or wounded, didn't matter. At the moment he had greater concerns. He slid the Colt into the holster.

Smothered coughs and a whimper penetrated the dense cloud. Plunging ahead, he groped soft flesh that shrank away from him.

"Don't be afraid. I'm here to help you."

Something held her fast when he tried to lift her. *The bastards had bound her.*

His lungs ached from an urge to fill them. Unable to see, he fumbled for the dagger he carried in his boot. With a finger between the ropes and her tender skin, he freed the girl.

Slinging her over a shoulder, he raced for sunlight and fresh air.

Darcy met them, latching onto his waist. "Watch out!"

A deep voice buried into his brain. "Hold it, Shenandoah."

Damnation.

The guttural warning contrasted with the musical *kerloo* calls of migrating whooping cranes.

Brodie's eyes watered too badly to focus, but memory served to assign the voice to the eldest Blanchard. Through the blur he couldn't tell if Bert pointed a weapon or not.

A crucial error not ridding Reno's carcass of the sidearm.

"I should've finished you off when I had the opportunity."

"Reckon that was your last mistake, Shenandoah."

One Brodie would gladly rectify had he eyesight and no child on his shoulder. He'd have to depend on wits to get them out alive.

"You've got me dead to rights." He inched toward the vague figure, trying to block the choking noises the little girl in his arms made.

"Damn right I do. About time you noticed."

"Let me put this little lady down and make sure they're both all right. Then you and me can unravel this mess."

"Good try. You think I'm stupid?"

"I don't have to tell you where two dead girls will lead. Folks might be lenient for the kidnapping, especially when I tell how you helped keep them from harm. But murder has the makings of a lynch mob." He took a few more cautious steps.

"Won't make a hill of beans. My best shot is killing all of you and running."

"You're not a murderer, Bert. No need to start now."

"An eye for an eye. For Reno and Nat."

"They drew their fate after what they put these innocent children through." Brodie uttered a low oath when stinging sweat trickled into his eyes. "Besides, remember how Reno and Nat left your poor shot-up brother behind with no more regard than a slab of spoiled meat."

"Take out that iron and throw it over here."

"Now how do you think I can manage that? With my teeth? You'll have to come get it."

"My mama didn't raise no fool. Do as I say," Bert snarled.

"Don't get nervous now. I'm going to put the girl down."

When he bent to do as bid, his vision cleared just enough to spy a horse moseying behind Blanchard.

Smokey? It had to be his old friend.

Brodie gently lowered Willa. From the corner of an eye he saw the horse rear, his forefeet knocking Bert to the hard clay.

If he didn't act now, Lady Luck might turn her back.

He leaped toward the figure, swinging a hard left and crossing with a right. Bert's harsh grunts silenced a family of squawking blue jays in the treetops. Quickly locating Reno's pistol, Brodie stuck it in his waist before hauling Blanchard to his feet. A length of rope looped over the saddle horn on Smokey provided ample binding of the outlaw's hands and feet. Only then did he turn to the animal that'd saved his butt.

"Good work, boy." He patted the smooth neck. Smokey snorted and nibbled on his shirt as if to say it's about damn time he got some credit for doing the hardest part.

Children's coughs mingled with sobs brought back his attention. He drew a pail of water from the well and knelt in the Arkansas wild rye to wash tear-stained cheeks.

"It's all right. You're safe, darlin'."

Willa's big eyes stared into his. The child shook when he put his arms around her. "I'm skeered."

"I know, but I would never hurt you."

"Who you be?"

"A friend. Your mamas sent me to bring you girls home."

Darcy sniffled and sat up. "Are you sure? Those men said they'd sell us and we'd never see the bayou again."

"Yep, I'm certain. They won't ever threaten you again."

"I want my mama. I need my mama."

Brodie didn't know whether to blame the moisture in his eyes on smoke or that Darcy's pleading gaze held the same lost fear Laurel's had. His gut wrenched as he cleared his throat.

"I'll have you back in Redemption before you know it."

"You promise?" Willa asked. "You won't leave me here 'cause I'm black? Mama says most folk hate people of color and not to trust 'em."

"Not all do. I'm not one of those. I promise."

❧

Purpose. That's what Ollie harped on and that's the way Laurel marched down the street—a woman with a purpose who wouldn't let a pitted, washed out road waylay her. She'd geared herself up for battle and chosen her weapon.

The clerk at the desk glanced up at the sound of the hotel door. "May I help you?"

"Zeke Vallens?"

"Let's see. That's number six at the top."

Her best shoes drummed the beat of a platoon's drill as she mounted the stairs. Pausing at the door, she first straightened the lace-rimmed bonnet and adjusted her skirt to hide the bulge within the folds. Long white gloves somewhat disguised the trembles. Fighting rising panic, she sharply rapped twice.

"To what do I owe the pleasure?" Vallens showed surprise. "If you'd have let me know in advance of your visit, I would've taken a bath. Or at least washed up first."

Her cheeks burned.

"You deviant, it's not that kind of call."

Horror swept over her when he tried to pull her into the room. She'd not be alone with Vallens. Not willingly.

The metal shaft in her skirt helped bring calm. Her grip tightened, ready to plunge it into his rotten chest.

Ollie had been bound and determined to pay Vallens a visit. Had Laurel not tricked the dear lady and switched places, it would've meant the grave for sure.

And still might. For someone.

No one had to tell her the grim reaper never lost.

She'd given that terrifying thought great consideration.

Anything to repay Ollie's kindness overrode the wish to keep far removed from this man's sight.

"You want others to overhear and know what sort you are?" Vallens touched her face, running a finger across her cheek.

The contact repulsed her. "I'm who I am and that's enough."

"Cain't rightly think of any other purpose you'd stroll over to see ol' Zeke. Figured you to hunger for a man's body."

Darkness surrounding her soul turned to pitch under the cynical stare.

"I haven't time or inclination to argue with you. I wish to strike a bargain." Releasing the knife, she moved to the small canvas bag it rested on. Adopting brazen courage she didn't feel, she jerked it out.

"What kind of deal are you proposing, little missy?"

"This two hundred dollars is free and clear money. I believe you'll find it adequate, considering no one will pay you a cent for anyone in Redemption."

"You're sure hell-bent on convincing me of that. Causes a man to wonder."

"Take it and leave. It's as fair a bargain as you'll get."

"Ain't in no hurry. I haven't completed my stay."

"You might reconsider. There'll be no more payments. The milk cow has dried up."

A quick pitch found the bull's-eye on his chest. He made no move to catch it. The blackmail money fell to the floor, scattering like dry leaves on a blustery fall afternoon. She whirled and beat a hasty retreat.

"I'm betting different," Vallens snarled after her.

❧

Three days passed after the unsuccessful venture. Despite Laurel's efforts, Vallens remained a fixture. The man's ominous presence cast a dark shadow over the town. No one knew why he'd appeared or why he stayed. Speculation that he stalked someone ran rampant. But who? Each person whispered a different name.

"If the Blanchard gang hadn't laid Sheriff Tucker to rest, he'd find out what the devil keeps Vallens here," George Adams had grumbled at a hastily called town meeting.

Laurel hadn't pointed out the obvious. Had the sheriff escaped the bullet, he still couldn't help because it would be his job of facing the murdering child thieves instead of Brodie.

And her heart wouldn't ache with uncertainty that perhaps the love of her life would never find his way back.

"How will we run the likes of Vallens out of town when he keeps us shaking in our beds? That dog of his snarls and we break our fool necks running backward. Someone should stand up to him." Jake the barber twirled the ends of his mustache.

"Like you, Jake? I could put a drop or two of strychnine in his whiskey," Curley suggested in a low tone.

Ollie took out her pipe and tapped it against the floor. "Your whiskey is poison enough. Don't rightly understand how that sidewinder keeps standing with the bottles he's poured down his gullet lately."

"What does that leave? Talk him to death?" John Miller, the blacksmith, quietly rose in the back of the room.

"Jeb Prater could've helped if he hadn't tried to bully Brodie Yates. Prater's not afraid of much 'cause he don't have a lick of sense." Jake leaned his matchstick frame against a wall.

The meeting had adjourned shortly after with simply a hearty wish for Brodie's return. Everyone knew without a doubt he could end the unwelcome angel of death's visit.

Laurel was sweeping the sidewalk in front of the café the following morning when a subtle change rustled the air.

Half expecting to find Vallens nearby, she did an about face, staring in surprise at the Appaloosa trotting down the street. Her pulse raced at the sight of the lean figure riding tall in the saddle.

Thank God.

The girls? She clutched the broom tightly. From this distance she couldn't tell who rode the other horses following. Shielding her eyes against the sunlight, she spotted two small heads bobbing on a dappled mare. Brodie held the reins of the third animal that carried a man whose hands were bound.

The broom went flying one direction, her feet the other.

"Ollie, come quick!"

When the woman poked out her head, Laurel swung her around.

"Tarnation, girl. You got buffalo fever or something?"

"Brodie's here and with little Darcy and Willa."

"Well, I'll be the son of a bug-eater."

The group halted at the hitching rail. Laurel tried to wipe away the smile, but it pulled rank and did as it pleased.

"You're back," she breathed, reaching up for Willa and swinging her down. She spoke to Ollie before helping Darcy. "Mrs. Hatcher just went into the mercantile and I think I saw Mrs. Carver head toward the livery."

"I want my mama," Darcy sniffled.

"Hold on there, sweetie. I'll get her here before you can say Singapore Jack." Ollie's skirts became a swirling wind.

"You brave darling." Laurel smoothed Willa's tangled hair, picking out a piece of straw. "We'll fix you up in no time."

Both girl's dresses hung in tatters from thin shoulders. Would their redemption be like hers—nothing but a dream?

Darcy's blue gaze gripped Laurel. "I'm scared."

"Not a soul will hurt you here. We won't let them."

Warmth of a certain gray-eyed rebel trapped her in his snare. He threw a leg over Smokey's back and dismounted, the motion setting off the snake rattles.

Lord, how she'd missed hearing that.

Breathless, her chest ached as though she'd run the length of the bayou.

A weary scowl deepened the lines around his mouth. It told her how difficult the task had been. Dust flew when he brushed at his clothes. Beneath the layers of trail grit, she noticed scratches on his arm. And dark bloodstains.

"You're injured."

Looping three sets of reins over the railing, he grinned. "A scratch. Nothing to get upset about."

"I can see perfectly well that it's more than that."

He stepped from reach, stiffening. "How's Murphy?"

"Doing quite nicely, thanks to Nora. You'll be surprised."

Until then, she hadn't taken account of the man on the other horse. He wore a sullen sneer. "What'cha staring at, Miz Uppity? I ain't no sideshow."

Repulsed, Laurel turned away.

"My baby!" Mrs. Hatcher hugged her daughter as the curious half of town gathered.

"Good work, son." Ollie had to go up on tiptoe and stretch to slap Brodie on the back. "I knowed you was made of fine-grained leather."

Since when? Come to think of it, Laurel supposed the change of opinion drifted to the more favorable side when Vallens moved in permanent-like.

Mrs. Carver arrived out of breath, her arms out-stretched. "Willa, child, come to your poor mama."

"What about the bank's money?" George Adams huffed from scurrying to get in on the commotion.

Brodie opened a saddlebag, pulled out a scorched canvas bag, and lobbed it at the banker.

Adams dumped out a handful of charred bank notes. "What happened to all the rest?"

"You accusing me of stealing?"

"I'd check his pockets there if'n I was you folks," Blanchard warned. "Can't trust these hired guns, you know."

"I'm saying it's mighty suspicious, with your repu-tation and all." George Adams shuffled his feet when Brodie advanced. "But then, I'm sure we have no reason to doubt your word."

"How did it get burned, Yates?" Jake demanded.

Thank goodness Jake wasn't a piece of raw meat or Brodie's glare would've seared him. A shake of disgust set the rattles in motion. He jerked the reins from the rail and led the horse carrying the robber toward the empty jail.

Ollie whacked Jake's arm. "You crazy fool. Let the man be. Cain't you see he's worn plumb to the soles of his boots?"

Darcy and Willa ran after the man who'd rescued them. "Mr. Brodie! Wait."

He stopped in his tracks. When he turned, both threw their arms around him. Laurel watched the tough gunslinger scoop up first one then the other through a misty gaze. She was so wrong. Brodie truly cared. It hadn't been merely a job she asked him to do.

"I don't know how to thank you proper, Mr. Yates," Darcy's mother said. "I don't have much money, but you're welcome at our door anytime day or night."

"Ours, too," Mrs. Carver added. "I can cook real good."

Eighteen

ONCE BRODIE MADE BLANCHARD NICE AND COZY behind a locked cell door, he hurried to the frame house on State Street. Color in Murphy's face reinforced Laurel's claims of progress.

After keeping vigil for half an hour with no sign of Murphy awakening, Brodie turned to needs of a more liberal sort.

The Dry Gulch Saloon had a fair amount of business for a Saturday morning. He hooked his heels on the metal rail and gulped a lukewarm mug of beer. The liquid wet down the first two coatings of dust inside his mouth but little else.

"Let me buy you one." Ollie brushed his elbow.

Sweet Georgia clay. The jackanapes was harder to get rid of than stink on a fresh cow patty. He wasn't in the mood for company. Leastways not of the ill-tempered sort.

Let him quench his thirst, soak in a tub for about a week, and he might possibly feel human again. Then he'd venture over to the café for an extra helping of pecan praline pie before all hell broke loose when the Yanks came for him.

Had he more than a speck of sense he'd ride on before the soldiers came.

Jake pushed Ollie aside. "Reckon the town owes you, Yates."

Brodie stared at the sloshed beer dripping from his hand. The thought of leaving became more attractive by the minute. Deep irritation grew at the circus that had followed him in.

"You should've recovered more of our hard-earned money though," George whined in a nasal twang.

"Son of a bluejacket. He done more than any of you sniveling two-bit chorus girls, including you, Adams." Ollie refilled the pipe from a pouch Brodie decided she slept with.

"Yates, would you be of a mind to reconsider the previous offer? We need a sheriff in a real hurtful kind of way."

"Goldarned it, Jake. You can't pour piss out of a boot. Don't you see the man's tuckered out? Let him get some shut-eye and put food in his belly before pestering him."

"Ollie Applejack b'Dam, don't you tell me what to do."

"Watch it there, Jake." The saloon owner entered the fracas. "Don't use that tone with the lady. You can take your flea-bitten hide outta here if you can't button your trap."

The gilt-edged mirror above the bar reflected a man in black who rose from a corner table. Patrons hastily parted, clearing a path through the hubbub. Brodie's hand moved to rest on the smooth walnut of the Colt without thought.

He swung from the long mahogany bar to face the stranger before he glanced downward. Beside the man stood a dog with its lips curled back. Snarls swept the area clear. Brodie returned the primal stare until knowledge he didn't scare easy penetrated the glittering depths. Finally, the beast cowered.

The mysterious stranger's low hat shaded his eyes. Yet some keen sense told of a dangerous glint. Although the man's threatening demeanor jabbed needles into each nerve ending, it was the jagged, diagonal scar that left bitterness in Brodie's mouth that no amount of spirits could sweeten.

He'd crossed shadows with such a disfigured man.

"Something's got the good folk of Redemption mighty stirred up. Quite a celebration I'd say," the stranger sneered.

"What do you want, Vallens?" Brodie cut to the chase.

"Ahh, Shenandoah. Wondered if you might remember me. Been a while, I recollect."

"Not a face I ever wished to see again. Now, what're you here for? Brodie had once stopped Vallens when the man had tried to burn down a house with a woman and children inside just to get her husband."

"Hey, mister," Jake yelled at a safe distance from the far end of the bar. "Better watch it. Yates just went up single-handed against the Blanchard gang. I warned you not to get him riled."

Vallens's sunken cheeks twitched. The funerary attire suggested an undertaker come to claim the next victim, with a devil-dog by his side.

"Or what? No lawman around to stop me from doing whatever I please. Town don't have no sheriff."

The guttural dare gave the wolf-dog courage. A growl rumbled. The animal leaned on his haunches ready to spring.

"Better think again, Vallens. It does now." Brodie's clipped answer stunned, leaving the rival at a loss for words.

"I see someone managed to lasso you." Murphy smiled weakly the next day, pointing to the silver star on Brodie's shirt.

"Sorta looks that way." Brodie touched the shiny badge that burdened him. "I swore and be damned I'd go to my grave before I'd wear a tin star."

"You could do worse, big brother."

Brodie placed his hat at the foot of the bed and rubbed the weariness from eyes that hadn't seen decent sleep in a week. "Thing is, I'm not cut out for upholding law or order."

He knew the Ten Commandments by heart simply because he'd broken every one.

"Beats me why you took it on."

"Zeke Vallens and his damn defiance. I had to put him in his place. Claiming the job just slipped out. I only meant to wipe the sneer off the smug piece of slime."

"He's here to cause trouble, isn't he?"

"Feel it in my bones."

Vallens had expertise at creating mystery. He took extra pleasure in making folks jumpy, unable to predict the next move.

Murphy's struggle to sit up ended in total failure. An ache swept Brodie as he gathered the narrow shoulders and raised him. He propped a mountain of pillows behind his brother, hoping to hide the concern that must show despite the mask he tried to wear.

"Appreciate it. Ollie says I'm so weak I can't even lick my upper lip. And I hate to admit she doesn't lie."

"It'll pass. When I left here I wouldn't have given a plug nickel for your chances of making it." Brodie wouldn't tell him how dearly it cost to ride out. Some feelings a man didn't wish to discuss. From experience those were better left unsaid.

"Getting back to Vallens…are his sights on you?"

"Aside from the army, I have no price on my head."

Although he did once, after a scrape out Tucson way when warring ranchers attempted to pin the murder of a prominent landowner on him. It'd taken might near a year to track down the culprit and clear up the mistake.

"I'd say having the army's target on your back would give Vallens reason enough." Murphy groaned from sudden movement, but waved Brodie away. "The scuttlebutt I hear says the man doesn't require much excuse to start trouble."

Brodie extracted the tobacco and papers from a vest pocket and rolled a smoke. "Want one?"

"Does a garden need water? These darn womenfolk coddle me worse than a newborn."

The complaint applied balm to the ache. Younger brother wouldn't be laid up too long. Brodie licked the edge of the paper to stick it and twisted one end. He no more had it lit and stuck in Murphy's mouth when Nora slipped through the door.

"Mr. Murphy! I tell you no smoke. Bad. Very bad."

"Get away, woman." He shooed her. "It's my house, by God, and I'll smoke if I darn well please. Don't you have some nasty-tasting potions to grind up or something?"

The pretty Indian swelled like a toad, her dark glare slinging arrows in all directions. Brodie ducked before one landed his way. One thing he'd learned—don't go up against anyone on the warpath, particularly one who wore skirts.

"Maybe half-breed go back to swamp. Maybe sick man not need Nora now." She crossed her arms and glared. "Maybe Nora let leeches suck you dry."

"Now, Nora darlin', I didn't mean it that way." Sugar dripping from Murphy's plea snapped Brodie's head around.

"Hmph!"

"You know I'm not well enough for you to leave." Sensing Brodie's curious stare, Murphy's tone became abrupt. "And don't let me hear that half-breed remark again. The color of a person's skin only proves our Creator likes variety. How bored we'd be if we all looked the same. You're a fine, intelligent woman, albeit far more handsome than most."

"And you are stubborn yellow-eyes."

The cigarette fell from Murphy's grasp onto the sheet. "Hellfire and damnation."

Quickly plucking the danger, Nora's hand collided with the patient's. For a brief moment a spark sizzled, held captive by the shimmer in their gazes.

Surely Brodie hadn't imagined it. Yet, the possibility intrigued. So much he trembled when he held a match to the slim, paper-encasement propped in his mouth. He couldn't stop the hope that tingled up his spine.

The supple doeskin garment Nora wore made no sound as she smoothed the sheet, tucking it around Murphy. Each gentle movement revealed extraordinary care.

Nora turned to address Brodie. "I offer prayer for safe return. Great Mighty One answered. My heart smiles."

Brodie met the brown warmth of her features. "Your heart isn't the only thing smiling, Miss Whitebird."

"The little ones?"

"A few days and the girls'll be fine." He emptied his lungs, aiming the smoke toward a cracked window in case her anger flared. "They suffered no worse than a bad case of fright."

Mere minutes had stood between the girls and an uncertain fate. Distaste lingered in his mouth. He'd rather not consider the what-ifs.

"They have a lot to thank you for." Murphy eyed the cigarette with longing. Nora held it outstretched by two fingers to avoid the smoke.

"You bring one bad man. The others? You take many scalps, Mr. Brodie?"

"They caught some luck. I let them keep their hair." His dry statements held a handful of remorse, thinking of Luther.

Ashes dangled from the tip of the cigarette. He looked about for a proper place to flick them. Giving up, he tapped them into the palm of his left hand.

"Good." Nora paused at the door and pointed a finger at Murphy. "No more smoke. You eat or Nora go home."

Murphy's grin stretched. "You'd best unpack then. Suddenly I'm hungry enough to eat the blades off a windmill."

A man would be deaf, dumb, and unconscious to miss the crackle in the air.

"I swear I just witnessed something," Brodie dropped casually when the door shut. "What's with you and Nora?"

"Don't know what you're talking about."

"And I'm a three-legged, blind donkey."

"I hoped you wouldn't notice." Murphy sighed. "When she touches me, it's as if a branding iron sears my insides. I've never felt this way before that I recall."

"Not even with Laurel?" His breath became glacial and harsh. Though she'd made it clear she wished no part of her former love, Brodie welcomed Murphy's interest in Nora.

"Laurel's different. She's the one I'm marrying."

Brodie wiped off a sick smile before it finished forming.

"Whatever you say, Mr. Expert Lady Killer." He took his palm full of ashes and raised the window high enough to dust them onto the lawn.

"Let's get back to your problems and leave my heart affairs alone." A coughing spasm gripped Murphy and several minutes elapsed before he could continue. "Damn, I hate this."

"Have patience. Getting blasted by an elephant cannon tends to hobble a man. You're lucky to do the slow poke shuffle."

"I can't abide much more of this." Murphy wiped his mouth.

Conversation drifted up the stairs. No mistaking the throaty caller.

"Laws a mercy. Shore is fine to see you, Miss James."

"Likewise, Etta. Is Murphy awake?"

"For a fact. Get your sweet self right on up there."

Laurel's delicate features brought a heart full of misery and a kick smack in the middle of Brodie's gut.

"Come here, Laurel my love. I need a kiss from my girl," Murphy pleaded.

She hesitated, meeting Brodie's quizzical stare. He turned quickly away, unable to bear the pain of their lips touching.

"You seem quite spirited today," she remarked.

"Don't know how you get that idea. Frankly, I'm upset. I dreamt you called off the wedding. Said you had no wish to marry me." Murphy closed his eyes for a moment. "Tell me it's nothing more than nonsense concocted by a figment of the mind. I don't think I could bear it should—"

"Don't get yourself in a dither over a dream, Murphy."

"Thank God. We do have to decide the details, however."

"What details?" Laurel's dress rustled in a hasty retreat to the window, where she gazed out, keeping her back to the two men.

Brodie wondered what had unnerved her. Surely not his presence. She knew he'd visit Murph at the first opportunity. And he harbored no illusion the upcoming nuptials would not take place, given his blessing pretty much sealed that. Still, her behavior reflected guilt of some sort.

"How could you forget our wedding date barely a

week off? Do we proceed with me laid up, or post-pone until full recovery?"

A wild, cornered expression shone on her face when she slowly turned.

Brodie favored putting it off—like forever. Murphy's directness flustered her even more, shown in the way she smoothed the quilt backward and forward.

"I believe we should discuss this in private."

"My brother doesn't mind. We're family."

"Just pretend I'm not here," Brodie piped up dryly, receiving a glare for his effort. "Murph, I daresay Laurel will agree it depends on whether you prefer tying the knot lying or standing."

"Exactly my point. Only a healthy man can do the marriage bed justice," Murphy agreed.

"That settles it. See how simple that was? Whatever would you do without your big brother?" A bit of hope rose. A marriage put on hold could turn into one that would never occur.

Laurel's mood seemed to lighten as well. "No need to rush. We have the rest of our lives. What's a few more months?"

"Not a chance, my love. I won't wait that long and give you a chance to back out. No sirree, two weeks from today, and that's final, one way or another."

The smattering of hope crashed around Brodie.

"Oh dear, look at the time." Laurel raced for the door. "Folks will kick down the door to get to the feeding trough. Ollie must wonder what on earth kept me."

Her footsteps padded on the stairs before Murphy spoke. "Where were we? Oh yes. What are you going to do with Blanchard?"

"A mighty good question. I'll have to think on it."

"I'll wager you've a trick or two up your sleeve yet."

Brodie scooped his hat off the end of the bed, pondering the advice. Magical feats hadn't run in the family, unless a boy counted the swift departure of a father who left in the dead of night with a painted lady.

The same misbegotten ways Brodie shared with Samuel Yates, it would appear.

Suddenly he had one more thing to cross off the list before bedding down for the night over at the jail.

The comforting hiss of rattlers ignited purpose inside him. "One thing I know: I'll make Vallens rue the day he rode into this damn town. If he's come to find trouble, I won't be shy about obliging him."

Nineteen

THE JINGLE ANNOUNCING A CUSTOMER DREW AN exasperated "spit and thunder" from under Laurel's breath. With Murphy pressuring her about wedding plans, the long day had stolen her spirit.

"Sorry, we're closed." She swiped crumbs from the table into her hand before glancing up.

"I'm not here for that."

The deep baritone unleashed a storm of flutters. Tiny droplets began to dampen the crevice between her breasts.

She might've laid blame on the warmth of his stare.

Assuredly, on the lopsided grin.

And most definitely, the lock of hair drooping onto his forehead bore responsibility for the flip-flop of her heart.

The quiet, gray-eyed rebel portrayed sleeping danger at best.

And at worst? Heaven help her.

"Ah, the new sheriff. I suspect you pay no social call."

"Only came to…" He suddenly yanked the hat from his head. Dancing rattles fussed with the fury of a whole den of deadly vipers. "To check on things before I bed down. Noticed the lanterns still burning."

"I have a cup of coffee left. Not exactly fresh though."

"A fair enough offer."

She led the way to the kitchen and thanked providence she'd brewed the last pot. Serving Ollie's thick mud might get her shot for her trouble. Sitting opposite Brodie, she wished the butterflies in her stomach would light somewhere.

He didn't want her, she reminded herself, clasping her hands tightly. He offered her to his brother free and clear.

"Would you care for something else?" What a dumb thing to ask. Having him mistake it for a proposition of some kind, especially the sordid variety, was exactly all she needed.

"Lil, I wish I was at liberty…"

Use of that name increased her vulnerability threefold. Awkward silence stretched, yet he added nothing more.

"I meant pie, of course. I'm glad you're back," she finally ventured. "Although letting them rope you into the sheriff job surprised me. You were dead set against it."

Brodie's stare wrestled with hers. "A man can change his mind. I had my reasons."

Blue blazes, it was as if he spoke in a foreign tongue. Nothing made any sense, and with each word she grew more confused than ever. What happened to his direct and to the point manner? "I expect Murphy's rapid improvement brought you relief."

"Nora has exceptional abilities. My brother is quite taken with her powers to bring him back from the brink of death."

The lifted cup and lowered gaze effectively hid the expression she sought to read. She couldn't ever recall him this guarded or mysterious.

Only irresistible.

Laurel rose to bank the fire in the wood stove to keep from doing something she'd regret. "Yes, we found Nora to be a godsend. By the time the good doctor finally arrived, the loop-legged man was in no shape to treat a sick cat, much less a human. I sent him packing."

"You make it most difficult for a man, Lil."

"Laurel," she ground out. "Hard for you? You waltz in and tempt me to forget…make my dreams disappear fast as mist in moonlight."

"How've you been…Laurel?" His brittle tone took her aback.

She didn't reply until she emptied the ash chute into the galvanized pail. "Who exactly wants to know, the sheriff or you?"

"Let me have that." He brushed her aside and took the pail before she realized he'd gotten up from his chair. "I'll set it outside. Ollie says Zeke Vallens threatened you."

He closed the back door and returned.

"The dear woman has many admirable qualities, but a closed mouth isn't one of them." The table hid Laurel's trembles, yet she met his rebel grays unflinching. "Should I admit the truth, he scares the devil out of me. His evil-eye gives me the shakes. And refusing to say why he's here keeps my nerves jumping. I'm almost positive he works for Will Taft. He's playing some sort of game in which we have no say."

Laurel kept Ollie's confession to herself. She had to respect the secret. She would go to her grave before she told.

"Has Vallens hinted that?"

"In a sense, but nothing concrete. I resorted to desperate measures thinking two hundred dollars would provide incentive to leave. Hindsight shows a clear mistake on my part."

Brodie's fingertips traced the curve of her quivering lips ever so softly. She rested her face against the texture of his palm, wanting more than a touch, but somehow knowing it wouldn't come. He'd never act on unbridled desire that made her pulse race, for he'd blessed her upcoming nuptials with Murphy. "What are we going to do?" The whisper bubbled from a well deep within her.

"About what?"

"Vallens. Bert Blanchard. The Union Army." Then she added before losing courage, "And us."

"I've wanted you since the first time I laid eyes on the vision of you in lavender and lace. I won't deny it."

"So much that you gave me to your brother? Strange way of showing it."

Disappointment swept her that he didn't refute it.

"Things change, notions and feelings a man most desires to hold on to fade over time."

This confirmed she'd become nothing but a memory.

"The night in Murphy's garden before you left— was it lust that made you hold me in your arms? Was it the needs of your body that made you kiss me breathless?"

"Just let it be. Why do females have to examine and pick apart every little thing?"

"I believe you answered my question. Now, if you don't mind, Sheriff, it's late." Her knees wobbled when she pushed to her feet.

The muscles in Brodie's jaw twitched. "Vallens lays one hand on you, he'll be a dead man. Put that in your bonnet and smoke it."

⁓

The midnight hour found Laurel sitting at the kitchen table when Ollie stole quietly in from the alley. The barely touched cup of tea in Laurel's hands had long grown cold. She cradled the cup as if somehow never putting it down would magically change the past hour. The noise of the latch unglazed her eyes.

"Out sparking with Curley tonight?"

"Son of a blue belly, I swear you have divining powers."

"It doesn't take a fortune-teller to know when a woman is happy. No one but Curley can do that."

"That man can sure start a fire in me, yes indeedy."

"Guess that's fine and dandy long as the gentleman stays around to put it out once he lights it."

"What's taken the starch from your sails, girl? You were in fine enough spirits when I left."

Frustration disturbed the night's quiet. "Brodie came by."

"No need to say more. Nothing quite worse'n to leave a lady with a heap of embers sizzling and not nary an attempt to cool 'em with so much as a drop of water."

Truth burrowed past the irritation and brought a flush. The warmth of his fingertips stayed on her lips.

"I hate to disappoint you, Miss Know-It-All b'Dam, but I have no embers, sizzling or otherwise." Denial came easier than admitting Brodie had trampled tender feelings. His spurning stung her to the quick. She raised her chin a bit higher. "Not that it's any of your affair. Furthermore, it appears a certain meddlesome woman, who I won't name, told Brodie about Vallens and his threats."

At least Ollie had the courtesy to appear sheepish.

"My grandpappy, bless his soul, always said that if a problem's got its teeth in your privates and you ain't big enough to shake it loose, find someone to help pry that mouth apart before it has you singing in the Jesus choir." Ollie squinted through one eye while rummaging in her pocket, probably for that blasted pipe. "Figured it wouldn't hurt to give our new sheriff a full tally of the situation."

"I would appreciate being consulted before you run to him with our problems."

"You ain't got me hoodwinked for a minute. That's not the reason you got your tail feathers bunched up tight, is it?"

Laurel exploded. "Brodie should either lay out where we stand or get the hell out of my life. He gave some song and dance about regret and notions and feelings changing."

Ollie finally located the pipe. She pinched some tobacco between finger and thumb, sticking it in the corncob bowl.

"Girl, I can see you're on the warpath. Lord knows

you have just cause. The man plain don't know his own mind. One minute he's hot, the next he's cold. Something you gotta understand. He's scared of horning in on his brother's territory. I've seen it a thousand times."

"I'm stuck in a lie in the middle of no man's land which I can't cross. But why does Brodie keep coming around? To jab me with a sharp stick? If he carried an ounce of regard you'd think he'd stay far away."

Unless he took pleasure from watching her bleed.

"Because he cain't help it, and it don't do a lick of good to piss and moan about it."

"Heaven forbid, is it too much to know why he's bound and determined to relinquish everything to Murphy? And don't I have a say in the matter?"

"Men like Brodie Yates develop lockjaw when it comes to discussing such."

"No other has ever made my toes curl, my skin tingle, or given me reason to feel safe in my own bed."

"Snatch that shootin' star before it vanishes into the sunset. Look at this old fool standing before you. I could've had it, only I let it get away. Wished I hadn't."

Laurel dearly cried for courage to throw convention to the wind. How blessed to lie in the arms of the man she loved without dishonor or regret and not have him push her away.

And yet, would she grab hold if presented a chance?

The journey had taken so long. She'd never gotten this close to redeeming her tattered soul.

To sacrifice it now?

Shameless desire scampered with naughty abandon.

Dear God, why did she have to choose between redemption and love with Brodie Yates?

❧

"Sheriff Yates, yeah right." Brodie punched the pillow. On his back in the darkness, he stared at the red glow of the cigarette and listened to Blanchard's snores.

What in almighty had he gotten himself into? A wandering glance met with the piece of metal he'd unpinned and laid beside him. Wayward moonbeams through the window bounced off it.

He didn't need the sparkle to remind him he'd messed up.

Men of his sort? They had no need for anything other than a fast hand and a moving target.

No ties.

No ladies who waited through long, dreary nights.

No Lil.

Maybe Murphy could develop a softness for Nora, then again maybe not. Brodie dare not bank on it. However it played, Lil deserved more. Of all the ones he'd come across, she alone held power to blot the nameless faces of men he'd sent to eternity.

The ropes beneath the feather mattress creaked when he shifted to finger the shiny object.

The badge's raised lettering spoke of ties and a purpose for staying. Roots could grow if given half a shot and a speck of rain. Resentment didn't rest so much in what the job represented, but the fact the little piece of tin stole freedom to leave when he chose.

Even as the wish formed, he knew he couldn't ride on until he rid the town of Zeke Vallens. For Laurel. Keeping safe those he loved took priority no matter his own fate. He'd not returned to Redemption blindfolded.

Risk came with his decision. Risk he accepted in

exchange for seeing Murphy and laying flowers on his mother's grave.

But now that he'd done that?

This is what you've searched for over the whole country and half of Georgia. It's the one place you can call home and know the full meaning of the word.

Damn the truth.

Smoke from the dangling cigarette probably caused sudden watering in his eyes.

Curse those roots that already burrowed beneath tender shoots.

When he ripped them from the fertile soil, it would make the god-awful pain gripping him now feel like a tiny pinprick.

Stay and fight or…fight to stay?

Either way he'd lose something—his life, redemption, or his sanity.

Damn Vallens's sorry hide to hell and back.

Had that skunk not taken up residence in Redemption, Brodie could've delivered the two little ladies and handed Blanchard over to the town's bravest—if he could've found one brave soul. He would've told his brother good-bye and ridden on.

The bayou held a million areas far better suited for hiding. Few white men had seen some of the dark, backwater places he knew existed.

Meanwhile, the bargain he made with himself, not to mention the man upstairs, to spare Murphy's life hung by a thread.

Thank goodness for sturdy kitchen tables and his knack for angering pretty women. Otherwise it could've led to disaster.

Fighting the urge to take Laurel in his arms and kiss her until he stripped the ache from his soul had sapped every ounce of fortitude and then some.

Pure weakness almost destroyed them both.

"Sweet Georgia clay. Why did I have to give her the go ahead to marry Murph? I pushed her straight into his arms." Brodie's noisy grumbling disturbed the prisoner. Bert Blanchard grunted and rolled over before he resumed snoring.

This silver star trapped Brodie. Circumstance forced him to see her each day and not touch. The odds worked against him. Resistance to the current would wear him down to nothing.

Certain reality about tempting fate... Something would break sooner or later.

Mulling over the likelihood of being worthy of Laurel's love and trust sent heat rushing to his middle. A perfect wish. And yet one that bore little hope of fruition.

A familiar need tightened and rose, drawing taut his buckskin trousers.

Damn her throaty voice and big violet eyes.

For argument's sake he let his imagination run wild.

He fancied crawling inside her and hanging out a Do Not Disturb sign. And then, he'd show Laurel exactly how much he loved her.

Twenty

"HEARD THAT GOLDARNED MUSIC BOX." OLLIE SHOVED a cup in her hand when she came downstairs. "Slept nary a wink."

"I tried to keep quiet. Sorry."

"Truth of the matter, it weren't that. Couldn't shake Vallens's ugly leer over at the saloon. The cunning devil's so mean he'd suck eggs from a widow woman's basket. Bet he'd even hide the shells on a neighbor's porch."

"Stay away from him. Far away." Laurel sniffed the liquid before she took a sip.

"Cain't very well do that when he slinks around, popping up here and there when a body least expects."

"Maybe you should tell Curley. He could help."

"Not ready to do that right yet. Don't want to see the disappointment when he finds out I'm a thief. I ain't ever had a man treat me as some sort of prize before. It's sorta nice and I don't want to hurry the ruination of it."

"Do you think hearing it from Vallens will make it less hurtful?"

Ollie twisted the dishcloth. "Maybe just a mite longer."

The sadness and agony in a voice that had always spat out exactly what was on her mind was disconcerting. Ollie had always been quick to speak whether a body wished to hear it or not. Laurel didn't exactly take comfort either in the drawn whiteness around Ollie's lips.

"I have an idea. We're down to bare cupboards and it appears our long overdue shipment of meat went by way of China."

"And overland by camel to Egypt," Ollie added dryly.

"Let's catch the steamer to Jefferson. The *Lazy Jane* docks in a couple of hours. A peaceful ride up Big Cypress Bayou and back might soothe our jangled nerves. We'll forget the Grim Reaper for a day. The sound of water swishing over the paddle wheels and staring up at big, fluffy clouds might be nice."

"You've lost your mind. Folks'll expect open doors."

"With low stores, we can't offer much anyway."

"Nope. I ain't going anywhere near that carpetbagging, rabble-rousing mess. No sirree. You go and I'll take care of these wheybellies. I can whip up a mean batch of corn pones and boil a big pot of beans. That'll suffice, I reckon. And if it don't, our customers can go jump in the swamp."

"You're the most stubborn, cantankerous woman I've ever met or I'll eat your hat."

"You saying I cain't serve up a few vittles?" Smoke curled, blocking the one-eyed glare. "You saying I'm old and not up to such a measly task? I was cooking long before you ever seen a pot."

"Well, I can see you've got your back bowed. That you can do whatever you set a mind to isn't the issue."

The state of a frail heart didn't make it past her lips.

Or leaving her with God-knows-what up Vallens's sleeve.

"I have no earthly desire to go mixing with blue bellies so thick you can't put one foot in front of the other without kicking one in the shins. No thank ye. Ain't anything I'd take joy in—except maybe the kicking part."

"What about your angel of death and waiting for when he'll pounce?"

"Curley's here. That swill-pusher's been dying to sling out something more'n whiskey. We'll do just fine, thank you." Ollie raised her skirt, tugged a crisp roll of bills from beneath a garter, and pressed them into Laurel's palm. "Might as well use some of these new gen-u-wine railroad notes. I hear they're liable to spend better than the rest. Leastwise folks tend to think they do."

Laurel felt weak. And suspicious.

"Don't tell me you've gone into counterfeiting."

"A fool thing to say." Ollie dipped down into her bosom and fished out a gold double eagle. "Buy a new dress or a hat, one of them frilly kind with flowers on it. Turning a man's head could loosen up his tongue on intentions. Even Yates'."

Laurel's watery smile doubted that. She hesitated.

"Girl, unless you go, we might as well board up the joint. You've earned a break for working your fingers plumb to the bone. I only ask one favor."

"That depends."

Some things a girl couldn't promise.

"I want you to get shed of that store-bought smile. Come home wearing a real one that grows from deep inside, the kind that lights up your face."

Laurel's throat caught at mention of home. Truly, Ollie was her family and the café was more than a place to sleep.

"And another thing—steer clear of them damn boot-licking soldiers and that stockade, you hear?"

～✦～

The jailhouse door shielded Brodie from view. To say the gaze that followed Laurel up the gangplank of the *Lazy Jane* could be construed by some as ogling might be wrong. He simply preferred to admire. From a distance.

Soft bayou breeze ruffled the mass of raven ringlets piled atop her head, seeming to taunt his cowardice. She blew a kiss to Ollie and waved good-bye as the boat slowly gathered steam.

The razor-tongued monkey-woman had paid an early visit, informing him of Laurel's outing.

"Just in case you're interested." She'd winked.

He wished in vain for the ability to turn a blind eye. Fact remained, everything the lady did caught his full attention.

With vanilla and pecan praline pie filling his head, he barely noticed the stage halting in front of the hotel. Jeb Prater hobbled on a cane toward the conveyance. With every step, the boy's eyes flicked in constant motion. Word had it Jeb decided the climate had grown a mite on the warmish side.

Then movement at Gordon's Livery drew his attention. How the town bustled on this Monday.

Vallens's horse reared coming from the stables, its forelegs flailing. Brodie winced when the man dealt angry blows from a short crop. Apparently finding defiance futile, the horse let Vallens mount and they trotted west.

"Now where is he going?" Brodie didn't enjoy the sensation of tarantula legs crawling up his back.

Wolf-dog sprang from the shadows, loping beside his master down the road that would take them to Jefferson.

In an instant, the solution over the problem with Blanchard whipped into mind. He yanked off the sheriff badge, tossing it aside, and snatched keys from his desk drawer.

"Get a move on, Bert, I'm taking you for a ride."

The prisoner sat up. "Ain't going to no hanging without a trial first. I have rights, you know."

A stroll along the promenade deck melted Laurel's tension. Fresh breeze hinted at nothing more than rain and coming fall.

No sign here of threats…or broken hearts.

A flock of hungry egrets eager for scraps of bread must've taken joy in pelting the boat with droppings to thus mar the tranquil day. She hastened from their line of fire to an overhang.

Darn Ollie's dead-set ways. She shouldn't have left her.

Preoccupied, Laurel almost dove over the railing when the steam engine flushed out in a loud blow-down. It shouldn't have lifted her two feet in the air, considering how many times a day the sound echoed up and down the bayou. Her unfortunate decision to stand directly above the outlet was to blame, for she'd received the full blast. The tragedy of the *Mittie Stephens* and sixty poor souls a couple of months ago shook her nerves. And Vallens.

She closed her eyes and tried to recall every wrinkle in Ollie's features, the sound of the little bell over the café door, and Murphy's happy glow when she vowed to marry him.

Instead, the deeply lined face sculpted by the wind of a thousand battles flashed before her eyes.

And a sweat-stained hat that rattled.

By the time the gangplank lowered in Jefferson, her jitters had vanished until a sweeping glance lit upon the huge stockade called Sand Town erected above the bayou at Texas and Common Streets. She'd take pains to stay removed from there.

Considerable change had occurred since she'd last viewed the town through the eyes of an innocent young girl.

However, some sights remained true to recollection. Bales of cotton lined the wharf. Dock workers formed a steady stream, unloading crates and boxes that bore the king of spades playing card. With few able to read, she recalled her father telling how each city's assigned card eliminated costly errors.

Pieces of her former self fell into place with the haunting tunes the deckhands sang while they worked.

She hurried down Walnut to Polk Street, taking care of business first and foremost. Thank her lucky stars for the office in town; otherwise she'd have to traipse all the way out to the smelly packing plant two miles south. This saved hiring a hack and paying the toll to cross the bridge.

A gentleman who might've passed for Jake's twin twirled a mustache when she entered the J.P. Dunn Meat Cannery.

"Yes, madam?"

"I'm inquiring about an order for Ollie's Café bound for Redemption three weeks ago. It never arrived."

"Let me check our records." The man opened a thick book and ran a bony finger down a list. "Hmm. It appears someone scratched through the name, thus we never shipped."

The odd and costly misunderstanding raised her ire.

"Why would anyone do such a thing? I can assure you, my good man, no one canceled the shipment."

"I wouldn't know of matters that go on in the female mind."

"Meaning?" She stiffened, glaring at the pompous oaf.

"To state it indelicately, women have somewhat, shall we say, notorious peculiarity for changing their minds on a whim. Give them this and they want that."

"Well, I never."

A graying man walked from behind a curtain. "Pennybacker, what the devil are you doing? Customers keep our doors open and pay your wage, which by the way I can terminate very quickly."

Pennybacker's face reddened. "Indeed, I beg your pardon. I deeply regret the error and my statement, madam."

"As do I," she mumbled.

Evidently not mollified, Pennybacker's boss

ordered, "If I were you, I'd get moving to the rear door. A farmer brought a load of hogs to take to the packing plant for slaughter. While you're at it, stay there until I decide you're fit to be around something other than dead carcasses."

"Yes sir, Mr. Dunn. I'm already on my way, sir."

Mr. Dunn swiveled back to her. "Now, tell me what I can do to fix the problem, young lady."

Laurel emerged with a promise that the beef and pork would be on the *Lazy Jane*'s return trip.

Sedberry's Apothecary on Dallas came next for a certain elixir touted for amazing cures. Perhaps it would fix Ollie's heart. That would indeed be miraculous.

Newly cut lumber prevailed over burned hulks of businesses left gutted by a huge fire the previous year rumored to be the handiwork of a carpetbagger named G. W. Smith. Carpenters worked in a frenzy, some hammering while others carried long boards up ladders. She swiveled this way and that to dodge catastrophe. The hubbub grated. Redemption's peaceful quiet had advantages. Eager to prevent a trampling and bypass an ogling group of soldiers, she crossed to the other side and didn't slow for several blocks.

A cameo necklace in the window of Ney and Brothers drew her. The white silhouette overlaid on onyx spoke of purity that a respected, fashionable lady would wear. Mindful to turn away from her reflection, she fancied tying the black velvet ribbon and letting the cameo rest in the hollow of her throat.

The daydream burst.

Ladies of questionable nature would never own such beauty.

Meanwhile, Sedberry's beckoned.

"Would you have some tincture of hawthorn berries?" she inquired of the gentleman inside.

"Yes indeed. However, I fervently hope someone other than yourself has need of it. What a dear shame to lose a pretty one in the flower of her youth."

If he only knew she'd long lost the flower of her youth. She'd aged rapidly.

"It's for another. How much do I owe?"

The man accepted the gold double eagle and bit down. "Can't be too careful these days. Some feller's coating silver coins and passing them." A warning came along with the appropriate change: "Follow the directions carefully."

Laurel slipped the precious bottle into her handbag. She closed the door behind her, praying she'd bought Ollie a few extra days.

Jars of candy and dry goods in J. M. Murphy and Company waylaid her. Redemption's small mercantile devoted its limited space to things less frivolous. Busy tallying a woman's bill, a male clerk gave her a fleeting glance.

"Make yourself at home. Someone will be with you shortly."

She spied the ready-made dresses hanging from hooks on the wall, more rare in the bayou than candy. She moved toward the stylish cut of a pretty blue, fingering the taffeta and silk.

"You have the figure for that if I do say so."

Laurel turned. A few gray streaks added matronly flair to the dark-haired woman. Twinkling eyes added humor.

"Oh, I can't buy it. I'm only browsing."

"Passionflower. That's what they call the color. Isn't that the most romantic name you ever heard tell of?"

The woman's bold examination gave Laurel warning pricks.

"You're not from here. I know every dog, coon, and hen house. I'm Mrs. Georgia Rutabaga of the Tyler Rutabagas. But say, you do resemble the James clan over at Turkey Creek."

Her heart skipped a beat. "I just arrived on the *Lazy Jane*. I wouldn't know them."

Mrs. Rutabaga whipped out a shimmering lavender hidden behind the others. "This was made for you. With those violet eyes I guarantee it'd capture a young gentleman's affections."

The pulse roared in Laurel's ears. She struggled to breathe but it got hung in the rawness of her throat.

"No!" The word burst harsh and brittle.

Alarm crossed the woman's face. "Oh dear. I wouldn't have upset you for the world and everything in it."

Laurel fought nausea and spun for the door, leaving poor Mrs. Rutabaga, of the Tyler Rutabagas, with her mouth gaping.

Barbershop, millinery, and stables passed in a blur. When Laurel regained her senses, she stood in front of a sign stating Excelsior Hotel. Years ago it'd carried the Irvine House name. She dropped to a bench amid the jangle of the departing stage.

Contact with the lavender had shaken her to the core. Time should've lessened that pain. Ollie assured her it would. The agony shouldn't persist fresh as the night she'd escaped.

Maybe she and being normal had forever parted company.

Streams of people entered and exited the hotel, each sending curious stares. Afraid they might approach, she moved on. Sidestepping blue bellies set her on an aimless path that led back to Dallas Street in front of the telegraph office.

A chance glance through the open door froze the blood in her veins. A black-frocked figure stood inside. The dog poised beside the man confirmed it.

That Vallens may have followed her made her head whirl. Did he telegraph Will Taft?

Laurel ducked into the nearest shop when he exited. Through the window she stared in horror when he gripped a young girl's arm. There was something familiar in the sweet dimples.

Shock rippled through her. Features of a forgotten vision took shape.

Resemblance to her sister was more than wishful fancy.

In the back of her mind had lurked the possibility of running into some of her family with them so near, but it hadn't seemed anything beyond a lost daydream. Until this moment.

The shiny cinnamon-colored hair, pert nose, and sparkling hazel eyes were unmistakable. Her sister had grown into a striking beauty. Quick calculation made Hannah, who'd been nine back then, fifteen years old. Laurel's age when the world turned upside down.

Vallens dragged Hannah down an alley while Wolf-dog chased an apple wagon much to his master's ire. Hate overwhelmed her.

She wouldn't let him steal her sister.

Keeping from sight, she followed. Luckily, barrels littered the alley. She ducked behind them, wondering why the girl didn't scream. Then she noticed Vallens' hand clamped over Hannah's mouth. A discarded piece of two-by-four fit Laurel's palm perfectly. Silently, she crept. Intent on subduing the struggling form, Vallens didn't hear her approach.

Cracking his head with a mighty blow, Laurel grabbed the girl and sprinted toward the bustle of town. The instant they gained the street, an arm reached out and pulled them around the corner.

The hiss of snake rattles seemed part of some illusion, but the voice lent credence.

"Get behind me, Lil. I'll take care of this."

Brodie blocked Vallens, who'd raced after his prize. "Touch them again and you die."

Laurel couldn't take her eyes from the bounty hunter. Surprise then anger switched places when they collided at the jagged scar. Brodie's frigid advice suspended the bounty hunter's hand in mid-reach.

How or from where Brodie had come didn't matter. Relief that he had quelled Laurel's shaking knees.

"Shenandoah. Or should I say Sheriff?" Vallens's foolhardy attempt to goad a fight would buy trouble he likely hadn't considered.

"I don't give a flying squirrel which you use, though if you bothered to notice, I'm not wearing a badge. I feel obliged to inform you that molesting young women does happen to still be a crime in Texas." The Colt hung low on Brodie's hip. His hands flexed, the cold rebel in him seeming once again to find a home on familiar ground.

Others less accustomed to the subtle tic of his jaw, steel gray in his glint, or defiant crooked smile might've missed the signs. But Laurel's and Brodie's souls had interlaced in those long, steamy nights, weaving a sturdy cloth no weapon could penetrate.

Only two things could unravel the threads.

Treachery and mistrust.

Heaven help her. She'd had plenty of both.

A mass exodus of every onlooker who suspected abrupt flying lead brought her back to the present.

"Don't want any trouble. Just having a polite conversation with the little miss." A sneer curled Vallens's upper lip. "No law agin that, is there?"

Hannah shivered, huddling closer.

"Leave them be unless you be next in line at the undertaker's." Brodie never blinked an eye, his gaze focused.

"You're mighty self-righteous for one who could end up in the stockade. A word in the right ear will take care of you."

The air Laurel sucked in struggled to fill the ache in her chest. Why had Brodie walked into a place fraught with danger when he knew the possible result?

Surely he couldn't think himself invincible.

Or think her worthy of such great risk?

Even while Laurel denied that bit of speculation, quivers raced the length of her body. No one would spin a weighted roulette wheel against the house and think to win.

Not on her account.

Dear God. It forever landed on black, the color of sin.

And the number thirteen.

Brodie's long legs were planted. "One thing I learned well during the war—men with holes can't make any noise. Just give me half a reason."

Arrogance twisted the scarred face into a hundred different roads, all of them leading to places the man shouldn't go.

"This ain't your town. You got no rights here."

"Why do men suddenly think they can *own* towns? Me and Persuader might dispute that logic. It's a damn good day to lose a bet."

Finally, Vallens raised his hands and stood back.

Brodie flashed a grim stare. "Laurel, take your friend and wait at the sheriff's office."

Blinding heat of the gray-eyed rebel bridged the fortress she'd built and brazenly stole her from its sanctuary.

Perhaps she'd wronged him.

Perhaps the cloth hadn't unraveled, merely snagged and needing repair.

And perhaps he did think her someone of worth.

Vallens spoke low, words meant for her alone. "Taft might consider a younger surrogate fair trade, I'm thinking."

The threat reached further than Vallens intended. Brodie grabbed his throat, pinning him against the rough stone wall.

"Should either lady get so much as a hair out of place, I'll come for you. No rock'll be big enough for your mangy hide to crawl under that I won't find you."

Twenty-one

BRODIE YATES FOUND SATISFACTION WHEN COLOR drained from Vallens's face, leaving the scar a ghostly trail to a past that persisted in haunting. His grip tightened. How easy it would be to give in and snap his old adversary's neck.

One thing kept him from murder—the lady who held his heart.

Each time he gazed into Laurel's eyes, he saw a painting of two bodies, complete with heads.

Those brief glimpses let him see the person he could become.

The one she believed he could be.

His hold slackened and released the rotten piece of humanity. Vallens straightened his drab frock coat. Brodie carefully watched not only the bold, but also each subtle movement, through narrowed slits.

He'd lived with hatred of one kind or another for most of his life. Though he sent more men to glory than any judge or jury, each occurred only when things reached the kill or be killed stage. Never had he stolen a man's lifeblood in anger.

The depth of rage he felt now scared the living daylights out of him.

The cold, lethal piece of steel at his side called to him.

Scum such as Vallens had cost Laurel six years. By God Almighty, she'd have an opportunity to reclaim her soul even if Brodie had to help it along. Icy daggers he shot the man in black might've sent him to hell and back, except Vallens avoided eye contact, preferring to edge toward his six shooter instead.

"Go ahead. I'd love to scratch this itchy trigger finger," Brodie said.

"Ain't over yet." Vallens's arm dropped limply. "There's a time and place coming."

"Name it. Me and Persuader will be there."

Brodie started toward the sheriff's office when wolf-dog lunged with teeth bared. Motionless and quiet, Brodie's eyes delivered a message that spoke the animal's own language. Wolf tucked his tail and lay down, appearing bewildered by his unaccustomed encounters.

Brodie found the two women pacing in front of the stone building of the sheriff's office. The bright glimmer swimming in Laurel's stare released a rush of emotion so intense he choked.

He longed to take her in his arms, comfort her, and kiss away each sorrow until they shriveled and died. But he couldn't. She belonged to Murphy.

With the toes of his boots touching her lacy petticoats, he let her fresh scent pillage the best part remaining of a lost love that used to be. He prayed for strength to pull himself from the whirlpool trying to suck him under.

"Don't worry. The man's not too bright, but I don't think he'll bother you." At least not until Vallens got reinforcements. But Brodie didn't share that tidbit with her. She was scared enough.

"What happens when you're not around? What will Vallens do then?" The half sob strangling her voice tightened his jaw.

Great Johnny Reb.

He'd rearrange each star in the sky and move Texas to the other side of the world if he held that in his power. Only it wouldn't fix anyone's problems.

Not hers, not his, and not the ache in his chest.

"That man, what did he want?" Except for the reddish hair and hazel eyes, the young woman who spoke could pass for Laurel.

"Zeke Vallens is looking for easy money. Selling human flesh wouldn't make him a bit squeamish." Brodie watched the fear in her white face deepen and swore under his breath.

"Sell me? To who?"

"It doesn't matter. We're not about to let him, so put that from your mind." Laurel placed protective arms about the girl's shoulders. "This is Brodie Yates. He's a friend."

"I apologize for scaring you, miss. Just be aware of the man's capabilities." He opened the door for them. "We don't warn lightly. I'll bend Sheriff Roberts' ear about the particulars so he'll know and watch out for you."

"I haven't thanked you for coming to my aid," the girl said.

Laurel touched her companion's shoulder. "Honey, there's no need. You'd have done the same."

"I should've paid more attention. Mama says I'm too trusting for my own good." Soft laughter stole from the girl's lips. "I'm Hannah James."

Brodie jerked about. No wonder she resembled Laurel. The warning shake of Laurel's head begged him to keep quiet. She hadn't told the girl who she was. He wondered why.

Hannah suddenly hugged Laurel. "Take pity and tell me again who you are so I won't feel like an imbecile."

Laurel gently pushed Brodie. "Go on inside. Hannah and I want to gab a bit out here. Lady talk."

"I suppose, but don't wander off."

Laurel pretended to adjust the laces of her high-topped shoe. Excitement of seeing the girl had swept aside caution. A fake name? A harmless thing really. Others likely did it on a regular basis. No one would know.

Except herself.

And living with lies grew old. Adding more could further hinder reaching the pinnacle of the thing she most coveted.

She took a deep breath. "My name's Laurel."

"That's pretty. I once had a sister by that name."

Pain spiraled, gouging a deep swath inside before it lodged in her chest. How foolish to risk discovery. Still, she couldn't stifle a thirst for tidbits about her loved ones.

A million questions poised on the tip of her tongue. "I gather from your tone you've suffered tragedy."

"It's dreadful." Tears welled in Hannah's eyes.

Laurel shifted her gaze to a distant spot, wishing she'd have moved the conversation to talk of a colder winter or how many drops of water it took to fill Big Cypress Bayou.

"Then, you shan't speak of it. Let's enjoy the sunshine."

"How silly of me. Mama says we must go on. Some days it's very hard. I miss my Laurel as much now as the day she vanished. Do you have any brothers or sisters?"

Laurel swallowed a startled gasp before she quickly replied, "I regret I don't."

"That's a pity. I can't imagine life without family."

Excruciating torture came in being unable to forget that very closeness. She'd not shared her family with anyone but Ollie.

"Your mother… Does she live near?" Laurel's voice dropped to a raspy whisper. "And what of your father?"

"We have a place on Turkey Creek. They continue to farm the same parcel of land they've owned for thirty-odd years. Of course, they couldn't now without my brothers' help."

The news made her breath quicken. Less than a half hour away by buggy. So near. And yet so far.

Hannah's tentative smile raised haunting memories. "Where's your home, Laurel?"

"Miles down the bayou," she answered vaguely.

"Papa and my brothers keep a tight rein. I've not traveled more than ten miles from the farm. I guess I can't hold that against them, considering what happened."

William Taft's ugly face loomed in her memory. Hannah didn't realize what evil awaited those who strayed unprotected from home.

"Here's a piece of advice from someone who knows—you haven't missed out."

"You've probably been just about everywhere. I think someday I'd like to visit St. Louis."

"No!" The word resounded like a rifle shot. Hannah jumped. Laurel softened her voice. "I'm sorry. I only wish to stress you're better off for having stayed close to home. The most precious things in life are here. Don't throw away what you have believing life is more grand and interesting elsewhere. Believe me, it isn't."

Her family had celebrated birthdays, Christmases, and baptisms without her. She'd missed each holiday and fun time.

She wondered about Jeremiah and his pet raccoon. About Millie who no longer had need of the baby blanket Laurel had sewn with uneven stitches.

And about the fading of her mother's hair.

But to get the answers to her questions carried too steep a price with no guarantee.

"Thank you again, Laurel. I almost felt my sister had returned." Hannah glanced up and down the street. "My brothers Quaid and Rafe must be worried about me."

"They're here?" More ripples swept through Laurel.

"Most likely at the saloon. The bottle eases powerful blame over letting our sister disappear. Papa'll have their hides though if they've gotten liquored up again."

Laurel's heart lurched. Other casualties lay in the wake of the crime. How ironic to have thought herself the sole victim.

Less than an hour later, Laurel straddled the big Appaloosa in front of Brodie. She was a tangled mass of nerves. Her sister walked out of her life again and ripped open unhealed wounds. Heaven only knew when she'd get that close to family again.

Between Zeke Vallens, the parting with Hannah, and half expecting a contingent of soldiers to surround the hated rebel spy any second, a hot frying pan looked more enticing by the second.

~

"Smokey, take us home, boy." Brodie gave a gentle nudge amid the creaking of saddle leather.

In horse-talk, the snort and toss of his head might've said the animal thought it high time to get out of hostile territory.

"I should've sailed back on the steamer," Laurel said from her place in front of him on the horse.

Male heat where her bottom rested snugly against Brodie's lap aroused yearning she'd worked night, day, and four years to forget. Such ridiculous ideas came half past late.

Notions and feelings change, he'd said.

"Not a chance, pretty lady. I'm not letting you out of my sight."

"You expect Vallens to make good on his threats?"

"I may have given him second thoughts when I told him what to expect with his persistence. But I'm not much of a betting man."

The clipped statement left no doubt as to what had transpired. Brodie must've laid down some strong advice, although it brought meager comfort. Icy fear held her in a glacial clutch.

"I'll stretch anyone out on a marble slab who tries

to harm Hannah, without batting an eyelash. What those monsters did to me they will never do to another member of my family, not while I live." Laurel's granite tone left no doubt of her feelings.

"So Hannah James is truly your kin?"

"My younger sister. Our meeting almost seemed designed by fate." She wished she could say likewise for the muscular arms resting on each of her hips, holding the reins.

His light touch made her feel most protected...

Most safe and valued...

She just wished that the bridge between them hadn't already washed out. Hope of crossing back over had long passed.

"I fail to understand why you didn't tell her who you are."

"Discovering the facts would add more grief, not ease it." She gripped the saddle horn tighter. "What can she remember, anyway?"

"Plenty. Why in God's name don't you go home?"

"I can't." The lump of hard clay sat in her stomach much easier than the bitter truth. "I won't."

"You can live with them fearing what happened yet never knowing the truth?" His voice held deceptive softness. "That's not the lady I knew."

"They believe I'm dead. That's the way it'll stay. That's my final word on the subject. It's much better for everyone." Laurel despised the brittle edge that again snuck into her voice. She could no more help it than stop loving the wrong man.

"Better for everyone except you."

The answer came like the soft, whispering wind.

His breath ruffled the top of her hair, sending shivers down her spine. If he knew the effect of his nearness, the fire their closeness ignited, he'd hustle her back to the *Lazy Jane* faster than lightning could split the heavens and singe a body's eyebrows.

"I'll be fine." Eventually, she added silently.

Smokey meandered through tall pines toward home. Moss-bearded water tupelo in the bayou reflected Laurel's spirit, for they also appeared old and weary from keeping constant vigil. Approaching fall also brought yellow color to the river birch and scarlet turning of black gum. A pair of loons played catch-me-if-you-can across the placid swamp.

"Have you ever seen a more beautiful place?" he whispered in her ear, his arms stealing around her waist.

Sick of fighting, Laurel relaxed. Thinking to rest against his hard chest for the barest moment would be a mistake. Still, she couldn't help it. Beneath flesh and muscle beat a steady rhythm she'd have to be dead to ignore—along with the rigid bulge poking her skirts, his erection clearly disputing his claim of notions fading.

A bittersweet smile formed. What she'd give to be free. Respectability and doing the honorable thing presented more difficulty than she'd dreamed.

"Sunlight on your hair would turn a raven green with jealousy. Your strands are so dark they're almost blue."

Laurel kept silent, torn between stopping what they both couldn't live without and fear he would. Lord knew she'd love nothing more than to have the gray-eyed rebel stroke her bare skin. Tingles fluttered up and down, inside and out.

Before she could nip passion in the bud, Brodie nuzzled her neck. The same gentle caress from long ago, his lips traced a path up to her jaw.

"Pure silk. Your skin carries the taste of fresh rainwater. You've driven me out of my mind ever since I rode into town." His hoarse declaration sent tremors of gladness through Laurel.

This was undeniable proof he'd lied last night.

Brodie Yates wanted her.

And yet despite everything Laurel couldn't let him say more. Them being together was painfully wrong. Regardless of his tender embrace, regardless of the dewy flush his kisses brought to her skin, and regardless how very much she wanted to welcome the glorious abandon that tempted her, she must honor one simple promise.

"We can't do this. I won't wrong Murphy."

"Then why does it feel so damn right?" he growled.

"I spent too many years in that hell-hole to throw away what I've gained." Laurel twisted to face him. "Do you know what it's like to see your reflection in a mirror or a window without turning away in disgust? I don't want to ruin finding out. One day I'll remove the black cloths from the mirrors and actually like the woman staring back. I have a chance to hold my head up, look honest, God-fearing folks in the eye, and not feel shame for a single, blessed thing."

"I reckon we both have a lot of backwater swamp to tread before we reach that point."

And trying to avoid alligators and evil in every shadow.

"Pushing away what I desperately want to accept is the hardest thing I've ever done."

"The thought of you married to Murph…" Pure torture thickened Brodie's voice. "I can't let it happen. You ask too much."

She twisted in the saddle and traced the crevices around his mouth, fingered the rebellious lock of hair that fell onto his forehead.

"Murphy found something decent in me. I won't dishonor him. Let me break the engagement first." She couldn't help but rub a little salt. "Besides, you gave your blessing, don't forget."

"You're devilish, you know that? It's a low blow bringing that up. For your information I didn't mean a word of it. Get one thing clear, little Miss Tease, I won't let you marry my brother. You're mine."

Though a crooked grin accompanied the statement, it brought out her Irish blood. "You won't *let* me?"

"You can wipe the war paint off your face. You know what I mean. You belong to me. Always have. Always will."

Smokey came to a standstill and swung his head around as if sensing a good argument and wanted to catch every word.

"Is that a fact? I think the excitement in town must've addled your brain. And should I wish to marry your brother, then that's what I'll do. I'm no child to order about."

Why had she said that? She didn't wish to wed Murphy.

"Of a certainty, I've never found anything but full grown woman." Snake rattles on the felt hat warned of danger. "Would you ruin three lives merely to prove a point?"

"If you think that, you don't know me at all."

"Then why in sweet Jezzie did you cause such a ruckus?"

"I didn't care for your lordly attitude."

He noticed at last they weren't moving and touched the animal's flanks. "Smokey, you flea-bitten snot bag, what'd you stop for? It's impolite to eavesdrop on a conversation."

"You're doing it again."

His deep sigh fluttered the top of her hair. "What?"

"Now you're bossing around your poor horse."

"He's used to it. Besides, he has no choice."

A great blue heron passed over and landed in the boggy marsh.

"Arguing is the last thing I want," he went on. "In my feeble bumbling I simply tried to make it clear how I feel about you."

"Me, too. I accept your apology."

One bit of good came from it all—the sparring had doused the heated passion that had come close to scorching them both.

"I'll thank you to keep your hands, and your kisses, to yourself for now. Never tempt me into sullying my honor again."

"Yes, ma'am. When I see how far you've come, I can almost buy an acre or two of your dream. Maybe putting down roots can give a man purpose other than staying alive."

"Like Ollie's grandpappy told her, 'If'n you don't take that first step, you ain't ever going nowhere.'" Laurel suddenly laughed, realizing what she'd spouted. "That old skinflinty woman's got me quoting chapter and verse now."

"Her salty tongue does tend to grow on you, doesn't it?"

Laurel touched the saddlebag to make sure the elixir rode easy and said a silent prayer it worked.

"If you're so all-fired het up on becoming a respectable lady, then quit rubbing the match against the flint." A groan followed the order. "Remember you still belong to me."

Laurel squirmed, trying to move from the snug pocket his legs had created.

"You keep doing that and I'm likely to forget about our agreement and your purpose. I'll sling that made-for-loving body of yours off this horse onto a patch of sweet grass so quick it'll make you dizzy."

Heat flooded her face. "I'm only trying to keep from—"

"Hellfire and damnation! Be still."

She sniffed, kept her back ramrod straight, and hands glued to the saddle horn. He had a lot of nerve blaming her, seeing how he'd insisted she ride with him instead of taking the steamer.

Men.

"Brodie, you never explained why you went to that devil's den, of all places. You're a fine one to speak of death wishes. Please say you didn't do such a dim-witted thing for my benefit."

"And if I did? What'd be wrong with that?"

The balmy afternoon sun blazed.

"Plenty, Mr. Rebel. You could've hired a street crier to advertise your presence and gotten less notice. Now, the Billy Yanks definitely know your whereabouts."

Guilt would make living with that burden impossible.

"I had a job to do and I did it."

"For me."

"Who I happen to care about. Besides, keeping you safe only played a part in my... How did you put it? Dim-witted plan? I needed to get rid of Blanchard. I told Sheriff Roberts how Redemption lacked a lawman. My solution to a problem."

"You already quit the job?" Her heart sank. Breaking ties to the town, his brother, and her seemed a sure sign he was ready to ride out. Talk about roots and saying she belonged solely to him confused the life out of her. She'd give anything to know what was going on in that head of his.

Did he simply seek another source of amusement?

Or torture?

Old doubts taunted her. Had he really moved that far from tricks and deception?

Yet, he'd ridden into the midst of the enemy and faced a death angel to assure no harm came to her.

"It would appear so, my dear. I'm not cut out to be a lawman. Redemption needs someone who likes low pay and a hard cot."

Twenty-two

LAUREL SHOULD'VE BLESSED THE SIGHT OF Redemption. Instead, regret and forlorn sadness bound her in a shroud by the time she slid from Brodie's lap to solid ground.

Ollie's bandy legs reminded her of the pump handle on a water spout when the woman scrambled through the café door.

"Goldarned it. What happened? I put you aboard the steamer and you come riding in on horseback."

"Vallens followed me. I'll give you the full report later." Laurel turned and got stuck in the anguished stare of a thousand disappointments. "I don't express gratitude well. They didn't exactly teach that in charm school. Take care, Brodie."

He handed her the precious package from Sedberry's. "Likewise. Promise to keep your guard up."

Against Vallens or himself? He failed to say. Perhaps both. And he'd not offered to expand further on why he gave up the sheriff job. Her suspicions didn't bode well.

Before he coaxed Smokey toward the stables, he

leaned and whispered, "Remember who you belong
to, lady."

The Appaloosa pranced down the street, carrying the tall rider. The fragrance of shaving soap and
leather—and the soft hiss of familiar rattles—wafted
on the bayou breeze.

Ollie crossed her arms and tapped her foot. "You
gonna fiddle-faddle there all day? The *Lazy Jane*
brought a whole passel of meat to do something with."

"Thank goodness. Glad the trip accomplished
something." Other than twisting her emotions six
ways to Sunday.

"Give me the lowdown. I'm about to bust a gut."

Laurel herded the woman into the café. "Which
version do you want, plain or fancy?"

"Pretty sassy, aren't you?" Ollie perched on the
edge of a chair in the kitchen, puffing away on the
pipe. "Fancy'll do."

The account evoked a longer string of "dadblast-
eds" and "son of a bluejackets" than Laurel could
ever remember in one sitting. Of course, she never
breathed a word of the ride home. That was her secret
to keep. Had she shared that, it would've brought out
the "damn scoundrels" and "scalawags" list.

"I'll blame myself, and rightly so, if harm befalls
Hannah."

"Cain't help what that mealy-mouthed swamp rat
does." Ollie cocked her head to the side and squinted.
"Did you tell your sister who you are?"

"I couldn't."

"You should've. The girl deserves the truth."

"Peace serves my family better than shame and

disgrace." Both had become regular visitors and neither made the pillow any softer at night.

"You have pretty odd thinking for a smart gal."
Ollie put the teakettle on to boil. "You think they rest
easy? Your sister's so broken-hearted she cain't bear to
speak of you, your brothers have taken to drowning
their guilt in a bottle, and your poor mama and daddy,
Lord only knows what they lug around day in and day
out. Don't sound like any peace I ever saw."

Laurel evaded Ollie's look that declared she'd been
nesting with a gaggle of loons all afternoon.

"After what occurred, it's simply not safe for Hannah
or them."

"A limp, sorry answer. Ever heard of secret visiting? There's ways, should you want to. Not knowing
whether you're dead or alive will eat a hole clean
through. Give 'em an end to the grieving. Let 'em
bury the past, dadblasted."

"Even if I could, I don't know how or where to start."

Ollie's callused palms rubbed hers, the dear face
becoming lost in a teary blur.

"That's what I'm here for."

When did the rightness of it become merged with
what she'd have to sacrifice? The loathing in her
parents' eyes would destroy what remained of the part
William Taft had left.

"I think of them each morning, and their faces are
the last thing I see at night. I die a little more inside
each day," Laurel whispered in agony.

"Then do it. Go see them. Set the past straight."

"And if they spit in disgust and turn away? What
then?"

"Being scared is as natural as breathing. The longer you hold off the harder it is to suck in air. Take it from an old sourdough, find a speck of happiness. Give 'em a chance, girl."

Doubts churned some of that Georgia clay Brodie spoke of into hard cement. How great were the odds they'd forgive and forget?

"I promise to give it some thought."

Evidently that satisfied Ollie. At least for the time being. "Now, what's in the package you brought from Jefferson? Too small for a dress or a new hat." Ollie rubbed her hands together. "Let me see."

"It's something for you. Tincture of hawthorn berries."

"Well, you can guzzle it yourself 'cause I ain't putting a drop of that stuff in my mouth. Nope. One of those carpetbagging leeches talked you into parting with good money, did they?"

Laurel sighed. This might be harder than she thought.

~⁕~

Beating the sun up the next morning, she decided Murphy would hear the truth, the whole, sordid, unvarnished truth.

He'd thank her for releasing him from scandal.

In a few hours, she'd breathe freely without laboring under the heavy weight of lies. She hopped from bed.

Ollie's open door and absence in the kitchen raised a few concerns, which she reasoned away. Probably spent the night with Curley, doing what lovers did. Color rose in her cheeks. She didn't care for such thoughts. Not that Ollie didn't deserve the full measure of happiness. Laurel merely preferred to not think of a parent figure finding sexual joy.

Like it or not, the woman had assumed a motherly role.

Still, Ollie hadn't appeared at a den of sin like the Black Garter looking for salvation. And she had spent a goodly amount of time in the cardsharp Frenchie Devereaux's company.

A hot cup of tea during the wait for appropriate calling hours helped clear her unsettling thoughts.

To say what she had put off too long would take every ounce of courage. Ollie had yet to make an appearance when the clock landed on eight and she grabbed her shawl.

"My lands, child. Come on in." Etta wiped the flour off her hands with the apron and took Laurel's wrap.

"Perhaps I've arrived too early."

"Not in this house. Mr. Murphy is raring to go. Now Mr. Brodie, he's another story. That one hasn't bothered to rouse for breakfast."

Even better. After narrowly averting disaster yesterday, she'd prefer to skip another encounter at the moment.

The intimate scene inside Murphy's room stopped her short. Nora bent over the patient, giving him a shave. The Indian woman's long braids snaked down each bosom and rested on Murphy's bare chest. Several seconds elapsed in which Laurel debated on leaving. But when she backed out, he saw her.

"Don't go," he called. "You're in time to watch Nora shear the sheep. I had hoped to surprise you."

Laurel took the empty chair and clasped her hands

to stop their nervous twitching. "I'll enjoy your helplessness," she said, eying the sharp straight razor Nora held.

"No mercy. A man in his sickbed and can't get a lick of respect from any of you females."

"Pay price for pretty smile and winsome ways." Nora scraped rough whiskers from a section of jaw.

Murphy winked. "I got Nora fooled. And here she thought I had the charm of a potato-digger."

"Better watch it. Remember who's holding the razor."

"Lady right." Nora's mischievous eyes glistened. "Ever hear them say the only good Injun is a dead one?"

Abruptly, Murphy's face darkened. "I warned you. Never say that again. Doesn't matter what your origin. Not to me. There are more important things in life."

Would he think differently when Laurel revealed her scarlet past? He appeared quite willing to overlook other things.

Nora shrugged. "I hear worse. Not deaf."

Uncomfortable silence lay in the wake of the exchange when at last Murphy's mood lightened. "Besides, Nora's worked too hard snatching me from the jaws of death. She'll not ruin her handiwork by slitting my throat now."

"Keep talking, yellow eyes, and we see."

Nora finished the task without further banter, gathered the utensils, and left.

"Come here, love. See how a clean-shaven face kisses."

How could she do the right thing when it sought to begin so wrong? Kissing wouldn't help the telling come easier. He noticed her hesitation and patted the bed.

Laurel's knees trembled when she stood. "We must talk."

"After you come and perform your pre-wifely duty first."

So much for doing the right thing.

He pulled her into his arms once she sank onto the mattress. Hope for averting close contact fled.

Desperate though she was to get things in the open, she had no heart for kicking a man flat on his back.

"Now, what pressing business do you have on the agenda?"

Strands of guilt twisted around her soul like ivy encircling a tree trunk—poison ivy. If only he knew she'd already changed her mind and given her heart to another. And worse, what would it do to him, how would he feel to discover his own brother occupied the place he once held?

Dear God, what a mess I've made of things.

∼⁂∼

Brodie wiped the shaving residue off and listened to voices from the next room. The early hour seemed a bit strange for Laurel to visit. He dressed quickly and opened the door.

"I want out of this bed and I won't argue about it!" Murphy's thunder echoed in the hall.

"Nora thinks it's too soon and I happen to agree."

Laurel's throaty voice made Brodie reconsider. He could do without another dose of the misery their encounters left. The last lingered in his mind like the frenzied cacophony of a flock of grackles.

Before he could move swiftly past, Laurel sped from the room and into his chest.

He lunged to break her fall, the contact jarring the

breath from him in more ways than one. Warning bells clanged when he found himself floating in smoky lavender pools staring upward.

Her pink, open mouth drew him and every rational thought vanished. Brodie savored the taste of her on his tongue very gently and with extreme laziness. Her stiff body relaxed under his caress as if it, too, had grown weary of fighting forbidden sin. She melted into his embrace, leaving him one wish—to hold her until each tomorrow faded.

Someone clearing their throat startled him back to awareness. Nora stood with arms folded. Laurel pushed away.

Sweet Bessie. The woman had bad timing.

"Mr. Brodie, what beautiful day."

"Yes, isn't it?" He caught a twinkle in the dark gaze.

"I come look for you. Please to help Mr. Murphy from bed. If crazy man insists on pulling wound open, we help him."

He shot Laurel a contrite apology which she ignored, choosing instead to turn away and smooth back the sides of her hair. Never would he deliberately embarrass her; she had to know that.

Lodestone to iron didn't pull with force greater than their bodies. The emotions she raised were by no means her fault, but his with which to deal.

Although, Lord knew he failed in that every time they came within a mile of each other.

Brodie lifted a rueful brow and strolled into the room. "Murph, you're giving these ladies grief, I hear."

"Don't you go starting on me, too. Dammit, I want up and I want up now."

"Where do you insist on going, pray tell?"

"Out of these four walls. I want sunshine and fresh air."

"I suppose that would be the garden. Then, take hold of my neck and I'll fix you right up."

"I have my own two feet, thank you very much." The dark stew Murphy was in indicated no sign of changing to a more even disposition.

Brodie knew it was useless to argue. He stepped back. "Whatever suits you beats the hell out of me."

Murphy took a couple of shuffling steps before collapsing to the floor. Brodie easily lifted and carried Murphy to a seat outdoors. Laurel and Nora followed with blankets which they tucked around him.

"Quit your hovering. You turn a man into a milksop before he can spit." But Murphy's bluster had lost its fire. A pale face and trembling hand bespoke of sapped strength.

"I get you coffee and plenty food," Nora said.

"Stop rushing it, will you, Murph?" Brodie lifted tobacco makings from a pocket.

"That's the problem." Murphy took Laurel's hand. "We've postponed the wedding day long enough. I want to make her my wife. In every way."

Despite the logic of waiting for Murphy to recover, despite the fact they had more at stake than destroying three lives by haste, and despite the love that anchored him to his brother, Brodie couldn't help fighting the bit. Plain and simple, Laurel fettered him with her insistence on respectability, which he admitted everyone could use a lot more of, even him. Yet, the encumbrance chaffed worse than the silver star had.

He desired her, and seeing no way out of the quagmire grated on raw nerves.

Rolling a good smoke—now that was something he could do well. He set about it with zeal. Dry papers, tapping the right amount of Bull Durham evenly in a row, and rolling it between finger and thumb, not too tight and not too loose. He'd call himself an expert. He lit it and passed it to Murphy.

"Thanks. Only a male can appreciate the value of tobacco."

Laurel's guilty stare warned Brodie not to make a peep, for he alone knew her weakness for fine cigars. The tip of her tongue slowly wet passion-swollen lips, sending a shiver through him. He could kiss her for the next hundred years and never lose the craving for that wild honey taste.

Warmth of the morning encounter left its brand. He soaked up her touch in a way parched desert soaked up spring rains.

Odd how nothing ever quenched this thirst.

"Coffee, Mr. Brodie?" Etta brought a tray.

It would do, he supposed. Anything to moisten until he figured out a way to get spring rains his direction.

"Don't mind if I do. Thanks, Etta." He accepted a cup.

All of a sudden a parade of citizens marched single file through the gate, past the sleeping crepe myrtle, and into the garden. Had they a trombone and some drums it would've completed the spectacle.

"Sheriff, we have news of a disturbing nature to report," Jake hollered, leading the pack.

"Whatever it is, you're in the wrong place. I'm not sheriff anymore."

"Since when? No one bothered to inform us."

"Since I don't want the job, that's when."

Laurel spilled the cup of tea Etta brought, filling the saucer.

"You can't just up and quit. We have to call a town meeting in which we require you to appear and submit a valid reason." George's whine coupled with the barber's sanctimonious quirks irritated worse than a dull blade on whetstone.

"Did you get that, Thomas? You're an attorney. Don't we have procedures to go through?" Jake twirled his mustache.

"What explanation can you offer for barging onto my property without an invite, ladies and gentlemen?" Murphy glowered at the crowd that continued to file into the yard.

"Accept our apologies, Murphy. Didn't see a choice." At least a contrite John Miller shuffled his feet, staring at the ground.

"We've come to report a murder," Florence Kempshaw blurted.

"What the devil are you babbling about?" Brodie's patience wore thin. "If this is a trick to get me to bend to your will, it won't work."

"At least we *think* he's met a foul end." Lawyer-trained Thomas Hutson attempted to accurately interpret.

"Think? Don't you know?" Murphy's bluster returned along with a bit of ire. "You interrupted a fine day with mere supposition?"

"Who in the name of God do you *think* met a foul end?" Brodie's cup rattled the small table Etta had brought out.

"Zeke Vallens, that's who."

Twenty-three

THE RED FLUSH THAT CRAWLED UP BRODIE'S NECK signaled a boiling point or Laurel would miss her guess. If he didn't throttle them all she'd be surprised.

"You caused this unholy stink over a man you despise and wished dead to begin with? And when exactly did this worry kick in?" Brodie unfolded his legs and several of the encroachers backed up a bit. "Besides, I ran into the man in Jefferson yesterday and I assure you for a dead man he appeared awfully spry. Probably still there or else he rode on to spread good cheer elsewhere."

"We have reason to suspect different," Florence put in.

Laurel bit her lip. She didn't know which caused more concern—that Vallens stalked Hannah, that he might have carried out his threat to inform the military regiment where they could find Shenandoah…or learning Brodie had quit the sheriff job.

Before she could stop it, Ollie's unslept-in bed came into her mind.

Where was the woman, and why didn't she number

in this parade given her weakness of not missing out on every dog, cat, and rooster fight?

She craned her neck, scanning the crowd until she located Curley, who stood alone at the back.

Laurel tried to stifle rising alarm. "What do you base your suspicion on?"

"Two gunshots around midnight," Jake said. "One broke an alley window of the barber shop."

"Did you happen to look out?" Murphy asked.

"I dove under the bed. I'm not crazy, you know." The crowd tittered.

"I heard 'em, too," John Miller added quietly.

"Did you get up enough gumption to check for a body this morning, Jake?" Laurel couldn't shake her unease.

The barber thrust out his chest. "Sure did. Not hide nor hair of anything dead—just some drops of blood."

"There you have it." Brodie stretched out his feet.

"Not so fast, there's more." George Adams put up his hand. "Vallens' horse is in the stables and his clothes still in the hotel. Haven't seen that mangy dog of his yet though."

"It doesn't prove murder." Laurel sorted the chilling facts in her head—gunshots, blood, and a certain missing woman.

She prayed Ollie hadn't taken matters into her own hands.

A new thought brought icy chills. Perhaps Vallens had disposed of Ollie. Heaven help them.

"It's your worry, not mine. Vallens can sleep in Hell for all I care." Brodie clearly wouldn't budge on the issue.

"You're sheriff until we decide you ain't," Jake

huffed. "You cain't just jump up and change your mind. Like I said—"

"You have a procedure. Yeah, I heard, and you can take your town meetings and stuff 'em up you know where."

"Well, I never!" Florence fanned her face furiously.

"What did you do with Blanchard is what we'd like to know," Martin asked, then ducked behind George Adams. He'd already received a dose of Brodie. The wimp did lean around to tack on a polite request. "If it ain't too much bother."

"Yeah, did you take him out and lynch him?" This time George did the asking. "I wouldn't put it past your sort."

Laurel wouldn't have them think for one minute Brodie would stoop so low. The stubborn set of his jaw said he didn't intend to dignify that accusation with an answer.

"Bert enjoys Jefferson jail hospitality," she said.

Brodie shot her a warning look for her trouble.

"That means every one of you who witnessed the robbery and abduction will have to traipse over there to testify when his trial comes up." The gray-eyed rebel grinned at the ruckus that prospect raised.

"I'm not going anywhere near that place until the army pulls out," George stated.

"Me either," the mumbling of voices agreed.

Curley spoke up from the back, "Who's going to volunteer to sheriff now? I nominate Jake since he has the loudest voice. Everyone in favor say aye."

A chorus of ayes bounced off the clusters of aster, chrysanthemums, and tall, noble oak tree.

Jake's eyes bugged out and his mouth worked. "Hey, wait a minute. This ain't legal, Curley Madison."

"Anyone opposed except Jake?"

Not a soul spoke.

"Folks, it appears you have a new sheriff," Brodie drawled.

"You can't do this. I'm refusing."

But the rank and file had already turned and headed back where they'd come from, leaving Jake scratching his head.

"Looks like you're stuck with it, Whitaker. Better pray Vallens met a foul end or you may have to earn your keep." Brodie propped a matchstick in the corner of his mouth.

Laurel would've taken delight in the color draining from around the handlebar mustache but she hurried to try to catch Curley. Wedged in the crowd, she found he'd disappeared from view. Hope sank. She'd not visit the saloon. She couldn't if her life depended on it.

❦

"Ollie, where in thunder have you been? I had no idea what to think much less what to…"

The sight of Ollie washing what looked to be blood off her hands at the kitchen pump stopped Laurel midsentence. She sucked in her breath when Ollie turned her haggard features toward her. Blood-shot eyes suggested no sleep.

"Son of a bluejacket. Cain't a grown woman spend the night how she sees fit without a body making a fuss about it?"

"With a failing heart, you can't blame me for worrying. I thought you might be lying dead somewhere."

"My ticker's fine. I went out and that's all I'm saying."

That Ollie wasn't forthcoming added a chill to her bones.

"You probably haven't heard the latest circulating the grapevine express. Someone may have murdered Vallens." She couldn't control the quiver in her voice. "And then I see you washing something red off your hands."

"And you thought I may have done the deed." Ollie cackled.

"You threatened often enough. I didn't have to stretch my imagination too far. You had more than good reason."

"We both did, you forgettin' that?"

"If you say it was you, no one ever need know."

Ollie swiped her hands on a towel and patted Laurel's shoulder. "Give me a bed and a couple of hours and we'll discuss it. I'm a little tired right now."

"That's all you're going to say?"

With a heavy heart, Laurel's gaze followed Ollie up the stairs. The woman might as well have confessed.

She'd never noticed before how closely the chimes of the clock resembled a death knell. They struck ten and it gave her a jolt. Two hours before lunch and she'd barely begun preparation.

Leaving suspicion and innuendo in bigger hands, she flew about. No time to make stew. She stoked the fire, remembering the smoked venison Mr. Dunn included yesterday to make amends for Pennybacker's slight. Smoked through and through, it only required heating. A quick trip to the cellar below and she had it in a roasting pan along with potatoes, carrots, and onions. Whip up a cake and bake the bread she'd set to rise that morning and customers would have a feast.

The only interruption she hadn't counted on was Jake.

The man opened the back door and made himself at home. The badge on his shirt accounted for the swagger in his walk.

Jake hooked his thumbs in his gun belt. "Need to ask you a few questions."

"I'm quite busy right now. Come back a little later."

"Cain't. I have a job to do in regards to Vallens's death."

"You mean disappearance—unless you've found a body?"

"Not yet, but I'm keeping on my toes."

"That might pay off in case the man should show up alive."

Jake ignored her and dropped into a chair. "How much do you know about Miss b'Dam?"

"You mean Ollie?"

"One and the same. How long have you known her?"

"A while," she evaded. "I've lost track, it's been so long ago. Are you thinking she waved a magic wand and Vallens went up in a puff of smoke?"

"I'm supposed to be the one asking the questions." Jake shined the tin star with his shirt sleeve. "Where did you come from before you lit in Redemption?"

Laurel actually might've had fun without a lunch crowd breathing down her neck. Yet, sneaking fear said he might accidentally get a little closer to the truth than she cared.

"Back East. Neither Ollie nor I had ties, so we decided Texas might give us a new place to start."

"Start what, may I ask?"

She measured some flour into a bowl. "This café, what else?"

"Just where did you get the money to purchase said café?"

The bell over the front door put an end to the interview.

"You know, Jake, I fail to understand what this curiosity has to do with Vallens. I suggest you wait. I'm sure Miss b'Dam would love to chew the fat with you on whatever subject your official duties would care to inquire."

"That's Sheriff Whitaker, not Jake."

"I hate to be rude, but I'm busy. If you wish to hang around though, I have an apron that would definitely bring out the best in you. And I dearly need the help."

He rose in a flash. "I just recalled a few other suspects I should pay a visit in my official investigation."

She breathed a sigh of relief that the man possessed a pebble-sized brain or he'd be dangerous.

Murphy heard Brodie's footsteps in the hallway long after dark. His brother returned from his haunts earlier than usual. The grandfather clock downstairs clanged the hour. He counted nine.

"Nora, don't you ever get lonely down in the swamp, away from everyone?" He winced as she undid the bandage.

"The swamp holds many mysteries—secrets long forgotten. I am one with nature there. Loneliness find no place in me."

The beautiful Caddo woman examined the leech's and their work in keeping the wound clean and free from yellowish-green ooze that could kill. Her gaze met his, and he lost his bearings in the dark pools.

The woman's quiet wisdom embraced his spirit where it traveled the by-ways leading to his heart. He only now realized the daily contact with her had extended beyond healer and patient. That worried him.

How could he promise to love and cherish Laurel, seeing how important Nora had become?

But he couldn't stop the persistent current dragging him toward an unknown destination.

"Do you want for male companionship in your world?" The question came in a husky whisper full of desire to know.

The wrong answer would pain him greatly.

Nora's curved lips came within inches of his as she leaned to work. The tip of a long braid fell over her shoulder, tantalizing his naked chest when it swished across the width of him. Tiny shivers coursed through him.

She appeared to weigh the reply with much caution. "Often in the midnight hours I would have such a want."

Her candor surprised him. He'd expected some degree of denial. The air crackled in the space between them. It pulled him deeper into uncharted, unexplored swamp water.

The dark braids skimming his sensitive skin inflamed his yearning more. An enticing pull crushed her lush breasts to him. No protest came as she allowed her body to follow the length of his. Each indentation filled with her softness, sealing them into a tight vacuum.

Murphy traced the curves her deerskin dress covered. No war drum rhythm was in Nora's rapid pulse, only the ceremonial beat of surrender.

He sensed a need in her as well. Their lips met on sacred ground in a kiss full of tenderness. Not until Murphy released her did complete reality of what he'd done enter his mind.

Remorse should've washed over any sane, engaged man. None came. Nor did regret for his actions.

In fact, he'd never before felt a love like this in his heart. He reveled in the newfound joy.

Her midnight gaze held questions, yet she said nothing, settling in the crook of his arm. Murphy drew the blanket over them.

"It's all right, Nora. Lie here. For now I want nothing more than your sweet breath whispering on my skin." He was too weak yet to do anything more. It would wait.

"Your heart cannot see sleeping danger?" She spoke low.

"I know only the beauty and total serenity of the moment. You, my pretty maiden, healed my spirit even while tending to my wound."

"And in daylight?"

What then, his conscience pricked? What of his commitment to Laurel?

"Tomorrow's soon enough to sort out propriety. Rest for now, my sweet Nora." He kissed the top of her head, tightening the embrace. "Let me absorb your wisdom and strength."

❧

Brodie sat on the side of the bed, pondering the sorry state of affairs.

Too early to go to bed.

Besides, he had yet to remove clothing or boots. And he may not. He reckoned he'd slept fully dressed more often than not, particularly after a snoot full of Mexican tequila.

Damn, he should've brought up some of Murph's private whiskey stash. For a moment he considered slipping back out.

He propped himself against the sturdy oak bed-stead that had belonged to dozens of Yateses before him. He bit the end off one of the three precious cheroots left. The smooth, mellow tobacco of these was preferable to the hand-rolled Bull Durham, but he couldn't justify the extra price too often. Only on special occasions when he most needed comfort did he indulge.

He considered tonight one that met those requirements.

Striking a match, he stared at the toes of his worn boots. They'd traveled many a mile, a lot of that through hostile territory.

Having spent the better part of the evening across the street from Ollie's Café, he wasn't certain if that classified as hostile, but then again, the atmosphere hadn't been all that accommodating either. Laurel's strange mood spooked him.

His feet had numbed up on him, watching for hours through the window, groaning aloud with each bend, twist, and sway of those alluring hips.

Herman Green and his wife, Mabel, had passed by with their wagonload of thirteen kids. From their bold stares, they must've heard the rumble in his throat. He returned the look, waiting to see if a kid fell out and call an alert because they'd never miss one. When all bumped, jostled, and stayed put, his thoughts had quickly returned to Laurel and her intriguing hourglass figure.

How snug her rounded bottom had fit into his lap yesterday. The rubbing friction had severely tested his control. He never again wished to come that close to tasting what he wanted and the devil take anyone who tried to stop him.

Then he wouldn't be content until he buried himself inside her up to his eyeballs.

Georgia clay. He'd break the news to Murph himself if it'd get her into his bed faster.

The bed squeaked as Brodie adjusted his pants, hoping to relieve a bit of pressure off the bulge that suddenly made them too tight.

Removing them would solve the problem. After all, he had the privacy of the bedroom. Yet, in some strange way he welcomed the uncomfortable sensation, for it reminded him of that damn painting of two bodies with heads.

One of these days, he promised.

He punched a pillow and stuffed it behind his head. His hand brushed the memory bag hidden beneath the dark shirt.

Three women whose lives intertwined with his... three women who had never received true justice, not Elizabeth Yates, not Aunt Lucy, and certainly not Laurel.

The men who'd kidnapped and forced her into that lurid world walked free and unencumbered while Laurel remained locked in a prison, perhaps unable to ever regain what she'd lost. Proof of that lay in the fact that her family lived only miles away, yet she couldn't bring herself to seek the solace they could give.

Justice? Hardly.

Losing one's family could yank a person's soul right from the mooring and leave a rotting plank. He knew from experience how bare it left the shore.

It scared the piss out of him to think what it might do to a sensitive lady like Laurel.

"Zeke Vallens, you'd better hope to God you're dead because you and Will Taft have a mess of answering to do."

Twenty-four

"GIT UPSTAIRS AND GRAB YOUR BONNET, GIRL. WE'RE taking a buggy ride," Ollie announced a full five days later after tense questions and speculation surrounding Vallens's vanishing act.

"A buggy ride? Wherever to?"

"Never you mind." The woman hustled Laurel toward the narrow stairs. "Do as you're told and you'll be a lot better off. Cain't go nowhere if you stand there dragging your behind."

"And what about the café that everyone expects us to open regardless on a Sunday? Last week the mere mention of closing for a boat trip up to Jefferson curled your hair. Not that it couldn't stand a curl or two. Beats me what Curley sees in those spikes. But then, I'm no expert on affairs of the heart."

"Exactly. And my hair is my business." Ollie twisted a wiry lock around her finger to make it reach for the ceiling.

"You didn't answer about the café."

"Folks ain't supposed to work on Sunday. It's the

Lord's day. Reason why we have until now was because we had to. Now we don't, so we ain't."

Laurel shook her head. The woman would have the last word or die. Somehow, she had trouble believing Olivia Applejack d'Dam had suddenly gotten filled with the holy spirit. A half hour later, they loaded a wicker picnic basket into a rented rig.

"You could've said we're having a picnic."

"Could've but didn't. Wanted to surprise you."

"You invited Curley to join us, I suppose?"

"Nope."

Ollie jiggled the reins, urging the horse into a trot.

"Am I allowed to ask where we're going in such a rush?"

"Dadblasted. I'm done answering questions. Sit back and put your mind on pleasant things."

Judging the attempt useless, Laurel moved slightly to keep the torn leather from poking her. Escape would be nice after the grinding their nerves had taken.

But, one gratifying thing…she'd gotten a little of the elixir down Ollie, which she considered a pure miracle.

The chestnut mare wound through the noble land full of cottonwood and pines. Clusters of white Indian tobacco blossoms blended with pink smartweed, painting a wondrous mural of the bayou. Big Cypress existed nowhere else on earth. No wonder the Caddo Indians, of which Nora belonged, called this home. How sad only a handful remained of the once huge tribe.

"Ollie, what do you suppose happened to the Indians who lived here in the swamp?"

"Heard tell most of 'em died, and them what didn't got run off by money-hungry land-grubbers."

"That's such a shame."

Potter's Point loomed ahead, a place of mystery. She prayed they'd steer clear of Rob Potter's grave. The sight made her skin crawl.

"Shame belongs to men like Potter, who lied, cheated, and stole whatever he took a notion." Ollie squinted at her through one eye. "You remind me of his poor wife, Harriet, in a kindly sort of way. The strength of that lady is still legendary."

"I grew up hearing the stories, but I'd not dare utter her name and mine in the same breath."

"Don't be so quick. Harriet had more reason than most to quit living. Instead, she fought with everything she had and defeated the odds. I'd say you might share part of that."

Love and happiness for her? Both seemed as far removed as the stars in the sky. She'd only glimpsed Brodie from a distance since that morning in Murphy's garden. Still, she counted a glimpse now and then a blessing, half expecting him to move on since quitting the sheriff job. It simply hurt to know he'd give someone with the plague less snubbing than he did her and the café. She cleared the lump blocking her windpipe.

"Horsefeathers. I'm an outcast. Six months hasn't changed anyone's opinion," Laurel said." Least of all those who mattered most.

Ollie pulled back on the reins to stop the rig and turned. "Reminds me of something my grandpappy said a long time ago, God rest his poor old soul. He said, 'If'n you go around calling a gold nugget a rock, ain't never gonna be nothing but a measly rock. But you shine it up and call it what it is, and you'll have a regular stampede on your hands.'"

Laurel blew out an exasperated breath. "Your grandsire talked in riddles, most likely just to flap his tired old gums."

The woman shook her head. "I call 'em pearls of wisdom."

"Well, I'm no gold nugget. You can spit and shine until there's no tomorrow, be my guest."

"Son of a bluejacket. Call yourself a rock and that's all folks'll see." Ollie clicked her tongue to move the horse onward. "There's a whole mess of jewels buried inside you—diamonds and rubies and those green sparkly ones, whatever they're called."

"Emeralds," Laurel provided.

"Yep, and them, too. Mostly you have a heart of pure gold, the finest grade a man ever could find."

The mare turned south away from the river and Ollie stopped beneath a loblolly pine.

"I reckon this'll do for a picnic. About halfway there."

"Tell me where we're going, you crabby kidnapper."

"Nope."

The wind gusted abruptly. She shivered, but not from cold. "Is it someplace I wish to go?"

"Yep, you do. Now shush and help me."

Laurel tried to ignore the quiet voice that warned the woman had some dirty trick up her sleeve and spread the blanket. They dined on cold fried chicken, a loaf of Laurel's homemade bread, and fresh pickles.

When they resumed the mysterious journey, the landscape became painfully familiar. She'd romped here as a child.

She clutched Ollie's arm. "Turn around right now."

"Sorry, girl. We've come too far."

"I can't. I truly can't." Icy cold crept over her. "Please."

"I'm taking you home, girl. Goldarn it, face your demons."

"Not today." A harsh roar in her head made her voice unrecognizable. Ollie, of all people, would force this on her?

"Nothing wrong with now. You can let go of my arm any time. That is if you can pry your fingernails loose from the skin."

"I never thought you'd misuse my trust."

"Hide and watch from the trees is all I ask. I ain't gonna make you go up to the house. You have to decide that yourself."

A dried soup bone gnawed on by a pack of wolves would've had more moisture than Laurel's mouth. Just before reaching the James farmhouse, Ollie found a thicket to pull the rig into.

"Skirt though the woods over there." The woman's face turned ashen. She clutched her chest. "I'm feeling a mite poorly."

"How gullible do you take me? This ruse is an all-time low, even for you."

A gasping moan and wide-eyed stare assured her that Ollie wasn't faking. Laurel fumbled to loosen the high-necked collar.

"Up and die on me and I'll never forgive you."

Ollie panted, "Ain't planning to…unless the good Lord…says otherwise."

The lid flew off the picnic basket. Laurel grabbed the crock of water, holding it to Ollie's pale lips. The

woman took several sips and didn't protest when Laurel
laid her over in the seat of the buggy.

"Give me a minute. My old ticker's getting awfully
tired."

"I think I should light a fire under this mare and get
to Jefferson." Laurel smoothed the lovable forehead.
She'd have to prop Ollie's head in her lap to sit, but
at least they'd reach help. She slid onto the seat and
reached for the reins.

"Maybe I should tell you something."

"Not now, Ollie. It'll wait."

"I think I killed Vallens."

Laurel froze. "You think?"

"Yep. I'm pretty sure, all right."

Oh Lord, the woman had not only thieved, but
murdered too.

That tied her hands. She couldn't take her to
Jefferson and risk having the soldiers arrest Ollie. Better
her dear friend die peacefully in the woods than strung
up for murder. Or cross over to the other side while in
the midst of those scalawags and carpetbaggers—Ollie's
worst nightmare. The woman would haunt her forever.

Slowly color eked back into the white face and Ollie
could breathe without grimacing.

"You killed the angel of death? You went out and
shot him, just like that?"

"I know my time grows short. Someone had to
protect you."

"Now's a fine time to confess, I must say."

"Better now than carry the baggage across."

"What am I supposed to do? I can't get you to a doctor
and have you blab the news and wind up in the stockade."

"I expect you to follow my wishes, and your heart. Go see your poor old mama and papa. I brung you this far, girl. From here it's up to you. You don't need me holding your hand."

"And leave you alone in the middle of the woods?"

"I'll be fine and dandy resting here. And after you get done with what you need to do, we'll go home. Now, quit dilly-dallying. Move them legs of yours and git, dadblast it."

Steel in Ollie's bark made her wonder anew. Ollie had never recovered this fast before. Heaven help the trickster if she was pulling Laurel's leg.

One little peek at her home wouldn't hurt, she supposed. They'd never know of her visit.

Strange excitement stirred when she found a path toward the wooden farmhouse. Her heart pounded faster with each step. Security in the trees and overgrowth gave her confidence. Each bird, blade of grass, the very wind seemed to whisper a welcome home. The hushed, silent land held arms open wide.

At last the house glimmered through silvery branches. Jagged pieces of her soul came together to form a whole.

From the leafy screen of her hiding place, Laurel watched. The familiar creak of the rocking chair on the wide porch encouraged a better look. The skirted figure leaned to pluck a kitten rubbing against her legs. Laurel crept closer.

White streaked her mother's dark hair. Common sense had prepared her for that. It was the heavy wrinkles that brought shock and dismay.

"Millie, come and get Boots," Mary James called. "Give the little thing a dish of milk."

"All right, Mama." A girl ran from the side of the house.

Millie? Laurel never imagined the baby, who hadn't even reached the walking stage when she'd been taken, had grown into a gangly six-year-old.

An elderly man stepped through the open door. Laurel's breath caught. She pushed the brush aside for a clear view.

"The darn kitten's supposed to catch mice. You keep feeding him milk and he won't have an appetite for the pests."

"Oh, Papa. He's a baby. When he gets big, he'll catch your smelly, old mice. Besides, Mama agrees."

"Jeremiah and Virgil's idea of drowning the litter in the bayou might have merit," Ben James teased.

"They better not." Millie snatched the kitten and ran as her father bent his lanky form to sit on the top step.

Misty-eyed, Laurel watched him take an object from the bibbed overalls. Blurred vision didn't prevent her from making out the mouth harp he'd carried probably since before her birth.

"Nice time of day, ain't it?" He cupped the harp in his palms and blew lightly across the reeds.

"Same as any other. Just sitting here waiting for the miracle I won't ever live to see," Mary James answered sadly.

"Don't get maudlin. Can't dwell on the past. Not good."

Crouched low, Laurel heard the catch in her mother's wishful thinking. Gut-wrenching pain lurched inside.

"I know, Ben. But a mother still can't turn loose."

"I curse that war. Me and the boys would've found Laurel if not for The Cause sending the country into uproar and chaos. I know that in my bones."

Despair flew straight across the clearing and punctured her heart. She shouldn't have come. What did she think to gain?

"Not your fault, Ben. You did all that was humanly possible."

Her father lifted the harmonica again to his lips. The first strains of "Home, Sweet Home" drifted in the air. Laurel shut her eyes, blocking the tears. Allowing herself to feel, to savor the taste of home was her biggest mistake. Now want and need suffocated her in slow death.

A barking dog drowned the music. Panic forced open her eyes. Ol' Blue Boy bounded straight for her lush, green shield.

"Wonder what he treed?" her father remarked.

"Probably a coon. Play some more, Ben. It soothes my frazzled nerves."

Laurel scurried, but not quickly enough. The bloodhound crashed through, knocking her over. Blue Boy had smelled her scent. The hound joyfully licked every exposed bit of skin. She buried her face in his fur, then took his muzzle that had turned gray between her hands.

"I've missed you. Oh God, I've missed you so much."

The dog couldn't contain his exuberance. He jumped on top of her, his floppy ears slapping her cheeks.

She jerked at a sudden, shrill whistle.

"Here, Blue. Where'd you go, you flea-bitten hound?" The yell came from a much younger male.

Heavy feet crunched the tangle of brush and fallen limbs.

"Hannah, are you up here? Here, Blue. I mean it, now."

Seconds separated her brother, Quaid, and her. She had to go. Yet, part of her wanted Quaid to find her. It would end the agonizing years of longing for her family.

They'd ask questions. Lots of them.

Condemnation and judgment would follow. They'd find out.

"I can't," she whispered into the beloved fur.

Sad brown eyes stared back in confusion of things he didn't comprehend.

"Go, Blue Boy, go home." She swallowed the rising sob.

The dog's low whimper seemed to say he didn't want her to leave again. She blocked the noise, lifting her skirts for flight. After a few leaps, she turned for one last look at the home she'd have to learn to forget, the animal that had remembered and loved her no matter what she'd done, and then at Quaid who scrambled up the small incline.

In her moment's hesitation, she found herself overcome by the glistening trickle running down Blue's face. Dogs couldn't cry. Could they?

Blue Boy tilted his head to the sky and released a mournful howl, raising gooseflesh on her arms.

"Hey, who goes there?" Quaid had caught sight of her through the saplings. "Stop!"

❧

Two days later, Blue Boy's grief-stricken howls remained burrowed deep in Laurel's memory, like earthworms into soft, fertile soil. The teary-eyed hound blocked her vision very often.

Plus, there was Ollie's confession of killing Vallens, but Laurel hadn't pried out much more on the subject. Ollie only claimed she left him lying in the alley and it mystified Laurel what had happened to the body.

To escape, she set a relentless pace from sunup to sundown.

"Stop it, Laurel girl. You're gonna drive yourself into an early grave."

"Work never killed anyone."

"Maybe not, but it dadblame sure makes it hard on a pitiful old woman." Ollie glared. "And I cain't find a blessed thing either. What did you do with my sparking dress?"

Guilt swallowed her. Until now, Laurel had never considered the clothing's importance. She had added the threadbare dress to her rag drawer.

"It practically fell apart in my hands. It doesn't even make a good rag."

"You have some nerve. That dress brought me good luck. Now, what'll I wear next time Curley asks me over to his place, nothing but my holey stockings and knit cap?"

Laurel tried to dodge the piercing stare. "Some folks might object to seeing that much of you."

"You been acting strange since that visit to your homeplace. Wish you'd found it in you to talk to your family."

"We've been over this a dozen times."

"Stop livin' in the dark. Spooks 'n such only prey in the dead of night. If you face that fear and stare it in the eye, daylight'll come. That's what grandpappy always said."

"I promise I will." Laurel kissed the wrinkled cheek. "A baby takes small, teetering steps before it learns to walk."

"Leastways you ain't crawling anymore. Reckon I can be grateful for that." Ollie wagged her head. "Cain't believe you threw away my dress."

"I'll buy you a new one."

"Don't want a stiff, store-bought dress. Cain't get in the mood for loving when I'm all bound up."

Laurel's thoughts turned in another direction and things that bound. She whipped off the apron and grabbed a shawl.

"I have an errand to attend. I'll be right back."

It was time to set things straight.

Twenty-five

"To what do I owe this surprise?" Murphy's wide smile crinkled the corners of his eyes.

Laurel fidgeted under the warm welcome. It made her job no less difficult. Nothing would deter her this time, not even if hell froze over, which it might before she finished.

"You have healthy color in your face at last." Indeed, he added certain bloom to the fading plants around him. "I take it you walked to the garden on your own steam?"

"Yep, and it didn't tire me a bit. Come, sit next to me." He removed a pristine white handkerchief from his pocket and dusted off the stone bench.

"Don't tell me you fired Nora. I didn't see her when Annie let me in." Or Brodie, who she prayed had business elsewhere. She perched on the bench.

"Nora has neglected her mother and herb garden long enough, so I sent her home. However, she comes to check on me every day."

A deep breath bolstered her courage for what she must do.

"I should've spoken of this matter sooner and intended to the day of the shooting. You've been so ill I couldn't bring myself to mention it until you recovered."

"Sounds all-fired important."

Laurel clenched her hands tightly in her lap.

"Please don't hate me in the end. You must believe I never meant to hurt you in any way."

"I could never hate you." Murphy's questioning glance didn't ease waves of remorse. She easily imagined how rapidly anger and betrayal could swap ends with the curious stare.

"Reserve that until you know." Laurel wet her dry lips. "I can't marry you, not now, not tomorrow, not ever."

She focused on the cracks in the walk. A few weeds sprouted between the mortar of the bricks—weeds that would take over unless a body kept them pulled. Once they got hold, getting them out required too much backbreaking work.

"You're breaking our engagement?"

"I should've told you sooner. I'm very sorry." She dared not glance up from the weeds. "I don't expect you—"

"Whew! That's a relief."

Shock sped through her blood. She whirled to face him and ran smack into the most whimsical gleam.

"You're not angry, disappointed, or humiliated?"

"Nope. I didn't know how to go about telling you I've fallen in love with Nora. This saves us more loss of sleep."

"You and Nora?"

Could she have misunderstood? Ollie always accused her of choosing to hear only what she wanted.

"I didn't realize how deep my love ran. It just sneaked up on me over time and in the course of daily contact. I woke up one morning and knew Nora and I were meant to be together."

"I'm elated for you both."

Yet, this twinge of desolation confused her.

"I haven't asked Nora to marry me yet. I first had to set things straight with you. No hard feelings, I hope."

"She's truly a lucky woman and had better appreciate what she has." Laurel realized the other burrs and thistles would remain unless she told him everything. "I have more to tell you, Murphy, some of which may lower your opinion of me drastically."

"Nothing can change what I already have come to know."

"We'll see." Another cleansing gulp of air helped. "I lived on a farm not far from here until a fateful day right after I turned fifteen."

For the next half hour, she bared her soul, told him about her life in St. Louis and what Taft forced on her.

"One night your brother came to the Black Garter."

"Brodie? So my mind didn't play tricks after all."

Now came the judging part she'd most dreaded. She didn't imagine the reproach behind the question. It didn't arrive unexpected. Surely any warm-blooded man would experience a sense of betrayal that she'd kept horrible secrets from him.

"I knew him as Shenandoah, and yes, he paid for the privilege of my services."

"You must've had a good laugh at my expense."

"On the contrary, we had no wish to keep you in

the dark. I never had anything other than the utmost respect and admiration for you."

"I hope those aren't simply words to mollify."

"They're not. Another thing—Brodie loves you. He'd cut off his right arm to prevent causing you a minute's anguish."

"I knew something ate at him. Couldn't guess what."

"The secret tore him apart." She slid off the bench and took Murphy's palm. "You gave me hope that I might one day live a normal life. Deceit goes against my nature, but belief I'd do more harm by confiding convinced me to keep quiet."

"That's enough. What purpose can dredging this up serve?"

"Hearing the whole sordid mess is the only way to absolve myself. I'm tired of living lies. You want the ugly truth? I tried to use you. In the struggle to redeem myself, I willingly did whatever I had to, even accept a proposal from someone I didn't love—the greatest sin of all."

"Sit back down. I'll not have you belittling yourself." Murphy pulled her back on the seat. "How did you escape from that hellish place? Did Brodie help?"

"He was wounded before he could return. Ollie got me out. We came to Redemption for a fresh start and opened up the café."

"My brother showing up must've soured things."

"He threatened to tell my secret. I begged him and bought a week's time so I might break the engagement in my own way."

"But the bank robbery took care of that."

"Yes. So I waited for the day when you grew strong

enough." She cast him a wry smile. "And to gain courage for the task."

"You could've left and I would never have been the wiser."

"I've gotten weary of running from my problems."

"My dear Laurel. You have innate goodness and honor that nothing or no one will ever destroy."

Murphy's declaration summoned the gold nugget story Ollie had tried to sell her. Perhaps the lump of coal she saw herself as had developed a bit of shine. No luster, mind you, merely a small glint. But she had one more truth to reveal before she could rest easy.

"I've saved this last part on purpose. I never meant this to happen, but it has and no amount of wishing can change it."

"I already know of your love for Brodie."

Spit and thunder. Did the man read tea leaves?

"I fell head over heels in love the first time I laid eyes on him in St. Louis. But when he never returned for me, I didn't expect to ever see him again. I figured he'd lost his life in the war or else his affection for me. Truth be told, Brodie Yates stirs a longing in my blood unlike any man. He walks near, and his mere presence makes me weak in the knees." Her voice dropped to a whisper. "I love him with all my heart and soul."

"A bullet might've laid me low but didn't take my sense. I'll have to admit you hid your truths far better than dear brother. I noticed how he followed your every move. He has a bad case of smitten-itis."

"Swapping tales about me?" Brodie's deep baritone made them both jump.

Laurel blushed that he'd caught them. Still, she had to admire the tall figure striding silently across the grass. And the tight cut of his trousers.

∽⟆

Brodie lounged inside an empty café after the last diner left for the evening. He preferred watching Laurel work from here much better than hiding in the shadows across the street as he'd done the last month. A need to have her beneath him, naked as a newborn, swelled a vital part of him until the seams of his britches threatened to split.

"Can I get you anything else?"

Coffee sloshed from his cup onto the table. He'd be remiss in thinking he affected her that much. Yet, he didn't fool himself. He noticed the tired lines in her features.

"Darlin', looking at you is feast enough. You wouldn't understand a man's appreciation for the sexy sway of hips in the quiet glow of lanterns...what it does to me."

"What on earth gives you the right to suddenly spout such things after pretending me or this café ceased to exist? Best take your endearments, suggestive talk, and ogling to another who might wish it."

Spots colored her cheeks bright pink. Flashing violet sparks declared battle and he had no dueling pistols.

Or walls to hide behind. Nothing but a white flag to wave.

"I had no idea you missed me that much." He felt a lopsided grin drift into place. "Thought you wanted time to yourself."

She wouldn't know how often he turned toward the café.

Only to stop.

"That's the thing, Brodie, your blessed desires are more important than a care about when or what a lady might wish."

He probably deserved a tongue-lashing for a lot of reasons, but not for loving her. That wasn't open for discussion.

Seemed odd that she continued to stand there tapping her foot instead of turning her back. The harmless compliment sure had made her mad enough to melt lead and make bullets.

"Murphy told me about your visit the other day."

"And you presume that changes everything and I'll fall in a puddle at your feet, grateful you remember I haven't left."

"If memory serves, dear lady, you set the boundaries. Do you recall the order to stop tempting? I suppose I could've fabricated that conversation—along with the pull of our bodies when we're near." Then he added softly, "Like now, when I want you so badly and I know you have the same yearning. Dare you deny that?"

Laurel did more crack-counting of the floor before she answered. "I can't. Dear God, I wish it weren't so."

A gentle squeeze of her hand, a tug into the chair he pulled out brought her onto his lap. He cupped her face and tucked a strand of hair behind the delicate ear.

"Will you resist should I beg to have you in my bed?"

Her head dropped wearily to his shoulder. He drew her into the shelter of his arms.

"I'm afraid."

"Of me? I left the chains and whip in my saddlebags."

"Of myself. I trusted you once and lived to regret it. What happens this time after you satisfy your needs? Will you ride on to other conquests? I've known men who want only that which is unattainable. Once they have it, the luster fades."

"Close your eyes and make a wish. I'll wave a magic wand."

"You can't turn wishful thought into reality when you don't know the nature of it."

"Oh, but I do. Therefore, I have the power."

Laurel leaned back. A teardrop poised on the tip of one sooty lash. More wetness glistened in the gaze that slid from behind the mask she had expertise at wearing.

For the first time he saw how deeply he'd hurt her. Anger, bitterness, and distance kept the depth of that pain hidden. Making up for misdeeds presented a mountainous task; still, he hadn't shown the reserve card up his sleeve yet.

Brodie lightly traced the curve of her jaw. "Do as I ask. Pretend we're at a masquerade. Be whoever or whatever you choose—bejeweled queen or beauteous gypsy maiden."

Laurel bit her bottom lip, but lowered her lids. "And you shall wear no disguise, Sir Rogue?"

"No need when I'm probably the most charming, debonair sort of chap you'll ever meet. Though I could be a ruthless buccaneer. I've always yearned to sail the seven seas on a frigate."

At least her frown vanished. He scooted from beneath her and dropped to one knee.

"I want you more than anything in this world. I assure you my interest lies not in conquest and I've never had the slightest desire for the unattainable. Will you share my bed, beautiful masked lady, before I die an agonizing death?"

"No…I wouldn't feel right making love in Murphy's house." A smile flirted with the edges of her mouth. "My bedroom is private and much closer."

He extinguished the lanterns before following her up the creaking stairs. In case Ollie occupied the room across, he closed the door with care.

She came into his arms and the heat of their kiss dispelled any lingering qualms either might have had.

"My pirate scoundrel, sure you won't have second thoughts?" Laurel asked, her voice husky with desire when he freed her mouth. "You know, the men in my bed too numerous to count? Worried that the color of your coin makes recalling your face impossible come light of day?"

"Darlin', your mask is slipping. Remember, you can be anyone you desire," he whispered in her ear.

A silver shaft of moonlight through the window bathed her slim form in unearthly beauty. The die was cast and the bullet mold safely put away. Brodie could no more turn back now than cease drawing air.

"This game… Does it call for capture and plunder?"

"Only the most painless, temporary kind. Worried?"

"I believe in our love and that destiny meant us to be together."

"You're a fire in my blood since before I arrived at this party and more so after spying you across the room. You drive me utterly, totally, indescribably insane." The words came out so hoarse and raspy he almost didn't recognize his own voice.

"Don't throw yourself on your sword this soon, my pirate."

The easing of a few buttons gave him access to her elegant neck. Trailing a path, he tongue-danced down the curve, exploring the rapid pulse at her throat before lace and fabric prevented further progress.

He made quick work on the remaining buttons, and the bodice and skirt slid to the floor in a rippling heap.

The thin chemise created a flimsy shield at best. He cupped a breast and expertly rolled a nipple to a hard nib. Laurel jerked his shirt over his head, apparently finding the fastenings too slow, before starting on the britches.

They tore off the remaining clothing in a fevered rush. Satisfaction came only after she bore meager similarity to the naked mural that hung over the bar in the saloon. He buried his face in the fragrant softness of her bosom. The beat of her racing heart mesmerized. He didn't know what the future held. Frankly, he didn't give a damn. He wanted only to freeze this moment and preserve it until time and eternity merged into one.

"When you didn't come, I presumed you didn't want me."

"Foolish lady. Don't you know I always will?"

His mouth met hers again. Her lips parted, allowing his tongue freedom.

Tasting.

Thrusting.

Each place Brodie drew flirtatious circles around raised prickles on her bared flesh. He curled his leg around hers. Exploration led him across her navel to the downy juncture of her thighs. Hot wetness encompassed his touch.

Laurel's fingertips grazed his chest hair and each brown nipple. And when she reached to grasp his stiff arousal, he shuddered and clenched his jaw to keep from giving in to pleasure so near he feared to draw another breath.

As if reading his mind, she stopped and became very still.

Between them no time and space existed. Brodie could no longer tell where her soft curves began and his hard muscle ended.

Vague thoughts intruded his passion-dulled senses. Faint remembrances of a line in the sand he'd drawn and now had crossed barely remained. He could never return there, for Laurel stole his good sense, his heart. She instilled a reason for seeking to become a better man than he'd ever been or even imagined he could be.

Pins from her hair dropped quietly to the floor, letting the raven strands cascade around his hands.

Laurel's silky caresses wandered lazily up his back.

Muscles long bereft of female attention quivered when she loitered to etch her name over each.

Her nimble touch flitted, inflicting torture of the most maddening kind.

And yet, he fought to hold himself in check.

Need to prolong the end dominated his crazed thoughts, for he wished to bring equal satisfaction.

She held his entire being in her hands and whether she believed it or not, she was all lady—a most respectable one, which he dared anyone to say otherwise.

The agonizing dawdle ended with the tangling of her fingers in his hair. Laurel pulled him still closer while the palm of the other hand dipped lower, further fueling the roaring blaze inside him. A sensuous burn inched upward, through the maze of muscle and sinew, knotting each in the passing.

Brodie realized he'd become more than flesh and bone. He belonged to her... They belonged to each other.

Finally, they'd become whole bodies with beautiful heads.

The humid swampland of Big Cypress Bayou on the hottest summer's day couldn't compare to the sultry film coating her skin. Rise and fall of lush breasts revealed desire at which the come-hither smile only hinted.

He'd never known such a bottomless, drowning hunger. The lazy storm that began at the onset developed into a huge cyclone that swept everything in its path.

Raw need rushed through his body as he lowered Laurel to the small bed.

"I want you, Laurel Lillian James. I need you."

"Groveling at my feet at last, are you?"

"I'm not greedy... All right, maybe a bit." He nibbled her earlobes. "I'll take whatever I can beg, plead, or bargain for. Is the plundering option still on the table?"

"You indeed have the heart of a dangerous brigand."

"Can't argue with that. At least I'm a happy one."

"Hush. Talking wastes too much energy, Sir
Buccaneer."

"That so?"

Their breaths mingled in a kiss that could've melted
lead and gave her to know he had lots left for pleasur-
ing her. Brodie fondled the weight of her heavy breasts,
and a moan tumbled from her throat when he rolled a
puckered nipple between thumb and forefinger.

A powerful onslaught of tenderness battered down
the last bit of restraint. He crushed her to him, shame-
fully reveling in all that he knew and more he hoped
to learn.

Ropes on which the feather mattress rested creaked
in protest. Yet other than a soft gasp, that was the only
noise when he filled her, fully and deeply.

Strange how he'd been here before, yet this seemed
the first time in which their bodies had joined.

In a sense, he reckoned it was.

They weren't the same two people. They'd grown
and changed in the passing years. Laurel had learned to
take what she wanted and speak her mind.

And him?

Thank God for an experienced woman.

Not only did she eagerly accept all he gave, but
returned pure, shimmering gold to his paltry silver.

Her grip held him fast as she shuddered. Warm
contractions pulsated around his imbedded length,
unleashing tremors that traveled throughout his body.

Long weeks of torment and waiting came to an end
in a surging release that shook him to the core.

The sheer curtains floated in a breeze through
the open window. Brodie locked the memory

away for safekeeping. He'd remember always this moonlit night, her dew-kissed softness when their hearts joined.

Even until the day they laid him six feet under.

Then, if God willed, in the hereafter.

Twenty-six

LAUREL NESTLED IN THE ONLY ARMS SHE'D EVER desired. Brodie's quiet breaths at her temple fluttered wisps of hair. She brushed back the rebellious lock from his forehead.

"I'm curious."

"Does it pertain to scuttling ships or plundering? Because if it does, I'll lay it to my seafaring great grandfather, Bartholomew Yates. I understand he did a fair amount of it."

"No, silly." She traced each line and crevice in his face. "I wondered why you adorn your hat with snake rattles of all things. They make such ungodly noise."

"They remind me how precious staying alive is."

The strength of symbols came in various forms, it seemed. A broken tooth had become such for her.

"I cut those off the biggest, meanest diamondback I ever killed. Had the rascal not shaken 'em, I'd be dead. Figured the noise would warn others to shy away and what would come if they didn't."

"A lot are too dumb. Look at Jeb Prater."

"When God handed out brains He certainly missed a

few souls." He nipped at her finger with his teeth. "But I have another reason, if you promise not to laugh."

"I swear not to crack a smile."

Anyone who let the harmless color of lavender frighten the wits out of them dare not sit in judgment of others.

"The hiss of those rattles sort of comforts. Reminds me I fear no man…only fate."

Or destiny. Thoughts turned to Ollie and her confession. She'd do anything to keep the dear woman free—anything.

"Have you ever been in prison for killing anyone?"

"I've gotten on the personal side of more calabooses than I care to recall, but missed being jailed for murder. Why?"

"I can't tell."

"Does this pertain to Vallens? You saying you shot him?"

Laurel pushed away and fumbled to raise the lamp wick, calling herself nine kinds of crazy.

"You should leave now."

"Whatever you say. What did I do wrong?"

Lowering her defenses proved definite impairment in sound judgment. She should've known better. The soldier she fell in love with wouldn't find her capable of murder. Sudden tears blurred the heap of garments littering the floor. Snatching them, a calculated throw landed the trousers in his face, covering narrowed rebel grays that set her pulse racing.

An object—a drawstring pouch—brushed her foot when she stood. Buttery leather molded to the shape of her palm when she picked it up.

"What's this?"

"Nothing of much value."

Brodie lifted the bag without sparing her a glance and drew on his pants. Anger lay heavy in the air, an ugly closure to the contentment their lovemaking had brought.

She'd mistaken him for a granter of wishes.

A lump formed in her chest as she fumbled with the buttons, not seeming able to find the holes.

"For God's sake." He spun her around and one by one put each button in place. "What did I say?"

"Vallens doesn't belong in our bed."

"I'll remember that." Brodie kissed the tip of her nose. "We're survivors. We know what it takes to make it to the next sunrise because we've seen our share of pitch-dark nights."

After pulling on his boots, he reached for his hat and gun belt and sauntered to the door. "You know where to find me."

Laurel swallowed hard as he stepped into the hall.

"Brodie?"

"Yes, darlin'."

"Thank you for tonight."

"For the record, which lady lurked behind the mask in our game of pretense?"

"Myself. I'm sick of trying to be something I'm not."

※

Brodie failed to stop by the following day. Evening drew to a close without her hearing the familiar noise she craved.

"You're a fool, a crazy stupid fool."

Ollie burst through the vacant dining room with Curley in tow. "What's that you say?"

"Can't a body talk to herself?"

"Reckon so if you've a mind. Girl, Curley wants to ask a favor." Ollie tugged at his arm. "Go ahead."

The ring on the plump man's finger sparkled as he twisted his hands. Laurel cast Ollie a suspicious glance.

"I'm at my wit's end. Ollie said maybe you could help."

"I'll surely do what I can."

"First off, Ollie sort of spilled the beans about your previous…line of work."

"You didn't!" Laurel sent the woman an angry glare.

"Hold on to your blooming mule train." Ollie wore a sheepish squint. "It merely slipped out during a—"

"Lull in the conversation? How could you?"

"Your secret's safe with Curley."

"What about those *you* guard so carefully? I don't suppose they happened to *slip* out while you shot the breeze."

"Now that I think on it…"

"Exactly what I thought."

"Ladies, blood sure would mess up this clean kitchen." Curley turned to Laurel. "Here's the problem. A pitiful little creature named Adeline arrived today wanting to work in the saloon. I can't turn her out with no place to go."

"Ain't no bigger than a corn nubbin," Ollie added. "Needs a chance to grow up afore she sets out to ruin herself."

"How exactly will serving liquor ruin her life?"

Curley squirmed. "Not what she has in mind.

She's determined to invite paying customers upstairs for a tumble."

Laurel's tongue scraped the rough edge of her tooth. "No, I won't go there. Not under any circumstances."

"Laurel girl, I understand your vow to steer clear of those places, but Adeline will only go on to Jefferson. Think about them murdering scalawags and riffraff."

"A person that stubborn won't listen to me."

Curley scratched his head. "You've been down that road. It might make her stop and think. If you won't talk to her I don't know what I'll do."

Not less than ten minutes later, Curley let Laurel in through the back of the saloon and pointed out Adeline's room.

Whiskey and stale, lifeless air mingled, taunting her.

Harsh laughter surged from below. A piano tinkled, no one minding it a little off-key. Chills enveloped Laurel. A male voice escaped under a closed door opposite the narrow hall.

"I've paid good money, dearie. Get undressed or else."

The salty taste of sweat drenched raw memories. Hurt and despair stung behind tightly closed lids. Her mouth dry, she leaned against the wall, too queasy to stand. A foolhardy move this was, stepping inside the one place she swore never to darken again.

Ollie's remembered plea stopped a lurch toward fresh air. Laurel had asked many times how long she had to wear the mark of shame.

The woman's reply sounded in her head. "Until it doesn't fit anymore." Lately, Laurel had begun to fashion a new, roomy garment.

A young girl answered her light tap. Curley might've bought the stated age of fifteen, but twelve or thirteen seemed more accurate. Ruffles and bows indicated the child would burst out of the dress long before the need to become a woman.

"Adeline?"

"Who's asking?"

"A friend…Laurel James."

Innocence in Adeline's sky-blue gaze twisted the knot in Laurel's stomach. The girl flicked her head in defiance, setting blond hair swaying.

"Don't need friends. None ever did me a lick of good."

"May I come inside?"

"I'm busy. Got paying customers waiting. Before the night's over I'm gonna have money in my pocket. Reckon it cain't be worse than doing other things."

A shiver swept through Laurel. Depended on the definition.

"Please, I promise I won't take long."

"Better not. I can spare only a minute."

The sparse furnishings repulsed her. But it was a rag doll's button eyes staring from the pillows that broke her heart. Loving hands had fashioned hair of yellow yarn and stitched a smile on the stuffed face. Funny how each new girl brought something to cling to.

For Laurel it had been her music box.

Careful scrutiny found etchings above the door, crude efforts to preserve true names. She blinked hard. Inside the third room to the right at the Black Garter scratched above the doorframe, it would read *Laurel*.

A flush deepened Adeline's cheeks as she quickly stuffed the doll beneath the mattress.

"Well?" The girl tapped her foot nervously. "This ain't no place for social calling."

Laurel perched on the edge of the bed, careful not to squish the little doll. "I see that. Where's your home?"

"Came up river from New Orleans." Adeline shivered as if bad memories walked across her mind. Her shoulders sagged when she sat beside Laurel. "Not home now. Ain't ever going back."

A shared misery. "I understand what you mean."

"How can someone like you know?"

"Because I've walked in your shoes. There are better ways to survive."

"Words come cheap, don't they?"

"Not if they offer a way out."

A ragged sigh disturbed the stale air. "Fever took my ma last year. After she passed, my pa…"

Laurel imagined the rest. A lot had the same story.

Adeline's defiance returned. "Like I said—my pa—he took me to his bed…forced me to do things. He told me I had to pay for Ma up and dying on him. I'm a disgrace."

Bile clogged Laurel's throat. She swallowed bitterness.

"The sin belongs to your father, not you." She folded her arms around the sobbing child, adding a few tears of her own. "Hush now, it'll be all right. Your pa won't ever hurt you again. I promise."

"You don't know him."

"We'll hide and keep you safe."

"Hardest part is not having a home, no family to call your own. You probably can't imagine that."

"Let me tell you a little story, Adeline."

After Laurel finished sharing her experience, she

stood at the small window, looking out at the darkness. "We are who we are. Hold your head high." She turned. "I want to hire you. Show up tomorrow morning at Ollie's Café. Can't pay a whole lot, and it's hard work. But it's a roof over your head and it's respectable."

Marching to the bed, she lifted the mattress and freed the rag doll.

"Don't ever let your treasures embarrass you. They're as much a part of us as the air filling our lungs. Both keep us alive."

∽

Laurel felt emotionally drained by the time she headed for the café. She'd hopefully started a child down a road that didn't lead to dead ends like hers always seemed to.

Preoccupied, she never saw the shadow leap forward until too late. She suddenly found herself face-to-face with the wild, glittering eyes of the wolf-dog.

The hated, fearsome beast froze her to the spot.

She scoured the buildings for signs of life. But they were locked tight for the night. Failing to see a safe place to run, she searched for a rock or piece of wood. None came to light.

What she wouldn't give to have the knife back in her pocket. She'd ceased carrying it when Vallens disappeared.

Speaking of which, she half expected to discover the hateful man leering at her. That he didn't come forth brought an eerie shiver. Ollie must truly have killed him.

Yet, the dog showing up meant something.

A soothing, calm voice could prevent an attack, she'd heard.

"Hey, boy, where did you come from? I'll bet you're starving. Let me pass and I'll feed you a big steak."

The animal whined low and pitiful. Indeed a stark change from the guttural growl. Then she noticed a dark splotch near the rib cage. The short fur had matted.

"You must've gotten in a fight. I'm going to move now. Nice and easy. I just want to look."

Laurel prayed her shaky legs wouldn't give way. She inched forward, trying to push aside the image of him lunging and tearing her limb from limb with his razor-sharp fangs. In daylight the animal's eyes had a grayish-green cast, yet the moonlight turned them an odd yellow. She stared into the frightening glimmer as she'd seen Brodie do.

"I won't hurt you. So don't bite."

Shock swept over her when she drew closer. Wolf-dog dropped to the ground in submission, watching each movement warily.

Common sense said she should run.

Before she could, treasured Blue Boy flashed across her vision. Animals depended on people for help. She couldn't leave anything hurt. Even wolves deserved a bit of kindness.

Besides, saving the dog might clear Ollie. Although at the moment she didn't know how. Maybe that would come later.

"I'm going to reach very slowly. I want to see what's wrong, that's all. Then we can both go on our way. I'll be gentle." The animal smelled her outstretched hand and once more whimpered. Thankfully, those sharp teeth stayed hidden inside a closed mouth, which added a bit more confidence. Laurel bent to touch the stiff, dried fur.

A gentle probe pushed aside the hair to reveal a hole where something had pierced the skin.

"Someone shot you," she crooned softly, her heart going out to the animal.

Ollie's threat to do so rumbled in the stillness.

A chill prickled her flesh.

The woman had many secrets—and a loaded pistol.

Wolf-dog licked her arm. His baleful yellow gaze melted her remaining fear, for it said he thought her a friend, not foe.

"Come on then. Let's get you home."

Laurel started for the café. Surprisingly, he followed.

When she entered with the dog, Ollie turned pasty white and caught the pipe from her gaping mouth before it tumbled to the floor. "Son of a bluejacket. Have you lost your dadblasted mind?"

"He's been injured, maybe shot. I couldn't leave him."

"You should've. We don't owe that vicious beast anything. Likely he'll pounce on our throats in our sleep."

"Don't you see? Vallens may not have met his Maker. You're clear. Perhaps you only shot the dog instead."

"Well, Miss Smarty, where's the angel of death then?"

Wolf-dog crawled onto a burlap bag she spread in the corner, but curled a lip at Ollie.

"Shh, you're frightening him. And if I knew where Vallens went, I'd tell you."

"I don't feel so good." Ollie's hands covered her stomach.

Laurel bustled to the pump with a bucket and filled it.

"Why don't you fetch Jake while I wash the wound? I'm sure he'll find this interesting."

"Ain't exactly the word I'd use." Ollie cackled and slapped a knee. "Jake's gonna piss all over hisself. Cain't wait to see it."

While the woman hurried to spread good cheer and tidings, Laurel cleaned off the blood. She spied a piece of lead embedded in muscle. While Wolf-dog devoured two large chunks of leftover meat, she ran upstairs for the tweezers. She was back down and hunched over the animal when Ollie returned. The bulging eyes of Jake Whitaker peeked around the door.

"Good God. I ain't wearing this badge. Vallens'll be spittin' nails at someone shooting his dog."

"Jake, you have experience in removing bullets."

The man crumpled to the floor, half in and half out. Ollie lifted a limp arm. "He fainted."

"Should've known he'd do this."

"Reckon I should drag him on in or push him back out?"

"Whichever is easiest. I need you here."

Huffing and puffing, Ollie pulled him in far enough to close the door. Together they removed the metal fragment and applied a bandage. Through it all, Wolf-dog remained amazingly calm. Laurel stroked the dozing animal's slender neck.

"No telling where he's been. I wonder why he

came to me of all people? It's odd how pure hatred can sometimes turn peaceable."

Ollie squatted on her heels. "Boggles the mind. How did things go with the young girl over at the Dry Gulch?"

"I hope we can afford another hand."

"Praise be, you hired her."

"It doesn't take much to make you happy."

"While you were upstairs, guess who I ran into at the bar?"

Tired eyes and pea soup for brains soured Laurel's mood.

"Who?"

"Yates. Trying to climb headfirst into a whiskey bottle."

Nothing except regret would make a man drown his sorrows. Or did Brodie wrestle with the idea of running out on her again?

The idea kicked her in the teeth and poured Ollie's tincture of hawthorn down her raw throat. Laurel closed her eyes to hide the vivid remembrance of their love-making. Walking a tightrope made one old and weary.

"Course, I tried to show him the error of his ways, but he'd slipped too far over the edge to pay me any nevermind."

Laurel's eyes flew open with a jerk of her head. "Please tell me you didn't meddle."

Whatever Brodie assumed, she didn't welcome Ollie's brand of help. Generally speaking, the dear woman botched everything. Ollie's wide-eyed innocence didn't fool her for a minute.

"Who, me? You know I'd never breathe a word to anyone."

Twenty-seven

JAKE HAD VANISHED BY BREAKFAST. THE WOLF–DOG
rose from his burlap pallet to sniff Laurel's hand. She
could imagine how fast the honorable sheriff ran when
he came to and saw the animal. And the door wasn't
even in splinters. Amazing.

"Bet you're wanting to eat, aren't you, boy?"

She rubbed his ears and upturned throat. Even the
worst of God's creatures responded to kindness. With
a master like Vallens no wonder he'd tried to eat
everyone alive.

"You're not so mean."

Ollie caught her hand-feeding meat and stale gin-
gerbread to the dog. "Stop that! Next thing I know,
you'll have an apron on him and waiting tables. On
second thought, the idea—"

A knock on the back door interrupted Ollie.

"Unless I'm mistaken, that's Adeline." Laurel let
the girl in, pleased she'd accepted the offer.

Ollie rushed forward. "Git yourself on in here,
little lady, and make yourself at home before
Laurel has you doing tricks and begging. I'm Olivia

Applejack b'Dam, by the way. But you can call me Ollie."

Adeline's blues sparkled with tears. Laurel marveled at Ollie's ability to make the loneliest orphan loved and wanted.

"It seems as if I've come home, thanks to you both."

Laurel took the ragged valise from the girl. "I hope you won't mind sharing my bed?"

"Anywhere beats the saloon. With the drunken sots raising a ruckus, I never got a wink of sleep."

Laurel laughed. "A few nights of Ollie's snoring may change that opinion."

Ollie swelled up like a toad. "I swear to my time, insult a woman in her own house, why don't you? You should make a body welcome, not run 'em off."

"What a beautiful animal." Adeline knelt to put her arms around the wolf's neck, showing no fear. "What's his name?"

"Reckon he don't have none other than Wolf-dog, leastways not that we ever heard." Ollie lit the pipe that had gone cold. "Don't belong to us, only keeping him…uh, for someone. He's sure taken a shine to you, young lady."

Inspiration hit Laurel. "He needs a proper name. Something more than Wolf-dog. Every living thing deserves self-respect. Adeline, any ideas?"

"I'm sorta partial to my mother's maiden name of Hannibal."

"Perfect. I like it. Then Hannibal it is."

Laurel led the way to the living quarters and watched the new help unpack meager belongings. The rag doll propped up by pillows added a fitting touch to the faded old quilt.

"Why is that covered?" Adeline pointed to the mirror.

She'd forgotten how strange another might take her phobia.

"I'm afraid I can't bear to see my own reflection." Or the color purple, though she didn't add that. The girl thought her an escapee from the madhouse already. "I can't seem to fix the problem. Not yet, at any rate."

"After Paw stole what belonged to me, all I see is something dirty and rotten. He turned a twelve-year-old into thirty. Seeing your mirror puts us both in the same boat."

"Shh, don't think about it. When Ollie spouts her golden rule enough, you'll soon learn that no one can roll back months or years and it don't do an ounce of good trying." She drew Adeline close and smoothed back the blond silk. "From here we keep our eyes on the future and focus on making ourselves better than we were before. Ollie says hopeless are those who refuse to step out of a quagmire once someone hands them a strong branch."

Unbidden pictures of the James family gathered on the porch popped into mind. She could take her own advice.

And she would.

One of these fine days, at the appropriate time.

"I'll wager you're a flapjack-eater."

"Oh shoot, I can eat a whole plate full."

✥

Brodie knew the roulette wheel of fate had stopped on unlucky black thirteen by the thunder of hooves halting in front of the Yates residence early Thursday morn, interrupting breakfast. Blood roaring in his ears almost drowned out the fists pounding on the polished cypress. Through the curtained window, robins in the garden appeared unaffected by the commotion. The nearby back door urged him to flee. A sane man would.

That is if said man hadn't grown tired of the chase.

If he hadn't let roots burrow so deep in Texas swampland, he could chop them loose with the sharpest hoe.

...and if he hadn't found Lil after all this time.

He forced down the bite of ham and calmly reached for another biscuit, spooning jam onto one half.

Murphy jumped to his feet when soldiers in blue barged into the dining room, followed by Etta who wrung her hands. They yanked Brodie from the chair, toppling it over.

"What the...?" Murphy glared, his voice thick with anger.

"Shenandoah, by the authority of the president of these United States and the governor of the rebellious Texas territory, I hereby place you under arrest." Two bars on the man's shoulders ranked the speaker as captain.

"I fear you've made a grievous error. This is my brother, Brodie Yates. I intend to register a complaint immediately," Murphy said. "Please leave my home."

"It doesn't make any difference what name he chooses to call himself. Apprehending the treasonous

Confederate spy will earn me quite a promotion," the captain blustered.

"May I remind you gentlemen the war ended over three years ago and Andrew Johnson issued amnesty for Johnny Rebs." Brodie spoke in a quiet tone, willing himself to avoid his brother's gaze. Brodie had known the danger that dogged his return.

The captain leaned forward. "We haven't forgotten the scores of men who died at Shenandoah's hand. No amnesty erases that."

Had the men not bound him, Brodie would smash the nose jutting a finger's width from his. Even so, he strained to free himself if for only a moment. The damn war would never be over as long as hate and revenge ran rampant. Men wouldn't let it.

"We can take you back in pieces if you prefer, you misbegotten scum of a whoreson." The captain shoved him toward the men filling the doorway.

"Yeah, General Buell didn't say it had to be pretty." The second voice spoke near his left ear—a lowly private no doubt who found bravery only after they had Brodie securely shackled.

Brodie turned. "Murphy, will you take care of Laurel?"

"No need to ask. You know me. We'll get this straightened out and soon have you back."

The group hustled Brodie toward the front, the captain pausing only to deliver a parting insult. "As far as me and the rest of the Union army are concerned, his neck promises to be all that gets straightened. A rope will see to that very quickly."

"My brother deserves a fair trial before execution."

"Before or after, it's all the same. Sit down, sir, or we'll take you, too."

"Murph, please. You'll make matters worse."

Glare of the morning rays usually required a hat. In the last twenty years Brodie could count on his fingers the days he'd stepped out bareheaded. Captain Blue Belly scoffed at his simple request, heaving him onto a horse.

People stared at the procession. Jake ran from the barber shop and Brodie caught the missing tin star on the weasel's chest.

His glance swung to the café. Laurel ceased cleaning the brand-new window when the rag slipped unheeded from her hand.

Her shocked lavender gaze shattered his heart.

He'd never hold her again, never feel her heart beating next to his.

And he'd never speak the words of love he'd carried silently inside for so long.

His luck had run out.

The reality that he loved her, without reservation and forevermore, came too late.

Moss-draped cypress standing proud and tall on guard shed tears he dare not allow. The giant trees spoke of dreams and plans turned to splinters. They told a truth few men wished to hear—that redemption came free of charge for those seeking it.

Ahh, but he'd been a body complete with a head for a little while, anyway. That consolation would have to do.

Brodie tried to drag his gaze from Laurel's, but he didn't have the power. That's when a lean animal leaped around Laurel's skirts.

Wolf-dog.

Did that mean Vallens hadn't died? A sick whirl whipped his breakfast into froth. Jake's shirt minus the badge made sense all of a sudden. Yet nothing explained why Laurel patted the beast's head without him ripping off her hand.

"How-do, ma'am." The captain halted the line of men and tipped his head. "Fine day, isn't it?"

"They shore grow 'em pretty here in Texas, eh, Cap'n?" a soldier hollered.

No doubt a bold leer accompanied the yell, accounting for Laurel's flush. Brodie strained to break the bonds, for he'd take joy in putting a fist in the coarse-mouthed Yank.

Before the captain issued the command to continue, Brodie watched her embarrassment fade. Helpless fear swept aside all other emotion. The beautiful features couldn't hide raw terror. A lump in Brodie's windpipe prevented the trickle of spit from passing through.

If he had one favor to ask, he'd use it to assure Laurel he'd gladly follow her to hell and beyond in order to keep her free of men the likes of Vallens and Taft... even it meant a walk right up the steps to the gallows.

Regret? You could say he had plenty to keep him company.

But never in protecting the love of his life.

The square-jawed captain displayed no mood to grant favors, not even small ones to ease a tormented soul. Brodie had trusted too little and so quickly thrown away what he'd battled great odds to find.

He glanced back when the column moved.

Sweet Jezzie.

Laurel stumbled, tears creating rivers down pale cheeks until she fell to her knees in the middle of the street.

"I'll love you always, my darlin'." His whispered breath couldn't rise past the hole in his chest. "For all eternity."

The ride gave him time to mask the misery that surely his face reflected, for he'd not give his enemy more reason to taunt. Arriving, Brodie noted the similarity of the Jefferson stockade to the shameless conditions at Andersonville and Camp Douglas. It was nothing more than a dungeon beneath the stars. Sole saving grace, if a man called it that, was they had no roof to trap the stench inside. Urine and decay that killed many with disease and dysentery could escape to some degree.

Sand Town. An accurate name for the place where men died in numbers, their bones returning to dust from whence they came.

His gut sank with reality when the immense fifteen-foot-high timbers of the prison's gate slammed behind.

Men in rags shuffled around the compound, their glazed eyes staring, welcoming him to a deplorable existence. Blankets spread on the ground indicated the sleeping quarters. The second thing to catch his eye was a gallows at the far end.

"There's no place like home, eh, Shenandoah?" The captain yanked him from the horse by the chains binding his wrists. "Don't get too accustomed though, you won't be here long."

"About what I'd expect from yellow-hearted Billy Yanks."

"Tsk, tsk. Mr. Shenandoah needs a few lessons in manners. Don't he, boys?"

Fists pummeled muscle and flesh, reminding Brodie of the value of keeping his opinions to himself. Pain in the midsection and kidneys doubled him over. His shackles placed him at their mercy, not that they possessed any for a Southern Reb. He slumped to the ground and prayed they'd tire.

Laurel's face flashed across his memory. The night they made love her sooty gaze had held anger.

He'd disappointed her once again. How many times did that make? Must surely set a record. And how many chances did a man get to right wrongs? No more, it seemed.

Useless to think about at this stage, for he'd not leave this stockade except in a pine box. That much remained clear.

Yep, he bore much regret.

Then a well-placed boot to the skull delivered Brodie into the black pit he'd dreaded.

Now he would never know when the last breath came.

❧

Laurel set about her business in a fog. Had Ollie not vetoed the notion she'd have put Closed on the door and curled under the covers.

"I think we've fed every mouth, belly, and hollow spot in the vicinity." Adeline finally sank into the nearest chair.

"Young lady, it's hard but honest work. You'll get the hang of it though. Gotta get your feet wet before you learn to dog-paddle." Ollie patted Laurel. "Girl, go talk to Murphy and get his two cents on springing

Brodie from that blue belly hell. You ain't gonna do much good here anyhow. Go put your heads together while I teach Adeline the finer points of dishwashing."

Within minutes, Laurel lifted the brass knocker at the house on State Street. Etta opened the door before she could let go of the shiny noisemaker.

"Lawsy, I'm glad you came. Mr. Murphy's in a tizzy since the soldiers invaded the privacy of his home. Them men snatched Mr. Brodie straight out of his breakfast chair before we knowed the reason why. Plumb disgraceful treatment of God-fearing folk."

Hannibal posted himself outside the entryway. His devotion to her touched Laurel deeply. She'd spent a good part of the day wondering who the animal would choose should Vallens reappear, for deep in her gut she knew the man would sooner or later. If he wasn't dead.

Laurel barely glimpsed her former betrothed's colorless face before she threw herself into his arms.

"What are we going to do, Murphy? It's all my fault."

"Come into the parlor. We'll figure out something."

"They're going to kill him. Probably without benefit of a trial, no less. They may already have."

"Not with the stink Mr. Loughery keeps raising with his editorials in Marshall's *Texas Republican* newspaper. He keeps an eagle eye on that bunch, particularly since most of the injustices occur against Jefferson's most influential." Murphy smoothed her hand to reassure, but worry lining his features said his reasoning didn't necessarily hold water. "Did you know Mr. Loughery even wrote the president of the United States, detailing a list of basic rights they've denied prisoners?"

"Letters. They're a waste of time and postage."

"Don't discount the power of words, my dear. Since he did, General Buell and his underlings have gotten more careful. I hear government spies watch and report back to Washington."

Laurel jumped up to pace the length of the room. "Brodie isn't influential or anyone of consequence. The soldiers can simply claim they shot him trying to escape."

The mere thought filled her mouth with bitter rage.

"Sit down. I can't think if you insist on pacing."

She returned to perch stiffly beside him. "Spit and thunder. He had to have lost his mind to come back with Texas under military occupation. And why did he have to follow Vallens and try to save me? He didn't take the danger serious enough."

"No, he did. And knowing my brother, he would gladly do it again."

"Why, for heaven's sake? Does he place so little value on his life?"

"You don't understand my brother very well. He does whatever it takes to ensure the welfare of those he loves, even if he finds death in the process. The answer to your question… He cares for you with his body and soul, so much he'd risk anything on this earth for your safety."

Brodie's crooked smile haunted her memory.

At least I'm not the one claiming something they're not, Lil. I hold no misconception of the sort I am.

Strange how it took losing the man she loved to discover a truth Ollie had tried to pound into her. No person could bring what she craved and thought never to have. It had to come from her.

Wearing a mask and pretending to be someone else didn't earn her a place of respect.

Strange she'd had it all this time and couldn't see it.

He couldn't die because of her foolish notions.

But he would. He'd chosen that.

Laurel gripped the tufted arm of the settee.

He'd die for her.

Twenty-eight

LAUREL FOUGHT SICKENING NAUSEA.

"I have an idea worth trying." Murphy steepled his hands, thumbs on his mouth. "It requires a trip into Jefferson, which I'm not up to…and a lie. It's a lot to ask."

"I'll say anything. Go anywhere."

"It may not work, but I believe it's all we have." Murphy quickly outlined the scheme.

Two hours later, Laurel walked down the gang-plank of the steamer at Jefferson and went straight to Epperson & Maxey, Attorneys at Law, tucked between the Rosebud Saloon and Mrs. Kinnear's millinery shop.

Laurel groaned when Georgia Rutabaga of the Tyler Rutabagas just happened to emerge from the hatmaker.

"Miss James, how delightful." The clerk of the mercantile pursed her lips. "I've spent sleepless nights worrying about whatever I said or did to upset you."

"You needn't give it a second thought. I'm fine. Truly."

Georgia Rutabaga peered over Laurel's shoulder. "Business with Mr. Epperson?"

Laurel suppressed a desire to tell the woman to mind her own business and tried to be gracious. "Forgive me, but I can't bear to discuss an extremely sensitive matter." She sniffled and dabbed her eyes. "I pray you understand."

"I must get home to Mr. Rutabaga anyway. How time flies."

After the woman rounded a corner, Laurel patted herself on the back for the stroke of brilliance, then calmed her shaking hands and turned the knob.

"Benjamin Epperson at your service, miss." A dapper man closed a large volume on his desk. Gray sprinkles shot through his once dark hair.

"Nice to meet you. I have it on good authority you might assist with a grievous problem." When the man raised a quizzical brow, she went on. "I travel seeking the head of Citizens for Peace."

Mr. Epperson cast a glance around then hustled her into an inner room. "Merely speaking the name in broad daylight gets innocent men killed. However, I have no knowledge any such organization exists and advise against pursuing this. Whoever claims otherwise committed a falsehood. I practice law."

"Murphy Yates of Redemption gave me your name. Perhaps he erred. I apologize." A sudden turn swirled her skirts about as Laurel tried not to show her despair. She stumbled, slamming her shoulder into a paneled wall.

"Wait, miss. You said Murphy Yates?"

"He's a friend. A contingent of soldiers took his brother to the stockade. A bullet wound during a bank robbery prevented Mr. Yates from coming himself."

"So the devils finally caught Brodie? Hate to hear that. I understand he gave them quite a slippery chase."

One that ended largely because of her.

"Then you grasp the importance of my need. Could you direct me to anyone who has affiliations with the Rising Sun?"

"Please follow me, Miss...?"

"James. Laurel James."

Benjamin Epperson tapped a code of sorts on what appeared an ordinary wall inside a coat closet. Laurel followed him inside a secret room. A small group of men leaped to their feet.

"No cause for alarm, gentlemen," Epperson said. "This pretty lady asks for our help. Mr. Crump, it's my opinion that we should consider obliging her."

In less than half an hour she tucked a hastily designed document into a satchel and headed for the tall gates that imprisoned her love. For the first time since leaving Redemption, she held hope of fixing the mess she'd had a hand in creating.

She only prayed it worked.

❧

Brodie had no strength to resist when pulled roughly from an airless sweat coffin designed to break a man's will.

"Commander wants to see ya," the voice yelled in his good ear, the one they'd overlooked in teaching the "lesson."

Getting a clear view of the figure through swollen eyes took some doing. And when a shove sent him sprawling at the feet of a woman who bore great similarity to Laurel, he decided the confinement and beatings had left him delusional.

They must've bashed out his brains to think Laurel would take tea with his tormenter like she was on a social outing.

"Shenandoah, good of you to place yourself at my beck and call." General Buell smiled and leaned forward. "Your lovely wife brings a document to my attention. It states your name as Brodie Yates. To wit, you can't possibly be the infamous spy because you were too busy marrying her."

A wife?

The brutes had indeed ruined his hearing, along with breaking two fingers and half his ribs, for he could've sworn the man called Laurel his wife.

"What have you done to my husband?" Laurel's strained voice told of her struggle to hold back a sob.

A hundred needles pierced his body when he tried to stand. Although lying on the floor presented tempting argument, he wished to meet the Yankee's smirk from an upright position. He didn't push aside the firm grip around his waist or gentle brush of Laurel's lips to his cheek as she helped him into a chair.

Thumb screws brought less misery than seeing her again.

Facing the only woman he'd ever loved shouldn't be where he must measure each word with the greatest care. Making amends called for softer surroundings far away from curious ears. Preferably amid a downy featherbed.

"I don't buy this charade for one minute, but I must compliment you on your excellent taste in women." Buell bit off the end of a fat cigar and struck a match to it. "No, it's going to take a lot more than paper. It looks phony to me."

Brodie felt Laurel stiffen. She clutched a handkerchief to her mouth. "I have no reason to lie. Besides, I have eight children I can march in here to prove he preferred bedding me over fighting a silly war. And you still haven't answered my question. How did my husband receive this beating?"

A marriage *and* children? Eight of them to be exact. How could he forget such a large number? One thing for sure, if he'd partaken of such pleasure, it would never slip his mind.

"Madam, I don't care if you parade half the children in the state of Texas through here. It won't prove he's not Shenandoah," the general stated dryly.

The raven-haired beauty's eyes widened. "Perhaps the word of a learned physician would carry more weight. Dr. Whitaker can explain why my husband couldn't join the cause because he took sick with cholera." She sobbed quietly into the lace-edged cloth. "But for the pure grace of God, I would've lost him. Once he recovered, a horse threw him and broke his leg—my husband's, not the horse's."

Brodie wondered where she got her acting skills. It was quite impressive.

"I declare, Mrs. Yates. That tragic concoction seems too good to waste. But I don't believe a word," Buell snapped.

"Disputing my wife's integrity, General?" Brodie snapped.

"Sure am, even if a Dr. Whitaker does exist beyond the figment of her imagination."

"Well, I never!" She placed a hand on her hip. "For the last time, I need an answer to my question concerning Brodie's condition."

"He fell. Does that suit you?"

"No. I intend to pay a visit to Mr. Loughery. One would think with the trouble he's stirred up recounting the atrocious prisoner maltreatment in the newspaper you'd take more care not to get on his front page again."

"Loughery's nothing but a rabble-rouser. Before it's over, he may find himself in my stockade if he doesn't watch out."

"Could I appeal to your sense of fairness and beg a private word with my husband?" Laurel leaned forward to touch General Buell's arm. "Please. It's so little to ask."

Brodie knew the effect of that contact; still, it amazed him to see how quickly it shredded the hardened man's resistance.

"I'm no ogre, my dear lady. Ten minutes, no more."

The door latch slid into place before either spoke. Brodie broke the silence first. "You should've stayed away."

How could he delicately explain that her presence poured salt in wounds that'd already festered?

She put her arms around his neck and leaned against his chest. "I couldn't stay away. Darn it, I can't find a spot that's not bruised or bloody. They've reduced you to shambles."

Brodie shrugged. "It's nothing I didn't expect. Comes with the territory."

"They didn't need to beat the living daylights out of you."

"Appears I made 'em mad."

Brodie winced when she gently brushed the lock of hair from his forehead. Everything about him hurt... mostly his heart. He stepped back from her. Give him back the thumb screws any day over this torture.

"Go home. Surely I don't have to lay out the risks to an intelligent lady," he rasped.

"I'm well aware of what's at stake. But I had to come. You're here on my account. I can't leave you to the mercy of these Yankees without trying to repay a debt."

"Darlin', so I'm reduced to nothing but a debt? Maybe it was a merchant behind the mask you wore that night."

"Don't give up." Her voice lowered to a whisper. "Murphy and I...and others will think of something."

"Dare I point out General Buell saw through your attempt, dear wife? By the way, remind me again when we said our vows? Was that before or after you sneaked out of Curley's saloon?"

Her lavender eyes registered surprise. "You saw me? I can explain. Believe in me. You did once. For God's sake, I love you. I wouldn't do anything to ruin that. In your own way, when you give yourself a chance, I think you love me back."

Love? It was too late for that... Too late for wishing for something he couldn't have.

"The only way I'm leaving here is in a box, understand?"

"Quitting at the first skirmish? Strange, I never thought they'd break the legendary Reb so quickly."

"Stop it. Forget me. Get on with your life."

"So we simply have dead dreams left? I mean nothing?"

The whisper came from hurt and misery that cut to the quick. He'd lost the one woman who could've brought peace.

"Don't look so sad, love. It's reality. We aren't starry-eyed schoolchildren." Brodie lifted her palm to his face. The smooth skin cooled a fevered cheek. "For what it's worth, I wish things were different. Only they aren't. A price comes for dancing to the music. You gotta pay that old fiddler for the privilege at some point."

"Don't say that. We deserve happiness and a chance."

"It won't happen. You can't rub the spots off a leopard."

He traced the moist line of her lips with a finger. When the tip of her tongue came in contact with his skin, he shivered with longing. She moved into the circle of his arm and burrowed her face into his chest. He closed his eyes tight to block the assault of her fragrance, soft curves that molded to his, and desire to have one more second with her.

"It doesn't matter. Once you're out of here, we can sort everything out," Laurel murmured.

Couldn't she see they didn't have a forward? Movement in any direction would earn him nothing but a walk up to the gallows.

He tried to smile only it hurt too much. "I dearly wish I could meet these eight kids of ours before that hearse rolls up to cart me away." He kissed the upturned mouth very gently, surprised he could still pucker.

The squeak of the door silenced a reply. "Time's over. General said…uh, you hafta leave now…uh, madam."

Brodie quirked an eyebrow at the brawny soldier's

sudden shyness. The man certainly hadn't displayed a speck of it when he drove those boots into his ribs.

"I'll be back tomorrow." Laurel's lips brushed his bruised cheek. "That's a promise."

"Let it go, I said. You can't save me—not now, not ever. Mind your own knitting and quit trying to mend things that are better off thrown into a trash heap. I'm not redeemable."

He had no choice but to push her away. Didn't she see the danger she was in? Although sending her back to Redemption would rip out his heart, he had to. But damn. Hurt in her pretty eyes drove a knife into his chest. If only he could hold her and kiss away her sorrow, make love to her one more time.

"I'd ask the General's permission first, ma'am." Then the soldier floundered. "I mean…he generally allows visitors only once a week. But he, uh…might make an exception."

"Heed me. Don't visit again." Brodie stared into the cloudless day, his voice brittle and hard. For her safety and his sanity, he could show no weakness.

Or his shattered heart.

Laurel stumbled through the gates. A sob rose, mixing with her tears. He saw in her a cat splattered with mud.

She could wash it off. Her quivering chin rose. Some she'd already scrubbed away. She could the rest.

He'd see. But first they must get him out and soon.

"Fancy meeting the beautiful Miss James in Sand Town."

In the midst of her pain and despair she'd failed to notice the man in the shadows.

"Vallens! You're alive and well despite rumors to the contrary. Folks in Redemption figured you for dead." The good news was they couldn't arrest Ollie for a murder she didn't commit. "Do you miss your hound?"

"Not particularly. Dog's a scrapper."

"You put Brodie here."

Vallens rubbed the jagged scar as though it ached down to his rotten soul.

"A word in the right ear works wonders and lures a woman from her safe surroundings."

Suddenly, everything began to add up.

"The mystery with the meat shipment has your name all over it. Correct?"

"Except Taft failed to show, forcing a change in tactics."

"I should've known it'd take more than a bullet to send you to hell."

"Reckon that's 'cause I'm already there." He moved aside to reveal a second figure.

"I do declare, you're looking splendid, Lil."

Laurel didn't need the rough edge of the broken tooth to recall the face that brought her nightmares to life. Icicles formed in the darkest corners of her being.

Will Taft's mouth settled in a grim line. "I'm out of patience with you. The woman who stole you away from the Black Garter cost me dearly. I want recompense. I will have both the money and you."

Terror rose, filling her mouth, gagging her with hopelessness. She glanced around for anyone who might help her.

"Grab a shovel because I'm dead to you. You'll never get Ollie or me. The money's gone, too."

"Reckon your hide will do just fine. I've never skinned a woman before. I anticipate the pleasure." The mouth barely visible in Taft's whiskered face turned up in a smile. "And you have two younger sisters."

Twenty-nine

LAUREL GASPED FOR BREATH. NO ONE COULD HELP HER now. Still she wasn't going to give him the satisfaction of knowing her terror.

"Touch my sisters and you'll rue the day you were born. I've come a long way from the child you stole. I fight much better."

A persistent bell rang somewhere in the middle of the afternoon. The clanging penetrated her dull senses that reeled from one surprise to the next. How very strange indeed. Perhaps a fire? Still no one shouted orders to form a bucket brigade.

"There you are, Miss James." Georgia Rutabaga appeared at her side, gently taking her arm. "Did you forget?"

"Forget?"

"The Garden Club tea I invited you to earlier. Come along or we'll be late. The ladies get impatient waiting for stragglers. Mrs. Crump grows most fretful when it comes to eyeing tea cakes and mouth-watering scones that she can't have until everyone arrives." The woman edged her out of Vallens's and Taft's reach with the expertise of a soldier.

"Oh yes. I'm so glad you found me." Although Laurel had no idea what was going on, she could've hugged Mrs. Rutabaga.

"Keep walking and don't look back," the woman murmured.

The bell continued to clamor as they traveled the streets, glancing back often to make sure they weren't followed. At last her rescuer unlatched the gate of a picket fence surrounding a dilapidated house. If the Garden Club met here, they were in dire shape.

Opening the door, Laurel found the lavish furnishings quite a shock.

"No one followed, did they?"

The question shot from a gentleman who took her hand. She recognized him from the secret room at the law office.

"I took every precaution." Georgia removed hat pins, lifted the feathered finery, and laid it on the marble table.

Laurel stared at the two. "I don't understand…"

"Alfred, please explain to the poor dear we're not kidnapping her before she faints dead away."

"I am a bit confused," Laurel admitted.

Holding her head, she sank into a silk upholstered chair Mr. Rutabaga shoved under her wobbly legs.

"We followed discreetly to the stockade and saw the two men accost you," Alfred said. "Vallens's and Taft's shenanigans have given them an unsavory reputation, to say the least. I alerted fellow Citizens for Peace with the bell and sent my wife to rescue you."

"I can never thank you enough. They've cost me and my family untold grief." Tears hovered at the near close call.

"We know of your abduction years ago," Alfred said.

"And your escape from that man's evil clutches." Georgia Rutabaga patted her arm. "You're safe here."

Within minutes the parlor filled with a group of men. Each wore grim features of fighting a cause they didn't expect to win, but would try with every ounce of strength in their bodies.

Laurel met Benjamin Epperson's concern head on. "General Buell didn't accept the document."

"I gathered as much. Never fear, we aren't giving up."

"That's right," Phillip Crump added. "We're not licked yet. I have a brilliant plan. Excuse us while we confer, Miss James." A wall panel opened up to another secret room.

Georgia Rutabaga took a seat next to Laurel. "You haven't let your family know you're alive and well?"

"I can't. I care too much." Laurel's voice broke.

"About them, or you?"

How quickly Georgia had seen through her. Laurel squirmed. Too many "toos" littered the path home.

"It's complicated. And risky. I will one day."

"Let me get you that tea while they talk, dear."

Over hot tea and fresh apple cake, Georgia Rutabaga shed light on the stark difference between the home's exterior and interior.

"The military marched in and immediately began confiscating the best homes. Making the outside so hideous no one would want to live here assured us it was the best way to keep it. As predicted, they passed us over. The Mabreys, Schluters, and several others wish they'd done likewise."

The old house and Laurel shared a kinship. Both resembled souls that ached with weary despair.

Her heart longed for something it couldn't have.

Brodie's swollen rebel grays hadn't disguised the truth. He'd taken her love when it suited.

Then discarded her as nothing more than ballast in a pockmarked pirate ship.

❧

Georgia Rutabaga's endless chatter the entire ride back to Redemption grew tiresome. Poor Alfred Rutabaga never had an opening to toss in an occasional word. Although grateful for the couple's armed escort, Laurel would've preferred a more quiet journey home. The day's events required mulling.

The misery Brodie dealt sat heavy in her chest. He'd never accepted her past, never had faith she could change.

She'd needed him to believe in her. To want her.

The grim lines in Ollie's face told of her worry. "It's about dadburned time!" she scolded. "Worrying a poor body to death oughta be a crime."

Wolf-dog rose from the pallet and bared his teeth.

"Shush, Hannibal. These are friends." Laurel kissed Ollie's cheek. "Couldn't help it. Now use your best manners to welcome Mr. and Mrs. Rutabaga from Jefferson."

"Didn't know you'd be bringing company, girl."

"I apologize for Ollie. She's not ordinarily this cantankerous."

"Am too." Ollie stumbled a little as she pushed Laurel away and held out a hand. "I'm Olivia Applejack b'Dam and I'm right pleased to make your acquaintance. It's not every day my girl brings guests home. Will you be staying for tea and crumpets?"

"I'm afraid not," Alfred quickly got in, "unless Miss James has further needs?"

"You've done more than enough. We'll be fine."

"I don't know, Alfred. I worry about leaving them."

"I insist." Laurel steered them toward the door. "I'll lock up so tight a cockroach can't find a crack."

"Think about going home," Georgia whispered in her ear.

By the time the Rutabagas' buggy faded in the distance, Laurel had bolted both doors, slid chairs under the knobs for extra measure, and checked each window latch.

"Hannibal, on guard." Then she selected the sharpest knife from the drawer.

Let Taft try to harm them now. One disturbing thought niggled. Would the wolf-dog choose Vallens when it came to it?

"Girl, I need you to help these old bones up the stairs if you've finished whatever it is you're doing. Rutabaga is the silliest name I ever heard."

Ollie generally didn't ask for help of any sort. Laurel didn't take that she did so as reassurance that everything was fit as a fiddle.

Also, the woman hadn't badgered her with a million questions.

"What's wrong, Ollie? Is it your heart?"

"Just need to lie down for a spell. I just cain't see."

The tick of the clock almost drowned the weak voice. Laurel shouldered the slight frame, taking care to not waken Adeline. Ollie collapsed on the bed in her room across from Laurel's. She didn't make a squawk when Laurel removed her shoes and drew up a worn quilt.

"Ollie, can I do anything else?"

"Stay with me."

Shallow breathing robbed the room of air. Laurel gasped from pain of fighting a battle she'd lose. She'd lived in dread of this moment since learning of Ollie's poor health. Her head told her she couldn't stall the inevitable, yet her heart wished to believe the motherly friend would live forever.

Fetching Curley entered her mind, except danger lurked outside the doors she dare not unlock. She prayed he'd forgive her.

Tears dampened her cheeks as she curled up beside Ollie and took the thin face between her hands.

"I don't think I told you how much I love you."

"Girl, no need to speak of things we already know. Afraid it's time to part company."

"Please don't die."

"Ain't of a mind to, but ol' Gabriel's tootin' his horn. Purtiest music I ever did hear."

Laurel strangled a sob. "Rest awhile and you'll be fine."

"Mama, I've missed your smile. What's that, Mama?" Ollie's voice became child-like. "Grandpappy, you came."

Chills tumbled end over end. Laurel had heard when a body neared the end that the spirits of loved ones would come carry them home. Only let her be wrong for this once. She smoothed back Ollie's faded spikes, wishing she could go with her.

"I need you a bit longer, Ollie. This world's a cold, forbidding place." Thank goodness Ollie didn't learn about Taft and Vallens. Laurel had spared her that at least.

Laurel took the knife and laid it beside her.

Ollie mumbled incoherently.

"Do you need something? Maybe a cup of your brew might get you raring to face another morn."

"Reckon the good Lord put me on this earth for a reason and that was to take care of my girl. You gave an old woman purpose when I had nary. Certainly filled my days with more love than an old crone like me deserved."

She kissed the fragile hand. "We're about equal in the giving department. You saved me when no other would."

"I failed. Tried to hang on till I got you with your folks. Promise you'll go to them once I'm gone. And don't be too hard on Yates." Ollie's murmurs grew more faint.

A blessing the woman didn't know about the shambled mess in her heart. It was nothing to share with a dying old friend.

The magnitude of an empty life suddenly washed over her.

What would she do, and who to turn to with problems?

"Shh, don't worry, I'll make do, Ollie."

"Say you'll go to your ma and pa."

A body had to keep a deathbed pledge no matter what.

Yet, how could she vow it, seeing the impossible nature?

Hot tears rose. She had jinxed everyone she ever loved.

"You should rest now, Ollie."

"Not until you promise."

Once the stubborn woman buried her choppers in something she wouldn't let go, not even in the throes of crossing the dark river. Laurel worked to form words she couldn't fulfill.

"I will. Now save your strength."

"I love you, my beautiful angel girl."

"Wait for me over there. I need someone to welcome me."

Laurel snuggled close and laid her head on Ollie's chest. A death rattle commenced that no amount of prayers could stop. Ollie had begun the journey. Soon the dear woman would rest and be free from pain. Laurel hoped the good Lord would overlook and take a liking to the crusty soul. Surely a heart big as the whole blamed state of Texas would go a long way in atoning for any faltering Ollie did on earth.

"Please, God, she didn't really kill Vallens. And she wouldn't have stolen that money from Taft if there'd been any other way. So, open the gates and let her in."

Midnight came and went. Angels folded their wings around Ollie and carried her safely to the distant shore. In the wee hours when dawn stole into the room, Ollie breathed no more.

Laurel clung to the shell her brave friend had occupied. Deep sobs wracked her as tears flowed onto the cold, stiff body.

The turning doorknob had Laurel grabbing the

knife. She clutched it with both hands. The mass of long blond hair brought relief.

"I thought I heard… Oh no, is something wrong with Miss Ollie?"

Laurel lowered the knife, wiping her weary eyes. "She's dead. Her heart played out."

Adeline sank to the floor. "What're we going to do? Two girls alone that everyone threw out with the slop."

"She did love us, for a fact."

"Who'll care for us now?"

"We will care for each other…together."

Laurel bathed every wrinkle of the body with loving hands before clothing her in a dress of satin and pearls. Aged tissue paper had encased the pale blue finery she found oddly hidden in the bottom of an old trunk Ollie brought with them.

A tiny box yielded another piece of the puzzle, for inside lay a shiny gold band. It glimmered through a sudden veil of wetness. Laurel brushed her eyes, slipping the ring on Ollie's finger.

Only a woman who'd loved deeply would guard those treasures all these years.

Laurel prayed the man was worth it.

Brodie's bruised, battered face lingered each time she closed her eyes.

Farewell words haunted every waking moment.

Quit trying to mend things that are better off thrown into a trash heap. I'm not redeemable.

Laurel found some faded letters tied with a red bow

in a corner of the trunk. She set them aside, unable to bear the heartbreak of learning that some stranger had spurned someone so precious. She tucked the letters written by Charles Farnsworth into the pine box. The grave would protect their private love.

A blustery day added gloom to the funeral. Little more than a handful came to pay respects. But that was fine. Ollie valued genuine friendship. She would've considered it sacrilege to have the scornful there for her send-off.

Laurel kept a wary eye out for Taft and Vallens, although knowing the sneaky pair as she did, they'd bide their time. That was their way.

Within the circle of Curley Madison's soft warmth, Laurel found courage to complete the journey she began with Ollie that night in St. Louis. Their paths separated here. Each would have to go alone. Perhaps Ollie would meet up with Charles Farnsworth to renew an acquaintance that must've had an untimely end. Laurel held on to that thought.

Nodding politely to Murphy, Nora, and Jake, Laurel pulled her heavy shawl closer. Adeline's heavy sobs punctured the somber quiet. The poor girl had seen much grief for someone so young.

"Curley, since we don't have a preacher I think Ollie would like you to say something befitting," Laurel suggested.

The saloonkeeper nodded, blew his nose, and cleared his throat. "Friends, we're gathered today to mourn the passing of Olivia Applejack b'Dam who the Lord Almighty saw fit to take from us."

He paused for a moment, struggling for breath.

"Many of you chose to see a rough, crotchety has-been. Not me. Beneath the layer of salt and vinegar was the finest, most beautiful lady I've ever met. She left a piece of herself within each of us. Ollie imparted wisdom and truth that we might not've wished to hear but had to anyway. Each morsel enriched our lives in ways we never guessed."

A purple and yellow bouquet of prairie flowers, spiderwort, and broomweed clutched in her fist seemed appropriate for Olivia b'Dam who lived life natural and free on her own terms.

"If a body's judged by the mark they leave behind, Ollie needn't worry because hers is wide enough to accommodate Texas and have room for Arkansas." Curley's voice quavered. He mopped his eyes with a handkerchief. "Dear Lord, don't get too mad if you catch her swinging on the pearly gates. Having fun is purely her nature. And she's a little on the sassy side, which you'll overlook once you take a shine to her. Amen."

"Hallelujah." Smiling, Laurel sniffled.

Through a haze of tears she winced as dirt covered the motherly woman. Adeline's hand strayed into hers and Laurel took comfort in the meager offering.

If only she'd done more to relieve stress on Ollie's heart.

If only she'd stayed instead of going on a fool's errand.

If only she could've taken Ollie's place.

Laurel swallowed the sob, mindful the woman didn't have anyone left to kill, run off, or hide from.

Murphy hugged her. "Don't blame yourself. She

lived on borrowed time. Just be grateful we had her as long as we did. Nora and I are here if you need anything whatsoever."

One by one, all left except Laurel, Adeline, and Curley.

"I can't leave her. What will I do without Ollie?" Laurel sobbed.

"Follow your dream, child." Curley's arm encircled her. "Just because loved ones pass don't give us call to slink away. Ollie would tell you to leave her to the grave and go on."

The advice stuck with Laurel on the long walk back to an empty life and through the task of moving her belongings to the room across the narrow hall.

"Are you sure Miss Ollie's things won't…?" Adeline fingered Ollie's worn dress they'd exchanged for the blue satin, unable to complete the thought.

"Give me the willies?" Laurel kissed the top of the blond head. "I honestly don't know. I can still smell that pipe. On the other hand, it'll seem she's watching over us."

"Like my ma. Sometimes I smell her perfume."

"I surely wouldn't doubt it."

Heaven must've had powerful need of livening up to have left them so bereft. Lord knows spouting Grandpappy's sayings would put big smiles on all the angels' lips.

"Maybe you should close the café for a day or two," Curley said, dropping by around sundown.

"Can't afford it." Laurel pushed a strand of hair from her face. "This business is our means. And it helps to keep busy."

Unless Taft had other plans.

"But, Curley, do you mind staying close?" Anger turned him beet red when she told him about Taft and Vallens.

"Those jackals! I'll set up a bed in the kitchen."

With the café locked tight and Curley snoring downstairs, Laurel felt relatively safe…from most things.

Ollie's gamin features poked from each shadow, while the scent of the pipe swirled in the still air. Fresh grief rose.

Then steamy recollections of a different sort entered the mix to keep her eyes from closing.

Silvery moon rays scampering through the window. Hard muscle sliding over hers. The crooked smile of a shameless rebel with gray eyes. All those memories brought tiny shivers.

And an ache for tender caresses unlike any other.

Thirty

"I SWORE I HEARD THAT FUNNY LITTLE CACKLE OF Miss Ollie's." Adeline set an armload of plates next to the bucket of hot soapy water. "Hard to believe we buried her yesterday."

Pain between Laurel's shoulder blades reminded her of how time dragged. She redoubled efforts on hardened stew in the bottom of the pot. She'd hid in the kitchen, assigning the girl dining room duty, thinking it might somehow be easier. Not so.

Danger lurked in the moonlight. Eyes watched, waiting.

And where had Hannibal gone?

Odd he hadn't scratched to get in since Curley let him out.

"Looks like you'd have more than enough to busy yourself with. Customers to satisfy, floors to sweep, tables to clear, mice traps to set." Laurel was instantly ashamed. Although she missed Ollie in every way possible, so did Adeline.

"That busybody Mrs. Kempshaw's taking her sweet

time. She's the last. I've gathered the dishes, wiped tables, and you know we never sweep the floors until all have gone. And I don't know nothing about baiting mice traps. Always get my fingers in the darn things." Adeline scooted out a chair and plopped down.

"I apologize for being ill tempered. Guess I'm tired."

"It's all right. Ain't complaining. At least it ain't the saloon."

Laurel flashed a wan smile. "I'm thankful you're here."

"Can I ask something? What kept you from going insane when those men forced you to…you know?"

The ugly word filled the space, an unmade bed in an otherwise orderly room that you tried not to notice but couldn't help it. Only this bed had every corner tucked in neatly and still a body couldn't erase the memory of mess and chaos. Hate welled for the man who'd stolen Adeline's innocence, making her a woman before she'd put away her dolls.

"I survived by doing what I had to. Thinking of my family, fresh green fields cleansed by rain, Mama's blueberry pie."

And waiting for Brodie's return.

"I prayed for God to strike me dead." Adeline's voice trembled. "I hated when my papa made me drink the potion."

Laurel's head snapped around. "The what?"

"Ain't rightly sure what's in it. Toads' innards wouldn't have tasted as bitter." The girl wrinkled her nose. "Made me drink it once a week. Said it'd keep my monthly coming."

Black haw tonic made from cotton root bark would

be Laurel's guess. The stuff worked well in preventing babies. Taft had forced the horrid liquid down her until a doctor supplied plant seeds from Queen Anne's Lace. A spoonful with a glass of water each morning spared a child they'd have ripped from her arms. She'd witnessed that misfortune in others.

"He was right on that count."

"Do you suppose I might not be able to make babies one day? I mean when I meet the man I'm going to marry."

"Don't worry. It has no lasting effects."

Laurel's heart lurched. The wondrous night in Brodie's arms, the rebel she wished more than anything to grow old with, may have left permanent proof of the love she'd fight to keep.

Even though the father didn't wish to become one.

And God forbid should he soon perish at the end of a rope.

A babe would assure keeping a piece of him always.

She shook away the thoughts. "You'll give your heart to the man of your dreams and have a houseful of beautiful blond babies."

Adeline chewed on her lip. "If Paw happens to find me, will you let him take me back?"

"I'll kill him first. You have a perfect right to live free from twisted perversions."

"And you? What if those men come?"

"I'll never again be any man's paid woman."

The door into the dining room moved ever so slightly. Laurel's heart leaped into her throat.

⤋

Brodie knew every speck of dust and spiderweb in the dark sweat box intimately. It was home. Probably would remain so until the appointed hour.

Deep black water amid the cypress held secrets, but in his lady love's sultry kisses he'd found the lost soul for which he'd searched...only to leave it scattered among the ruins of broken promises like moth-eaten rags on a peddler's cart.

Hell and be damned.

He forced aside despair as boots crunched on the rocks littering the stockade. A key grated in the lock. The abrupt glare almost put out his eyes that'd seen far too much horror.

"Come along, Shenandoah. Got a visitor."

Georgia clay. He'd begged Laurel to stay away. Another encounter with the raven-haired temptress would drain him. Ahh, but he'd savor something to carry besides the lavender scrap of lace in the memory bag the general had ripped off his neck.

He stumbled, faint from hunger. The soldier jerked him to his feet. Seconds later, the blue belly shoved him into a room.

"Yates, so we meet again. This time under more, shall we say, favorable circumstances." A hint of a smile twisted the jagged scar into a well-traveled road pitted with deep ruts.

"Fighting a bound man would seem fair-minded only to you."

"You don't scare me," Zeke Vallens sneered.

"That so." Brodie kicked a chair into the wall, relishing Vallens's sudden jump. A quick curl of his foot around the leg flipped the seat upright. The leisurely drop into it hopefully masked his pain. To expose his suffering would reveal a chink in the fortress. "How like you to come to gloat."

"Ah, you misjudge me. I wished to inform you of Will Taft's arrival in town. He means to reclaim what's rightfully his."

"Damn you!" Brodie lunged, driving his full weight into the man. Zeke Vallens staggered against the wall.

"Guard!" Vallens's yell alerted the soldier posted outside.

The soldier ran into the room shouting, "Reb, in the corner or I'll shoot your sorry hide."

"Better get him out, blue belly." Brodie lounged easy, though he dared anyone to interpret his black stare as cordial.

Zeke Vallens retrieved the hat that'd fallen off in the scuffle and wedged it on his head. "Good day, Shenandoah."

"Heed my words. Harm Laurel, and you and Taft'll answer."

"To who, pray tell?"

"You'll see. I'd pay attention." Hate silenced the rumble in his belly. If only it fed a soul's gnawing hunger as well.

The black-hearted devil's smile wobbled a bit in leaving.

The young soldier cast Brodie a wary glance. "Come peaceable, Reb. I wouldn't want to have to call for reinforcements."

What rankled most was leaving Laurel at the mercy of evil. He couldn't protect her. He couldn't soothe her trembling limbs.

Good God, he couldn't even love her like she deserved.

Guilt rode like a dark shadow, blotting out the sun.

"Private, do I get a final request before execution?"

"If it's within reason, I'd suppose."

"How about a letter? Think you can deliver it?"

"I'll see to it, but not sure how soon."

"I'd prefer it happen today. It's imperative."

With it written, Brodie found the metal box a tad less dark than before. Something he'd learned about people in the war let him believe the private would keep his word. With luck the letter should get in the right hands by nightfall.

Even though he might not stick around to see the outcome.

&

Beyond the stockade walls, Zeke Vallens flipped open a timepiece. Satisfaction came that he'd given Yates something to chew on. The visit might pay off in the event he lost control of the situation. The night would tell whether it'd been profitable.

Plans oftentimes took a volatile twist.

His jaw tightened. The pliable leather fob curled around his hand. He returned the watch and reached inside the somber frock coat to pluck a tintype from his pocket. The face in the small likeness stared into the blackest crevice of a heart the years had turned to stone.

The lady had once had the clearest blue gaze. She'd overlooked the parts no one else could stomach and saw something redeeming.

He'd disappointed her on many occasions, though she never let on.

Damn. He breathed a grateful sigh she'd never know of the despicable things he'd done.

Zeke flipped the tintype to hide the gentle soul's calling, tucked it away, and lowered the brim of his hat.

～

Panic bubbled, spurring Laurel into action. She threw back the kitchen door and stood nose to nose with Florence Kempshaw.

"Why on God's green earth are you eavesdropping?"

Florence stepped back and huffed. "I can smell rotted garbage a mile off. I knew your story didn't quite wash."

"Whatever you think you heard—"

"More'n enough to run you out of town."

Laurel's fists doubled. She yearned to punch the gossip. "One thing about me, Florence…I don't scare easily."

"We don't need your kind. When I get done, you'll wish you'd stayed in that whorehouse in St. Louie!"

Over Laurel's shoulder, Adeline gasped. Laurel had been about to tell Florence to take whatever steps she deemed appropriate. After all, baring the secret would disarm its power. But she must consider the repercussions on the girl.

"Every story has two sides. Care to listen?"

"You're not fit to associate with decent, God-fearing folk, and it's my duty to let others know."

"Mrs. Kempshaw, Laurel is the most generous,

caring person I've ever known besides my mother." Adeline's voice quaked.

"You're tainted too, girlie. Unless we put a stop, you'll turn this joint into a billiard parlor behind our backs. I'm not stupid. I know what goes on in those dens of iniquity."

It appeared Redemption's finest would soon get an earful.

"Since I can't appeal to someone who has no compassion, we have nothing further to discuss."

The woman's thin lips puckered up as if she'd bitten into a green persimmon. "Olivia b'Dam must've been in cahoots with you. I'll wager she was one of your sort, could tell by that wild hair. Kept a path hot to that saloon."

Laurel's blood boiled. "Get out of here before I forget the sort of real lady I am."

"And those Yates boys. Praise be you didn't marry and bring them ruin. I shudder to think how a faithless harlot tried to play them for fools."

Laurel shoved her. "Out! Out before I snatch you bald."

The beady eyes grew round with fear, but her courage returned once she had access to running room. "You and little missy pack up. No one'll spend another cent in this flea-infested establishment. I'll fix you."

The door slammed against Florence's heel, propelling her onto the sidewalk faster than she intended.

"I should've taken a butcher knife to that old biddy." Laurel's voice shook.

Tears welled in Adeline's blue gaze. "I hate her."

"Ah, honey." Laurel pulled her close, smoothing

the pale locks. "Don't waste a second on someone who has nothing to do except judge others and delight in spreading poison."

"Will we leave?"

A short while ago she would've. But Ollie had taught her how to build a fire and make a stand. She prayed those flames didn't heat a bunch of tar for the chicken feathers Florence was already gathering to roll Laurel and Adeline in.

Ridden out of town on a rail had to be very disgusting.

"We're staying put." She firmly bolted the door, sliding a chair beneath the knob. "Running is for sissies. Let's finish up so I can tuck you into bed."

"But it might get plenty ugly."

She tucked a long golden strand behind Adeline's ear. The word that brought shivers went a bit further than ugly.

"My dear, try as I might, I can't foresee the future. I'm rusty in foretelling such. But Ollie warned never do anything in haste. Or maybe it was her grandpappy. Don't know about you, but I'm ready to fight if that's what it takes."

"Will they send me back home?"

"Absolutely not. Get that out of your head. We're a pair. Nothing can separate us. Honey, I swear on a stack of Bibles."

Lord, give her strength to keep the promise, for their enemies consisted of a small army.

Where on earth was Hannibal when she needed him?

Swinging toward waiting work, her toe caught the ridge of an uneven plank. A table's sharp edge drove into her thigh.

Pain shot both directions at once. Laurel gritted her teeth to silence a sob.

Life always had a damn board sticking out ready to trip a hardworking body. The uphill battle to reach leveling-off ground had beaten the whey out of her. Up was the only visible trail through the forest. She saw no place to rest for a while.

Oh for the day she'd reach a tiny ledge.

With thoughts going helter-skelter, she jumped when someone pounded on the door. Taft and Vallens wouldn't bother announcing; they'd kick it in. Adeline wielded a broom.

"Miss Laurel?" Curley's boom was a relief. "It's me."

"I didn't expect you for another hour or so," she said, opening the door.

"Whistle Dixie and pass the ammunition. Closed the saloon early. No customers. Worse'n when I ran out of whiskey once."

"Let me guess. They've linked you to my lily-white character?"

"Ollie'd whale my hide to bring such a grim face. She claimed a smile lifts a body's spirits faster than wild horses in a stampede." He planted his girth at the kitchen table and raised his feet for Adeline's broom.

"I haven't exactly seen reason to smile."

"I heard the rubbish…right before I knocked out two of the rumormongers' teeth."

Frayed nerves and untold sorrow transformed into peals of laughter. Once Laurel started she couldn't stop. Adeline and Curley pronounced her a bona fide lunatic.

"You shore have a strange way of showing spunk, girl."

Laurel sobered the next minute, wanting to cry. "I can just hear Ollie, her head cocked to one side, squinting through pipe smoke." She launched into an imitation. "Grandpappy always said how a predicament could always be worse. When given a choice between attacked by a mountain lion or getting gut-shot, choose the lion. Best to get the dyin' over with fast. Yessirree."

Curley swiped at his eyes. "That woman sure knew how to live and how to die. Some folks can't do either. Least, not well."

"All I ever desired was a quiet place to bury the last six years, start fresh, and live a normal life. Is that greedy?"

"Shoot, a dream isn't anything more than thirst for something a bit better than what you got." Curley patted the back of her hand. "You're entitled to all the water you can drink. You have a lot of giving inside."

A knock on the door came again.

Shaking, she stole quickly behind the saloon-keep. Perhaps they'd already come for the tarring and feathering. She snatched Adeline against her. They could do what they wanted with her, but not a blameless child whose only crime was having a depraved father.

Curley flexed his hands before jerking it open.

Murphy leaned on Etta's son, Jacob, for support. "Madison, I'm relieved to see you. I need a word with Laurel." He met her worried gaze. "In private?"

"Sure thing. I take it you know about the newest quagmire?"

"It's why I've come."

Adeline and Curley vanished before Murphy

accepted the chair she offered. Tight lines around his mouth signified something awfully important for the friend to call this late.

"Oh God, it's Brodie!" Laurel put a hand to her mouth. "Mr. Epperson couldn't save him."

Perspiration dotted her upper lip. The image of her beloved dangling by the neck on a high platform sent jagged piercing pain into her heart.

Murphy placed a quick hand on her shoulder. "No, Brodie's still in the stockade. He sent a dispatch tonight." He turned to the young boy with him. "Jacob, will you wait by the buggy? I won't be long."

"You're in no shape to go gallivanting around town." Laurel tried to ignore the unease that leapfrogged up her spine.

"Your welfare causes great concern. Vallens paid Brodie a visit earlier, to rattle him, it would appear. I come on my brother's behalf." Murphy reached for her palm. "And I also come in regards to another matter. There's a plague of loose tongues running rampant."

"I must commend Florence. Her news swept faster than the gold discovery in California."

"I have a solution to the whole rotten mess."

Thirty-one

"MARRIAGE TO YOU! DID YOU FALL AND HIT YOUR head?" Murphy's offer both stunned and dumbfounded Laurel.

"It will silence talk—in addition to providing safety for you."

"And Nora? Have you forgotten the woman you love?"

Anguish filled Murphy's eyes. "You have no one to protect you. It's the only solution."

"A pretty sad excuse for throwing away love. The letter you received from Brodie... This ludicrous notion is his, I take it."

The man still persisted on tying her to his brother.

Murphy released her hand and slumped deeper into his chair. "He can't save you. Guilt does things to a normal man. Brodie is much more. In him emotion cuts like a deep river. Marrying me would ease his mind."

A horde of butterflies flittered in her stomach. Memory of hard, muscled flesh robbed the room of oxygen.

Dear Lord, she'd never use the term *ordinary* for Brodie Yates.

His devilish grin made his kisses irresistible, his touch melted the finest steel, and the mere heat of his gaze aroused passion she'd never found in another's arms. The rebel-eyed man had created a stairway to the stars and shown her how easily she could pluck one and tuck it into her heart.

A small part of her, the panicked part, wished they'd never met. The loss wouldn't be nearly as devastating.

Another part cried to climb those stairs one more time in his arms. To feel his heartbeat beneath her ear. To inhale the scent that was his alone and know that she'd had something other women only dreamed of.

Brodie Yates completed something in her.

She'd manage without him. She had grit. But part of her would never be the same. And she wished to do more than manage. "Your generosity amazes me. I don't see wings sprouting, but you're an angel all the same." Her fingertips grazed Murphy's cheek. "Sacrificing what you and Nora have...for me...I won't allow it. Ollie, God rest her soul, was fond of reminding me that I'm way past grown. I carry my own burdens these days."

"But—"

Laurel pressed a finger to his lips. "Shh. Yes, William Taft frightens me to death." So did getting tarred and feathered, only she didn't add that. "But you know what? They don't have me yet, and with any luck they never will."

"He and Vallens will come eventually."

"When they do they'll find I'm tougher than I used to be."

"You won't reconsider or come to the house for tonight?"

A sharp knife, Ollie's old pistol, and a good brain could outsmart a whiskey-soaked brothel owner.

"Go, give Nora a big hug, and tell her how lucky she is."

He got slowly to his feet. "I'd take it real personal if anyone hurt you."

That made two of them.

Later, she swore Curley's snores vibrated the café. She allowed a smile. Intruders wouldn't have to use stealth at this rate.

Laurel's frazzled nerves twisted into bow ties.

She wished Taft would hurry so life could resume some semblance of normalcy, whatever that was. Days absent of worry or heartbreak she could number without using her toes. For the hundredth time, she touched the knife and pistol, wondering about Hannibal. Maybe the dog filled some gator's belly.

The door to her room squeaked and Adeline poked her head in. "Can you sleep?"

"No need to whisper."

"Mind if I scoot in beside you?"

Laurel threw back the cover, glad for the company. It made her feel braver about what she had to do at daybreak.

❧

Laurel dressed early, taking extra pains with her hair. She leaned near the mirror. An amazing thing had happened since Ollie's passing. Seeing her reflection didn't bother her anymore.

Adeline sat up, rubbing her eyes. "I overslept?"

"Go back to sleep, honey."

"You can't leave me. You promised." Adeline sobbed and the bedcovers tangled in the girl's haste to stand. "I'll be good. Please, let me come. I beg you."

The brush clattered onto the dresser as Laurel hurried to embrace her. Still sobbing, Adeline snuggled into the comfort, gripping her tightly. Laurel hadn't the courage to admit she couldn't offer safety or security. She couldn't guarantee they'd keep their home, or their lives, one more day. Because of her past, trouble would call. This she knew.

She smoothed back Adeline's hair. "I'd never sneak out and leave you behind, honey. We're family."

"Then why are you dressed up?"

Laurel's chin rested on top of Adeline's golden silk. "I wanted to look my best before I do battle."

"I wish everyone would let us live in peace. We never did anything. Mrs. Kempshaw is plain ol' mean."

"People fear what they can't understand. We threaten them. It's not so much what we've done that frightens Florence, but what might occur as a result of who we've been." Laurel set the girl firmly aside. "Now, young lady, I'm going to fix you and Curley some breakfast. Forget this nonsense about leaving you."

A hot cup of tea did wonders to help organize her speech. Their snoring protector didn't rouse until she set a plate of flapjacks, eggs, and steaming coffee on the table.

Curley grunted, pulling on his boots. "Wherever you think you're going this fine morn will be on my arm."

She untied her apron and grabbed the shawl beside it. "My errand requires no chaperone, but thank you anyway."

"Use your noggin, Laurel girl. It's foolhardy to go out."

"I'll be back before anyone realizes I'm gone."

A few minutes later her footsteps pounded on the sidewalk. It didn't escape her notice that several women hastily crossed to the other side. She ground her teeth and plowed on. It was fair to say her skirts snapped with electricity as she stepped smartly and with purpose.

Florence Kempshaw's modest residence showed neglect. The woman was much too busy destroying lives to tend to repairs, it appeared. Laurel rapped on the weathered entrance.

"You! What gall," Florence exclaimed when she saw Laurel on her stoop.

Quick thinking and plenty of ire put Laurel's foot between the door and the jamb. "I will have a moment of your time."

"Won't spare a second for the likes of your kind."

"I don't give a rat's hindquarters if you despise the very ground on which I walk, you will hear me out." She pushed past the surly woman. "Shut your mouth or you'll attract flies."

"I'll yell if you hit me."

"Much as I'd delight, I'll refrain…unless you provoke me."

A good deal later, Laurel emerged from the long chat wearing a satisfied smile. That fire blazed in her chest put it mildly.

It had simply taken a poke with a sharp stick to get her back bowed. The good folks of Redemption, lumping in Taft and Vallens with that mess, didn't know who they dealt with.

The time had come to stand up and be counted.

Throughout the day a steady stream of customers kept Ollie's Café open. It heartened her that a few of Redemption's regulars drifted into the eatery besides the passengers on the steamboats and barges.

Moonbeams now trailed through the back window. Laurel adjusted the wick of the oil lamp and counted her blessings. Not a soul had come yet with tar and feathers, thank the Lord.

Perhaps "letting the hide go with the tallow," as Ollie would put it, had accomplished something.

Florence had actually listened. And even though the gossiping woman hadn't met Laurel's stare, Florence showed slight thawing. The tale of Laurel's abduction had even sparked a hint of human decency as evidenced by the flicker of sympathy.

The clock neared ten when fists pounded on the door. Laurel gripped the knife in her pocket.

Curley lumbered over with his rifle ready. "Who's there?"

"It's me, Arlo." The shout belonged to a worker from the Dry Gulch.

He slid back the new, heavier bolt that he'd

installed at Laurel's request. "I told you not to disturb me without good cause."

"You hafta come quick! Some fellers got liquored up bad. They're breaking glass, furniture…and bones."

Deep regret colored Curley's tone when he turned to Laurel and Adeline. "Ladies, I have no choice but to leave you alone. Lock up and don't answer to anyone. I mean it."

An eerie quiet descended after Curley left. Laurel and Adeline finished straightening up the kitchen for the next day's business. All the while, she listened for Hannibal's scratch. The animal's long absence puzzled her. He'd be hungry.

Adeline yawned. "I'm beat down to the soles of my feet."

"No use in us both waiting up. You go on up, honey."

The clock's loud ticking along with the creak of boards above where Adeline moved about filled the kitchen. Then the noise overhead ceased, telling her Adeline had crawled into bed. Laurel rested her head in her hands. Brodie filled every crevice, every corner of her mind. Thoughts of his welfare formed images of the twisting, agonizing kind.

Had she misplaced her trust in the Citizens for Peace? Were they unable to save the man she loved?

An hour stretched into two and yet Curley didn't return. Perhaps he figured they'd gone upstairs and didn't wish to awaken them. Or…the thought of rabble-rousers killing their friend turned her to ice. Losing another would further test her ability to survive.

She pondered venturing out to the saloon, swiftly

rejecting it as unwise. For now she'd stay put. That was the best thing.

Checking on Adeline, Laurel lay down fully clothed on Ollie's bed. In case trouble called she'd be ready.

It seemed she'd just dozed off when low whispers jarred her awake.

Wooden planks complained beneath someone's weight.

Intruders lurked in the hallway.

Even if Curley had found a way past the bolts, he'd not come upstairs. And nothing would drive Adeline from bed unless she was ill, and the girl hadn't stirred or made a peep.

The knife slid into place, the pistol into her palm before her feet hit the floor.

A muffled scream froze her midway across the room.

Walking on tiptoes, she slowly opened the bedroom door and peered around the door frame. Shadows moved along the hall in the murky light.

They had Adeline.

Laurel ran after two male figures who hauled Adeline's kicking form, catching them at the head of the stairs.

"Put her down this instant!"

Will Taft whirled. "Who's gonna make me?"

Laurel shivered. The face that spawned nightmares and dominated daylight hours stood before her. Well, her wish came true, only now she'd give anything to put the genie back into the lamp. Chewing nails hadn't been all that bad, she told herself.

She raised her chin a notch and swallowed the fear that strangled her. "I am. I'm going to stop you."

"What's a scrawny-ass harlot gonna do?"

"Lessons you taught in survival might not work in your favor now, Taft." She leveled the pistol at his gut. "I said get your hands off the girl."

In the dim light she saw his eyes widen. "You're full of surprises, Lil."

Adeline jerked free and scooted behind Laurel.

Laurel ordered, "Vallens, lead the way downstairs. Remember, this six shooter will put a big hole in your boss should you make one bobble. I swear to God I'd dearly love to."

Things turned into chaos at the bottom when Vallens suddenly darted from sight. The man hid, ready to pounce. Added to that, Taft lowered his hands. His body shielded them. What seemed a good plan at the onset shifted in hindsight.

She shoved the cold metal into his spine. "I will kill you."

"You sure you know what you're doing, Lil? Don't reckon you ever shot a man before."

"With you it'll be awful easy to remedy that."

Taft cleared the steps, leaving Laurel on the last one. "Zeke, why don't you show Lil our trump card?"

The death angel raised the wick on the oil lamp and held it toward a bound, gagged female.

A cry sprang from her lips. "Hannah!"

Taft's hoarse laugh pierced the air. "Give me that pea shooter or your sister's brains will spatter the walls."

Laurel's arm sagged. She'd pretty much lived her life, but Hannah and Adeline were young. Banking that Taft had too much at stake to damage his goods didn't reassure her enough to take that gamble.

Taft's fist caught her mouth the moment he took her pistol. She slammed to the floor. The metallic taste of blood wasn't something a person forgot the taste of. Hate crawled from the dark corners of her soul.

"You rotten piece of cow manure!"

"What a pity. I went to enormous trouble arranging this little tea party and you haven't the slightest gratitude."

The sinister mouth with its taunting sneer leaned too near Laurel.

She aimed the wad of spit just right. It hit him squarely and ran down the bridge of his nose. Her bold impulse earned her a kick that brought stars. But seeing the smug veneer slip made it worth the glimpse of a dented, bent halo Laurel would surely wear up there when she joined Ollie.

Her breath came in short gasps. "I have friends."

"Zeke, explain why poor Curley Madison can't come to her aid."

Vallens shifted his hold on Hannah. "Madison feels a mite poorly at the moment. Taft arranged the fight at the saloon and made sure the saloon-keep was out of the way."

Perhaps that didn't translate to dead. She prayed it didn't. Outsmarting them was up to her. One thing about it, they'd have hell getting Hannah, Adeline, and her to St. Louis. Taft had better rethink his plan. No swamp scum would soil Hannah and Adeline. She'd stop him somehow.

Blocking pain that hurt to blink, she struggled to her feet. "No one will pay a red cent to lie with a corpse."

"Silly twit, I have fresh merchandise. You're

expendable. In fact, you'll make a prime example for those who think to escape my clutches," Taft sneered.

"Except it's a long way to Missouri," she needled.

"We ain't going anywhere with you." Adeline launched herself onto Taft's back, raking her nails across his face.

Laurel fingered the knife in her pocket, eyeing the two men. She had just one chance.

But once she buried the knife in Vallens, could she get to the pistol fast enough?

Thirty-two

BRODIE YATES BROKE FORMATION, SPURRING THE loaned horse into a hard gallop. If this nag possessed Smokey's long gait, he'd not have doubts circling his head like vultures. Cold sweat dotted his brow. The half-dozen men who ate his dust could sway the odds.

They had to beat Taft and Vallens.

Thanks to Citizens for Peace, General Buell deemed him a free man. Brodie wanted no part of staying in the stockade until morning, and the general had no desire to test President Grant's patience.

Sheer terror they'd be too late booted off the devil's scorn that usually shared his saddle.

This night it would have to find its own way. If it dared.

Which brought his intelligence into question. If he had some, he'd be riding in the opposite direction instead of riding hell-bent for Redemption. Buell would be after his head when he discovered the document was a forgery.

But Laurel was in danger. His gut never lied.

He had to keep her safe or die trying.

The memory bag Brodie snatched off Buell's desk molded to the warmth of his skin. It still held each treasured item.

Something Murphy said bumped across the ridges of his conscience. *Never let a woman who lights up the dark, lonely places of your soul go.*

His lady did a damn sight better than merely light up dark corners of a moth-eaten soul. She built a bonfire.

The right choice meant he wouldn't be alone anymore.

Or filled with haunting coldness a flame couldn't touch.

He was anxious to give marriage a whirl. Had to get the begettin' started soon. Eight little ones posed quite a chore.

First he'd have to talk Laurel into having him. A fellow with nothing but a reputation and a six-gun to back it up would have a devil of a time.

Running from every name-seeking fast gun between here and San Francisco wasn't much to ask a woman to share.

Unless… Thoughts of losing Laurel froze his blood.

He bent over the flying mane, leaving the road to cut through the pines.

❧

Though Taft had confiscated Ollie's pistol, Laurel took comfort in her weighted pocket. She focused on the two men. Taft stood nearest, therefore was the logical target. She shortened the space until Vallens's black gaze met hers in silent warning.

At least she hadn't revealed the knife.

Taft grabbed a handful of Adeline's hair and yanked,

pulling her off his back. He held her tightly in a vise. Laurel winced at the girl's cry.

"Leave her alone. She's merely a child."

"You were too once. Or has it been so long you forgot? This sassy one's gold hair an' face of an angel will make me the envy of everyone." Lust glittered in Taft's gaze. "And I can't tell what treats are in store for your sweet sister. She'll take to whoring. Just like you." He spoke to Vallens. "Load Sis in the wagon and I'll be along directly."

Something human crossed the angel of death's features. "I agreed to locate the two thieves who parted you from your money. The one in the grave ain't no fault of mine. I'm done."

Vallens with a sliver of conscience?

How absurd to think he'd become an ally. Balking could buy him an extra favor or two from the good Lord, however.

"I have a .45 that says different," Taft snapped.

The two swapped glares. Taft shifted his weight back and forth. The clock ticked loudly. Vallens didn't back down.

"Threatening women is easier than threatening a grown man. I'm walking out of here, so I reckon you gotta do what you hafta."

Hope plummeted when Vallens moved to leave.

She met the horror in Adeline's blues and nodded slightly, flicking her head toward the dining room. If the girl understood, she'd run the second Laurel made her move.

"I'll pay a bonus, you low-down swindler."

"It takes one to know one. You don't have the

kind of money to buy me." The man in funeral attire opened the door. Wolf-dog bounded in. "Dog, I told you to guard outside."

To see Hannibal in good health brought a moment's joy from the dread that was pulling her into a deep, dark sinkhole. Brief compassion might not overcome the animal's wild instincts that Vallens encouraged.

Silver flecks in Hannibal's stare bore no sign of recognition when the dog looked at her. One didn't have to possess keen insight to know that bared fangs and the bristled neck weren't shows of affection. Sorrow rippled inside her.

Wolf-dog kept his stance, ignoring the order to retreat.

Vallens continued toward the pitch-black night.

She must make her move. With a deep breath to calm her, she gripped the wooden handle and jerked the knife high.

Hurtling it in Taft's direction, she aimed for any part of the hated enemy. A person would think defending those they loved made it easier to bury the tip into a body. And yet, nothing prepared her for the sight of a six-inch blade plunged to the hilt in Taft's arm.

Or the smell of blood swimming up her nostrils.

"You stinking harlot!"

A flash of fleeing nightgown reassured her of Adeline's safety for the moment. It was the last she saw before Will Taft flung her to the floor and straddled her stomach. She knew the sickening crack of bone. Murder filled Taft's eyes.

Fury in the raised fist told her the man would not stop this time. She closed her eyes and waited for the coming pain.

The blows never had a chance to destroy delicate tissue.

Hannibal sprang with a feral growl, more vicious than anything Laurel had ever heard. The animal ripped into the uplifted arm, tossing his head from side to side.

"Zeke, damn you! Get this beast off."

Laurel scrambled into a corner and huddled.

Vallens turned. "I warned you about the animal, Taft."

"Call him off! Name your price."

"Said I won't be bought."

"I'm pleading. Please."

"Just gonna get Dog off. Nothing else."

Wolf-dog avoided the boot, sidling in Laurel's direction. She wanted to pound both men into ever-lasting hell. But she hugged her most unlikely protector, vowing to feed him the biggest piece of meat she could find. Sorrow ebbed back from the gray eyes.

But the danger wasn't over. A mangled limb didn't stop Taft. In considerable agony, he rose slowly, pulled out a Colt, and stood over her.

"I've had a gut full of you and this mangy wolf."

The cold barrel touched her forehead. Laurel clenched her teeth. Ollie had better get ready for visitors.

"Cain't let you do that, Will."

Laurel's eyes flew open. She held her breath. Vallens had pressed his Colt to Taft's left ear, knocking the six-gun from his boss's grip.

"Get outta my way, you chicken-hearted bastard."

Vallens held fast. "I ain't gonna let you ruin more innocent lives. Your flesh trade stops right here, right now."

"Since when did you suddenly get religion?"

Vallens met Laurel's gaze. "I've watched you, even tested you for signs of weakness. Why would someone work so hard when you could line your pockets with riches? It seemed farfetched. But I came to admire your courage." Then he addressed Taft. "Then, I got word you killed my daughter to keep me in line. You shouldn't have done that."

"Spare me the hymns," Taft spat.

"You're for real, Laurel James. I do believe you'd fight to the death to protect everything you stand for."

Had Ollie reached down to soften the heart of stone?

Though barely audible, her reply held grit. "Make no mistake. I would."

"This ain't over, Lil." Taft measured the distance to the door where a man could disappear into the inky night.

"You're wrong about that, you sorry slaver. Go ahead, I'd love for you to run." From the open doorway, a man's soft suggestion carried the deadly hiss of snake rattles. Laurel whirled to find Brodie blocking the entrance. He held a cocked rifle. "Vallens, put down the Colt or I'll make you eat the damn thing."

Laurel wondered if she only imagined the lean figure. Yet, the heat caressing her face appeared beyond the scope of an apparition's power. Oh Lord, she hoped he hadn't broken out.

"He's on our—" She never got to finish.

"Drop it, you two-legged jackal." The brittle order said Brodie had spied her bruises and he meant to make someone pay dearly. "Take a deep breath because it'll be your last."

"Please, it's not what you think." She scrambled to defuse his anger. Murder would for sure earn him the gallows.

"Maybe you don't know that I'm William Taft and this woman rightfully belongs to me." Taft found his tongue once Zeke Vallens didn't threaten to fit him for earrings.

Flinty sparks shot from the gray-eyed rebel. "Reason enough to shoot you on the spot. Where I come from, Will Taft is Cajun for skunk piss. And you're truly misinformed. No one *owns* Laurel."

Adeline peeked curiously around Brodie's bulk.

"I suppose you'd be Yates," Taft sneered.

"Welcome to Judgment Day, you piece of filth."

Soldiers swarmed through the back door before anyone could explain the situation, adding more confusion. Laurel threw herself in front of Brodie. Although she hadn't a clue how to prevent it, she'd not let them take him again.

"Which one is the Confederate spy, Shenandoah?"

Laurel inhaled sharply. Shouldn't they already know the jail escapee's appearance?

"Sergeant." Vallens pushed Taft forward. "He's your man."

Air slowly left her lungs. She went limp. "Yes, indeed. He's Shenandoah. I'll testify to that." She leaned into the warmth of Brodie's broad shoulders a moment to banish the chill before running to Hannah. "He'd have murdered us all. The man bound and gagged my poor sister. I'd appreciate a knife to cut her loose."

"They lie." Taft's face mottled with anger. "You

had the right man in your stockade all along, you bumbling idiots."

"Private, shackle this man and throw him on a horse."

"Lil, tell 'em who I am. Zeke, tell 'em." Taft fought to break free of the soldiers' grasps, losing in the end.

Taft's desperate cries echoed until hoofbeats drowned out the man's voice. She prayed he'd not convince them for many years. Or at least until Brodie had a head start.

Vallens moved toward the night. "Dog, we'd best get moving."

"Hannibal, his name is Hannibal." Laurel braced herself against shooting pain when she helped her sister stand. "I want you to remember that, Mr. Vallens."

"A fool name. I expect I will remember though."

Brodie swung the rifle dead center. "Thought you'd walk out scot-free, Vallens?"

"No." Laurel planted herself in front of the rifle.

"I understand not wanting blood spilled on the kitchen floor, but he isn't leaving. Move out of the way."

"We figured him wrong, Brodie." She crossed the space to touch Vallens's arm. "Zeke saved my life. I won't forget it."

The man tipped the brim of his hat to her. "I'm leaving Hannibal here. He's more yours than mine now."

Laurel knelt and placed her arms around the dog's neck. "Thank you, Mr. Vallens." But when she looked up, the man had vanished into the star-studded darkness.

Curley ran up, holding a wet cloth to his head. "What on earth happened? One minute I'm headed for the saloon and the next a steam engine slams into me. Yates, what in saint's name are you doing here? Don't tell me you broke out."

The pair of rebel grays that fastened on Laurel seemed to dare her to try escaping his clutches. She didn't for one minute consider doing so.

If she could have her choice of any place on earth to be, she'd choose Ollie's Café in Redemption.

The crooked grin that played across Brodie's features stole her breath. "General Buell discovered he had the wrong man, thanks to Laurel."

His heated stare caressed, promising nights of passion and untold delight in making up for lost seconds. Moisture pooled in the crevice between her breasts while tingles of anticipation swept her from head to toe.

"It's about dadgum time," Curley grumbled.

"Are you truly my sister, Laurel?" Hannah tugged her from one kind of dangerously deep water only to plunge into another.

The moment of reckoning had arrived. She chewed her lip.

"How would you feel? I'd understand if you hate me."

Hannah hugged her. "Don't be a goose. You can't know how happy I am. And proud. I want to run home right now and tell Mama, Papa, and the rest I've found our Laurel."

Brodie threw Laurel an I-told-you-so stare.

"I'll just mosey on and leave you folks to talk away the night," Curley said. "Maybe I'll go tell Ollie what she missed. Things ain't the same with her gone."

Untangling Hannah from around her neck proved a daunting task, for her sister clung worse than thistle. Laurel wouldn't have traded it for anything. Well...

except for lying bare as a newborn babe, with the man of her dreams crawling inside her.

Only that would have to come later.

"Hannah, Mr. Yates will take you home at daybreak. But promise not to tell a soul about me."

"I can't do that. They have a right to know."

"See?" Brodie rubbed the small of her back. "I'm glad others agree."

"I intend to do it, but I'll choose the right time."

"Whatever you say, darlin'. You're so tired you can't think clear." Brodie scooped her in his arms. "I say a bed looks mighty welcome."

Tomorrow Laurel would worry about impropriety. For now, she loved the beat of his heart next to her ear. She snuggled deeper into the breadth wrapped around her. "Adeline, will you make Hannah welcome? I'd appreciate it, dear."

"Consider it done." Then Adeline leaned closer and winked. "I like him. He's the right one for you."

Upstairs, he started for her old room before Laurel realized. "I sleep in Ollie's room now. She died in my arms the night I returned from the stockade two days ago."

"So that's what Curley meant by that strange remark."

"Adeline has mine. The girl's afraid of ghosts. I find it peaceful in here though with Ollie's spirit around me."

"She'd better hide her eyes because I intend to love you like you've never been."

He eased her to the patchwork quilt and made quick work of stripping off his clothing. Then he slowly undressed her, planting kisses on each new patch of exposed skin.

"My stars, Brodie, at this rate daylight will come before we even get down to the best part." She gasped when his tongue meandered down the crevice between her breasts to draw a wet heart on her stomach.

"Complaints so soon, darlin'?" He propped on an elbow and let a fingertip continue the journey. "We make quite a pair. You're more battered than I am, I do believe. Are you certain you're up to this after the hellish night you've had?"

The last few hours had fled. Laurel brushed back the rebellious hair from his forehead and stared into his eyes. She prayed they'd never have anything worse than a few scrapes to complain about. Although a breeze blew in from the swamps, ruffling the curtains, Brodie's sultry breath feathering across her bared flesh kept her heated.

"I'm positive. I have this need…"

"Do tell."

"We should start on those eight little ones before we grow too old," Laurel said, nibbling on his ear.

Moments later a moan crept from her throat. He touched places no one had charted—dark, moist places that had never experienced the thrill of human contact. The gentle gunslinger's tender lovemaking brought mist to her eyes. Redemption hadn't come without sacrifice. It took forsaking preconceived ideas and letting ash return to ash. Their souls flourished. And still their love would take constant nurturing.

Light pressure located old scars on the solid body of her warrior. There were fresh ones also. Those created an ache inside Laurel so deep that not a parcel of daylight penetrated.

"Fine wine always tastes better when sipped, precious."

"But…" Her rebuttal got lost. Scandalous pirates had that effect when they pilfered a woman's jewels.

Dampness covering her inner thighs assured her he'd have no trouble sliding inside. She wanted him now.

A patient lady would grind her teeth and wait.

A desperate one wouldn't.

Laurel pulled Brodie atop her. Male brown nipples surrounded by fine down begged for homage. Flicks of her tongue taught him to dally with her senses. A shiver rewarded her efforts, turning the nibs into hard protrusions.

"Ahh, pretty lady, you shouldn't do that."

Thirty-three

Dawn crept as silent as a thief into the room. Brodie pushed back raven strands that reminded him of rare, expensive silk from Laurel's face and kissed each bruise. A tic jerked along his jaw. Thought of how close she'd come to dying chilled his bones. He'd littered her life with disappointment and setback and riddled her heart with cracks and holes. His chest constricted.

Brodie lifted her hand and turned it over, marveling at the strength there. He kissed her palm and each fingertip.

"Thank you, beautiful Lil."

"For what?"

"Loving me. Letting me love you back. Forgiving me."

"Ollie made me promise to not give up on you."

"I'm sorry you had to deal with burying her alone."

"We don't have a choice in those matters. I'm a big girl."

"I know the tragedy of burying family. Deep loss

becomes a part of you. A body never truly stops missing them."

"Even for a little boy forced to become a man too soon."

He quirked an eyebrow. "Murph told you about Mother?"

"Are you mad? I wanted to discover what made you tick."

"Surprised at him. Learn anything else?"

Laurel's satiny curves molded to his large form. Her fingers tangled in fine chest hair. "You're not some big, bad ogre. Compassion and respect comes out of hiding more than it suits you. I also see how you guard a fervent desire to belong."

"Do tell." Needles of discomfort pricked. He may as well have posted his secrets in *The Jeffersonian*.

"Those qualities most endear you. After Ollie died I discovered we don't ever truly know a person, and perhaps that's the way it's intended. But there's something that intrigues me."

"I can't imagine any tidbit that escaped your notice."

She raised and leaned over him, her lush breasts leaving imprints above his heart. He inhaled sharply. His memory bag dangled from her hand. "When I asked about this earlier you told me it was nothing of much value. Please, may I look?"

Brodie had never revealed his private stash to anyone. Each sentimental treasure revealed something of him—things he'd clutched fiercely when the world slept.

Still, he had to begin trusting. That meant letting the woman he loved into the dark pain. He swallowed hard.

"Be my guest."

She removed Aunt Lucy's letter. Then came the gold band that glistened in the early morn. Her questioning gaze caught his. "My mother's," he murmured.

Laurel placed it tenderly on the letter as though sensing his agony. Murphy's lock of hair joined the ring. Brodie held his breath. The last item held the most significance. Her reaction to it would determine their future. "Oh, my love." A rush of tears darkened her violet gaze. She cradled the scrap to her heart. "Lace from my skirt. You kept the memento. Putting it in such good company must mean—"

"I love you. I always have."

"You hid it well."

The split lip, compliments of Taft's fist, trembled. He pressed his mouth very lightly to the wound, moved along the jaw line to a dainty earlobe, before placing feathery kisses on her eyelids. She'd suffered too much over the years, something he'd have to live with. If he could. Memories hurt.

"That's because you were set to marry the wrong man."

She groaned. "What a horrible mistake. I didn't love Murphy, though I thought it would be the answer."

"You've reason to change your mind?"

He loved the wrinkle in her brow when wheels of thought turned inside her head.

"I realized after the soldiers took you that no one can bring redemption to another. I'm proud of who I am. I don't need to marry anyone to prove I'm good and decent."

"And generous and beautiful to a fault." Brodie

shifted onto his side. "You pounded a few things into this lamebrain. The stockade took my blinders off. You're right. The past has nothing to do with the future except shape us into the people we are." He squared his jaw. "I was a jackass. I'm sorry. Other than a reputation as a broken-down gunslinger, I'm no prize."

"I never asked for anything more, Brodie."

"You know it eats at a man to be unable to provide."

Laurel turned away. Her husky voice held a quiver. "You think I'm merely an obligation?"

"Darlin', you mean life, death, and the hereafter to me." He inhaled her fragrance and plunged. "That's why I humbly request your hand in marriage."

Laurel swung back. "Of all the dumb ways to ask."

"I haven't had much practice. Is that a yes or a no?"

Anger and confusion darkened her features. He hadn't a clue whether the roulette wheel would stop on red or black. Hell, he couldn't even tell where the chips had fallen. He just pitched them out. Perhaps it was too late for winning his hand.

"I can't. I truly can't."

Ice water in place of blood didn't flow too easily, Brodie discovered. "I've messed up real bad. I just hoped—"

"Hold on, rebel, I'm not finished. I can't vow to love and cherish until we settle some things. First, how do you feel about swapping a Colt for an apron? I warn you, it's a big switch."

He chuckled and kissed the sweet, honeyed mouth. His fingertip traced the curve of a bruised cheek.

"I feel like the luckiest man alive. Gunplay and fast

draws don't compare to the excitement of being with you." He nibbled an enticing shoulder.

"I'm afraid."

"Makes two of us, darlin'. We'll face our fear together."

"What assurance do I have you'll not up and leave on me?"

"The word of a Johnny Reb. Does that mean anything?"

"What about the ugly whispers? Can you face those?"

"They best not let me hear 'em." He itched to give the gossips a dose of the Brodie Remedy.

"Gossip is hard to silence. They may run us out of town."

"Let 'em try. Let's get married right now, this very day."

"Spit and thunder, you're not in any hurry, are you?"

"I'll make an honest woman of you," he growled. "My name hanging on the end of yours will solve most problems. They'll think twice before opening their big mouths." At least folks would know who looked out for her. "Anything else?"

Sweet Jezzie, he prayed not. Her naked body was doing things beyond his control. No telling what would happen if he denied the urge much longer. He inched a finger up and down her long legs in sensual, tiny circles. He yearned to fill every lonely nook and cranny inside this beautiful lady with his love.

"Just one more thing. This honest woman business...I can't build a life on lies."

"Then it's about time you went home." His grin came from the place where old memories died and new ones were born. "To make it perfectly clear… you're accepting my proposal?"

"Aye, aye, Sir Pirate." Laurel ruffled the hair on his neck and drew him near. Her throaty whisper made him tremble. A little thing he predicted would never change. "I love you, Brodie Yates. Don't you be forgetting it."

"I'm sure you'll remind me a few thousand times."

"We've spent a lifetime thinking of what might have been. I prefer focusing on bright tomorrows, not to mention moonlit nights we'll share."

"Umm, moonmist. Knew that scent was familiar."

Laurel slid from beneath the nuzzling assault on her neck.

"You said that was the musky aroma of moonbeams bathing an aroused woman. Impossible in broad daylight."

He massaged the tips of her breasts between forefinger and thumb. "You certain?"

"Adeline…Hannah…" Her breathless words trailed.

"They can wait."

Several hours later Laurel wiggled into the saddle atop Smokey. Adeline and Hannah rode in the buggy. A horde of flutters whipped her stomach into froth.

"Thought you learned what happens to little girls who insist on rubbing a man the right way." Snake rattles on his worn Stetson hissed. Brodie looped the reins around the horn and wrapped her in the security of his arms.

"What will I say to my family?"

"The truth. Quit worrying. I'm right here with you."

Miles passed until at last they wound down the lane

through tall sycamore and pine. Rounding the last bend, Laurel glimpsed the house. Adeline and Hannah climbed from the buggy. Blue Boy abandoned the porch, racing for her.

She slid from the saddle and ran to meet the dog. "Blue, I've brought someone special. This is Brodie."

Brodie dismounted and rubbed the dog's droopy ears. "Hey, fella."

"Everyone, look who I found," Hannah said.

A woman stepped onto the porch, shielding her eyes from the sun. Laurel slipped her palm inside Brodie's.

"Saints be praised. Hannah, you gave us such a fright when you disappeared. I saw it happening all over again."

"Two men abducted me, but Laurel fought them. It's her, Mama."

"Laurel? Our Laurel?"

Brodie gave Laurel's hand a reassuring squeeze.

"Yes, it's me, Mama."

"Hannah, get your papa from the barn." Tears streamed down the aged face Laurel had so often dreamed about. Mary James gathered her lost daughter close. "I can't believe it, child."

Laurel had tears as well. "Many nights I laid awake, my soul dying bit by bit, willing myself back here. Now I am."

"Baby girl, rest on my shoulder. Soak up all the love I saved special for you. Everything's right as rain now."

Long-deprived senses soaked up the aromas of vanilla and fresh-baked bread. She had come to the birthplace of her roots. She snuggled into the soft haven, barely aware of footsteps.

"Laurel?"

Strain lingered in her father's question. Dread lodged like a week-old biscuit in her throat. She pulled from her mother's arms. Where had Brodie gone? She couldn't face the stern disapproval alone. But Brodie had disappeared.

Raising her chin, she met her father. "I'm home, Papa."

Ben James hugged her. "All these years and here you are."

The stripes of his bibbed overalls blurred.

They accepted her, just as Ollie had vowed. So far.

"Your face, child. What happened?" Work-roughened fingers touched her wet cheek.

"It's a long story, Papa. A wise woman once said a person without scars never fought for anything they believed in. I'm happy to say I'm home because I stood fast and won."

"You should've seen my sister," Hannah seconded. "Without her courage, I'd be bound for Missouri right now."

Laurel spotted her love, standing apart from the rest wearing a lop-sided smile. She tugged him forward. "This is Brodie Yates. He asked me to marry him." She turned to Adeline. "And show Adeline Cade a warm welcome. Our family just got larger."

"Lordy. Not only do we get our Laurel back, but we have another son. And a new daughter, to boot." Ben slapped Brodie's back. "Thank you for watching over my little girl."

"Don't give me credit. Miss Olivia Applejack b'Dam had the honor, Mr. James."

"Plain old Ben, that's what everyone calls me. That

Olivia sure has a fanciful name. I'll have to ride back and meet her."

Hotness lurked behind Laurel's lids. "Ollie's a little busy polishing a halo and trying to be as good an angel in heaven as she was on earth. We laid her to rest a few days ago."

"I would like to have known her," Mary murmured.

"She's watching and grinning from ear to ear."

Brodie draped an arm around her. "That she is."

"Hey, sis. Glad you found the way back," Quaid said.

"Us, too," chimed the rest of her siblings.

"I'm waiting for that long story, girl. Let's go inside."

"I'll make some lemonade." Mary James rushed up the porch.

Brodie's hand prevented Laurel following. She couldn't conceal panic in the gaze she favored him with. The shaky footing wouldn't become solid without his help. He couldn't back out.

"Aren't you coming?"

He brushed her jaw. "I have some business in Jefferson while you visit with your folks. Don't worry, I'm not about to let you out of my sight for long."

"Is it wise? The general might believe Taft."

"Not a chance. Shoot, that forged signature of Andrew Johnson almost convinced me." His soft kiss held desire and promise. "I'll be back before you know it."

"I can't bear us to part. Silly of me, huh?"

"I'm glad. I'll bring a surprise."

"Something sneaky up your sleeve?"

"Who, me? I'll never tell." Grinning, he untied Smokey.

Keeping an anxious eye out the window, she bared the whole ugly mess since that fateful day, including how Ollie helped her escape. Hannah filled in the ending, which allowed Laurel to give the shady lane her undivided attention. No sign of Brodie.

"You should've left that low-down scum to us. We'd show him what happens when you hurt a James," Jeremiah proclaimed.

"I hope he has to live with nasty pigs," Millie said.

Mary James held Laurel's hand as if afraid she'd disappear.

Ben James blew into a faded kerchief. "I failed in my duty."

Through a misty haze, she stared at the love and harmony in the faces that surrounded her. Grief had aged her father and mother beyond rightful years. She despised Taft more for that than anything.

"Stop blaming yourself, Papa," she said. "The man is getting his due. We can't go back and undo what happened." Her glance encompassed them all. "Hope that I'd see you again sustained me through all the dark times. And yet, shame kept me away after Ollie freed me. I was afraid you'd think badly of me."

"Don't be ashamed of anything, Sis," Virgil's voice broke.

"Amen," her papa agreed.

Blue Boy's pitiful howl appeared to add agreement.

Twilight had turned the sky orange and purple by the time Laurel heard the big Appaloosa. A dignified stranger riding abreast of Brodie drew frowns. Perhaps the man had turned down the lane by mistake.

She flew into Brodie's arms the minute he swung

from the saddle, not caring that people watched. Worrying about proper things tuckered a body out. She'd learned not to waste good time. Folks would think what they wished anyway.

This man was hers.

No reason to hide the love she'd almost lost.

"You're back."

Need reflected in the rebel grays made her pulse race. He planted a long kiss, letting her know he could assume a pirate's plundering duties in the wink of an eye. Her knees went weak. She leaned against Smokey for support when he released her to reach into a saddle bag for a mysterious bundle.

"Did you bring a guest?" Laurel asked.

A tall, reed-like man in a frock coat tied his horse.

"Reverend Thompson has agreed to wed us tonight. I didn't think you'd fuss about having the ceremony with your family."

"Tonight? I somehow pictured myself in a grand gown."

"What's going on?" Ben James rose from his favorite roost, wood shavings falling from his lap.

"A wedding, Papa."

Mary James beamed. "Land's sakes! This calls for a feast. Don't know what I'll scratch up befitting the occasion, but I'll scare up something. Girls, come and help me throw it together."

Adeline, Hannah, Millie, and Mama scurried into the house, chattering like magpies.

"Reverend, I don't entertain often, but I'm a real good listener. Ever whittle?" Her father offered a chair.

Laurel's attention never wavered from Brodie.

He was a gunslinger.

And a scoundrel.

But the man kept a length of lace next to his heart, and she loved him with every fiber of her being.

"Darn Ollie. She couldn't have waited just a few more days." Unshed tears clogged her throat. She plucked at the string securing the package he clutched. "It would make this perfect."

"I don't have the power to bring her back." His husky voice cracked. "But I did fetch something else."

"The preacher, and whatever that is you're holding."

"Always mean what I say and say what I mean." Unspoken promises hung heavy in the swamp breeze.

Deliriously happy, Laurel floated. "Fork over that gift or I'll sic Blue Boy on you."

Brodie's twinkle shifted. "He's mighty vicious, all right."

Accepting his elbow, Laurel navigated the steps in a trance, unable to take her eyes from the lines and crevices that added character. Each one told of the many roads he'd traveled in order to get where he was.

"Still waters run deep," Ollie had once remarked.

Laurel couldn't wait to begin exploring things she'd only begun to learn.

Brodie poked his head into the midst of a lot of pots and pans banging. "Mrs. James, I'd be obliged if you'd suggest a place for a moment's privacy."

"Use my bedroom, son. It's safest from interruption."

Laurel took his hand. "I'll show you."

Safe from prying eyes, he placed the gift in her hands. She ripped off the brown paper. Rich folds of a beautiful dress unfurled. Thickness rose in her throat.

"My darling husband, you truly amaze me."

"Every bride should have a wedding gown. You don't mind it being lavender? The color brought us together."

"Mind?" The purple satin brushed her cheek, as whispery soft as a baby's breath. She blinked back tears. He'd given a present of great significance. The past was behind at last and they had nothing ahead to fear.

"I hope it doesn't bring back bad memories."

"That you selected lavender means more than you'll know."

The wedding gown slid to the bed as her arms went around his neck. She inhaled the faint scent of leather, tobacco, and shaving soap. The mirror reflected a daunting pair.

Bedecked in the lace-edged work of art, they stood hand-in-hand before the reverend. The man who was stronger than the mightiest storm, taller than a swamp water cypress, who moved heaven and earth to set her world straight stole her thoughts.

Through a brilliant mist, she watched Brodie shake the gold band from the pouch inside his shirt. Parting with the ring meant trust and commitment. She didn't mind the imperfect fit.

"I pronounce you husband and wife."

Fiery passion in the kiss sealed the union. He swept her up into his arms, her feet dangling amidst yards of lavender and lace. Albeit a bit scarred, she'd found her soul mate.

Blue Boy's howls nudged them back to earth. Scowls emphasized Brodie's craggy features before he put her down.

Brodie rubbed the hound's ears. "You belong to her, but you have to learn to share though, because I love her, too."

Heat in the rebel grays held her prisoner. A flush rose. Being undressed by roguish eyes tended to do that. The dewy sheen coating her skin was a good omen.

Epilogue

BRODIE SETTLED INTO THE LIVING QUARTERS ABOVE
the café while a new house took shape on the land
adjoining Murphy's.

The parade of nameless faces no longer tormented
him. Truth to tell, he strove to remember the empti-
ness of former days and nights. Allowing love into his
heart had freed him.

"What'll happen to me?" Adeline's mouth had
trembled.

Both he and Laurel assured the girl she'd always
have a bed under their roof no matter what. When
the girl gained experience, they'd turn over the deed
to Ollie's Café to her.

Florence Kempshaw dropped by to eat a big helping of humble pie. The rest of the town followed suit,
which brought relief. The devil take anyone who
harmed Laurel.

They'd deal with him first and find it a pretty big
chore.

"I'm anxious to hear what prompted you from

running her out of town to smoking the peace pipe?" he'd asked the busybody.

Florence had flushed. "She risked death to keep Vallens and Taft from taking those girls and stood up and fought to stay when it would've been easier to leave."

Now, in the garden, his gorgeous wife captured his full attention. He'd never tire of watching her.

Laurel held a bouquet of purple pansies. "Are you ready?"

"For anything, darlin'. Let me grab my hat."

The flowers added flair to Olivia Applejack b'Dam's bleak grave. He missed the jabs the crotchety woman had delighted in poking him with now and again. She'd grown on him before he ever realized he wanted her to. Ollie thought she could paint over the crust so no one would see the size of her heart. She'd fooled him for a while—until he peeled aside the layers.

A cool wind blew raven tendrils across Laurel's face. He held her tight, brushing them back to dry the tears. He blinked hard when she knelt to adjust the pansies.

"I did it, Ollie," Laurel said. "I went home. You were right about my family. I also think you pegged Brodie for the handsome rebel he is. We're married now. I miss hearing your cackle and your mother hen ways, but you probably know that, too."

Brodie ached with loss left by his mother, Aunt Lucy, and Ollie. The palm he laid on Laurel's bowed head shook.

"Her spirit lives with us, darlin'." He tried to swallow but it got stuck on the way down. He suddenly sniffed. "I swear if I don't smell smoke from that damn corncob pipe."

Laurel smiled up through misty eyes and drawled, "My grandpappy always said, 'Girl, ain't nothing to dying. It's the living that takes talent.'"

All of a sudden, the breeze ceased. Not a leaf, blade of grass, or ripple of air moved. Amid the hush, a red bird landed on one of the flowers she'd brought. It chattered, scolding.

"Great Johnny Reb. Ollie always insisted on the last word."

"That she did." Laurel accepted his hand and came into his arms. "Ollie b'Dam, you try to behave yourself and mind your manners up there. Don't try the good Lord's patience with all those righteous sayings."

Arm in arm, they strolled for the café. A strange horse and rider galloped from the woods and into town.

Brodie tensed.

"Who could that be?" Laurel shivered as if sensing danger.

"The only thing you should worry that pretty head about is the lusty lover who'll be in your bed come sundown and taming his wild streak." He tweaked her nose.

"A pure waste of time. I like you exactly as you are."

The stranger pulled alongside and sized them up. Brodie pushed back the felt hat, releasing the rattle's hiss. He returned the hard, piercing stare, noting the twin ammunition belts crisscrossing the stranger's chest and the pistols at his hip.

"Lookin' for a feller. Goes by the name Shenandoah."

Laurel sucked in a sharp breath, but kept silent.

"Rumor has it the army took him to the stockade in Jefferson to be hanged. Others claim he headed east to St. Louis. Mentioned something about the Black Garter."

"Obliged." The man tipped his hat and took off.

Unease gripped until the stranger rode past the saloon and disappeared into the woods.

Laurel let out a pent-up breath. "I thought for a minute you yearned to do something rash."

"Can't go around shooting strangers. What would our eight children think of their paw?"

"That he's the keeper of their mother's heart?"

"Absolutely. But there'll be more seekers to come. My dear Mrs. Yates, think you can handle life with an ex-hired gun?"

"Strange question, seeing who you bedded up with."

"You're a lavender-eyed vixen, you know that? Had to seine through a bunch of ugly rocks to find the right stone. Mighty glad I did, too." He flashed a crooked grin, winked, and switched his battered Stetson to her dark head.

"I declare, Brodie, you need to brush up on how to sweet-talk a lady." The rattles hissed when she leaned back to brush the lock of hair from his forehead.

"Don't have any call to practice now. You're mine."

Promising secrets peeked around the edge of her smile. Lush hips filled his hands. He nibbled gently on a mouth that fit perfectly the curve of his. Her lips knew him and didn't hold any slights that might've occurred against him. A sight better than he deserved.

Brodie moved to the pulse in the hollow of her throat before she pushed him away, laughing.

"You may just change your mind." Laurel crooked a finger for him to follow, which he'd blindly do to the ends of the earth. "Come, my love, I want to find out which apron best fits."

"Now, darlin'…" He discovered she paid his glares less mind than a pesky fly.

But Lord, did those curves sway when she moved.

"Everything comes with a price. Ollie once said we're all rare jewels that need polishing. I would say we're both gold nuggets."

Call it passion, call it lust, or call it fulfilling a dream—his soul was no longer lost. He'd discovered it in Redemption where it was born.

*Keep reading for a sneak peek at book two in
Linda Broday's Men of Legend series*

the HEART of a TEXAS COWBOY

One

*North Texas
Spring 1876*

SOME OLD WIVES SOMEWHERE PROBABLY SAID THAT blood on a wedding day forewarned of things to come. But he didn't have any patience for curses or omens today. Becky Golden was the only girl he'd ever loved. They were perfect for each other.

Nothing would stop him from making a future with her. Nothing.

Houston Legend sucked a drop of blood from the thumb he'd cut on a piece of shattered coffee cup. "Great," he muttered. He'd probably get blood on the highfalutin ascot he was trying to tie. One good thing—it was black.

"Houston, get a move on. You're going to be late for your wedding." His brother's bellow was louder than a snorting, snot-slinging steer on the rampage. The huge stone house that served as headquarters for the famous Lone Star Ranch picked up his voice and bounced it around the walls.

"Hold your horses!" Houston Legend fumbled with the fancy neckpiece that his beautiful bride-to-be had insisted he wear.

The bedroom door flung open and his younger brother Sam poked his head in. "What's the holdup?"

"This damn tie. For two cents I'd wear my normal clothes." Houston shot a longing glance at his comfortable trousers and shirt on the bed. He seldom wore a neckpiece and when he did, it was a simple western tie. "This isn't me. I think it's called an ascot or some such nonsense, but with this thingamajig on, the only ass in the room is me."

Sam strode forward. "You can do anything once, big brother. Becky wants her wedding perfect and you're gonna give it to her. Let me see it."

With a flick of his wrists, Sam had the silk neckpiece tied in nothing flat. "Where's your stickpin?"

Houston handed him the diamond pin. "You're not wearing your sheriff's badge."

"Not on duty." Sam reached for the black cutaway coat and held it for Houston. "Besides, it ruins the look of my suit."

A former Texas Ranger, Sam had given up the job when he married Sierra Hunt and adopted an orphaned boy two months ago. Sam was now sheriff of Lost Point, Texas—a place that until recently had been an outlaw haven. The town was an hour's ride from the Lone Star, so that made their pa happy. Stoker had said if Sam couldn't live on the ranch, he wanted him nearby. Houston was glad he hadn't gone far. He liked having his brother around.

"Shouldn't need the badge today. At least I hope not." Houston nodded and shot him a grin. "Were you nervous when you and Sierra tied the knot? My hands are shaking."

"Mine shook too the day I wed Sierra." Sam shot him a narrowed glance. "Becky's the right one, isn't she? I mean you don't have any doubts or anything."

Houston paused for a moment in thought. Although they'd grown up together on different ranches, he knew the exact second he'd fallen hard. Becky was ten and Houston had been twelve. It was right after they'd buried his mother. Although he protested, his father made him go to a barn dance at the Golden ranch. She wore a blue dress that seemed woven from his dreams and the soft lantern light shining on her hair reminded him of daffodils. He knew right then that there would never be another girl for him. Lord, how his heart pounded when he took her in his arms. Becky pushed away the dark shadows of his life with rays of sunshine. He'd known then that she was his one true love for all eternity, and he still knew it now.

"She's the one," Houston assured him.

"I wish Mother was alive to see you," Sam said quietly. "You'd make her proud." He wandered to the window and pushed the curtain aside. "I wonder if Luke will show up."

With one last glance in the mirror, Houston turned.

"Hope so. I miss him, you know. I really like having our outlaw brother in the family—it's easier than having a lawman like you, anyway."

Sam moved from the window and flicked off a piece of lint from Houston's shoulder.

Houston slapped his hand. "Stop it. You're not Mother."

Paying him no mind, Sam straightened the ascot. "I worry about Luke out there all alone, searching for the man who framed him for murder. He needs us."

"It's what he chose," Houston reminded him.

Music drifted upstairs from the piano they'd lugged outside for the ceremony. Both bolted from the room. Houston would never hear the end of it if he kept Becky waiting at the altar.

A few minutes later, he pushed through the door and stepped onto the wide porch. Though this was a ranch, it was so large that it was more like a town, complete with a mercantile, school, telegraph office, and its own doctor. The early May afternoon was beautiful with sun splashing onto rooftops and white-washed buildings.

Everything was perfect, and not a cloud in the sky.

He and Sam strode to stand next to the preacher they'd brought all the way from Squaw Valley, the nearest town with a church. Overhead, the Texas flag fluttered in the breeze and the sun caught on the huge bronze star that hung suspended twenty feet away. The brilliant rays passed through the cutouts in each star point, creating a beautiful image at Houston's feet.

Reverend Smith fought a sudden gust of wind

that sent his long red hair tumbling, blocking his vision. Remaining ramrod straight, he calmly parted the copper strands in the center like a curtain and peered out. Houston covered his mouth to keep from laughing.

The pianist launched into the wedding march and all eyes turned. Houston's tongue glued to the roof of his mouth. Becky was truly a vision with her golden hair hanging in ringlets from the crown of her head.

How had he landed such a breathtaking woman? Must've been fate. She slowly made her way to his side and took Houston's hand. Crazy with love for her, he stared into her soft brown eyes and squeezed her palm. He mouthed, "I love you for all of eternity."

The sound of a horse whickering outside caught his attention. Guests had been arriving all day. When he glanced up, he spotted his brother Luke, standing apart from the rest next to his black gelding. He'd made it after all. Their gazes met and he nodded to Houston. Houston nodded back, happier than he'd ever been in his life.

Just as the good reverend opened his mouth to speak, a single shot rang out. It happened so fast, no one had time to react. As if in a daze, Houston heard Becky cry out, watched her collapse. He caught her in his arms before she hit the ground.

Blood oozed from a hole in her chest and stained her beautiful blue dress.

About the Author

Linda Broday resides in the panhandle of Texas on the Llano Estacado. At a young age, she discovered a love for storytelling, history, and anything pertaining to the Old West. There's something about Stetsons, boots, and tall, rugged cowboys that get her fired up! A *New York Times* and *USA Today* bestselling author, Linda has won many awards, including the prestigious National Readers' Choice Award and the Texas Gold Award. Visit her at LindaBroday.com.

hurdy-gurdy dancer